Veil of Darkness

a novel of the Seven Deadly Veils, Book Three

Diana Marik

Veil of Darkness ~ Seven Deadly Veils, Book Three
Copyright © 2018, Diana Marika Preston
Cover Art by Kris Norris

Published by Diana Marik
Released January 2018

Praise for Diana Marik's Veilverse

Veil of Mists

"I am obsessed with this series. Diana Marik has created a high intensity series that grabs you and doesn't let go."
—Lisa Reigel Reviews

"Danger and deception know no bounds in this riveting second installment of the *Seven Deadly Veils* series. Complex liaisons deliver the action and suspense paranormal fans crave." —
RT Book Reviews

"Completely captivating! I LOVE this series and can't get enough of RRRemare. So much happening in this book...deception at its finest! Just when you think you have it figured out, everything changes. Definitely couldn't put this book down and one hell of a ride."
—Paranormal/Urban Fantasy Book Lovers Haven

The Blue Veil

"Marik's compelling delivery commands readers' attention; the easy, seamless passion and intensity between characters is a welcome companion to a perfect balance of action and suspense." —
RT Book Reviews

"The characters are edgy and intriguing. The plot is suspenseful and sexy. I'm drawn into this series and fascinated by the world that Ms. Marik has created."
—Comfy Chair Books

"I am so Team Remare. This novella just keeps us hooked."
—Sik Reviews

"Just one word...Remare. Love that dark and dangerous vampire."
—Paranormal/Urban Fantasy Book Lover's Haven

Veil of Shadows

"The suspense is as dramatic and intense as the action, and paired with Marik's steamy sex scenes, will leave readers satisfied on many levels. Off-the-chart chemistry." 4 STARS HOT
—RT Book Reviews

"I flipping LOVED this book. I was drawn immediately to the main characters of *Veil of Shadows*. The characters are edgy, sexy, and intriguing. Her writing style drew me in and kept me fascinated; the suspense kept me on the edge waiting to see what would happen next. *Veil of Shadows* is fast paced and action packed. I highly recommend this book to fans of paranormal romance and romantic urban fantasy."

—Comfy Chair Books

"Ms. Marik has made this new paranormal world come alive and leave me begging for more."
—Sik Reviews

"I absolutely LOVED it! With so many awesome characters, can't decide who I love the most! Refreshing story that completely captivated me. I simply couldn't put it down until the last page."
—Paranormal/Urban Fantasy Book Lover's Haven

Dedication

For Nora, I miss you, cuz. You are not forgotten.

Acknowledgments

I would like to thank all my fans in the Marik's Mortals Fan Club and to all my wonderful readers who've written to me with such kind and warm wishes. Your affection is much appreciated. Also, I want to thank my editor, Jessica Bimberg, for your many encouragements and keeping me on track and to my fantastic cover artist, Kris Norris. You guys rock!

Chapter One

In the training area of House Valadon, a fencing match was quickly drawing a crowd of Torians. Tristan, the youngest of the group, whispered, "Damn! See the way they spar. They're impossibly fast."

Katya agreed. "They look like they could kill each other."

"They're testing each other. Note the tips of the swords—they're protected." Morel, a high-ranking Torian and Lord Valadon's third, joined them. "You've seen them practice before."

"Yeah, but not like this." Tristan ran his hand through his long locks. "They fight like they mean it."

"They should." Standing casually with his arms crossed over his chest, Morel nodded. "That's what makes them both so good at it."

"Have I exhausted you already?" Ignoring the comments of their onlookers, Remare grinned at Valadon before drinking the water Escher, their butler, had provided for them. He then used the small towel to wipe the sweat from his face and chest. It was rare that Valadon, their lord and ruler, had the time to practice, but tonight, he'd been in the mood for a vigorous workout. And Remare would not deny him.

"You're the one who calls for breaks, not me," Valadon amusingly chided.

"Shall we continue, then?" Both opponents, dressed only in loose fitting pants, took their stance on the mats. Remare tucked a strand of hair behind his ear that had broken free from his leather tie. He'd been too busy with his investigations to have it cut. One corner of his mouth rose. "If you think you can keep up with me."

"Would you like to make a wager on who wins this round?"

"I would, but then, I would have to collect, and your room is so far from mine." True, their rooms were at opposite ends of the corridors, but it was hardly a trek to the other side. Remare resumed his position with feet carefully placed wide apart for optimum balance, his left hand behind him and his right holding his sword at the ready.

Valadon smirked at Remare's jest as he mirrored his pose. "*En garde.*"

Immediately, the match was underway with the foils clashing against each other with the requisite hits, feints, and ripostes. Remare heard the spectators' trepidations and effectively blocked them from his concentration. They need not be concerned. With his favorite sword in his hand, he was in his glory. He loved sparring with Valadon, the only one in their House who could match him for skill and speed. He lived for workouts such as these. The sounds of steel echoing throughout the room was music to his ears.

His eyes trained on his rival, he enjoyed watching Valadon trying to outthink him. They long ago had learned the tells of the other, each waiting until the other made a mistake.

Remare didn't make mistakes.

Although Valadon carried more muscular bulk than him, Remare was able to move more rapidly with his trim physique. Sweat was rolling off his brow as their speed increased. However, his heart rate remained steady as they continued to thrust and evade. He knew Valadon was enjoying their match as much as he was. Their footwork took them from one end of the mats to the other, rarely changing position.

Remare briefly glanced at Aiden signaling from the side, and that single, momentary lapse gave Valadon the advantage to down Remare's sword.

With the onlookers applauding wildly, they both laughed and patted each other on the back, congratulating each other on their endurance.

Valadon took the hand towel Escher offered and dried off his face. "What is it, Aiden?"

"Your speed is incredible; it's amazing you've never injured each other."

"When you've sparred as often as we have," Remare drank from his water bottle, "you know how to avoid causing harm."

"There's a communique requiring your attention. I've transferred it to your email account."

When Aiden seemed to be hedging, Valadon asked, "What else?"

"I'm afraid it's Nick. He hasn't reported in. It's two hours past the time he was supposed to check in."

Valadon sighed. "I thought we had put a stop to my nephew's reckless behavior."

Remare put his hand on Valadon's shoulder. "Go, answer your email. I'll track Nick down. It's the end of the semester. He's probably out celebrating with his friends from the university."

All the humor that had been present in the High Lord's voice vanished. "Do so. And, then, have him report to me."

***

"Concentrate."

"I am."

"No. You're not."

"Yes, I am." Miranda Crescent barely stifled a growl. She'd been practicing for the last few months with moderate progress.

"Try again," her soft-spoken mentor instructed. "Block out everything else."

Straightening her spine, she extended her palm and focused. The energy grew warm between her and the vase on the mantel. The tips of her fingers tingled. She could do this. She could manipulate the air surrounding the vase enough to move it. As an *Elemental*, Miranda had some talent in telekinesis. However, her real power, where she really excelled, was with fire—there, she had little problem proving her control. She had similar talent with air and water, but with moving objects—yeah, that took some work and practice. A lot of practice.

Despite her attempt, the vase barely moved. Shoulders sagging, she groaned in frustration.

"Try again. Focus, Miranda. Keep your eyes on the vase. Picture it in the space you *want* it to be, not where it is already, nor in the process of movement."

Miranda closed her eyes and regulated her breathing. Her greatest fear was not in failure, but in disappointing the one vampire who gave so generously of his time to her. She was, after all, the one who'd asked Blu, aka Guy de Montglat, for his help. A strict tutor, firm in his approach, he had far more patience than she. Which made sense since he was an ancient. Although his deceptive appearance was that of a college grad student, sometimes Blu dressed in sophisticated suits. But, tonight, his usual garb included a blue T-shirt and jeans, thereby earning his nickname. Wavy blond hair complemented his timeless face, but it was his penetrating hazel eyes that betrayed his age. Those orbs contained a world of knowledge.

Ever vigilant, Blu remained standing with one hand casually stroking his chin while his other arm wrapped around his waist. "Keep your eyes on your target. Breathe. Now, move it."

Determined to impress her mentor and prove his lessons weren't in vain, Miranda deeply inhaled and narrowed her eyes. The air energized around her, and the familiar prickling sensation flowed through her body. With deliberate concentration, she centered her power and directed it at the vase.

Unexpectedly, it shattered into a thousand pieces, the shards flying about the room.

"I said move it, not explode it!"

"Oh, God!" Her heart sank. "Please tell me it was a reproduction and not an authentic piece." Miranda knew before she'd asked everything was valuable in Blu's living space beneath the New York Public Library. The original benefactors of the library had constructed several apartments for use by their exclusive members. Most had been redesigned for the special reading rooms upstairs. But this one had been sealed and long forgotten by the time Blu discovered it and decided to make his home here. She rushed to pick up the pieces at the foot of the fireplace.

"My dear, everything I have is genuine. Do not fret. It was not a favorite, as you are."

He must have cut himself on the broken porcelain because as he smiled at her, two drops of his blood hit her square in the mouth. In her attempt to spit it out, she sputtered and accidentally swallowed his blood. How vampires could like the coppery taste of blood was beyond her. He simply licked the cut, the wound healing instantly.

"Show off."

He grinned at her. "Not at all."

"Now, Guy, maybe you're being too tough on Miranda."
Sitting at their intricately carved dining table, Dr. Felicity
Walcott, Blu's longtime companion, looked up from her
laptop.

"Certainly not! She asked for my help, and I was
instructing her as I know best. I simply wanted to see how
far she'd progressed."

Miranda noted the hint of British aristocracy in the
voices of two of her favorite vampires. Dr. Walcott had been
her friend and trusted advisor at New York University when
she'd been an undergrad working on her degree in Art
History.

"She'll have plenty of time to practice when we're away
on holiday. Oh, look, those two eagles are back at St.
Patrick's Cathedral." Felicity pointed to the screen. "It says
the city wanted to call the ASPCA to relocate them to some
preserve upstate, but the church officials said the eagles
were welcome to stay as long as they wanted."

"You're going on vacation?" Miranda didn't hide her
surprise, nor her excitement. "Where?"

"Guy is taking me on a three-month cruise in the
Mediterranean."

"As much as I love your fair city, I prefer the warmer
climates of Greece and Italy." Blu deposited the broken
pieces of the vase in the wastebasket. "New York winters
can be a bit harsh."

"I'll say." At least Miranda would be on semester break
from teaching at NYU for the next six weeks until the spring
semester started. In the meanwhile, she'd focus on her day
job at City Museum where she worked as an authenticator
of rare works of art. A position Felicity had helped her
attain.

"Miranda, why don't you take some time off from the museum and join us, for at least part of the trip? We have friends in many of the coastal towns that are quite lovely."

"A splendid idea," Blu agreed. "We'd love to have you. I can keep a better eye on your progress that way."

Miranda sighed at the prospect of getting away from the cold. "Not a chance. After my summer in New Mexico and then the Paris trip, I don't see another vacation happening any time soon."

"Pity." Blu shrugged. "I would have loved to introduce you to our friend, Robert. He'd be delighted to meet you. He makes his home on Sardinia, now, off the coast of Italy. So many vampires had to leave their ancestral homes during the world wars for more remote areas in the Mediterranean islands."

She'd miss them dearly when they were gone. Miranda enjoyed visiting Blu and Felicity in their elegant living quarters with the pale blue walls with the Rococo trim and myriad paintings. The antiques on the various shelves and the baby grand piano in the corner gave the place a quaint and comforting ambience. It felt like she'd stepped back into the eighteen hundreds.

"I've checked the databases for known purchases of Impressionists, auctions as well as private sales, and I can find no mention, not even a hint, of the missing Renoir."

"Thanks, Felicity. I knew it was a long shot." Miranda joined them. "I just feel so bad for Alistair Calder. I told him I would make certain inquiries, discreetly, but I've come up with nothing."

"I should think that painting is in the home of some wealthy collector on the far side of the world by now."

"Most likely," Felicity agreed with Blu. "Don't feel too badly for Calder. His Chelsea gallery is doing quite well. A real hit with the uber-chic millennials who frequent his showings."

"Good to hear." Miranda picked up one of Felicity's pens and started twirling it. Another thing they had in common, beside their love of art, was antique fountain pens. Miranda's father had collected several of them. A question surfaced, which had been in the back of her mind for some time. "Blu, have you met any people," she shook her hand for emphasis, "like me in your travels?"

"Rest assured, as unique as you are, Miranda, you are not the only one of your kind. There have been several *Elementals* throughout history. Even now, there are those who possess your talents. And, like you, they *wisely* keep their talents hidden. Remember what was done to women during the Inquisition. Though, I must admit, most, from what I'd heard, had power over just one of the elements. You have talent in all four. A rarity, indeed."

Miranda wanted to ask him more questions, but the sound of her phone ringing had their heads turning in her direction. "You get reception down here?"

"Yes, of course. We get a great many things here," Blu teased. "Pizza included."

Rummaging in her bag, Miranda found her phone. She smiled when she saw the caller ID. Only one person made the butterflies dance wildly in her stomach—Remare.

Chapter Two

At Nightshade, the popular vampire nightclub, Miranda was quietly sipping her cranberry and vodka and enjoying the sights of the dancers below. The vivacious proprietor, Rosalyn, who sported a magnificent mane of red hair, was a good friend. Miranda had instantly liked the vampire because of her witty sense of humor. From her seat at the cocktail table near the railing on the second level, Miranda gazed down at the bar and her two Were friends, Maxine and Sasha. Since their apartment building was being exterminated, they'd temporarily moved in with her. In gratitude, they cooked her hot meals and made sure her home had never been cleaner or better organized.

She was surprised they were mingling with the vampires. Usually, they stayed with others of their own pack and partied at their home base, Werehaven. Even Sasha, the young Were who had been brutalized by vampires and members of a rival Were clan, seemed to be cozying up to a handsome, dark-haired vampire. For a long time, Sasha hadn't been capable of socializing with anyone other than a few members of Black Star. It had taken much TLC from the clan to make her feel comfortable around others. Maxine had been pivotal in providing support; they'd become inseparable ever since.

"Don't worry; if he said he'd be here, he'll be here," Rosalyn whispered in her usual sing-song voice.

With the music playing, Miranda had barely heard her arrival. "Do I look worried?"

"No, you look like a woman patiently waiting for a lover who is running late."

Miranda tipped her drink in her direction. "Good to see you, Roz. I've missed you."

"Likewise. Perhaps, now, you'll visit more since the university is on break. By the way, I didn't forget your promise to come with me to that new boutique in SoHo. The Gala is next week, and I need a new dress."

Miranda sighed. She'd nearly forgotten. She'd promised Jordan, her boss, she would attend, but socializing with New York's upper crust wasn't her idea of a fun night out. She already had her dress picked out, but since she liked Roz, she'd accompany her to the boutique. "Let's make plans soon, then. Text me so I won't forget."

"I will." As she straightened her spine, her voice sounded whimsical. "Oh, the vampire in question approaches."

Inhaling, Miranda caught a whiff of an old growth forest. Her body tightened in anticipation. It always did whenever Remare appeared. She mentally ordered the butterflies in her stomach to desist from their acrobatics. His familiar scent made her skin tingle. So did the way he rolled the *r*'s when he said her name. It had been months since she'd seen him. Her part-time lover—who had been too busy for the last two months to stop over at her place or even send a text. Evidently, work took precedence, as did his boss, Valadon. Part of her was angry Remare'd been unable to make time for her. But an even larger part, she reluctantly admitted, was excited to see him.

"Good evening, Rosalyn, Mir-randa."

"Good to see you, Remare. Shall I have one of my servers bring you a bottle of your favorite Cabernet?"

"No, just a glass. I can't stay long tonight."

"As you wish." Before she departed, Rosalyn put a hand on Miranda's shoulder and whispered, "We'll get together soon, Miranda."

Patting Roz's hand, she silently nodded.

When she finally peered up at Remare's strikingly handsome face with his raven-black hair and dark eyes, her heart sped up, and her body felt like it was glowing. Always elegantly dressed, tonight, he wore a dark suit under his cashmere coat. Eyes narrowing, she almost cursed him for the effect he had on her. She'd nearly forgotten how alive he made her feel. "Hello, Remare."

"It's good to see you, again." When he smiled, his perfectly even white teeth gleamed with just a hint of his incisors. "You look wonderful."

Sensations of his fangs embedded in her neck, gently sucking her life force, suddenly emerged, and her body throbbed in places she found hard to ignore. She quickly crushed the erotic memory. "Been a while."

He removed and then casually tossed his gloves on the table. "Yes, unfortunate events have delayed our meeting."

She suspected from his sensual smirk he knew, without any doubt whatsoever, the effect he had on her. Would always have on her.

His voice was low, seductive. "I've missed you."

Miranda tried not to be taken in by his charm, but Remare was so goddamn handsome, her hormones were jumping up and down, like tiny cheerleaders welcoming the home team. She silenced the traitorous bitches. His hair had grown longer than she remembered, but his goatee and slight beard that traveled up his jawline were neatly trimmed. She remembered how soft those hairs felt brushing up against her skin. He was drop-dead gorgeous without it. With it, he was lethally sexy. "And whose fault is that?"

He sighed as a waitress set his wine down and left. "I explained, the last time we spoke, that ValCorp has been unusually busy. We have many ongoing investigations I must be present for." He tilted his head the way he usually did when he was being sarcastic. "I'm sure, with your highly perceptive mind, you understand the demands on my time."

She wasn't going to argue the point, at least not tonight. She sipped her vodka, wishing it had more ice. "You said something on the phone about Nick missing."

"Yes, I was hoping you remembered more places where he might have gone to tonight." Drinking his wine, he glanced around the club. "I had our people check out the areas you mentioned earlier, but still, there is no sign of him."

She leaned in closer to him. "You do realize it's the end of the fall term, and the students are out celebrating." Dismissively, she waved her hand in the air. "I'm sure he's just lost track of time."

"Be that as it may, he still has a responsibility to check in." He met her eyes, and Miranda sensed his weariness. "He has not done so. We tried to track him down by the GPS in his phone, but apparently, it was left in his car."

Miranda wanted to help find Nick. Not only was he High Lord Valadon's nephew and heir, he'd been her favorite student and assistant. "All right. Keep in mind, I usually don't socialize with students. Occasionally, I've met them for tea or a quick bite near the university. However, I've overheard them talking about some local cafes and bars. I can't give you the exact addresses; I just know landmarks. Down in the West Village, a lot of streets don't run north and south or east and west like they do in Midtown. Even I sometimes get lost, and I grew up not far from there."

When he moved closer, his lips a breath away, her heart rate increased. "Will you show me?"

"Of course." She stood and gave herself points for keeping her hormones in check. Remare helped her with her jacket, his hands sliding seductively over her shoulders.

When she gazed down, Max and Sasha were smiling giving her the thumbs up.

Once outside, Miranda shivered and quickly put on her gloves. "It got cold out." She sniffed the air and peered at the overhead clouds. "We're going to get rain tonight."

Remare took her elbow. "Then, let's not linger." He gestured to his black Mercedes SUV, and once inside, she closed her eyes and inhaled his deeply masculine scent. A sense of contentment she hadn't felt in some time washed over her.

"Okay, let's go south of Washington Square Park then hook a left on Bleecker. Wherever you can find parking, do so. We can cover more ground on foot."

When they approached the area, Remare saw a car vacating a parking space; he pulled in quickly and smoothly. This part of Manhattan had some of the best ethnic restaurants the city had to offer. It was going to take time to check them all. "Do you realize how many bars and cafes are in this area?"

"Yes, our people are already checking north of the park and the East Side."

Miranda pointed to a café/pub she'd overheard her students talking about. They searched it, but Nick wasn't there and no one had seen him. She was amazed how quickly and easily they settled into a routine. She would mingle among the patrons, looking for Nick, and Remare would show Nick's picture to the bouncer or bartender. Each time, it was the same: No one had seen him. It was frustrating, but she liked working with Remare, again. He had a way of getting people to open up. She admired his professionalism; he was one hell of an investigator, very methodical, organized and precise.

A lot like her when she was at work, she smirked. But was she ready to forgive him for being silent for so long? Not just yet.

When they finished searching the eighth or ninth tavern, Miranda went to the bar for a bottle of water. "I was thirsty. Want some water?"

He nodded and then paid the bartender, leaving a hefty tip. Once outside, they gulped down some water, and Remare twisted the cap back on and handed her his bottle.

She gazed down at her shoulder bag. Why did men do that? Gabriel used to do the same thing whenever they'd gone to a Broadway play and he had nowhere to put the playbill. Sometimes, she got stuck carrying his keys and wallet. "I guess I'm supposed to hold it?"

He made an expression that seemed to say, *"Of course, that's what women do."* He scrutinized her somewhat worn shoulder bag. "You have the rather large purse."

Sighing, she tucked both bottles away.

After visiting the twelfth club without success, they climbed the few steps to street level. Rubbing her hands together for warmth, Miranda gazed up at the night sky. It was getting colder outside and rain was imminent. "You know, he's probably safe and warm in the home of a friend. Socializing."

"The thought has occurred to me." Remare started texting. "None of our people have had any luck finding him, either." They started walking back to his car. "You've been somewhat distant tonight."

Distant? He's calling me distant? "I haven't heard from you in months. What did you expect?"

His eyes narrowed. "I thought I explained the constraints on my time."

Not caring if he heard her or not, Miranda muttered, "But you found time to socialize with the blondes at Nightshade."

He waited until a young couple passed them then took her by the arm. "What are you talking about?"

She really didn't want to have this conversation with Remare on the streets of New York; she was tired, her feet were aching, and she could feel the pressure building for an oncoming migraine. She usually did before a storm. "Oh, c'mon, Remare, your picture was plastered all over social media with you dancing and partying at Nightshade...and other places." *Work constraints, my ass!*

He started smiling and then began laughing.

Her heart had felt pierced with a jagged knife every time she'd looked at one of those photos, and now, he was laughing. *Laughing? Where's a hot iron poker when you need one?* She started walking toward his car.

"Miranda, you must be joking." He stopped her by grasping her hand. "You couldn't *possibly* take those photos seriously."

She smiled sardonically. "Why not?"

His eyes glittered with humor as his lips trembled with mirth. "There was nothing between me and those women. Surely, you know that."

"I do? Kinda explains why you haven't called. You know, Remare, if you needed variety in your diet, all you had to do was say so."

When he continued smirking, Miranda wanted to rake her nails across his face. But that would be like defacing the *Mona Lisa* or one of the rare paintings she authenticated at the museum. Truly, his face was a work of art.

He sobered. "Miranda. If I thought, for one moment, you would take any of those photos seriously, I would have told you not to."

Rubbing her arms, she avoided his eyes. "Why not?"

He grasped her shoulders and started massaging them with his thumbs. "Because, my beauty, I had those photos staged. If you look carefully, some of those pictures are from years ago; others were taken when you were in Paris," he grinned, "with your fiancé."

"Ha! Don't go there. You know damned well Orion isn't my fiancé." She took two steps then turned toward him. "He's quite happy touring Europe with Bastien." She remembered the picture he'd sent to her of some cottage in Amsterdam he was thinking of buying. "Our so-called engagement was done to protect his reputation when damaging images started appearing on the social media sites questioning his gender preferences. It was your boss' idea to publicize the engagement."

"And did I ever make assumptions about you with him?"

She flung her hand in the air. "There were none to make."

"Precisely. I see we need to clear this matter up. Ask me why I had them staged."

"Don't care." She continued walking.

He quickly halted her momentum by grabbing her arm. "Ask me." His voice didn't offer any retreat.

"Fine! Gee, Remare, why were you so cozy with the blondes at Nightshade?"

He pulled her closer. "Because, my dear Mir-randa, Valadon was becoming suspicious of me." He exhaled a deep breath. "Apparently, my abstinence from other women has become a topic of speculation at House Valadon. He even accused me of having an affair with Rosalyn since I sometimes conduct business there."

Miranda's jaw dropped. "Rosalyn? She's with Jason Morgan. Isn't she?"

"Yes, and quite happy from what I understand." He exhaled. "Others started wondering why I was no longer with Irina, who also started asking questions. I thought it best to let them think I was into 'variety' as you so put it."

Miranda disliked the stunning blonde who had once been Remare's lover. She was one of the most beautiful women in the world whose icy stare reminded Miranda of the look one gave a hated competitor. She took a deep breath and tried to process what he was saying. It was beginning to make sense. But he wasn't off the hook, yet.

Her head pounding, she pointed a finger at him. "And...you promised to take me up to The Cloisters on your boat. It was the one thing I asked you for. *The one thing!* I know your work is demanding, but you said you'd take me and then didn't." She knew she was being petty, but his silence had stung more than she wanted to admit. Her burgeoning headache didn't help.

"I did try to take you!" Remare lowered his voice as a man walking his dog passed them on the street. "You had to attend a seminar down in Washington, DC."

Her temper spiked. "I had plenty of free weekends; you waited until you *knew* I was going to be out of town."

Frustration laced his voice. "You did not inform me of your travel plans until after I rearranged my schedule. I volunteered to go with you, but if I remember correctly, you did not want me with you."

Miranda was moved by his defenses, and a smile tugged at her lips. "You would have been bored."

"Perhaps." His sexy smirk returned. "But I would have sufficiently hidden it."

Shame had her gazing down.

He pulled her tighter to him. "So, am I forgiven?" His dark brown eyes hinted at laughter.

"Maybe." She kept her arms around him. "But you still have a promise to keep."

"I did not forget. We can go during the winter break. I assume the museum will give you time off for the upcoming holidays."

"Not a chance." She shook her head. "It's way too cold and stark there during winter."

"In the spring, then?" Remare's smile melted something deep inside her.

"In the spring." Her hands massaged his back. "With the flowers in bloom, it will be pretty up there. I just wanted to show you it in the fall with the leaves changing colors. It's spectacular, and it's my favorite museum in the city."

"I know." He kissed her forehead. "Get in the car. You're freezing. I'll take you home. You're probably right about Nick being with his friends. My men can finish canvassing the area."

"No. Take me to NYU." She rubbed her forehead. "I have one helluva headache coming on, and I left my migraine medicine in my desk."

He opened her car door. "As you wish."

Chapter Three

Cerise entered the private entrance in Riverside Park and walked through Red Claw's main meeting room like the queen she longed someday to be. Calvin and Arturo were fighting in the ring, each covered in claw marks and blood. Shouts of encouragement rent the air as Arturo threw Calvin against the bars and hit him with a series of brutal upper cuts. Unlike Lizandra's prissy Black Stars who used their amphitheater for music as an entertainment, here, combat was a way of life. The cage, where they held weekly contests to determine the strong, was their mode of exercising their more aggressive natures.

She blew Arturo a kiss as she passed by her uncle's lieutenants who nodded to her. As the niece of the King of the Weres, they accorded her the respect she deserved. She searched the gallery for her uncle who usually attended the matches. "Where's Edgar?" she asked one of his soldiers.

"He's in the back with Dori and the others."

The Were Queen was such a fool, Cerise sneered. She didn't even know she had a spy in her midst. When she reached her uncle's room, she knocked and then entered. Since she had good news to share, she knew her presence would be welcome. God help anyone who brought the Were King bad news. She shuddered.

Edgar Renworth was surrounded by three women as naked as he was. Sweat rolled off his glistening body. His sensual smile of contentment made his face appear handsome. The scent of sex, raw and powerful, permeated the air. "Well, niece, I hope your news is as delicious as these beauties." He groped the ass of one of the women who seemed to purr in his ear.

"The package has been delivered."

"Did you make sure our other guest was starved to the point of madness?"

"Of course, he was delirious with hunger."

Edgar shoved the women to the side and pulled on his leather pants. For a man quickly approaching fifty, he was in amazing shape. His muscles flexed as he dressed. "This calls for a drink. Finally, Valadon will know what it is to suffer." He pushed back his hair and went to his bar. "And you're sure no one followed you or saw where you took him?"

"No one saw us. I made sure of it."

Renworth tossed his head back and roared with laughter. "I think we need a celebration." He poured himself some scotch and drank it down. "Let them know I'll be entering the cage."

Cerise's eyes widened as a thrill went through her. It was a rare treat to see her uncle fight in the cage. He always won. But not before he shredded whatever opponent was unlucky enough to be with him. The clan would go crazy when they found out Edgar Renworth, Were King of Clan Red Claw was ready to battle. No one ever challenged him. They feared him too much. He was the strongest among them and the fastest.

And he never showed mercy to anyone.

Even when they begged for it.

***

Seething in rage, Valadon quietly rode his private elevator down to the lowest level beneath his House. Magritte, their supreme ruler in Europe, had grown impatient at his refusal to visit their High Court. Apparently, the "accidents" occurring on his properties throughout Europe had increased. He knew she was behind them. First, there was the train derailment, then the fire in one of his grand hotels, and now, one of his freighters had collided with another ship in the Mediterranean. His people had been looking into each of the incidents and could find no tangible proof that Magritte was involved. Of course, they wouldn't. She was too careful to be implicated. But he knew her methods. She would not rest until she got what she wanted.

And, right now, she wanted him.

And that, she would never have. He ground his teeth in aggravation.

When the doors opened, he strode over to the underground river where Gabriel was kneeling and inspecting the vials of water he'd ordered. Valadon's temper softened. Of all the people Valadon had turned in his twelve hundred years existence, Gabriel was his favorite. His light brown hair and golden eyes were striking, as was his handsome face.

So reminiscent of his ancestor.

As a human, Gabriel had been a good friend and physician when Valadon's people had needed him. He'd taken the young doctor's humanity, even though he would have died had Valadon not turned him when he did. As a vampire, his progeny had never entirely forgiven Valadon for turning him. He wondered if Gabriel ever would.

"I've collected the samples from the river and the surrounding ground you requested." Gabriel stood and wiped the dirt from his pants. "I can work these up in my lab and have the results to you when I'm finished."

"Work them up in the labs here; I don't want any of the samples leaving ValCorp's property."

"All right." Gabriel seemed to be searching his face. "You look pensive. Is everything okay?"

He sat on the stone bench near the underground river and rubbed his forehead. "I have a lot on my mind these days." Not the least of which was wanting his son, the vampire he'd turned nearly a century ago, to return to ValCorp and his House. Ironically, it was only after Gabriel left House Valadon that their relationship seemed to improve.

His son had left to pursue his research in vampire genetics with the hope of someday becoming human, again. A dream which would never come true. He'd also taken the only woman Valadon had loved in centuries, Miranda. Even though she'd not returned to him when her relationship with Gabriel had ended, he still believed the day would come when she did.

He had plans for that day.

Gabriel closed up his satchel. "Were there any more contaminants found in the bagged blood?"

"No, except for the ones we detected, there have been no further taints." ValCorp maintained their own private blood bank and vigorously screened their blood for any toxins that might be harmful to vampires.

"Your enemies have started up, again."

Valadon sighed. "Yes, they have."

Gabriel sat beside him. "What else have they been up to that you wouldn't discuss on the phone?"

Valadon detested reading the latest reports of the missing vampires. These were his people who looked to him for reassurance. He was supposed to be protecting them, yet several more vampires had disappeared in the last few months. Detective Vetti, the human liaison on the police force, had also cited more humans had vanished, as well.

Valadon had his people researching known members of the HOL—the Human Order of Light, a well-funded hate group whose intolerance of vampires was well-known. He had their movements carefully monitored. Remare was pulling double duty in his quest to root out their more prolific members. Other members of his Elite force had been working diligently to discover the leader of the heinous hate group. Irina and Gregori had been on several assignments identifying and locating their enemies.

To this day, they were still unable to find the man members of the HOL had simply referred to as *The Regent.* He sneered at the thought of the HOL's leader daring to challenge him. They may not have a name, yet. But they were getting close.

And, now, toxins were found in the very blood they needed to survive. Intolerable. He would make certain this problem was quickly eliminated. And, for that, he needed Gabriel here at ValCorp. "Are you content with the Rockefeller foundation? Are they treating you well, there?"

"So far." His son smiled up at him.

Valadon knew any attempt to lure him back to ValCorp would be futile at this point. But, in the future, he would find a way to make certain his son did, in fact, return to him.

Gabriel's face got serious. "If this area," he arched his arm in a circle, "has become polluted, what will you do?"

Valadon looked solemnly at him. "We may have to move elsewhere."

Chapter Four

"It's okay, Stan, I just left something in my desk." Miranda waved to her favorite night security guard at NYU. Stan was a tall, thin African-American who worked nights to help pay for his college education.

"Working late, Professor Crescent?"

"Yes, we're all very busy at the end of the semester. I'll only be a few minutes."

When Stan looked at Remare, the vampire just smiled back, and Miranda could swear he used one of his mind abilities to be let through. When she glanced back at Remare, he had one of those innocent looks on his face as if to say, *"Who me?!"*

The lights automatically flashed on when they entered the lecture hall where Miranda held her classes. At the front of the room, she rummaged through her desk as Remare strolled up the aisle. "Where does Nick usually sit?"

She pointed toward the uppermost section. "Third row from the back. Aisle seat."

Studying the layout of the expansive room, he moved up to the last row. Leaning against the support beam, he crossed his arms over his chest. "I came to see you here one night. You were up at the screen, discussing the history of one of the Impressionist artists." His lips curved in a manner suggesting pride. "You were very proficient. The students were rapt in your lecture."

Not sure if he was just being charming, she raised one brow. "Which artist was I teaching?"

"Monet. No, Manet. Edouard Manet's *Olympia*, and who had the stronger influence on him: Goya or Delacroix. Nineteenth century, France. Correct?"

Nodding, she was secretly thrilled he'd come to see her and had been impressed with her work. "It's my demented sense of humor. When you've been teaching for a while, you learn to develop one. Otherwise, they would either start daydreaming or texting." Miranda opened the side drawer. "Found it." She retrieved the bottle of water from her shoulder bag and took her pills. "I swear, we're in for a storm tonight. I only get these headaches before it rains."

Something caught his eye, and he bent to retrieve a folded piece of paper. "Unfortunately, I was summoned back to ValCorp before I could invite you out for a bite."

"I wish I had known." She would have enjoyed having dinner with him. "What did you find?"

He showed her the paper. "It's an address. Not Nick's handwriting, though."

No, it wasn't Nick's handwriting, but she knew whose it was. "It's over on the East Side. I know that neighborhood. I went to school with a girl from that area; it's not a very good one. Close to the East River. They never rebuilt some of the old apartment houses that were damaged in the last war where the bombs dropped. There's a lot of vagrants in the vicinity."

"I found this beneath Nick's desk. Why would he have it, Mir-randa?"

During finals, she made the students put away their electronic devices, and some resorted to passing notes. She didn't want to tell him it was Cerise's handwriting, but when Remare gave her that look, there was no holding back. "To meet a girl, probably."

"Which girl?"

"I'm not sure." But she had a pretty good idea which one.

"Don't tell me he is still seeing that young Were?"

"Not really sure." But she was. "Do you think we should check it out?"

"You are going home. I will investigate."

Miranda knew a bitter argument would result when he found Nick. As a Blueblood, a purebred vampire, Nick wasn't supposed to date outside his own race. "If he is with a girl, don't you think it's better I come along with you?" With her presence, she thought any argument between the two headstrong vampires would be alleviated.

"You knew this." His eyes narrowed. "Why didn't you tell me earlier he was still seeing this girl?"

"I don't know where Nick is. It's possible he's with her or someplace else. It looks like her handwriting, but I could be wrong. Hey, wait!"

He turned on his heel, muttering something in Italian, and Miranda practically had to jog to keep up with him.

Once outside, Miranda sensed the coming storm. They quickly got in his car. She was only able to convince him to take her along by telling him she knew the area fairly well. After a few more mutterings, with words she knew only from certain films, he'd agreed. When they got to the East Side, the area seemed deserted, dark because of the broken or missing light bulbs on the utility poles. The breezes from the river blew old newspapers around, and the smell from the brine permeated the air. They circled the area until they found a parking spot a few blocks from the given address.

Miranda scanned the once chic neighborhood that now resembled a broken-down war zone. Many of the buildings were in disrepair, neglected. The mist rolling in off the water made the region creepy. "I don't like this. I haven't been down here in years. Some of those buildings look abandoned, and I bet there are criminals lurking around."

He shut the ignition off. "Why would Nick come to such a place?"

She knew his question was rhetorical but offered, "Students like to party wherever they can. Sometimes, in train cars, abandoned train stations or empty warehouses. They like the danger aspect. In Paris, they liked to party in the Catacombs."

When he just grunted, she couldn't refrain from asking, "Oh, c'mon, when you were younger, didn't you have celebrations in out-of-the-way places where you knew you wouldn't be caught?"

Again, with the sarcastic look. "Will you stay in the car?"

"With the state you're in, not a chance." Miranda grabbed her bag as he reached for his sword cane. She'd never walk alone in this neighborhood at night, but with Remare by her side, she felt reasonably safe. She'd seen how lethal he could be with a sword. They'd barely gone a block when a shadow moved in front of them.

She knew instinctively he was a vampire. Young from the vibration he was throwing off. But something was different about him. His pitch was off.

Fangs emerged from the dark-haired vampire as he moved slowly toward her. His face was handsome, almost boyish. He had a fallen-angel quality that suggested *other*, but also not. She should have been frightened, but somehow, his approach was non-threatening. She sensed a pervasive sadness in the vampire and almost felt sorrow for him.

"Move away, George. She's not for you." Remare kept his tone mild. "She's a member of House Valadon and, as such, under the High Lord's protection."

He stopped as soon as Remare mentioned Valadon's name. "She's not for me." His voice, barely a whisper, suggested vulnerability.

"No. Move along. Find your dinner someplace else."

Bowing to Remare, he crept back into the shadows.

"Something was wrong with him. I sensed his hunger, but there was something different about him."

"Always perceptive. George isn't dangerous, but he's not right either. We call his kind shadow-dwellers. Loners."

"What do you mean?"

"For whatever reason, his master didn't finish turning him. He's half-vampire, half-human and will remain so. Unfortunately, his mind is fractured. No House will accept him."

"And you say he's not a threat?"

"Not so far."

Miranda couldn't get over that feeling of loneliness the vampire was emitting. "What happens to vampires like him?"

"They usually learn to fend for themselves. Some, however, become the pawns of older and more powerful vampires."

"Can't something be done for them?"

"There are places for those like him. Most choose not to go there, preferring the outside world they once knew."

"Why would a master not finish what he started?"

Grimacing, Remare seemed uncomfortable discussing George with her. "Any number of reasons. It could be he changed his mind. Or that his blood wasn't compatible. Some humans think they want to become vampires then, when faced with the reality, panic and try to stop the process once it's begun." He rubbed her knuckles with his thumb. "Mistakes are few. But they do happen."

She glanced backward and pondered where the vampire had slunk off to. She wondered who took care of him. He looked so alone, as if yearning for something. She was curious how many others there were like him.

Miranda gazed up at the sky as a flash of lightning struck the water. She knew the storm was coming quickly in off the ocean. When the skies broke, it would be like a monsoon. She could feel the electricity in the air. It made the tips of her fingers heat, and she considered the possibility of tapping into it. The air was heavy with humidity, and the putrid smell of the East River was growing stronger the closer they neared to it.

As they walked toward the river, they passed a few homeless people sharing a liquor bottle. They were trying to light a fire in a metal drum to stay warm. Some looked dangerous. Miranda didn't like the idea of anyone freezing; she snapped her fingers, and instantly, the fire started in the can as they walked by. She grinned at their startled sounds of surprise.

Remare eyed her speculatively.

"What?" Now, it was her turn to look innocent. "They were cold."

"Do you *not* know the benefits of keeping a low profile?"

Miranda looked at his cashmere coat and expensive suit. "Oh, yeah, like we blend."

They were only a block away when Miranda heard voices sniggering behind them and glanced at Remare. His face betrayed nothing, but she knew he was aware of their new followers. Their fetid stench gave them away.

When they turned to face their would-be attackers, she knew they were high on something. She could smell marijuana, probably laced with other chemicals, and booze reeking from them. The trouble with drugs was that it made people unpredictable. Whether or not they knew Remare was a vampire, she couldn't tell. But, when one of them brandished a knife, demanding cash, Remare burst into fighting mode, and then, the others joined in.

Miranda had been taught self-defense by the Were Queen herself, Lizandra, and knew how to aim a well-placed kick. The electrically charged particles in the air made it easy to form a ball of energy in her hand. When one of the men rushed her, she ducked and threw the power orb his way. He slammed into the side of the building and slid, unconscious, to the ground.

Remare moved so fast she could barely track the swings of his sword cane. Two men were on the ground; they lay, bleeding, on their sides. Behind him, a third picked up an old beer bottle and aimed it at the back of Remare's head. Miranda raised her arm and used her power to shatter the glass. Startled, he took off running.

When another rumble of thunder, much closer this time, rent the air and made the ground tremble, the rest of the assailants scrambled and ran off.

Her heart pounding, she joined Remare. "What, no decapitations, this time?"

He smirked at her humor. "They were human. I only use the sword with vampires." Adjusting his coat, Remare nodded in her direction. "Let's get this over with, so we can go home."

Miranda had no desire to stay in this neighborhood any longer. Especially when it started to rain. In buckets. "I agree."

Chapter Five

Valadon waited until the last of his Elite Torians had entered his stately conference room to start his meeting. His traditional black and gold colors decorated the room from the ebony table to the dark oak walls, on which hung many of his prized paintings with gilded frames. He had an army of mid-level Torians who waited on his command within the walls of ValCorp and in the surrounding area. But the ones present were his closest advisors, those he considered his family. Each of them had bled for him, proving their loyalty many times over the long and tempestuous centuries they had been together.

Only one was missing, his trusted second, who was tracking the movements of his nephew, Nick, and would join him later.

"I'll keep this meeting brief. In front of each of you, you will find a folder containing information on the missing vampires who have been reported to us."

Tristan, his master of weapons, asked, "Do we have an exact count on how many have disappeared?"

"Exact, no. Some vampires may have no families or close friends to report their absence to us. However, we do know at least twenty-three have gone missing in the last six months. That number is sure to increase." Valadon motioned for Aiden, his communications expert, who was standing off to the side, to continue.

"If you will look up at the screen." Aiden used his laser pen to point out several faces at various public events. "You will see those who either have been known to have dealings with or have been proven to be members of the Human Order of Light."

Katya, Tristan's lover, asked, "How current is this data?"

"This is the most up-to-date information we have." Aiden added, "As you know, Irina and Gregori have diligently been working on infiltrating and monitoring the movements of certain high-ranking members of the HOL."

Valadon interjected, his voice deeply authoritative, "Let me be clear, our intel is the work of not only our trusted Torians," he bowed his head in deference to Irina and Gregori, "but that of our human and Were friends, as well." He sighed in remorse. "One of the Weres died in his attempt to help us. Unfortunately, he was working solo at the time. That will not be the case here. Each of you will work in pairs and be in constant contact."

Aiden continued, "Each of your folders contains photos of the bodies we were able to recover. As you can see, the amount of mutilation varies, but the cuts are nearly identical. In most of the cases, substantial amounts of blood were drained. Vampire and human alike."

After the moans and angry grunts died down, he said, "This figure here," he pointed to a man who seemed to be attending a formal cocktail party, "we know was Emerson Whitney," he clicked the remote to the next slide of another figure, "and this was Cyrus Langhorn. Both were killed in a fire out on Long Island nearly a year ago."

"West Gate Estate." Irina's voice was cold and harsh "That's where the members of HOL had an exclusive party. Several others died there, as well."

"Yes, including Walter Pettigrew." Aiden clicked the remote again to a screenshot of several men enjoying a game of golfing. "We've been collecting data on known associates of theirs, and they've been under constant surveillance. Their dossiers are included in your folders."

Valadon's voice resonated. "Each of you will closely monitor the members you've been assigned."

Tristan looked up from his folder. "Who's the man in the background? He's been in all four shots."

Valadon's face turned icy, as did his voice. "Notice how his head is turned in each of the slides as if he knew he was being photographed. He usually stays in the shadows. Until now, no one has been able to ascertain his true identity, although it is believed he's European in ancestry. From what our sources have gathered, he is the enigmatic leader of the HOL. My Torians, we suspect he's the one they refer to as...*The Regent*."

A rush of voices echoed in the room, and Valadon quieted them with a raised hand. "We will go with the presumption he is as wealthy as the others and attends many of the same social engagements. There's one coming up soon." His eyes narrowed in contemplation. "We owe thanks to Jason Morgan and his father, Wilson, for providing us with the data."

Aiden nodded. "They've certainly proven their loyalty. Jason has been gathering intel for us for some time now, but even he can't determine *The Regent's* true identity. He's worried they may be on to him. They're being cautious. Old friends are not as forthcoming with information as they used to be."

"Protection has been provided for him and his father. Morgan informs us the others live in fear of their leader. Find this Regent." Valadon banged his fist on the table. "Cut off the head, and the rest will scramble. Any questions?"

In unison, everyone shook their heads.

***

Stuart Blackmore, CEO of Ehrlich Industries, reclined in his Park Avenue penthouse and admired his newest acquisition. Collecting Impressionist art gave him great pleasure. He stroked one tapered finger down his jaw and wondered if he would send this particular painting to his estate in Austria or keep it here in New York. There was still time to decide.

He gazed around his study at his other works of art he had accumulated, some through legal means and others through more nefarious methods. Smirking, he pressed the hidden button beneath his desk, and a panel on the opposite wall slid open, revealing his prized Renoir. He'd had to pay the art thief a sizeable amount, but nothing compared to what he might have had to pay if the painting had gone to auction at Sotheby's. No one else knew he had the painting, and he planned to keep it that way.

As he studied his paintings, he wondered how many forgeries were hanging in the homes of his acquaintances. He knew, in his collection, there were no forgeries. Unlike some of his associates, he'd invested well, and the revenues from his pharmaceuticals company, as well as his various other holdings, were performing very well. They had better, he thought. It took a great deal of money to fund the research necessary for his DOL Project.

In the past, his ancestors had been accused of committing crimes against humanity for the experiments they'd performed on the prisoners. Little did the authorities know of the other tests presently being conducted. Fools didn't know the half of it, he sneered. When they'd finally discovered the underground labs of his forefathers, all empirical proof had been disseminated or destroyed. Didn't they realize great medical breakthroughs came at the expense of great sacrifice?

How fortuitous it was he had made the acquaintances of those like-minded individuals who could continue with his grandfather's research. One, in particular, was Frank Peralt, his chief chemist and VP of Research and

Development at EI, and with modern technology and the profits from the pharmaceuticals, the experiments would continue without interruption.

Several other members of the exclusive group Ehrlich belonged to had elected to sell off their art in order to contribute to the cause. Of course, they'd had to hire extraordinary forgers to replace the original works that were now in the homes of collectors in Asia. The forgeries were exceptional; even he had difficulty discerning the copies from the masterpieces. As did the authenticators the insurance companies insisted on.

The image of one beautiful authenticator came to mind. She'd been studying the Van Gogh in the Ormont home and might have seen a flaw in the reproduction, had she not decided to eavesdrop on his conversation with his fellow conspirators.

He pressed a different button beneath his desk and watched as another panel slid open to reveal a large blank screen. He used his remote to turn on the disk of Professor Miranda Crescent casually strolling along the corridor in the Ormont home, admiring the paintings. She really was quite lovely. He wondered what it would feel like fucking her. Before he killed her, of course. If she was wary about one painting, she may grow suspicious of the others. That he could not allow to happen. He always enjoyed playing with his prey before he saw it vanquished. But, first, he would ascertain how much she knew about the forgeries.

"How astute you are, professor." He lifted his brandy snifter in salute. She'd been reportedly involved with the detestable vampire, Valadon, the one vampire Ehrlich was sworn to destroy. For centuries, his family had been systematically eliminating the vampires, and he would see that legacy continue. They'd come close to killing Valadon, but complications ensued, and the vampire lord had been able to evade his assassins. No matter, the war was better fought from within than without. It would take longer, but Ehrlich would see the eradication of the vampires if it was the last thing he did.

He studied the fine length of Crescent's throat. There were no marks. That pleased him. The latest media reports had her engaged to a handsome young musician, but he didn't take those reports too seriously. He swirled his brandy in quiet anticipation. He had plans for the young professor.

He reached for the button to shut the panels but, then, as no one was present, decided to use his *Elemental* powers and, raising his hand, closed both panels.

Chapter Six

"Knock, again. You can't just go barging in on them. This is someone's home."

Remare examined the old row house as the rain continued falling. "It appears no one has lived here in some time." As there was no bell, he knocked, again. When there was no answer, he took out a small leather case and used his tools to pick the lock. Opening the door, they stepped inside. Good thing, too, because at that moment, the sky opened, and the rain came down in sheets. It was dark, but the lights from the bridge on the East River offered enough illumination for Miranda to see the wall sconces. She flicked her fingers, using her power to light them.

The musty scent greeted them as they entered the domicile. The furniture was old but clean in the sparse living area.

As they moved into the kitchen area, Nick came rushing down the stairs. His hair was disheveled, and his shirt was wrinkled. *"Don't shut the door!"* he yelled as he started buttoning his shirt. "Too late." He blew out a breath. "I think the lock is on some kind of timer. It's locked."

Not dissuaded by Nick's remarks, Remare tried the doorknob and then jiggled it roughly. Angrily, he turned to Nick. "What the hell are you doing here? We've been searching for you for half the night. You're supposed to keep your cell phone with you at all times. Is that so difficult to do?"

Nick groaned, "I forgot. Some of the students wanted to go out and celebrate. I just lost track of time."

"Did you, now?" Remare moved closer and sniffed the air around Nick. "Apparently, you had someone to celebrate with. *Intimately!* A Were, if I'm not mistaken."

Miranda winced at Remare's sarcastic tone, and her stomach sank for Nick. She'd never seen a vampire blush before, but Nick's face was definitely glowing. Not wanting to witness Nick's further humiliation, she went off to the kitchen to see if there were any candles in the drawers. She tried to block out Remare's tirade about rules and obligations. With Nick's parents deceased, he almost sounded paternal, like he was Nick's father giving him a tongue lashing for staying out all night.

When Nick's voice equaled Remare's in volume and pitch, she joined them and tried to ease the situation. "Calm down. Arguing about it is not going to make this situation any better."

"We would not be in this situation if Nick had remembered to take his phone."

"Look, I already apologized—"

"Stop! Just stop." She put a calming hand on Remare's arm. She hated seeing the anger in his eyes but knew it sprang from concern for Nick's welfare. "We're here, now. It's pouring cats and dogs outside. Let's just try to make the best of it until the storm passes."

Remare muttered something she could not hear as he took off his coat and hung it on the newel post.

"I'm going to get my shoes." Nick explained, "I left them upstairs."

When Nick departed, Miranda glared at Remare.

His eyes narrowed. "What was that look for? He should show respect to Valadon and to me."

Miranda lowered her voice. "You didn't have to yell at him that way. You humiliated the guy."

He followed her into the kitchen. "Good, he should be embarrassed."

"Will you keep your voice down? He apologized, so get over it." Miranda started opening drawers to see if there was anything to make tea with. With the rain coming down, a soothing cup of tea would do wonders for her headache.

"You don't understand."

"I do understand. It's you who don't understand. I know he's under a great deal of stress with all the obligations and responsibilities you love to throw on him." She exhaled. "Nick's a good guy. You and Valadon have got to cut him some slack."

Remare started to say something then appeared to change his mind. "I know we may seem to be strict with him."

"Seem to be?" Miranda smirked at him as she found a couple of mugs in the cabinet. "I'm going to make some tea. Want some?"

"If there's anything edible in those cabinets, I wouldn't risk it."

"I wouldn't try it, either. I'm using the bottled water we got at the bar. I have some teabags I keep in my purse. And, if we're lucky enough, a couple of sugar packets." She dug them out of her shoulder bag. "Jasmine green tea. Mmm, one of my favorites."

Arms crossed, he leaned against the fridge. "I thought you liked mint tea?"

Miranda remembered the pound of fresh mint tea he had bought her from McNulty's, her favorite tea shop, and had placed in her cabinet. She still kept the note she'd found inside the bag he had written her. "That's for special occasions."

Finally, a hint of a smile.

"So, do you want some?"

His eyes darkened as he stared at her lips. "Yes."

"Man, it's really pouring out there." Nick joined them in the kitchen.

"I'll call in and let them know Nick's safe." Remare tried his cell phone, but there was no service. "Great! We're in a dead zone."

The sound of the thunder shook the old house. "Because of the storm?" she asked.

"Maybe, but I suspect this area probably hasn't had cell service since the last war."

She took another mug from the cabinet. "Nick, I'm making tea; would you like a cup?"

As if cold, he rubbed his hands together. "Sure. Thanks."

***

It was nearly three-thirty in the morning when Gregori tossed and turned for the last time. Looking over at the empty space on his bed, he slid his hand over the cold bare sheets. For too long, that side of his bed remained empty. The hell with it, he thought, and decided to get up. He wasn't getting any sleep tonight. He needed to work off the energy that had been building all night. He slid his workout pants on and a muscle shirt and headed for the training area.

Gregori liked working out in the early morning hours when the place was empty and he could concentrate on his own routine. After three miles on the treadmill, he started his repetitions with the weights. The strongest of the Torians, he could bench press more than any other soldier and had the muscles to show for it. He knew he wasn't handsome like the other Elite guards—his face was too rugged, but his body was well-defined. He made sure it stayed that way.

During his last set of reps, she walked in. He didn't even have to open his eyes to know it was her. The scent of her lilac perfume was enough. The bane of his existence, the one who kept him up at night. The woman who had refused his advances to share his bed. Some called her, *The Ice Queen*, but to him, she was simply Irina.

And he craved her more than any other.

"I take it you couldn't sleep, either." He used a hand towel to wipe the sweat from his face.

"The storm continues raging outside."

He loved the sound of her Russian accent. His own had disappeared decades before, but hearing her inflections made him yearn for the home of his youth—a home which no longer existed. Both had grown up in Russia during the time of the czars, but where he was the son of a fisherman in a small town near the Volga River, whose parents had loved him and encouraged his studies, Irina had a much different upbringing.

The child of poor farmers, she'd been sold to an aristocratic overlord, Count Dravenoff, to be a companion for his young daughter. From the accounts Gregori had heard, the first few years were decent enough. She'd been taught the same studies as the Count's daughter and had been instructed in horsemanship, where she'd quickly excelled. But, when she became older, the Count had noticed her beauty far surpassed that of his own child. He'd raped Irina when she was barely a teenager and told her that her duties now included servicing him.

When she'd taken one of the horses and fled back to her parents, they beat her and told her she should be grateful she belonged to Dravenoff. None of the other girls in the village would ever have as much as she did. She would have fancy dresses, live in a castle and never know hunger.

Irina had cried and begged to stay, but when the men came for her, her parents had turned their backs on her.

In his rage, the Count had shot her beloved horse and had her punished by sharing her with his friends. Years later, he gambled her away to another overlord, Ivan, who made Dravenoff sound like a prince. Gregori knew Irina still bore the scars from her time in his camp.

"The storm will pass. It's still early. You should be sleeping."

"You're a fine one to talk." She nodded to his weights then took a dumbbell and started working her biceps. For a slender woman, she was in fantastic shape. Her body was long, lean and very desirable. And, with that mane of white-blond hair and piercing blue eyes, she was hauntingly beautiful. Something stirred deep within him.

He closely examined her face. "You've been putting in too many hours, Irina."

"Valadon needs the information." She switched the weight to the other hand. "You saw those pictures of the dead."

"Yes, but you don't have to work yourself to the point of exhaustion."

"I'm not. I'm just worried." Putting the dumbbell down, she rubbed her hands together as if for warmth. "Remare has not come back tonight."

Gregori exhaled. He'd known they'd once been lovers, but Remare's interests lay elsewhere. He would not be jealous of a vampire who had shown no interest in Irina for months. The truth was Remare's only concern was in tracking down Valadon's enemies and destroying them. "You still yearn for him?"

Her eyes glared as her temper spiked. "I said I was concerned, not that I yearned for him."

"Aiden said his last transmission indicated he was going to check out one more place and then call it a night." Like the others, he believed Nick to be cozy in some female's bed and would show up tomorrow. "Remare probably went back to his town house in Sutton Place. It is the weekend, and he, like the rest of us, needs his down time." When she remained tense, he changed his tone. "If there was a problem, he would have called for backup. Remare is no fool. He's the most powerful of us all. You saw the way he sparred with Valadon tonight."

"Yes." She sighed then met his eyes. "You're probably right."

Gregori smiled at her reluctance and the irony of the situation. She had a man before her who would worship her body and soul. And, yet, she still hadn't let go of the vampire who had proven he wanted nothing to do with her. "Come." He rose and took her arm. "I'll take you back to your room."

They were silent as they walked down the corridor to her room. When they reached her door, he silently prayed she would invite him, but he knew she wouldn't. "Will you sleep, now?"

She shrugged. "I'll try." She looked up at him, and he saw a vulnerability she rarely showed others. "One of the dead was a girl who couldn't be more than fourteen. They cut her to pieces."

Gregori moved a stray strand of hair from her face. "I know. We'll find the monsters who did that to her. And destroy them." He turned to leave and was a few steps away when he heard her voice, barely a whisper.

"Gregori." Her voice was music to his ears. "Do you want to come in for a nightcap?"

He shook his head; he couldn't possibly have heard her right. His desires had him imagining things. Irina never invited him in to her private quarters. The most amount of time he ever spent with her was either in the training rooms, the rifle range or when they went out on missions together. He turned to look back at her.

When she stood there with the door held open with the lost look of a woman who needed comfort, his protective instincts kicked in. God, how he wanted her. "*Da.*"

Chapter Seven

Remare quietly entered the bedroom and closed the door behind him. He removed his tie, and then, toeing off his boots, he undid the first two buttons on his shirt. The mattress dipped as he lay beside Miranda on the bed. She could pretend to be asleep, but what would be the point? He could sense her level of consciousness.

In the darkness, a solitary candle flickered. "Is your headache any better?" His voice was soft and sensual.

"A little." The migraine medicine had helped, but the storm raging outside with the rain pelting against the windows only added to her sense of unease. Turning toward him, she saw the slow rise of his lips and was amazed at how handsome he really was. She breathed in his masculine scent. Remare always had a dangerous aura about him, upping his sex appeal. And the goatee only added to his allure. Stroking the fine line of beard along his jaw, she could easily see how the women at Nightshade would be attracted to him.

He took her hand in his and kissed her palm. "It's been a while since we've been alone."

"I know."

He pulled her closer and kissed her forehead. "You're not still angry with me about the photos?"

"No." But, when he tried to kiss her again, she slowly stood and stepped a few feet from the bed. "I'm not angry. But I've given some thought to what you said." She met his eyes. "You thought I was jealous of the women you were dancing with in the photos." She began pacing. She'd always been able to collect her thoughts better when she was in motion. "I'm not."

When he tried to speak, she raised a hand to stop him. "Let me explain. I know I'm not gorgeous like those women." She shrugged. "I know I never will be. That's not what bothered me."

When he started to rise, she gestured for him to stay. "Hear me out. I've been thinking of little else, and I want you to understand why I reacted the way I did."

His dark brown eyes held concern and warmth. "Go on."

Crossing her arms over her chest, she leaned her arm against one of the posts of the bed. "This goes back to when I was an undergraduate at NYU. I was spending as much time as I could with Lizandra and the gang at Werehaven. I guess I was nervous about moving to Paris to do my grad work."

"I remember there was one night at Werehaven, I couldn't sleep. Fragments of nightmares haunted me, chilling me to the bone." She rubbed her arms as if cold. "Call it anxiety, insomnia, whatever you want. I got up in the middle of the night and sought Liz out. I could talk to her about anything, and she wouldn't judge me; she'd understand. Did I ever tell you how I met Lizandra?"

He shook his head. "No, I don't think you ever did."

"It was down at the old Waverly movie theater. I was a movie fanatic—got that from my Aunt Meg. One night, after the movie let out, I went to the café across the street for tea and dessert, and I noticed her. We were both eating the chocolate decadence cake, looking equally guilty for enjoying the sinful pleasure of it. I'm not sure who started talking first, but we compared our thoughts on the film. We seemed to hit it off right away, and then ran into each other the next week. And the week after that. You know when something just clicks and it feels so right?"

Remare lifted up on his elbow. "You had much in common. I'm glad you were able to develop your friendship with her."

"After that, she started inviting me uptown to her family's place. God, can they cook." Miranda leaned her back against the post. "Her brothers, grandfather, everyone was always making me things. Food is a way of life with them. Then, one day, she asked me why I never invited her to my place. I didn't realize I had offended her. I rarely, if ever, invited anyone over. After my parents died, my aunt encouraged me to spend more time with friends, but I didn't want to." She shook her head. "Instead, I turned my attention to books, studying. I pretty much kept to myself."

"You weren't ready to socialize, then?"

"I chose not to. I didn't want to see the families of my classmates; I didn't need to be reminded of what I'd lost. So, yeah, friendships—not so much in my life. At least not until NYU. I explained to Liz I didn't realize I had upset her, so I invited her over to my place. One of the few things I could cook back then was grilled cheese sandwiches—the best kind are with Swiss cheese and tomatoes. After a while, she asked me if I was embarrassed of her because she was a mixed-race person. Stunned, I just looked at her. She'd introduced me to her family, but I hadn't introduced her to one single member of my family.

Holding on to the post, Miranda closed her eyes. "I remember she was ready to walk out." She bit her lip. "It was hard for me to get the words out, but I finally told her I didn't have any relatives. I'll tell you this much: Orphans hate admitting they have no family. That stopped her dead in her tracks. She just turned and gaped at me."

"What about your aunt who raised you?"

"My Aunt Meg left me after I turned eighteen. We weren't very close. Oh, she took care of me, taught me the essentials, but she always had such a sad expression on her face. Distant. She introduced me to the family lawyer, Arnold Rossman, who explained my parents' will and trust and the finances I needed to know. The night I graduated from high school, after a fantastic dinner of roasted lamb and red potatoes, my aunt informed me she was leaving. She said it was too painful for her to live in the house anymore. Frantic, I didn't want her to go. Aunt Meg was all I had left of my family. I told her we could sell the place, move elsewhere. She wasn't interested. She said, as I got older, I reminded her more and more of my dad, and she just couldn't deal with it anymore.

"Did you ever hear from her, again?"

"In the beginning, I got postcards from her, birthday and holiday cards. Over time, they lessened and finally stopped."

Remare's voice was unswerving. "I could track her down for you, find out where she is. If that's what you wish."

"No." Miranda shook her head. "She gave up seven years of her life raising me. I'm respecting her wishes. She's entitled to her life."

Nostrils flaring, Remare mumbled something in Italian she didn't quite hear. He met her eyes. "If you change your mind, ValCorp has many resources. It would not be difficult to locate her."

"Don't." She exhaled. "Getting back to Lizandra. She took it upon herself to adopt me. Made me attend holiday parties with her family. I told her it wasn't necessary; I was used to being alone. She wouldn't hear of it. I tried to explain to her that, for about ninety percent of the time, I'm good with my life, and I like the solitude."

"And the other ten percent?"

"Yeah, solitude sucks."

Remare smiled up at her.

"Anyway, that night at Werehaven when I sought her out, I went to her rooms. It was dark, but my night vision has always been good. We were pretty close, so I didn't knock when I entered her bedroom."

His brows rose. "You walked in on her with another Were?"

"Oh, yeah, I did." Miranda reflected on the memory. "Good sense should have had me leaving and closing the door. But I didn't. She was in Gavin's arms. Both were naked. I just stood there, transfixed, watching. I had friends from NYU who got frisky with each other, weren't exactly inhibited about sex." She raised a shoulder. "I suppose I knew as much about sex as any college student, but what I saw that night between them...captivated me. I'd never seen that level of intimacy, that soulful, heartfelt tenderness before. The love between them was so apparent, so real—I couldn't comprehend its depth so I stayed there, spellbound."

"I remembered tears started forming in the back of my eyes. Lizandra turned her head toward me. I thought she'd be mad. But she just grinned and then told Gavin. He looked up at me and smiled. I would have left, but she gestured for me to join them. I shook my head and reached for the door. She called out to me. She knew I suffered from nightmares about the car crash that killed my parents and...other things."

As if he couldn't hold back any longer, Remare reached up and pulled her down beside him.

Miranda continued, "Liz hugged me close and told Gavin it was all right. That everything was all right. Gavin embraced me, too; he kept running his hands up and down my arms and back to soothe me. He kissed my neck and shoulders. They chased away the cold and gave me warmth. Both of them cuddled me, brought me into their secret world until the tears stopped. It was pretty damned erotic." Miranda rubbed Remare's shoulder, her thumb drawing circles on his neck. "That night, the energy between us was electric. They knew I had alienated myself too much, created too much distance between everyone else. They gave me the connection I so desperately craved."

His eyes narrowed. "Did you—?"

"It wasn't about sex, Remare." She held his hand. "It was about acceptance. About understanding the depth of loneliness and offering a piece of yourself so your friend doesn't feel isolated from the rest of the world. It was so fucking *precious* to me. To know they cared enough to welcome me into their lives, to their passion, their friendship, to become a part of them. It meant the world to me."

She met his eyes. "I haven't felt anything that deep, that intense...until you. That night in your apartment, I felt we had something sacred, something beyond the ordinary. You made me feel so cherished, more alive than I've ever felt before. It was magical."

His voice held sympathy and a hint of reprimand. "And you thought, when you saw those photos, it was not equally precious to me. That I have that level of intimacy with other women."

Miranda gazed down at their linked hands.

"You need not have been so concerned, Mir-randa." He pulled their clasped hands over his heart. "Never doubt me. You are my heart. In a world filled with darkness, you are my light. No other has *ever* affected me the way you do." His breath mingled with hers. "No one else ever will. Don't you know that?" He snaked his hand around her neck and pulled her close. His leg brushing the inside of her thighs, he plundered her mouth in a kiss so hot it seared her very being.

Their tongues dueling, Miranda lost herself in his embrace, swimming in an ocean of intimacy, the intensity of which was both frightening and exhilarating. She dug her nails into his back, needing something to hold on to. To ground her as her emotions spun high and wild. He returned her fervor by plunging his hand in her hair and tugging gently as he devoured part of her soul.

And no one, not one single person, not even Lord Valadon, could ever touch what they shared.

***

Cerise walked down the corridor in her uncle's mansion in Riverside Park, a veritable fortress containing many artifacts from the generations of Were packs before them. Edgar Renworth had a penchant for weapons and collected antique guns and daggers dating back centuries. He even owned a few cannons, but why, she had no clue since they'd never been fired. At least not since she'd been alive. She giggled at how phallic the weapons were. Spears, swords, knives, guns, fucking cannons—all a representation of their maleness, their power. And Uncle had to have the biggest balls around. She was surprised he didn't have a missile or rocket launcher hiding somewhere within their compound. Knowing Renworth, he probably did.

He also liked collecting fine art. Many paintings and tapestries containing battle scenes lined the walls of the mansion. And one beautiful portrait of the pack master's deceased wife.

She hesitated outside his bedroom. Leaning against the door, she snickered when she heard the laughter of two distinct female voices in the throes of passion. After the pack master's bloody victory in the cage, women had swarmed him, wanting to feel the excitement of his touch. It didn't matter how many Renworth chose, there were always more waiting, wanting to fuck their leader, if for nothing else than the sheer pleasure of claiming to be one of his favorites. As Were King of the Red Claw Clan, Edgar Renworth could have any of the females in the pack he chose.

And choose he did, whenever and as often as he wanted. His appetite for sex was almost as voracious as his craving for power.

Although Cerise enjoyed the view of the river, Renworth was not satisfied with his territory along the Hudson River Park and desired the Were Queen's land in Central Park. He saw the potential in such prime real estate and was determined to have it. There had been several skirmishes and one legal battle ending in their defeat. It had rained blood in the mansion that day. Cerise shuddered. Many of Red Claws had been viciously torn apart in the cage by the wrath of the Were King. Renworth did not take defeat well, but the pack master was far from done. He was always planning, calculating risk and probability.

He hadn't become a media mogul by playing by the rules. If he couldn't obtain the region by legal means, he would resort to more nefarious methods.

Most members in Renworth's inner circle knew their king despised the vampire lord ever since Valadon had out-maneuvered him in acquiring a prestigious and lucrative communications network. But Cerise knew his animosity went much deeper. She'd been a mere pup when she'd overheard the pack master arguing with his late wife. Julienne was the most beautiful Were in the clan and one of the best fighters. No one could best her. They were the power couple to end all couples. Everyone admired them wherever they went. But jealousy was an ugly hag, and gossip began to surface about Julienne. Cerise suspected certain females vying for Edgar's attention purposely spread those rumors. Weres could be very possessive of their mates, and Edgar had accused Julienne of cheating on him with Valadon.

Two days later, Julienne had died in a horrific car accident. And, that night, Edgar had welcomed two new lovers to his bed. Cerise often wondered if he kept her portrait as a sentimental gesture or as a warning to anyone who would betray him.

When the laughter died down inside the bedroom, Cerise knocked on the door and then entered the opulent sleeping quarters of the Were King. The scent of sex was heavy in the air.

"Cerise, what news?" Renworth pulled on a robe and went to pour himself a drink. The two nude women on his bed didn't bother covering up.

"All has been done as requested. The vampire lord's nephew will not survive the night."

"And our special guest? Have all the arrangements been met?"

"Yes, everything has been done to your specifications. He will find his way through the underground access tunnels we provided into the house where I left Nick sleeping. All the windows have bars on them, and the doors have been sealed shut. There's no hope of escape."

"Good." Renworth bared his teeth and seemed to be considering her. "And you have no remorse for the young vampire you've been sleeping with for the better part of a year?"

Grinning, she accepted the drink he poured for her. "None whatsoever, Uncle."

Laughing, he raised his glass to her. "You shall be rewarded, then." As he drank, his eyes gleamed with anticipation. "As soon as I have confirmation of your success."

Chapter Eight

After checking on Nick, who was still asleep on the couch, Miranda gazed outside. The wind seemed to have picked up and was battering against the house. When the lid of a garbage can nearly crashed into the window, she realized why the occupants had installed bars. That, and to keep the undesirables out.

When she returned to the bedroom, Remare rose up on his elbow and grinned at her. As sexy as he was when he smiled that way at her, as if they had some secret pact only lovers shared, her heart ached. If it was only lust, she would have walked away a long time ago. But their relationship was so much deeper, more complex. He held her spellbound.

"You know, there is still so much I don't know about you." She leaned against the bed post.

His voice was husky but still sounded amused. "Then, ask what it is you want to know."

"How did you and Valadon meet?" She'd been wondering about their friendship for some time. She'd heard rumors but wanted to know more. His unwavering loyalty to the High Lord had to have been forged by some incredible experiences.

"That," he sighed, "is a very long story."

Miranda pointed to the window and the raging storm outside. "It doesn't appear we're going anywhere anytime soon. Tell me."

"All right." He patted the space on the bed near him, and she lay down beside him. Remare closed his eyes as if in memory. "It was a very long time ago. Valadon grew up in an area outside Paris, and I grew up in Rome. When we were old enough, our parents sent us to University. Valadon studied economics, and I focused on learning war strategies. Our countries were always at war with someone back then and needed good commanders. As we both belonged to noble families, it was expected we would serve our main court in Paris after our education had been finished."

He turned toward her and ran his thumb along her cheek. "There are many things about my past you will not like, Miranda." He exhaled. "Our survival depended on us doing many unspeakably ugly things. Our ruling queen was ruthless in exacting treaties with the human aristocrats. At the time, she needed to be."

She sensed Remare wanted to tell her things, private matters, but was reluctant. She took his hand and rubbed her thumb over his knuckles, the way he often did with hers. "I didn't expect your life was easy and fairytale-like."

"No." He stroked her hand. "It was hardly so. Our sovereign court was rife with corruption and twisted indulgences only the very rich and powerful luxuriate in."

"Is that where you met Valadon?"

"We'd been friends at school, but our education wasn't complete until we went through our council's training program." His eyes drifted shut. "In order to secure adequate hunting grounds, our leaders had to negotiate accords with the human courts. There were no readily available blood banks back then." He linked his fingers with hers. "We either hunted for our food or it was provided to us by the aristocrats in exchange for certain favors. Often, our treaties included trade."

"What did you have to barter?" Miranda asked, although she had a pretty good idea.

"We watched your kind for some time, began alliances with those we trusted so that we would have human associates to keep us protected during the daylight hours.

When your kind erected castles and instigated the feudal system of lords and vassals, so did we. Having lived so long in caves, we explored and mined precious metals and stones. We traded with them. We became lords and rulers over our own lands, pretty much as your ancestors did. Valadon understood economics better than I did and had our people build ships to negotiate with other regions. I led armies against those who threatened us."

"But that wasn't enough for your high court?"

"No. It wasn't. Human rulers came and went; each new king or queen had different demands. They were fascinated by our otherness, desired our beauty, and hungered for our touch. Our queen implemented courses for our youth to please the humans. In return, they kept us protected."

Miranda knew nothing came without a price. She hated asking but felt compelled. "What did you do?"

"The training regimen all younger vampires from noble families went through was to improve our skills in the carnal arts." He smirked. "Some aristocrats have quite eclectic tastes. At first, I was intrigued by the teachings. We were assigned to different lords for periods of time. I was taught to seduce and be seduced." His hand waved nonchalantly in the air. "In the beginning, the houses we served were acceptable." He sighed. "And then, there were those that weren't." A slight tic started in his jaw.

"Remare, you don't have to tell me anymore."

"You should know, Miranda. Who we are." He ran his knuckles across her jawline. "Where we came from." He pushed up on the bed and leaned his head back against the pillow. "Magritte was our queen. No other vampire was older or more powerful. She decided who we would go to and when. As my mother was from Britain, I was assigned to an outpost in northern England."

"Your mom was British?" Her brow knitted. "I thought you were all Roman. Your accent."

"No, my father was a Roman general who served as advisor to the human monarchy. He met my mother when he was stationed in Britain."

She was beginning to read his prolonged silences, her empathy strong. "Your mother wasn't a vampire, was she?"

He ran one finger down her cheek. "Ever perceptive, Miranda."

"Intuitive, I guessed." But, somehow, she'd known. It was something in his voice—the way he'd hesitated. "That's why you're not a Blueblood, nor have your own territory."

"I could have my own territory, Miranda. I chose not to. The reasons are many."

She heard the prevailing sadness in his voice and wanted to silence his pain. "You don't have to continue."

His eyes said otherwise. "I must."

Miranda laid her head on his chest and liked when his arm circled her shoulders. His embrace offered comfort.

"The lord I was assigned to was a temperamental, arrogant man who gave free reign to his indulgences. When business was good, he was decent enough, but when a deal did not work out to his expectations, he drank heavily."

Miranda remembered he once spoke of the cruel lord who had punished him by making him witness the repeated violations of a young girl he'd had feelings for.

"Lord Acton enjoying making those around him suffer. Whether they were human or vampire didn't matter to him. A true sadist, he took pleasure in the pain of others. Especially those who openly defied him."

Sensing his pain, she knew this wasn't going to end pretty. "And you defied him."

"Often. And suffered the penalty for it. I had petitioned our court for a transfer, but Queen Magritte would not hear of it. Her word was final. Or so she thought."

"Acton found out about my request to Magritte and had me beaten to within an inch of my life. Of course, he had me starved first so that I was already weakened. I knew, if I didn't escape, he would have eventually killed me. I had one of the servants get word to Valadon, requesting his assistance. He sent his people with horses to help me get back to Paris. By the time I got there, I was barely alive. When he saw the condition I was in, he gave me his blood and then negotiated my release with Magritte."

"I know." He had mentioned this to her one night, months ago.

"But I did not tell you the price he was forced to pay for my freedom. You asked how Valadon and I became close. I will tell you."

"Magritte had fallen in love with Valadon. She was a powerful queen, but she was still a woman. Valadon was her favorite above all others in the court, and there was very little she would deny him. But everything comes with a cost. And hers was exceedingly high. She had been Valadon's personal trainer, taught him all there was to know about carnal pleasure. She expected him to please her when and where she demanded."

"Not too indulgent, huh!"

"The very rich and powerful often are. As much as she loved Valadon, he did not return her affections. And no amount of training could hide that painful truth from her. She grew angry, impatient with his disinterest. And, when Magritte became angry, she became vindictive."

"He'd used me as an excuse to avoid having to spend time with her. My wounds were such that I needed blood constantly to help with the healing. Acton had used a fire poker on me, and as you know burns are the hardest scars to heal, and in my starved state, I could not adequately heal all my wounds. Valadon continually fed me his blood so that my body could repair itself.

"In her wrath, she watched as Valadon tended to my wounds and resented it. Gravely. She decided to punish us both."

"But you didn't do anything."

"I left Acton's castle without permission. That was an act of defiance she never fully forgave me for."

Miranda's heart ramped up. "What happened?"

"She contrived to hurt Valadon as much as he had wounded her. She had us brought before her and our entire court. She publicly admonished us for deliberately conspiring against her. It was not true, but there was no arguing with our queen."

"Valadon contended he was tending to me, and there was no conspiracy. We did not know, at the time, that was the opening she'd been waiting for. She declared if Valadon loved me more than he did her, he could prove it to the court."

Miranda's stomach began contracting.

"I'm sure you heard the rumors that persist to this day, Miranda." He rubbed circles behind her neck. "Have you never wondered if they were true?"

She was honest with him. "I never gave them much thought."

"I've often been amused when I've heard the whisperings of others who weren't there."

Miranda was compassionately drawn to this proud man who was baring a part of his soul to her. Reassuringly, she leaned in and tenderly kissed him. "I don't care what happened back then. It was so long ago."

"It was. But I want to tell you so that you know the truth." His eyes narrowed. "You may not like most of it."

It was Magritte whom she disliked the most from his tale. Smiling, she laid her chin on his chest and remembered a phrase he often used. "Tell me."

Moving a strand of hair from her face, he returned her smile. "All right." His voice was thick with emotion. "You amaze me, Mir-randa, with your courage."

She wanted to tell him it wasn't about bravery, but more about the bond they shared.

"Magritte commanded Valadon fuck me in front of the entire court. *'Let's see if your actions match your words.'* Valadon was infuriated she would make such a request. He is not one easily manipulated and defied her in front of her own court."

"My God, what did she do?"

"To hurt him and prove to her court she was our supreme ruler, not to be questioned or challenged, she ordered me whipped. I was still weak from my injuries. She wanted me dead so Valadon would suffer, and others in her court would know never to oppose her."

Remare rubbed a thumb over his brow. "I will never forget the look of resentful defiance on Valadon's face. Finally, he capitulated. *'As my queen demands.'* She had desired his love, and he would never give that to her, but he was going to show her, and everyone else, what she would never have. You see, Magritte wasn't the only one capable of being vindictive. We were disrobed for the viewing pleasure of the audience. Someone had extinguished most of the torches in the room so the mood was that of evocative intimacy. Magritte sat on her throne, smug satisfaction in her eyes. They wanted to see the violent fucking of two men; the passion and the fury of a man who had been forced to submit. They did not know Valadon as well as I did. He would not give them the satisfaction.

Heart thundering, Miranda worried at just how Valadon would elicit his vengeance.

"Instead, Valadon decided to seduce the court, showing genuine affection instead of bitterness. He'd mind spoken to me in advance what he intended. Touching me as a lover does his beloved, he kissed my wounds, smiled and even laughed with me. His sensual tenderness was designed to enthrall. Remember, Magritte had been his teacher. He knew well how to elicit the reactions he desired. With every caress, every kiss, the audience was entranced by his skill. Sighs and groans of yearning could be heard throughout the throne room. Even Magritte allowed one solitary tear to roll down her face.

"Instead of a violation, of forced sex between two men, Valadon reminded them what many had forgotten: What it was to love and be loved. What it meant to sacrifice your dignity, your body for a person you cared about. He had every person in that court longing for his touch, to know what it meant to be loved that much, that well. To experience true passion.

"Hot damn, Remare." Miranda's heart was banging against her chest. "Magritte must have gone insane from jealousy."

"Hate is the other side of love, Miranda. And, from the expression on her face, I don't think she ever despised Valadon as much as she did that night. We knew we would have to leave her court soon after. The territories, here in America, had opened up, and Valadon petitioned for one of them. Of course, she denied him. It wasn't until the revolutions here in America and in France that she yielded. Wars cost a great deal of money, and Valadon had negotiated our freedom by promising to pay a portion of his profits from his holdings in America to the main court. Magritte reluctantly agreed. She was many things, but never a fool. Necessity superseded her pride."

Exhaling, he turned to her. "So you see, Miranda, that is the root of the rumors you may have heard. I wanted you to know the truth."

Miranda had suspected only through sex could they have such shared intimacy. But, now, she realized it wasn't just physical longing for each other that offered the serene closeness, the blissful connection of souls everyone desires, but few actually experience. It was the unremitting trust one had in the other that bound the hearts of those who truly know how to love.

"Your secrets are safe with me, Remare." She caressed his neck. "I will never betray you the way Magritte did Valadon."

"I know." He smiled and kissed her forehead. "That is why I told you."

Chapter Nine

Nick was sitting solemnly when Miranda went to check on him. Holding his jaw in his hand, he looked sad and despairing. Her heart ached for him. The storm had yet to abate with the howling wind and downpour. She sat across from him. "When the rain stops, we'll get out of here."

"And, then, what?"

She shrugged. "We go home." When she saw her statement had little effect on him, she added, "He means well." She tried to assuage his hurt look. "He's just concerned about you."

Nick snorted. "And he criticizes me about *my* choices! Valadon is going to go ballistic!"

Miranda was taken back by his comment. She and Remare had only kissed. There was no scent trace, so how could he... "We were only talking."

"Really? I'm not blind, Miranda. Your lips are swollen, and your face is flushed. I see the way he looks at you, and you at him. I saw it when we were in the archives trying to find the missing painting and, again, tonight."

Her heart racing in fear, she was shocked he had known and worried he might have said something to someone. "Has anyone else said anything?"

"No. Not yet. But Valadon's not a fool. Sooner or later, he's going to figure it out."

"You won't tell him?"

"He won't hear it from me. But one of you should tell him. He's not going to take kindly to his best friend..." he seemed to search for a better word than what he initially was going to say, "hanging out with the woman he loves."

Miranda hung her head in frustration and rubbed her hands. "We haven't been together much." She grimaced. "We've both kept our distance."

"Tell that to Valadon." Sarcasm laced his voice. "I'm sure he'll be *very* understanding."

"Miranda will not be the one telling Valadon anything." Remare stood against the entrance to the living room. "If anyone tells Valadon, it will be—"

Before he could finish his sentence, a loud roar thundered throughout the room, and a creature Miranda had once seen in ValCorp's cave tore through the room. Before Remare could reach for his sword cane, the monster cut him with piece of jagged metal across his leg. Blood gushed in a high arc as his body was thrown back by the force of the hit. He'd slashed Remare's femoral artery. Nick was up and moving way faster than anything she'd ever seen before. The invader growled in outrage. He threw Nick's body against the bannister with a sickening crash, the sound of splintering wood echoing through the room.

She must have been in shock, because as fast as everything was moving in real time, in her mind, the events were playing out in slow motion. Everything was registering as if it was on some sort of bizarre time delay. The phantom turned toward her. Before she even summoned them, her hands held two giant fireballs. Instinct must have kicked in because the red flames were hotter than anything she'd ever conjured.

In a virulent, harsh voice she was beginning to realize belonged to her Dark Angel, she threatened, "Taste the darkness."

Eyes wide in terror, the creature put its arms up to fend off the fire. Howling in agony, he ran back inside the closet. In its attempt to flee, she heard his movements descending downward. Miranda quickly grabbed a chair and shoved it under the doorknob, bolting the door. *Damn! There really were monsters in the closets!*

She swooped down to help Remare, who lay in a puddle of his own blood. His hands desperately tried to halt the flow pouring from his leg. His head had also suffered a gash when he'd hit the wall. Grabbing a scarf from her jacket, she tried to stem his bleeding by tying it around his thigh.

"Go help Nick. I've got this." He unbuckled and removed his belt then wound it around his leg as a tourniquet.

Miranda didn't like the awkward tilt of Nick's head as he lay sprawled, unconscious. She could tell, from the angle of his body, his shoulder must have been dislocated. From the blood on the wall, he probably had a concussion among his many other wounds. "Nick! Nick, can you hear me?" She tried rubbing his good arm and then his cheek, but there was no answer. She was glad for his somnolent state; otherwise, the pain would have been unbearable. Slowly, she dragged his body to the couch and carefully laid him down.

Remare pulled himself in front of Nick, leaving a bloody trail behind him. "Let him rest. He's a Blueblood. His body will heal."

Her heart was thundering. "That's the creature I saw down in the cave. At ValCorp. Remember." Miranda strained to catch her breath. "I tried to tell you then I'd seen something, but you didn't believe me."

"Not quite human but still human," he choked out, his face contorted in pain.

"From the war." Miranda agreed. "The media reports said people who were trapped underground twenty years ago had survived but were horribly disfigured. There was no way the rescue workers could get to everyone. They were entombed too far down. They're *not* urban legends."

"Those wounds looked like radiation burns. I've seen similar in pictures of victims of Chernobyl. His clothes were melted into his body."

Miranda nodded. "That horrifying stench smelled like burnt oil and something putrid."

Remare laid his sword across his legs. "Make sure that door is better bolted, Miranda. It may come back."

Miranda didn't want to go anywhere near it, but she grabbed a tall metal lamp and used it to secure the hold. After making sure the chair was tightly locked in place, she joined Remare.

Her voice trembled. "How many of them do you think there are?"

"No way to know." He shook his head. "I didn't believe you when you first mentioned them. I still can't believe a human could survive for so long buried underground."

"Scavengers. Somehow, they could climb high enough to forage for food, water. How come the rescue people didn't search longer?"

"Maybe they didn't think anything would endure being trapped there, Miranda."

"But, with medical treatment, maybe they could have been helped. Did you see how deformed his face was?" Miranda shuddered at the horror it must have suffered.

"I don't think there was much a medical team could have done." His voice sounded strained. "It will be dawn in a few hours." He pulled her down beside him. "More than likely, the creature will return." His eyes met hers. "I need blood to regain some of my strength."

Miranda retreated. She didn't like sharing blood. She wasn't a vampire. When he'd bitten her in the past, she was good with it because it was only a taste. But, now, what he was asking for was substantially more. He'd be feeding from her. "Nick will need some, too. His bones are broken."

"I need to be able to fight. To protect you and Nick. His strength and speed were quicker than I imagined."

Nodding, Miranda was ready to offer him her wrist then hesitated. "If I give you this, all three of us will be weakened. Right now, I'm the only one at full strength."

"Even at half-strength, I'm still stronger than you. Please, Mir-randa."

She was touched by the sincerity in his voice and his profound need to protect, but logic persisted. She ran her hand along the sword's cane. "I can do this. I scared him with the fireballs. He'll hesitate when he comes, again."

"No, Miranda. I will not hear of it. I will fight it. You take care of Nick."

She gazed at Nick's sleeping form. "You taught me how to handle a sword. Remember?"

"That was sword dancing. Not fighting."

"Lunging, thrusting. What more do I need to know?"

"You *don't* have the strength!"

She looked at the anger and the pleading in his eyes. "Right now, neither do you." Her heart was pounding. "You're always protecting someone. Let me do this."

"No!"

In a burst of speed, she swiped the sword from him and backed away. His eyes blazed in rage. Her eyes flashed back at him. Any other arguing was cut short by the sound of the creature approaching. Apparently, he had gotten over his aversion to fire and was banging against the door. It would be only seconds before he burst through. She removed the sword from the cane. "Any helpful hints you might have would be welcome, now."

His breaths became pants as he tried to stand, blood pouring down his leg. Before he could utter one word, the beast broke through the door.

Emotions warring within her, Miranda found the courage to attack the creature. Her body vibrated with rage, and her eyes flashed red as if sparks were emanating. No one and nothing would harm the ones she cared for so deeply. As the beast rushed her, determination transcended fear, and her need to protect erupted in a violent swing of the sword.

***

In the communications room at ValCorp, Morel looked up at the monitor. "That's odd, Remare's GPS just went on. The storm must have passed."

Aiden, who had been talking with his wife, Bree, looked over at the screen. "Pull up the grid."

With a few keystrokes, a map of the Lower East Side came up. Morel focused on the blinking light. "I thought he went to his home in Sutton Place." He pointed at the map. "Instead, it appears he's in what the locals call 'Old New York'. Bad neighborhood. I thought it was deserted. Some of the buildings there were never repaired from the last war." He rubbed his jaw. "What would he be doing there?"

"I don't know," Aiden barely whispered as if thinking aloud. "I'm going to try him, again, see if his phone's working." There was still no service. "No answer."

Morel ran his thumb over his lower lip. "I don't like this. I'm going to check out the area."

"Take back up with you. We don't need any more of our people going missing."

"Will do."

***

Miranda hoped her blood would help heal some of Nick's wounds. His face seemed so angelic in sleep. Even in repose, his instinct to feed was strong, and he sucked greedily at her wrist. When he had taken enough, Remare gave him the mental command to stop, as he had assured her he would.

"Nick really does resemble his mother." She moved a curl of his hair behind his ear. "I used to stare at Bianca's portrait in the archives. There were times when I felt as if she was trying to talk to me."

"Ghosts, now, Miranda?" Remare smiled slyly up at her.

"Funny." She slid beside him. "No. Just a strong sense I would have liked her immensely, and hopefully, she'd feel the same about me."

He stroked her cheek with his thumb. "I think she would have." His voice was labored.

"Okay, your turn." She moved her wrist to his mouth.

He held her arm tenderly in his hands. "Thank you, Mir-randa."

Her stomach fluttering, she became sensuously aware as Remare's fangs lengthened and penetrated her flesh. Eyes on her, he drank steadily; as if they were communicating a bond only a vampire and a human lover would know. It woke something primitive, primal, making her body feel more alive, even as her energy waned. When he sensed her weakened state, he removed his fangs and sealed her wounds with his tongue.

"You need rest, Miranda. You've fed two vampires, now."

"I know." She gazed over at the dead body lying in the corner. With a force she hadn't known she'd possessed, she'd been able to decapitate the creature. Of course, she'd gone for the knees as Remare had instructed her to do and had sorely missed. But, on the reverse move, the monster hadn't seen her strike from behind. She'd killed him. Emotional exhaustion pulled at her. She could rest, now.

Remare heard a buzzing in his coat and reached for his phone. Luckily, with the storm passing, Morel had been able to get a text through. "Morel is on his way. There's sporadic reception, but he was able to track us with the GPS."

"Thank God." She snuggled closer to Remare, knowing as soon as help arrived, she'd have to draw away. He must have thought the same because he pulled her tighter to him and kissed her temple.

When there was the eventual knocking at the door, Miranda's strength gave out, and she slipped away into peaceful oblivion. Whatever questions they had would have to wait.

***

When she awoke in ValCorp's infirmary, Valadon was standing near her with his arms crossed over his chest and a half-smile. "It appears I have to thank you again for saving the life of my nephew and second."

His deep, melodic voice was music to her ears. She pulled at the tubes taped to her arm.

"No. Leave those in. They're full of the nutrients your body needs. You need to replenish your blood. How do you feel?"

"Fine. A little light-headed." Her voice sounded gravelly. "How's Nick? Remare?"

He gestured to the two beds to her right. "Dr. Amira is keeping Nick in a medically-induced coma until his body heals sufficiently. Remare's leg is also being treated. He is lightly sedated to aid in the healing. The creature you killed nearly amputated it."

Miranda tried to sit up.

Valadon adjusted her pillows. "Remare needs a respite, so I've ordered him on bedrest for twenty-four hours." He snorted. "I insisted on forty-eight, but even injured, he likes to argue with me."

She mumbled, "Tell me about it. Any way I can get a shower? That creature was rancid. I can still smell him." Valadon's scent of ocean breezes was much nicer.

"I'll have one of the nurses assist you. Clean clothes will be provided. Remare told me what you did." His emerald eyes glittered. "It was foolish of you to confront the creature. You should have let him fight it."

Miranda had to clear her throat. "Where is it, now?"

"In the labs. I'm having Gabriel analyze it. He was fascinated when they brought it in and asked to do the autopsy."

Miranda thought the decapitation was pretty much self-explanatory. "I want out of here."

"So do I. Let Dr. Amira examine you. If she gives you the green light, I would like to take you to dinner. You could do with a steak." He glanced at his wrist. "After feeding Remare, so could I."

Miranda's stomach picked that moment to grumble.

"Ah, you're awake." Dr. Amira pulled the curtain back.

Miranda remembered the kindhearted doctor with the soft brown eyes from the last time she'd been in the infirmary. She'd treated Miranda for the burns on her legs. The scars still hadn't healed. "Hi, doc."

"How do you feel?" Dr. Amira covered her hand with hers.

Safe. "Hungry. In bad need of a shower."

Dr. Amira used her stethoscope to check Miranda's vitals. And then wrapped the blood pressure cuff around her arm. "Good. You have remarkable healing abilities. I'm pleased you're feeling better."

Miranda was glad, too. "How long was I out for?"

"A couple of hours. Your color has returned, and your vitals are steady. I heard you might be having dinner with our High Lord." Dr. Amira glanced up at Valadon and then started removing the IV. "I think that's a wonderful idea. I'm going to discharge you. But I want your word, no physical activity for at least a couple of days until your strength is fully returned."

Miranda gave her the thumbs up.

Chapter Ten

After going home and changing for her dinner with Valadon, Miranda walked down to the infirmary to check on Remare and Nick. She'd been tempted to take a quick look at her beloved archives but decided she'd rather see how her boys were doing. When she saw Remare was upright in bed, reading a book, a sigh of relief escaped her lips. Someone had shampooed and styled his hair and made sure he was cleaned up. Gazing at his hands, she wondered if he'd also had a manicure. His long, tapered fingers looked smooth against his gold and sapphire ring.

"Glad to see you sitting up." Miranda checked the title of the book. "You're reading a Sherrilyn Kenyon novel?!" She started chuckling.

"It was the only book in the drawer. The nurses took all my electronic devices away. They said it interfered with their monitors. I think they lied."

He still looked clammy so she put her hand to his forehead. He should have been healed by now, or at least close to it. She inhaled the air around him. "You look a little worn; how are you feeling?"

"I've been better, but Dr. Amira says she'll probably discharge me tomorrow."

She wondered about that. "Mind if I have a peek at your wound?"

His eyes narrowed, but he acquiesced to her request. "If it pleases you."

Miranda pulled back the blanket and looked at the dressing stained with a dull grayish-green color. She spotted a box of gloves on the wall and the extra bandages on the patient table. Slowly, she peeled back the gauze. "I think you have an infection."

Not liking what she saw or the emanating odor, she retrieved her micro-goggles she used when doing authentications from her shoulder bag. Her eyesight was good, but she used the special goggles so she didn't miss the minutest of details. After putting on a pair of the latex gloves, she bent over and examined his injury.

"Well, this is a sight I never expected to see." Valadon's melodic voice drifted over her.

"Hi, Valadon." In clinical mode, she turned to face him, still wearing her goggles. "Can you hand me that plastic tray on the table?"

Surprise flickered on his face. "May I ask what it is you are doing?"

"This cut doesn't smell right, and it's oozing." She used her thumb to carefully touch the skin around the injury. When Remare hissed in pain, she stopped.

"I think you have some metal fragments imbedded under the skin. With your rapid healing, I suspect your body started repairing itself before expelling the shards." Removing the glove from her right hand, she leaned closer and used her powers to draw forth the tiny slivers and, without touching them, dropped them in the receptacle Valadon provided.

When she nonchalantly placed her gloved hand on Remare's groin for support, she did not think it would elicit the smirk on Remare's face or the rise of Valadon's brow. *Men!* When she was done, she counted eight pieces barely the size of eyelashes. Gesturing to the table, she said, "Hand me that bottle of betadine solution."

Valadon chided, "I didn't realize nursing was one of your skills."

"Hanging out with the Weres, I've watched how Lizandra bandages them up after they've been fighting too vigorously."

After cleansing the wound with the antiseptic and securing a new bandage, she handed the tray containing the particles to Valadon. "I think you should have these analyzed." She removed her gloves and tossed them in the garbage. "There's this weird smell to them."

Valadon sniffed the shards and then signaled to one of the nurses. "Have these brought down to the lab. Tell Gabriel I want a full analysis."

"Yes, right away." The nurse hurried off.

As Miranda returned her goggles to her purse, Valadon's deep tones echoed around her. "How are you feeling?"

"Dr. Amira said, if the wound stopped draining, she would discharge me tomorrow. And, now, thanks to Professor Crescent, I believe it has. Where are you two going for dinner?"

"Miranda seemed to enjoy *One if By Land* the last time we were there, and I thought she could do with a good meal after nourishing you and Nick."

"Sounds like a plan." Smiling, she wrapped a scarf around her neck, then put on her jacket. "I'm starving."

"Your chariot awaits." Valadon grinned at her then turned to Remare. "And you rest up. I want you in my office tomorrow morning. Much has been happening here, and I want to keep you apprised."

"Send me the files; I'll work on them tonight."

"No." He reached for the book Remare had been reading and read the title. "Finish your tales of Styxx tonight. Tomorrow, we'll discuss business."

Miranda didn't want to leave Remare alone in the hospital bed, but she really was hungry, and Valadon had promised it would just be a casual dinner and they would make it an early evening. Her face warming, she spoke mentally to Remare. *"Feel better."*

"I already do. Thank you. And, Mir-randa," he gazed at Valadon, *"no dessert."*

Miranda grinned. *"I wasn't planning on getting any."*

***

After a sumptuous dinner of mushroom soup and the elaborately prepared Beef Wellington, Miranda relaxed with Valadon in their private dining room. She loved the old-world ambience of the eighteenth-century restaurant. The oak paneling and exotic plants only added to its charming atmosphere. Valadon had shown his consideration by calling ahead and having their dinners ready by the time they arrived.

"Dessert?"

"Oh, no." She patted her stomach. "I'm full."

"Are you sure?" He teased then, when their server appeared, ordered, "Chocolate mousse truffles."

Sure, vampires didn't have to watch their weight.

When the waiter brought their dessert, Valadon tormented her by slowly, evocatively savoring the morsels. Miranda wanted to brain him then used a spoon to taste the mousse. It was heavenly. He grinned when she moaned. As much as she enjoyed dinner with him, there was something niggling at the back of her mind. "Valadon, I've pretty much told you all that I remembered about the house we got stuck in, but I still have questions, as I'm sure you do."

"I'm listening."

"Remare told you I saw one of those creatures down in your cave. He didn't believe me at the time." She shrugged. "Said it was just an urban legend, like the alligators."

"Yes, he told me, and I'm very sorry he didn't believe you." He wiped his mouth with the linen napkin. "I've had extra security measures implemented in the underground cave."

"Yeah, but how did the creature get all the way over to the East Side? Don't you find it strange that it just so happened to be in the same house Nick was in? Bars on the windows, doors on a time-lock?"

"Yes. Odd, indeed. Our people are investigating the basement and the tunnel beneath it." He tapped his fingers on the table. "I'm not comfortable with the evidence indicating the digging was done recently. We're looking into it."

"Good." Miranda tried to stifle a yawn.

"You're tired." Valadon signaled for the check, and after signing for it, they left. She wanted to walk a few blocks; after a hard rain, the air smelled cleaner. But, given Valadon's affection for her, she wasn't sure that was prudent so she rode with him back to ValCorp."

"I can have my driver drop you off at your home."

"No. I want to check on Nick and Remare one more time."

"They're resting. You can check on them tomorrow, after you've gotten some sleep."

Bossy, as always. "I'll sleep better knowing they're okay."

"All right, then."

Once in ValCorp's parking garage, his chauffer opened the door. Valadon said, "We'll be up in a moment. See to it that a pot of Turkish tea is waiting in the dining area for us."

"Very good, sir."

Miranda's heart began racing; she wasn't comfortable being alone with Valadon in his limo. The vampire lord was just too damned handsome in his dark suit, overwhelming with his presence. She knew he still had feelings for her and felt bad she couldn't return them. His masculine scent was playing havoc with her hormones, and if he started releasing his pheromones, she wasn't sure how she'd react to his allure. "We should get upstairs."

"In a moment." He exhaled, as if collecting his thoughts. "There's much I want to say to you, but I'm not sure how to say it."

"Valadon, you don't have to—"

"I do. What you did for Remare and Nick was incredibly brave and...foolish. Remare is a trained soldier. You should have let *him* kill the creature."

Miranda rolled her eyes. "He was injured. Besides, I'm not defenseless. Lizandra, as well as several other Weres, trained me in self-defense. I can take care of myself."

"I know, but you shouldn't have to." When she tried to speak, he raised a hand to silence her. "I've been trying to come up with something to show my appreciation, but you didn't seem to like the diamonds nor the Jaguar I tried to send you."

"You don't have to buy me gifts, Valadon. I'm sure Nick or Remare would have done the same. *Friends* don't have to reward each other. A simple thanks suffices."

"Be that as it may, I still want to give you something." He grinned mischievously, and she was moved by his warmth. "So, name it. Whatever you want, just name it."

Miranda nearly gasped. A billionaire was telling her to ask for anything she wanted. Her breath caught. Her eyes blinking, she couldn't think of a solitary thing. The genie had popped out of the bottle, ready to grant her a wish, and she couldn't even imagine such a gift. She didn't need jewelry, didn't want a car. Her salary covered her expenses, so what could she want? A thought came to her, and she slyly grinned. "You know, there is one thing."

"Name it."

She turned to him. "Access to your archives. I loved working down there with Nick. And you have books not available anywhere else." Miranda often dreamed of completing the two courses necessary for her PhD in art history. Someday, she would take Felicity's advice and finish her research, and Valadon had the books in his archives to make that dream come true.

"Miranda, you already have access. I never rescinded your permission to use the archives as you see fit. You can borrow any of the books you want."

Warmth suffused her heart. "Seriously?"

"Of course. There's only one stipulation. I ask that you don't reveal the contents of my archives to anyone else. My privacy is important to me."

"I would never do that." Her research was important, but Miranda had another reason for wanting to visit the archives. "I can stay down there and study with no expectations, no interruptions?" She remembered how she'd nearly succumbed to Valadon's allure when they'd been alone in the library.

"No, I'll see to it you are not interrupted. However, I will send Escher down to you, on occasion, to see if you need refreshments."

She could hardly contain her joy. "Then, that is what I want."

"Then, that is what you shall have." He took her hand as they exited the limo.

During the elevator ride up, Valadon asked, "Will you join me for tea in the dining room?"

Miranda shook her head. "I just want to see Nick and Remare one last time, then call it a night."

"All right, then." He took her hand and kissed her knuckles, his eyes never leaving her. "Thank you, again, for saving the lives of the two people I cherish the most. My

driver will take you home when you are ready to leave."
When the elevator dinged on his floor, he stepped out and
tipped his head to her as the doors closed.

Miranda exhaled in relief. She hadn't realized how tense
she'd been. She hoped, one day, Valadon found the affection
he so richly deserved in the arms of another. Happily, she
walked down the corridor to the medical wing, thinking
about the archives. The first thing she would do when she
got the time was explore the biographies section. Bianca
had been haunting her thoughts, and she wanted to learn
as much as she could about Nick's mom.

When she entered the infirmary, Nick was still
comatose, and Remare was resting with his eyes closed, his
book by his side. She passed Remare and checked on Nick.
She slipped her hand into his as he lay silently on the bed.
More and more, he was beginning to look like his handsome
uncle. She moved a strand of his hair from his face. "When
you get older, you're going to have to fight the girls off with a
stick." She kissed his forehead and then made her way to
Remare, who was watching her every step with heavy-lidded
eyes.

"How was dinner?"

A feeling of contentment washed over her. "Subdued."
She pulled a chair closer to his bed and sat. "Valadon had
work to get back to, and I didn't want to stay out too late."
She took his hand in hers. "Your color's improved. How are
you feeling?"

"Better." His eyes gleamed. "Now that you're here."

"Likewise." She picked up his book. "Would you like me
to read to you? I'm told my voice has a soothing effect.
Usually by students who nearly fall asleep in my class."

"Yes. I would like that very much."

Miranda propped the book up by his good thigh and
used one hand to hold it open. Lacing her fingers around

Remare's hand, she gently squeezed, needing to feel his warmth. "Let's see where you left off."

***

Valadon finished his tea and closed the report on his desk. He rubbed his neck. As long as sleep was evading him, he would check on his second and his nephew. He stopped to ask the on-duty nurse if there had been any change in their conditions. There hadn't been. When he strode to Remare's bedside, a feeling of unease settled in his stomach. Miranda was hunched over, her head nestled on the side of the bed. She'd fallen asleep on the book she'd been reading to Remare. Her body was twisted at an angle that couldn't possibly be comfortable.

When he moved closer, he saw their clasped hands. She'd only been providing support, he thought. When he lifted her up, she cried out in alarm for Remare, who swiftly woke with a growl. His arm protectively surrounded Miranda, pulling her close to him. His eyes were glazed with sleep as his fangs elongated. He looked ready to attack Valadon.

"Remare, awake." He spoke soothingly, not wishing to agitate his second any further. "I was just taking Miranda to the other bed." He gestured to the one adjacent to Remare's.

Distrust, laced with protection, surfaced. Remare's body language screamed possession.

"She was bent in a twisted position." Valadon tried using logic with his oldest friend. "She'll be more comfortable here."

With ever watchful eyes, Remare let go of her arm. His nostrils flared as the red rims of his eyes pulsed.

Valadon lay Miranda down and pulled a blanket over her. "I didn't realize you had become so protective of her."

Now fully awake, Remare said, "She's been through a lot. I just reacted. After the incident with the creature, I just...didn't want to see any harm come to her. She's quite brave, you know."

"Yes. I do know." Suspicion grated. "If you're up to it, I expect you in my office first thing in the morning. We have much to discuss."

"I'll be there."

"See that you are." He turned and left. Envy was a green-eyed monster Valadon had no time for. But seeing how Miranda had instinctively reached for Remare, clung to him, and he to her, chafed at Valadon's heart. But logic prevailed—Remare was only being protective. After what they'd been through, of course, his second, his oldest, most loyal best friend would want to shield Miranda from any harm.

Still, the vexation of jealousy would not abate.

Chapter Eleven

Irina turned over the body that had washed up on the shores near Battery Park. Immediately, her hand went to her stomach. Her usual cool, detached persona did not permit displays of emotion, but seeing how the young girl had been tortured and cut open made her nauseous. The girl couldn't have been much more than fourteen. Her light blonde hair, dirty from the water, covered the side of her face. A vampire, her nascent fangs were just barely visible. Irina ran her fingers lightly over the girl's jaw. "Don't worry, *dorogoy rebenok*, dear child, we'll find those who did this to you." She slowly rose, her voice full of sorrow. "May the angels watch over you." Though, in her case, they never had.

Listening to her partner's conversation with the human detective, she watched as their medical team retrieved the body for transport.

"We'll take her back to ValCorp. Our people will perform the autopsy." Gregori informed Michael Vetti of the NYPD special task force set up to work with vampire law enforcement. "Thank you for calling us."

"I've been on the force for nearly twelve years." Vetti shook his head. "Seen a lot of bad things, but this is one of the worst. These killings have got to stop. Too many victims of this nature, Gregori. Two days ago, we found the remains of a young male, human, who had similar wounds on his body. I think whoever did this was rushed and didn't take the time to weigh them down properly." He rubbed his bare hands together and blew on them for warmth. "It looked like his body was experimented on."

Gregori gazed out at the open water. "Yes, I've read the reports."

Vetti frowned. "Are you, at least, close to finding the ones responsible?"

"Not yet, but we will be."

Irina joined them. "The investigation is ongoing." Her voice was icy, and her Russian accent more pronounced. "Those responsible will soon meet with vampire justice."

"Valadon has most of his Elite Torians working on this. He won't stop until we get answers." Gregori shook Vetti's hand. "We'll be in touch." He opened his car door and sat silently for a moment. Irina suspected he knew how seeing a young female vampire who had been tortured affected her. With her blonde hair and angelic features, the girl could have been her when she'd been younger.

She knew he sensed her suffering, but she wouldn't allow another to witness her vulnerability. He was wise to respect that. "Let's go back to ValCorp."

He turned toward her. "You should get some rest. I'll file the reports."

"No. I want to go to the firing range." Already an accomplished markswoman, she would not stop until every shot she made hit the targets with deadly precision. And all the rage she kept bottled up was spent.

***

Valadon walked silently down to the Hall of Memories. It was the one place he could visit when he wanted solitude and the pressures of being the leader of New York's vampires weighed heavy on his mind. Another vampire had been found. A body mutilated the way the others had been. It was bad enough the HOL had taken adults, but to do that to a young male was unconscionable. Valadon went to the reflecting pool, lit by the tiny lights strung across the cave's wall. Gazing at the water, he sat on the stone bench and contemplated the events of the last few days. The pond offered him a measure of peace—something he greatly desired.

"You still come to this forsaken area." Gabriel joined him on the stone bench. "I thought I might find you here."

Valadon smiled at his progeny. "It's one of the few places I can clear my mind. Did you finish your work on the creature?"

"Yes, I sent the results to your email." Gabriel shook his head. "I thought the sightings were all urban legends. How he was able to survive this long underground is beyond me. The pain he must have suffered from the radiation burns is unfathomable. There was still some microscopic residue of radioactivity on the corpse and in the fragments you sent to me. But they were dormant."

"I've received the other reports, as well. The underground hole in the wall had been recently breached, as well as the one in the closet. The creature was led there for one purpose: to kill my nephew."

Gabriel's eyes blazed. "Do we know who?"

"Not yet, but we will." Leaning forward, Valadon lowered his head. Visiting the Hall of Memories always brought back fond remembrances of his beloved. Lena had been on his mind much these last few months, probably because she had died in winter, the season of death. He closed his eyes and let out a breath. "Gabriel, there is something I want to tell you." Somberly, he said, "Something I should have told you long ago."

"What is it?"

"Something I've hesitated in telling you, because I wasn't sure this was information you would welcome. Especially since your resentment toward me has seemed to lessen since you moved away."

Gabriel rubbed his hands in the manner Valadon did and bent to stare at the water. "I think I already know. Enough of your Torians have told me over the years, you didn't intentionally decide to prolong my misery by turning me." He lifted his shoulders. "I believe it's finally sunk in," he met Valadon's eyes, "you couldn't let go. You thought what you did, in turning me, you were giving me a gift." He gazed back at the water. "I get that, now."

Valadon's paternal instincts surfaced. "I never meant to make your life more difficult. I just wanted you to live. You're right; I couldn't let you go." He put his hand on Gabriel's shoulder. "You were too good a friend. And an honorable man."

"Still am." He chortled. "I think my hatred's abated."

"You prefer living among the humans." Valadon reluctantly said, "It seems to suit you. You look happy. Much more than when you lived here."

"I am. I enjoy the work I'm presently doing, and working with others in the field of genetics."

Enjoying the rare moment of harmony between them, he asked, "So, am I forgiven after so many years of anguish between us?"

"Forgiven?" He smirked. "Let's just say, I think we finally understand each other."

"At long last." Valadon returned his smile. "But that's not what I wanted to tell you."

"Oh, what is it, then?"

It was time, he thought, to tell him the truth. "Centuries ago, there was a woman I fell in love with. Desperately and completely." Valadon imagined her smiling face in the pond. "She was human, and our main court was very particular in deciding who among the humans could be turned. For political reasons, I was denied my petition to turn her."

Gabriel crossed his arms over his chest. "Knowing you and your resolute determination, I'm surprised you didn't anyway."

"Looking back, I should have. Though, she may have suffered greatly if I had done so."

"What became of her?"

"She died. In my arms. When I first met her, she was young and so full of life. She loved poetry and tales of adventures." Visions of Lena being happy and laughing surfaced in his mind, and he felt her warmth despite the cold, dank cave. "You would have liked her; she had a good heart and a gentle touch. Though, she could also be quite stubborn, at times." He glanced at Gabriel. "A lot like you."

"And you never found another woman like her in all these long centuries?"

"No. I did not. But I did keep track of her children and her children's children and all the ones who came after." Sadness pervaded his heart. "Almost all of her line has died, either due to illness, wars or accidents."

He closed his eyes in regret. "Only one survives to this day." When his gaze met Gabriel's, he uttered what he'd longed to tell him. "You."

***

"Where is that stupid cunt?" Renworth screamed in rage at his lieutenant. "She should have been here an hour ago."

"She's on her way." Victor Gren's voice was his usual calm. "There's no way she could have known Valadon's second would show up at the house."

Cerise leaned against the door and trembled at her uncle's wrath. He would be merciless with her, and she only hoped she'd still be able to walk when he finished with her. She slowly opened the door. "Uncle, you sent for me?"

"You stupid bitch! You failed me! Valadon's nephew still breathes, as does his second. He beheaded the fucking beast."

"I don't know how he could have found Nick. I made sure he left his phone in his car. There was no way to track him."

Renworth's eyes blazed as he stalked toward her. "I'm only going to ask you this one time, so be truthful with me, or I will rip out your guts."

"Of course, Uncle, always."

He grabbed her arms, his claws cutting into her flesh. "Is there any way Valadon can trace this back to me?"

"No. Uncle. No. There's no recording or anything. It would be a simple measure of his word against mine. We were drinking, heavily. All the kids from school saw us. We can easily say he was too drunk to have heard correctly and went to the wrong address."

"Lucky for you, Valadon's nephew is still in a coma. So, it will come down to your word, not his. Tell me one thing, how did Remare find Nick? No one should have been able to; it was a fucking storm outside, and communications were down."

"I don't know, Uncle. I swear I don't know!"

His voice turned steely. "You didn't have a change of heart and warn the vampire, did you?"

Cerise couldn't keep her body from shaking. "No. Never. I swear. I didn't warn him."

Renworth backed her up against the wall, and his hand traveled to her throat. Raising her from the ground, he threatened, "If this comes down on me in any way, blood will be spilled." He tightened his hand around her throat. "And you know whose blood it will be."

Her heart beating frantically, Cerise tried to swallow but couldn't. Even when he released her, she barely could suck oxygen into her lungs. There was no way Valadon's second should have been able to locate Nick, but if there was, it would have been through some high-tech implant. But she'd seen every inch of Nick's body, and there was no evidence of any embedded devices.

Maybe with the head injury, he'd be confused when he woke up. His memory wouldn't be right. But, if it was, she was in deep shit.

Her mind was already racing for plans for her escape. If it was proven they had conspired to kill Nick, she wouldn't have to wait for Valadon's enforcers to kill her. The man across the room would do it and wouldn't blink twice about it. No one at Red Claw Clan would shed any tears over her death.

Fuming, Renworth slugged down his favorite scotch. Valadon would be furious when he figured out what had happened. The Were King would not allow the vampire lord to exact vengeance on him. Seething with rage, he thought of his friend in the HOL. Perhaps it was time he made another generous contribution to their cause. If the progress they were making against the vampires was to be believed, he wouldn't have to worry about any retribution from Valadon for much longer.

Smirking, he reached for his phone.

Chapter Twelve

"Where did you learn your culinary skills? Dinner was superb." Miranda had no idea cooking was one of Remare's specialties. "I don't think I've ever tasted Veal Masala prepared quite that way."

"I'm a vampire of many talents." Raising his eyebrows, he smiled with a wicked glint in his eyes. "As I'm sure you remember."

She grinned back at him. "I remember." It was good to see him back on his feet, uninjured.

"Bree and Escher have taken to watching a cooking show on TV, *Lydia's Kitchen*. I've watched a few episodes, as well." He sipped his wine. "Lydia has several restaurants here in the city. If you wish, I will take you to one of them."

Miranda suspected he'd been a little peeved she had dinner with Valadon while he'd been laid up in the infirmary. She could have told him he had nothing to worry about. The High Lord had been friendly but not overbearing.

She raised her glass to him. "Looking forward to it."

"Come." He put down their glasses of wine and took her hand. "Let me finish the tour. You have not seen the upstairs as yet."

"Okay." If the upstairs of his Sutton Place town house was anything like the first floor, she was sure it would be equally stupendous. His house sported high ceilings supported by marble columns. Remare had a thing for marble and crystal; his vestibule, hallways and stairs were all polished to such a shine she was almost afraid she'd slip on the floor. His living room was a study in blue with lush drapes and textured wallpaper. There were several finely-crafted flower arrangements and a baby grand piano off to one corner of the room. To the right was a bar with a Baccarat crystal decanter and wine glasses.

She'd expected old-world charm, but Remare preferred modern furniture with deep, rich fabrics. At the far wall, his entertainment center had a huge TV with twin bookcases containing a myriad of DVDs and books.

On his walls, his taste in art ran from the classics to contemporary. The Edward Hopper painting had been one of her favorites. He had a few objects d' art, but nothing overwhelmingly ostentatious.

But the room she loved the most was his study with the huge ebony desk and the lapis lazuli fireplace. This was where his affinity for the traditional shone. Light blue Aubusson carpets partially covered his parquet floor. His bookshelves were lined with leather bound books. Miranda could picture him working diligently at that desk. Of course, she would be reclining on one of his twin chesterfields with a good book in hand.

The kitchen was all stainless steel with modern appliances, but the connecting atrium at the back of the house with its assortment of plants was heavenly. Remare seemed to have an affinity for orchids. The Georgia O'Keeffe painting only emphasized his taste. Gazing outside, she wondered if he ever dined at night on the adjacent terrace. "This room is fantastic. With the bay windows, you have a great view of the East River, but the study is my favorite."

"For someone who has spent much time in libraries, that doesn't surprise me." He took her hand and led her up the marble staircase with the elaborate wrought iron bannister.

When they reached the second floor, he opened a door to a room decorated in warm earth toncs. Just like her bedroom, peach was the dominant color. "This looks strangely familiar."

She examined the oak secretary similar to the one where she did her research in her home. There were several art history books, as well as an assortment of fountain pens—one was even a rare, intricately designed Montegrappa that had belonged to her father. Upon further perusal, one brow rose. "Is this mine?"

He laughed. "I believe you stole one of my shirts. So, I took one of your pens."

Her face blushed. "I meant to return it," she lied. He was never getting his shirt back; she liked sleeping in it far too much. When she peered in the closet, several of the outfits were designs by Cesare, ValCorp's leading designer. He had created them for her at Remare's request. He'd seen the fabrics and colors she'd preferred in Cesare's office when he'd wanted her to have a new suit for an underground auction they were attending. She turned to look at the vampire in question. "You did all this for me. Why?"

"Your comfort is important to me. When you come for visits, I wanted you to know how welcome you are."

Miranda was moved by his words. "Thank you."

Nodding to her, he then led her to a room at the end of his hall. The master bedroom. He flicked the lights on but kept them low. Miranda stood rapt at the expanse of midnight blue dominating the room. As feminine as her room had been, this one screamed masculine authority. His collection of swords was mounted on one wall, and his king-sized bed was an ebony poster bed big enough to fit ten people. If they all slept on their sides, she chuckled. "Massive. And elegant."

"Were you referring to me?"

Rolling her eyes, she pointed to his bed. She walked along his wood floors until she came to the huge bay window overlooking the Queensboro Bridge, its lights glittering in the night. "This view is spectacular."

"Yes. I bought this house over a century ago because I liked the view of the river." Lowering the lights even more, he moved toward her. His arms circled her from behind. Miranda quivered as she leaned her head back on his shoulder and caressed his hands. It had been so long since she and Remare had alone time.

Turning in his arms, she lifted her hand to his jaw. His fine line of beard was soft to her touch. "I've missed you."

"And I've missed you." When he kissed her, Miranda felt the world slipping away. Whatever magic was between them flared to life, the intensity almost frightening. He tasted like wine, and she was intoxicated at simply being in his embrace. When he broke from the kiss, his eyes were as seductive as his half-smile. Hunger eclipsed all other emotions. "Help me turn down the duvet."

And she did. His eyes never leaving hers, he slowly undid the buttons of his shirt and casually tossed it on a chair. Miranda knew he was waiting for her to mirror his actions, but she was too spellbound by the sheer masculine appeal of his body. Remare was a vampire who believed in keeping fit, as evidenced by his tight six-pack and muscular arms. She knew his thighs were equally well-defined. Most people thought vampires had light complexions, but Remare had olive tones reflecting his Mediterranean background. When naked, his body revealed no tan lines, just one hundred percent male.

He gestured for her to undress, but Miranda hesitated, wanting to drink him in as much as she could. Seeing him standing nude had her mesmerized. She knew every inch of his body and how talented he was with it. Her heart ramped up. The thought of having him inside her again made her body throb with lust. "You know there's something I always wanted to do with you."

His wicked smile hinted at sin. "There are a great many things I want to do with you."

She shared his desire, but first, she wanted something that had been denied to her. "Do you have a music system here?"

"Yes, of course."

"There's this one song that haunts me. It's by the Australian singer, Delta Goodrem. It's called, 'Angels in the Room'. Will you play it for me?"

He reached into his nightstand and retrieved the remote then pointed it at the wall. A panel slid open to reveal speakers. Miranda finished undressing until she, too, was naked. Swaying to the sultry, poignant lyrics, she walked seductively toward him then slid her hands up his chest and asked, "Will you dance with me? I know we've sword danced in the past, but I want one slow dance with you. I want to feel your arms around me."

He brushed his hands over her shoulders and along her arms until his fingers met hers. He planted a kiss on her knuckles. "If that is what you want, it will be my pleasure."

They started slow dancing, and Miranda was moved by the singer's haunting lyrics of desperate longing with the beautiful pain of desire. She loved the way Remare held her, the quiet strength he imbued to her. The way he held her to him as if she belonged to him and no one else. Inhaling his forestry scent awoke something primal in her.

"A lovely song, Mir-randa. I've never heard of her before, but I like her music." His voice was huskier than she'd heard before.

"So do I." She massaged his neck, loving the way his silken strands felt gliding through her fingers. "I used to play this song late at night and imagine you holding me, just like this, as we danced naked."

Male satisfaction shone brightly on his face. "I enjoyed visiting you while you slept."

He had set the alarm for her house and knew the password, which she had yet to change. He'd called her "his favorite pain" and had programmed that as her PIN. "When was this?"

"About a month ago. I couldn't sleep. I kept reaching across the bed for you, but you weren't there, so I went to see you. You were sleeping so peacefully I didn't have the heart to wake you. So, I watched over you."

Touched by his words, Miranda stopped dancing. "I wish you had told me."

"I just did."

She lifted up on her toes and kissed him with all the simmering passion she'd kept locked away. Her hands explored the muscles of his back, and her nails trailed down his spine to land on his butt. She kissed his jaw and licked her way to his neck. She wouldn't bite him in the way of vampires and draw blood, but she could take his flesh inside her mouth and suck. A hiss escaped his mouth as she gently bit down with her teeth.

She wanted to taste more of his salty skin and took tiny nips down his chest. She circled his nipple with her tongue then sucked it into her mouth. His body hardened, and she smiled in feminine awareness. She licked his other nipple then kissed her way down to his abdomen. She looked up at him and hoped he saw all the longing she barely contained. A tic started in his jaw, and Miranda continued her exploration of him.

She trailed brushes of her tongue along the fine line of hair leading down to his groin.

Taking his cock in her hand, she gently stroked him, her fingernail gently grazing the vein from base to tip. A growl sounded low in his throat in warning, and she nearly chuckled. Instead, her tongue replaced her fingers, laving his cock lovingly as she gently caressed his balls. When she sucked him deep into her mouth, she heard him curse in Italian and tried not to laugh.

His eyes were heavy-lidded; his hunger seemed to be pulsating with desire.

He pulled her up by her arms. "Come, my sorceress, before you bewitch me any further." He lifted her up in his arms and carried her to the bed. Miranda giggled at his eagerness. The joy of being with him, knowing she could drive him insane with her touch, gave her such a sense of female empowerment. She kissed him thoroughly, exploring every inch of his mouth, loving the taste of Cabernet. Vampires were cold blooded, but under the smooth, cool texture of his skin, Miranda felt the heat of his beating heart.

Remare had enjoyed sex for centuries, but no woman had ever driven him as insane with lust as Miranda did. Her soft touch as she explored him had nearly undone him. The warmth of her hands had branded him hers. When had he allowed another to have so much sway over him? Never! Positioning her in the center of his bed, he then knelt between her legs and inhaled her tangy aroma. Recently waxed and glistening, she was beautiful. Venus had nothing on her, and he enjoyed studying her sultry body. Every inch belonged to him. To pleasure or torment as he desired. He would not take her fast and hard as his body was dictating him to do. He wanted this night to last.

Taking her foot in hand, he massaged her instep then worked his way up her ankles to her calves. Extending her leg up, he kissed the scars she kept hidden. He was pleased she'd taken off her dark stockings, knowing her minor imperfections meant nothing to him. The amount of trust she had in him was overwhelming. He loved her body and wanted her to know she was his.

He tongued the inside of her knee and watched as she trembled beneath him. Her muffled cry of pleasure pleased him. He gently sucked the skin until her moans rent the air. He licked the inside of her thigh and paused as his tongue traveled up her femoral artery. His fangs elongated, throbbing with the need to feed. He needed a moment to get his feral beast under control. She'd fed him once this week, and he would not bleed her a second time so soon after. His heart was pounding to take her, but he wanted to torment her the way she had done to him. He spread her legs wide, her ankles a yard apart, and stared down at her.

"Do you want me, Mir-randa?"

Her breath caught, and her nails dug into the sheets. "God, yes! Now! Please, now."

"Not a chance." He laughed with wicked intent. "You tortured me; now, it's my turn." He inserted one finger inside her, feeling her warm, damp arousal coating his hand. He plunged deeper, stroking her inner walls until he had her writhing in anticipation. He enjoyed learning her sweet spots. Where she merely panted and where his ministrations made her twist and turn in passion. He didn't consider himself a sexual sadist, but right now, seeing her lust contort her body aroused him to new heights.

Another finger joined the first, and he stroked deliberately slow, keeping her on edge and watching as her passion built. When her hands gripped the sheets and her nails nearly ripped through the silk in blistering arousal, he pushed a third in her tight channel and pumped hard enough to throw her over the edge.

When she screamed out his name, it was sweet music to his ears.

He rolled her over to her side and spooned her from behind. Her breathing was labored, and he would give her a moment to collect herself. When her body started trembling with aftershocks, he held her close to his chest, pulling the blankets over them.

After a moment, he asked, "Are you all right?"

"No." She panted. "I think you killed me."

He chuckled. "If you were dead, you would not be talking. And your body would not be so warm." He trailed a finger down her glistening back.

She turned toward him and stroked his jaw. Tears of pleasure stained her face. "No one has ever made me feel the way you do."

He took her hand and kissed it. "I feel the same, Miranda. You make me feel things I've never felt before." When the lights from outside caught her beautiful face, her eyes seemed to glow red and gold. When she smiled up at him, his heart expanded. "I want to ask you something, but I'm not sure this is something you would want to discuss."

Concern marred her face. "What is it?"

"It's just something I've given careful consideration to and was curious about your opinion."

"Go on."

He hesitated, started to speak, and then hesitated, again. "Have you ever wondered, did you ever want...?"

"What?"

He brushed a strand of hair behind her ear. "This is just something I want you to think about. I would never pressure you or expect you to do anything you weren't ready for."

Her eyes sparkled in understanding. "You want to ask me if I would ever consider becoming vampire."

He knew Miranda was highly intuitive, but it still surprised him she could so easily read him. "Yes, but there is no need for an answer, now." He reassured her. "You're not ready. I just wanted to know if you think the day may come when you might be."

"Honestly?" She heaved a breath. "The thought scares the hell out of me."

"Why?"

"Gabriel told me what he went through when he was turned. He described it as a living hell."

"Gabriel was not properly prepared." Remare shook his head. "He was not aware of the physical and mental changes he would go through. I would tell you all you needed to know, so the transition would not be as intense."

She placed her hand on his shoulder. "You've given it some thought."

"I have. A few decades with you will not be enough. Through the centuries, I've taught myself distance, witnessing the deaths of many humans I called friend. I don't want to watch you grow old and wither away. I couldn't bear it. Something inside me would shatter."

When Miranda looked away, he held her chin with his fingers. "People think we are cold, indifferent. That we consider humans pets because your life span is so much shorter than ours. But that is not true. If we are detached, it is because we have learned not to care so deeply for a human because watching a loved one die tears us apart."

She smiled up at him. Her compassion nearly undid him. "You're right. I'm not ready to make that decision. It's a huge step. Would you ever consider becoming human?"

He grinned at her courage. "That is not possible."

"But what if it were? Would you ever want to give up being a vampire?"

He exhaled. "No. Being a vampire is all I know. All that I am. I would lose my strength, my cunning, my ability to survive." He looked at her. "I could never protect you."

"I would never ask that of you, Remare. I know your vampirism is a part of you. Truthfully, I would never want you to give it up." A wicked grin surfaced. "I've grown used to your fangs."

He growled seductively, his fangs prominently displayed. "Is it something you would consider? Something you may want to do...sometime in the future?"

"I don't know." Her eyes narrowed as she seemed to contemplate. "Before I would make any decision, I would have to know a helluva lot more about vampires."

"There's no rush, Mir-randa. I will not pressure you. It would have to be a decision you are completely comfortable with. I just wanted you to know; it's something I've thought about."

She caressed his face with her thumb. Closing his eyes, he basked in the tenderness of her touch. How this woman could make him feel so vulnerable amazed him.

"Valadon said I could use his archives."

He cocked his head. "Why? Are you going to work for him, again?"

"No. At first, I wanted to research the biographies of the artists. I have this crazy dream of someday going for my PhD."

"You should go back for it. If it's something you truly want. I would help you with it."

She ran a finger down the side of his jaw. "How?"

"Any way I could."

Miranda stroked his shoulder. "It's just a thought, right now. I have no idea what I would do my dissertation on. I'm in no rush to decide."

"Then, take all the time you need."

"I will. When I was in archives, I saw biographies of philosophers, histories of your people. Remare, I want to learn more."

He exhaled. "Some of our history is not pretty."

She laughed. "And ours is?"

He kissed her forehead. "You amaze me, Mir-randa. You always do."

His desire for her throbbing in near painful need, he maneuvered his body so that he could penetrate her. Sliding inside her silky sheath, he reveled in her warmth. He wanted slow and easy so he could watch her face glow with passion and remember this night. In her eyes, he saw truths he never knew before. No, decades would never be enough with her. He wanted centuries of hearing her laughter, seeing her smile. There were so many places in the world he wanted to take her. Share with her the many wonders he'd seen.

But, before he could, he would have to tell Valadon about his bond with Miranda, and neither one of them was ready for that. However, he was sure the day would come when Valadon would accept his relationship.

Remare gazed down at the female who haunted his dreams, the one he wanted to travel the centuries with. The woman he belonged with. Miranda, his beloved. Increasing the speed of his thrusts, the pleasure building inside his balls, he rode the heat of his desire as it grew and grew until their worlds collided in a firestorm of ecstasy.

And she was right, her collapse resembled death, *la petite mort*. Panting, her body was coated in a fine layer of sweat. And so was his. Basking in the afterglow of their passion, he absorbed her warmth deep into the very fiber of his being.

It was a bliss that had become sacred to him. Something he would fight for.

And, if necessary, kill for.

Chapter Thirteen

After scanning the horrific pictures of the dead girl Gregori had forwarded to him, Valadon sat back in revulsion. What monsters could do this? Her body had shown such grievous signs of torture. Quietly seething in rage, he could only hope the mutilations were done post-mortem. He wanted to tear the hearts out of those responsible for such an atrocity. He was a king, the leader of his vampires. His people looked to him for protection.

And he had failed them miserably.

As he studied the images and the angle of the wounds, memories of an old nemesis came to mind: Francis Peralt, the fiend who had conducted heinous experiments on his kind. He'd been sanctioned by a secret brotherhood of the Church to find a way of prolonging life. The corrupt officials, wanting to know why some beings lived longer than others, had encouraged Peralt's demented research. Human aristocrats, not satisfied with one mortal lifetime, had wished to live eternally like the gods they believed they were. But King Robert had signed execution orders on the perverse alchemist. Peralt had been dead for centuries.

While his fingers tapped silently on his desk, memories stirred in his mind of Miranda giving him an old copy of Peralt's writings and drawings she'd found in his archives. Reaching inside his lower drawer, he pulled the book out and thumbed through the pages. *Demon children,* Peralt had termed vampires. Valadon sneered. Peralt had thought, by consuming vampire blood, humans could live eternally. How wrong he'd been.

Valadon wondered if there were other copies of this book floating around. Could someone have obtained a copy of Peralt's experiments? Someone in the Human Order of Light?

Irina had managed to snare a high-ranking member of the hate group—a man whose wealth had deteriorated and was in severe need of financial assistance. The High Lord smirked. William Tolliver had become a valuable informant. He would assign Irina the task of finding out if Tolliver, or anyone in the HOL, knew anything about Peralt and his atrocities.

They were so close to finding the installation where the mutilations had taken place. His Torians had been working day and night to discover their secret meeting places. Valadon rose and paced the length of his office. He suspected the HOL wouldn't conduct the experiments in Manhattan; there were too many law enforcement agencies seeking them. But it had to be some place near—a location where they could gather and conspire together. He would not rest until he discovered their hidden facility.

But, for now, he had another pressing task to deal with.

Nick had finally woken from his coma and had reluctantly given him the name of the girl who had sent him to the house where the creature had been. It had taken some doing, but Valadon had finally convinced his nephew there was the possibility he'd been set up. Cerise Renworth was the niece of a bitter rival, Edgar Renworth, the Were King, whom Valadon had outfoxed in a major business acquisition. Could Renworth harbor such animosity for so long to attack his nephew? Valadon wouldn't put it past the bastard. Cerise's trial was scheduled to start soon, and his chief legal advisor assured him the tribunal of the Council of Others would find in his favor.

And, after that, he would deal with the HOL. They would learn the meaning, once and for all, of vampire justice.

***

Inspecting the new specimens scheduled for testing, Stuart Blackmore walked along the corridor of the underground installation he was using for research and development. Long ago, he'd dropped the use of Ehrlich, his father's last name, in favor of his mother's. As far as his people were concerned, Blackmore was acting president of Ehrlich Industries, while the elusive and enigmatic Mr. Ehrlich, founder and CEO of EI remained in Europe, presumably playing golf somewhere.

Of course, no one knew his more dubious moniker of *The Regent,* and never would. He smirked. He had killed many times in the past to protect his secret and wouldn't hesitate to do so again if anyone ever discovered his true identity. It was fascinating to witness how his victims handled their impending deaths: Some were cowards who had begged for their miserable lives, their futile pleas, an insult. But the ones he enjoyed most were the brave souls who stoically went to their deaths. He took exquisite pleasure in watching them succumb to his power. They didn't humble themselves to beg or show fear; they had honor. Like the young male who had recently tried to escape. His look of defiance as they eviscerated him had been something to behold. He would have made a fine soldier if he hadn't been born vampire.

Blackmore examined the glass-enclosed cells where his latest guests were housed. Dr. Peralt's experiments were proceeding well. How ironic, in trying to prolong human life, Peralt had come up with ingenious formulas to deteriorate the health of vampires. Soon, Blackmore would be able to instigate his DOL—the Dawn of Light Project, the eradication of the vampires. They were so close to developing a toxin that would finally annihilate the vampires.

Blackmore studied the vampire behind the protective glass of the cell. Like the one last week, he had perceptive eyes, ever watchful of all the activity in the facility. Handsome youth. Dark hair, sturdy build. How fortuitous they'd been able to abduct a true Blueblood. Blackmore had almost given up hope in finding a purebred. He read from the chart: University student, Columbia, age twenty-two, aristocratic features, highly intelligent, no wounds, and no infirmities. Of course not; there wouldn't be any.

The youth rushed him, indignation etched in his features. "What do you want from me? Why am I here? You have no right to keep me prisoner!"

Blackmore had to give the vampire credit for not showing any fear. If he had any idea what was in store for him, he would have. "You are here to serve a purpose."

"If it's money you want, my father will pay the ransom."

"Oh, no." Blackmore turned to leave without looking back. "What I want is far more valuable." He continued walking toward the testing center where Dr. Peralt was working.

In his lab, Frank Peralt used his electronic microscope to study the effects of the blood orchid's compounds when mercury was added to the solution. Centuries ago, he'd cautioned physicians and chemists not to focus on plants and herbs so much, but to find cures in chemical combinations. His followers had called him *"The Father of Toxicology"*. The earth issued forth generous amounts of minerals to be mined and used purposefully for chemical engineering—some for curative purposes, others for contagions.

But, now, with the rare orchid, found only in the jungles of Peru, and with the secretions of a certain arachnoid, he was able to develop a poison of ominous durability. In Europe, his experiments had been limited to the animals indigenous to the area; however, with the addition of plants and creatures from around the world, the possibilities were endless.

"How's the progress coming on your latest experiments?"

Peralt turned to see Blackmore, his friend and benefactor, leaning against the doorframe.

"Good. Come in and see for yourself." He flicked on the screen mounted on the wall. "Observe how the spider's venom combines with the orchid's and what happens when I add mercury and a few other elements." The solution attacked a human cell, destroying it. "See what happens when I add the same solution to vampire blood." The cell seemed to mutate as if fighting off the toxin, shriveling and weakening in the process.

"Nothing fatal as yet?"

"Not yet, but we are getting close."

"I trust that you will. We brought in a new specimen, a Blueblood. He's in Cell-4. I want you to use his blood in your experiments."

"I will, indeed."

Blackmore nodded and then left.

Finally, they'd been able to capture a purebred alive. He could continue the experiments he had started so long ago.

The world had laughed at his methods, called him insane for his revolutionary ideas. How provincial they had been in their beliefs. They didn't deserve the medicines he'd created that made Ehrlich Pharmaceuticals a world power. Of course, he had created some of the diseases that necessitated the treatments. Research was expensive and needed income from the sale of prescribed drugs to continue.

Peralt rested his head back in memory. His experiments with chemicals had elicited cures for the many ailments people had suffered from. But, instead of thanking him, acknowledging his superior intellect, championing his efforts, they derided and damned his techniques.

Perhaps, now, they would be impressed with his latest alchemical remedy. He just needed a little more time to perfect the dose to destroy the vampires. The new scientific equipment Blackmore had provided for him would speed up the results of his tests. Procuring the services of Dr. Anya West had been a great help. His research assistant shared many of his beliefs and understood the necessity of sacrifice. She wasn't squeamish when it came to the more unorthodox experiments needed to be conducted in the ongoing tests.

Once he got his formula revised and complete, the world would know of his greatness.

Then, he would repay the green-eyed vampire who had damned him to a life of eternal hunger.

Chapter Fourteen

"You still favor the Luger?" Gregori asked, removing the head gear that diminished the thunderous reverberations of their discharges. Like the rest of the Torians, he practiced regularly, and like everything else in their compound, ValCorp's firing range was state of the art. Some of the younger soldiers preferred the simulations, but he was used to the paper targets. He pressed a button, and the silhouette floated steadily forward.

"Yes. It feels good in my hand. I like the control." Irina examined her target and seemed pleased her shots were all centered at the heart.

"You should try the SIG Sauer." He preferred the semi-automatic. "It's quicker and has adjustable grips."

Irina studied his results as it moved closer to them. Gregori preferred head shots, as well as the heart ones. She admired his control and unwavering focus in weapons expertise. "Show me."

Gregori unlocked the panels and retrieved the grips that would fit her hand. "Try this. It's lighter than the Luger and more proficient." He moved behind her and held his larger hands over hers. He breathed in her scent and fought against the erection straining against his pants. He backed off once she was in position. He knew, after seeing what had been done to the young female, Irina needed to vent her rage and feel she was in control, so he'd suggested they practice their shots. Her breathing had seemed to ease, and for that, he was thankful.

Replacing the ear protectors, he watched as she fired off several rounds. Nearly all her shots were centered. One or two were off, but that was expected when firing a new pistol for the first time.

"You're right." She maneuvered the gun in her hand. "It is more lightweight, and I think the shots fired quicker."

He nodded. "Had enough for one night?"

Irina rubbed her neck. "I think I might do a few laps in the pool before turning in."

Gregori waited but knew an invitation wouldn't be forthcoming. He sighed. She had retreated into her shell and would stay that way. "You go ahead; I'll finish up here."

She was halfway to the door when she turned. "Will you join me?"

Gregori hesitated as he placed the guns back in their cases. He'd already resigned himself for a night of solitary gun cleaning. His brow raised in surprise. "I thought you might want some alone time."

"I..." She seemed conflicted then turned away. "Suit yourself."

Tristan, ValCorp's resident weapons master, appeared. "Man, you've got your work cut out." He patted him on the back. "You really know how to pick them."

"She's a colleague." Gregori huffed. "Just a friend."

Tristan grinned. "Sure she is."

"You didn't see the condition of the girl we brought in today." He rubbed his brow. "I think it shook her."

"Yeah, I heard about that. It would rattle anyone." Tristan took the cases from him. "Go. I'll make sure these are cleaned and returned to you."

"Thanks."

***

Irina nearly finished her laps in the dimly lit pool. She'd kept the lights low because the practice session at the range had given her a miserable headache. The demands of the ongoing investigations were taking their toll. The stress of seeing the mutilated body of the young girl hadn't helped. She'd seen corpses before and hadn't reacted this way. She supposed it had to do with the girl's age. She'd been so young. Swimming slowly to the edge of the pool, she heard footsteps approaching. Gregori.

She knew the way he moved, the cadence of his steps, even his masculine scent. Her body reacted. It had been so long since she'd been with a male. She told herself it was just a basic need, nothing more. Just the body yearning for an essential requirement.

She continued swimming until she reached the edge and peered up at him. He was beautiful, his muscular body without equal. She knew Gregori was built, she'd seen him shirtless before, but never with only a pair of bathing shorts before. The muscles of his thighs were defined, and for just one moment, she wondered what he looked like underneath.

"I had Escher make us a fruit platter with some cheese. I thought you might be hungry." A bottle of wine, with two wine glasses, dangled from his hand.

"Leave it on the table. I just want to finish another lap." She was halfway to the other side of the pool when she heard the water splash; her pulse soared. What was wrong with her? Her nerves must be strained. That's all. After the day they'd had, whose wouldn't be?

He swam close to her. "I think you had a good idea in swimming. It's relaxing."

Silently, they swam side by side the entire length of the pool. She climbed the few steps and dried off with one of the towels. She knew her light blue one-piece suit clung to her wet body and left little to the imagination. "Thank you for getting the fruit." She hadn't eaten much, but now, her stomach growled in anticipation.

He climbed out of the pool and wiped the water from his eyes. She handed him a towel. "I'm glad you brought the wine; I could use a drink about now."

Gregori undid the little metal foil around the top of the bottle and then frowned at the cork. She smiled. He'd forgotten the corkscrew.

"Let me have it." She took the bottle of wine and then covered the tip with her mouth. Using her fang to penetrate the cork, she was able to maneuver the cork in tiny pulls, back and forth, until it was out. When she looked up, Gregori was staring at her with his mouth open. "I'm a woman of many talents."

"I never doubted it." He took the bottle and poured the wine. *"Nostrovia."*

Taking her glass, she nodded then sat at the table where he joined her. Sipping the wine, she felt her body loosen and closed her eyes in bliss. "Excellent."

"Try the strawberries; Escher said he got them today." He took one from the tray and offered it to her.

Irina wasn't sure if it was the wine, or the late hour, but she reached forward with her lips and bit the fruit, the juice leaking down her chin. How strange, the more she seemed to relax, the tenser Gregori became. "Strawberries have always been my favorite."

"Mine, too." He chose a slice of cheese and popped it in his mouth.

Irina found it amusing that she liked watching him eat. When they had devoured most of the fruit and all of the cheese, she suggested they go in the hot tub before heading upstairs.

Gregori adjusted the controls for the steaming water as she poured the last of the wine in their glasses and brought them to the edge of the hot tub. Gliding into the heated froths was like sliding into heaven. She moaned in pleasure as the powered bubbles caressed her body. When he joined her, she handed him his wine. "I haven't been down here in ages. I'm glad we came."

He sat down beside her on the tiled seat. "We need to relax more often. I think we get so caught up in our work, we forget to indulge ourselves."

"Agreed." She chose that moment to sink to the bottom of the Jacuzzi and then burst upward, nearly laughing. "Try that. It feels good. Like being reborn."

He did, but he stayed down longer than she had, and for a moment, she worried. She reached under the bubbles for his shoulder, but instead, his hand found hers and pulled her under.

Wrapping his massive arms around her, he burst up and out of the water. Water dripping down his face, he held her securely against his chest.

"Irina."

He said her name like it was holy, sacred. His dark eyes met hers, held them for a moment, and then, he moved closer until his mouth hovered over hers as if he was giving her the opportunity to deny him. She expected fierceness, but he surprised her with his tenderness, slowly exploring every area of her mouth. She thought, with his strength, Gregori would crush her, but he held her as if she was a precious gift. Her skin tingled, the heat from the water coating them in warmth.

"I think we've both waited long enough for this moment." His eyes were heavy-lidded and his voice deeper than she'd heard before. Before she knew it, his lips plundered hers in a searing kiss that had her body feeling like molten lava. Gone was any tenderness. Gregori was not a man to be denied. His kiss was hot, demanding. And she returned it in kind. Before she knew it, he was sliding the straps of her bathing suit down her arms and past her hips.

She gracefully stepped out of it. He threw the wet garment over the side of the hot tub.

Gregori looked like a vampire who hadn't fed in eons. His fangs elongated at the sight of her naked breasts. Not to be undone, she tugged at his shorts, and in an instant, they, too, were gone. He pulled her to him for another scorching kiss. His cock brushed up against her, and a moan of desire escaped her lips.

A growl tore through his mouth. He lifted her up and out of the hot tub and onto the tiled floor. Droplets of water rolled down his skin. He looked down at her with ravenous eyes. Her heart thundered in her chest as her own fangs lengthened. She seductively raised one knee up and let it fall to the side, baring herself to him.

He was on her in an instant, nuzzling her neck, jaw and shoulder. Her hands dug into the muscles of his back, her nails grazing his hot flesh. She loved the way his slick, smooth skin felt under her touch. His tongue traced a path to her breast, then he lightly scored her tender flesh with his fang. He circled her areola then sucked her nipple into his mouth. Hard. She cried out at the pleasure shooting into her core, raking his shoulders with her nails.

Gregori gave her a smoldering look before starting his descent. He laved her navel and butterfly kissed his way to her core. He pulled her long legs over his shoulders; Irina groaned as passion filled her to the point of bursting. Her cries of pleasure echoed throughout the pool room as he gave her orgasm after orgasm, her body wracked with tremors.

Gregori's breaths came hard and fast, but his movements were slow as he covered her body with his. Keeping his weight on his elbows, he brushed her wet hair from her face. He whispered, *"Dorogaya,"* before he kissed her, again. He'd called her his darling, and Irina, for a moment, felt worshipped. Then, he entered her, and her world shattered into a thousand blinding lights. Another orgasm tore through her. He moved slowly inside her, watching her.

She knew her face was flushed with desire when she reached up and kissed him. "This must be what heaven feels like." She wasn't sure if she'd spoken the words aloud or not, but as he moved inside her, the world slipped away. All its horrors, violence, and ugliness no longer existed. Here, there was only bliss. Each of them kissed by the warmth of heaven.

As her passion grew, so did his, and when she felt his body begin to tremble, she wasn't sure whose screams rent the air more.

Chapter Fifteen

"You spend too much damned time at a desk behind your computer."

"I know, but I've been busy."

Breathing heavily, Miranda stopped her bicycle at Central Park's Bethesda Terrace for a water break. Even though Lizandra had kept their pace moderate, it was still faster than what Miranda was used to. "I used to run up and down the stairs at work for exercise." She slugged down some water, grateful for the late autumn breeze. "I haven't had time for that either."

"Um-hmm." Leaning over, Liz gazed at her butt. "It shows!"

Grinning, Miranda admired the angel at Bethesda Fountain. A bead of sweat rolled down her face. "You know, this has always been my favorite part of the park. I love it here. Especially when the leaves are all changing color." Inhaling the cool, crisp air, she watched as the bare branches swayed with the wind.

Lizandra agreed. "Yeah, mine, too. Too bad they're almost all gone, now." As if reading Miranda's mind, she said, "If you think we're stopping at the Boathouse Cafe for a bite to eat, you can kiss my round black ass."

"Who me?" Humorously, her eyes widened in mock surprise. "Not a chance. Not when I know how good the food is at Werehaven."

"So, you gonna to tell me why you cancelled the other night?"

Bowing her head, Miranda couldn't suppress her smile if she tried.

"Ri-ight!" Liz bent her head. "I don't see any bite marks on your neck."

Miranda sniggered. "That's not where he bit me."

"Well, hot damn! It's about time. How long's it been since you got any?"

She sipped more water. "Too long, but Remare made up for it."

Liz gave her a droll look. "Do tell."

"He asked me to consider becoming vampire."

Now, it was Liz's turn to gawk. "What. The. Fuck?!"

"Yeah, I know." Miranda rubbed her hands against her thighs. "I'm not comfortable with the idea, either. He's not pressuring me. Said he wouldn't." She shrugged. "He just wanted me to think about it."

"Are you?"

"I don't know. Not anytime soon. There's too much I don't know about vampirism, and I'm not one to rush into anything."

"Gabriel know?"

"No one knows, and we're keeping our relationship secret."

Liz huffed. "You know if Valadon ever found out, there'd be hell to pay."

"That's why it's secret. But there is something else I have to tell you. Let's go sit down there." They walked their bikes along the path to where the angel stood perched atop the fountain. For some reason, this place always gave Miranda a sense of peace, especially when it was nearly deserted. "Something happened you should know."

She relayed the events at the house where they'd been attacked and her uncertainties about Cerise.

"That bitch!"

"Yeah. I kinda suspect she set Nick up."

"Ya' think?!"

"At the time, I was more concerned with surviving the creature. Remare's leg got cut bad, and Nick was banged up pretty seriously."

Swallowing some gulps of water, Liz seemed to be considering her. "You told me your powers were improving. How big were the fireballs?"

"Pretty big. It wasn't until the day after I figured Nick had been set up. Remare and Valadon agree. They've been searching for Cerise."

Lizandra's eyebrow rose. "They haven't found her, yet?"

She shook her head. "Not as far as I know."

Evilly, one of Liz's eyebrows rose. "I'll find her."

"How?"

"Weres are the best trackers. Leave this to me. I'll get her here. She likes to hang out by the carousel. We'll send her a little message. Say it's from Dori, her uncle's little spy." Liz's eyes narrowed the way they usually did when she was thinking. "She's probably in disfavor with the Red Claw King. If he hasn't killed her already for her failure, she'll come running, hoping to win her uncle's trust, again."

"What will you do to her?"

A sinister smile brightened her face. "I'll get the truth out of her."

Miranda wouldn't ask how. She knew werewolves could be brutal in defending their turf. More so when fighting rival members of other packs. "You can't kill her. Valadon wants her in for questioning. He thinks she was sanctioned by her uncle."

"Oh, I won't kill her." There was something ominous about her tone. "But she'll be begging for death by the time I'm through with her."

That's what Miranda was afraid of. But Weres weren't human; they had their own system of justice.

And so did the vampires.

***

"This is only an inquest, not a formal trial, so I want you and Nick to stay behind the glass in this room." Valadon spoke softly to Miranda. "No one knows he's awoken, except for my most trusted Torians, and we're keeping it that way for now. As far as the Renworths know, he's still in a coma." His eyes met hers. "I'm glad you're here. Nick could use the company." He sighed. "He hasn't handled learning of Cerise's betrayal very well."

Miranda nodded. *Who did?* Betrayal was one of the bitterest pills to swallow. She'd seen the way Nick had looked at Cerise during her class, his affection obvious in the way he smiled at her. Cerise's eyes never held that same sparkle.

Valadon tugged the tips of her hair. "Thank you for getting the Were Queen to assist us in the hunt for Cerise." His lips twisted upward. "She does have a way of getting to the heart of the matter."

"Nick became one of her favorites when he visited last year. Her protective streak is very strong." Not unlike the vampire king himself, she thought, meeting his emerald eyes. His fondness for his nephew was something special. Valadon didn't often show emotion, but as an empath, Miranda sensed his deep-rooted feelings he kept carefully guarded. She'd seen the way his face became bereft when gazing at Bianca's portrait in the archives. From all reports, Valadon and his sister were very close. The deaths of Nick's parents had hit him hard. And he intended to keep Nick safe, even if his nephew didn't welcome such attention.

"I appreciate you taking the time to come today, though I wish it was under better circumstances."

She was glad her deposition stating she'd witnessed Cerise giving Nick a piece of paper just before the finals on the night they'd been attacked was all that was required.

When Valadon had asked her to be present, just in case they needed her during the inquiry, she'd agreed, trusting the High Lord to see to her well-being.

When he escorted her into the viewing room, which resembled the ones detectives used to observe suspects, she was glad to see Nick sitting up. Though the look on his face said he'd rather be anywhere else but here. Her heart ached for him.

"Katya will keep you company and answer any questions you might have." Valadon kissed her hand in farewell. "I'll see you afterward." He nodded to Nick. "No one leaves this room until the inquest is over. Understand?"

Nick nodded.

Valadon bowed and, with a solemn expression, left.

"This room is soundproofed, so you can speak without fear of being overheard." Katya pointed to the control box. "If you push that button in front of you, you can listen to the testimony given. Push it, again, and it shuts off the sound."

"Thanks." Miranda thought Katya's presence was more due to the fact that Nick looked like he was ready to bolt. Valadon didn't want him anywhere near the inquest, but when Nick insisted he had a right to hear what went on, Valadon relented that he could witness the proceedings but not be a part of it.

"I'm glad to see you out of the coma." Sitting next to him, she brushed his arm. "How are you feeling, Nick?"

His eyes held hurt, betrayal, but most of all, pain. Valadon had explained to him that the evidence proved Cerise had purposely led him to the house where the creature lay in waiting. His old business competitor and nemesis, Edgar Renworth, was not only Were King of the Red Claw Clan, but also Cerise's uncle. It was alleged it was on his orders she had set the trap.

Nick didn't want to believe it. He said he'd known Cerise for months and she'd never hurt him. But Miranda suspected Nick knew; on some level, he knew. His heart just wasn't ready to accept it.

He sighed. "I've been better."

"I know." From the front row, they could watch the events of the inquiry as they unfolded. There were two empty back rows behind them. She grasped his hand for support. "I am so sorry this happened."

"Yeah, me, too."

From the way he twitched in his seat, Miranda couldn't tell if he was still suffering from his injuries or if he was uncomfortable at having to witness his ex-girlfriend being accused of pre-meditated murder.

When the proceedings were about to start, Katya dimmed the lights. "They can't see or hear anything inside this room, but it's best to keep the lights low."

Several people entered Valadon's spacious conference room. To the left, Valadon, Remare and Irina sat at a long table. Miranda's spine straightened at how formidable Remare looked. Even through the glass, she could feel his magnetism. On the other side, Edgar Renworth, his chief advisor, Vic Gren, Cerise, and a Were Miranda didn't know sat. "Who's the tall woman with the black hair?"

"That's Alexa Cantrell, counsel for the accused. From what I hear, a total bitch."

A long raised platform with tables and chairs were set up for the tribunal, which would include a Were, a vampire and a human. They would decide today if enough evidence was present for a formal trial. When the three magistrates entered, wearing the long robes, Miranda wasn't surprised Lizandra Wells entered first.

Renworth had strenuously objected to her presence on the tribunal. But Valadon explained it was only an inquest and any judges chosen for a trial would be different from today. And, since no one from his own clan could be on the tribunal, Renworth was forced to relent. The animosity between the warring clan chiefs was palpable. Lizandra returned his icy stare and then turned to smile at the mirror, knowing Miranda was behind the glass. Next in was an older vampire with a few gray hairs at his temple, the chief magistrate.

"That's Victor, our sage. He's very knowledgeable about our laws. He has a reputation of being firm, but fair." Keeping her voice low, Katya nodded to the last magistrate, a dark-haired man of medium build. "And that's James Wyatt. He's a human judge who agreed to be part of the tribunal."

Then, the door opened, and a young man, immaculately dressed in a gray suit and carrying a briefcase, entered. His blond hair was stylishly short. "That's Chase Lambert, Valadon's chief counsel. He's our best litigator."

Miranda frowned. "He looks awfully young."

"Think so?" She smiled slyly. "Once he gets started, there's no stopping him." She nodded appreciatively. "He's fucking brilliant."

Nick twisted in his seat as if his side hurt.

Miranda listened as the chief magistrate went through the motions of introducing everyone and then explaining how the inquiry would proceed. Victor explained the charges against Cerise, who appeared calm and detached, but even from a distance, Miranda could detect her apprehension. When asked how she responded to the charges of conspiracy to commit pre-meditated murder, Ms. Cantrell rose and answered, "Not guilty."

Then, Mr. Lambert rose and used a remote to light the screen on the wall between the magistrates and the lawyers. "We'll present evidence today to show that Ms. Renworth deliberately and knowingly led Nick Valadon to a house where the foundation had been recently excavated." He pressed a button to reveal images of the cement blocks from the foundation had been cut away for an opening. He zoomed in on the ground where proof that drilling had been done was clearly visible.

"Secondly, we'll prove, through depositions that Ms. Renworth had an ongoing relationship with Nick Valadon and that she desired advancement within the ranks of Red Claw Clan by plotting the death of Nick Valadon to curry favor with her uncle, Edgar Renworth, known to have adversarial feelings of animosity toward Lord Valadon." He pressed the remote to show pictures of Nick and Cerise together around NYU's campus.

Nick cringed when he saw the images of him and Cerise together. Apparently, Valadon had been keeping a closer eye on him than he'd thought.

"Your honors, we have motivation, means and opportunity to prove our case." He then handed copies of the affidavits to the magistrates, as well as opposing counsel, and gave them time to peruse the information.

Gregori and another dark-haired vampire with a neatly trimmed beard entered, carrying a black box, and laid it on Valadon's table near Remare.

Miranda asked, "Who's that?"

"Scorpio. We call him 'The Scorpion' because he's known for his stinger. He's the leader of the mid-level Torians and our main interrogator." Katya added, "He's also the only dhampire in House Valadon."

Half-vampire, half-Were. She wondered if his Were blood kept him from being one of the Elite Torians.

"Tell her the truth, Katya," Nick snarled. "He's an executioner, one who takes pleasure in torturing Valadon's enemies."

Miranda gulped. "What's in the box?"

Katya hesitated then said, "It contains truth-inducement implements."

"Seriously?!" Nick groaned. "Call it what it is."

Torture devices. Lizandra had warned her the Council of Others had similar judicial proceedings as the human ones, but also some unique methods of persuasion never allowed in a human court. Miranda's stomach recoiled.

It was one thing to know your lover was an assassin. Remare had killed to protect the members of his House. Hell, she'd even killed to stop the HOL from torturing him. But to see the man you trusted with your heart, your very life, inflict torture on another being, Miranda wasn't sure she could handle it. She started eyeing the exit.

Nick looked like his stomach was ready to roil, as well.

"Can we leave, now?" Miranda asked.

"Not until the inquiry is over. Valadon's orders." Katya went to the corner where the water cooler was and got Nick and Miranda a glass of water.

Nick gulped his down, and Miranda slowly let the cool liquid quench her dry throat.

Not wanting to see what would happen next, she asked, "Maybe we could close the curtains, then?"

"We may not need to." Katya pointed to the window. "Watch."

Lambert resumed his questions. "Ms. Renworth, do you deny inviting Nick to the house where the creature was located?"

"I deny it." Ms. Cantrell whispered something to her. "Yes, Nick Valadon and I were involved, but he must have gotten the address wrong, because that is not the house I invited him to."

"And what address did you invite him to?"

Miranda knew Cerise was lying, and when she looked at Nick, she could tell by his crestfallen face he did, too. As far as the Renworths and their council knew, Nick was not available to dispute her claims. "They think you're still comatose."

Katya smiled. "We've been withholding that piece of information."

"I see." Lambert then flicked the screen to show a photocopy of Cerise's art history final with her handwriting clearly visible. "Is this a copy of your final you were given at NYU?"

There was no sense in denying it. The date and her name were clearly marked on the top of the page. "Yes."

Lambert then proceeded to display on the screen a partial copy of the note Remare had found near Nick's seat at NYU. Lambert maneuvered the papers to show the handwriting was identical. "Your honors," he handed the judges folders, "this is an affidavit from Professor Thomas Gaines of John Jay College of Criminal Justice. It is his professional opinion, after using his Identification Analysis System, that the handwriting is an exact copy. Ninety-nine point three to be exact."

"Where is he going with this?" Miranda wondered aloud.

He then displayed the whole note, revealing the exact address of the house where they were attacked.

A fine layer of sweat blossomed on Cerise's upper lip as she nervously gazed around the conference room. "No, there must be some mistake! That's not what happened." Her eyes lit on her uncle and she gasped loudly.

Miranda didn't have to be a Were to know the scent of fear permeated the room.

Covering his face, Nick sank deeper into his chair. Miranda put her arm around him and rubbed his shoulder.

There was a murmur of voices until Victor banged the gavel, quieting the conference room. Edgar Renworth looked like he wanted to lunge from his seat and attack Lizandra. Unflinching, she quietly stared back at him.

"How did they get that note?" Nick asked. "I thought I'd lost it."

Miranda didn't want to admit she'd been with Remare at NYU when he'd found it. "It doesn't matter. Remare is quite thorough in his investigation." She stared out at her lover, wondering if he knew she was sitting behind the glass.

After much outrage, accusations and counter-accusations, Renworth got up and stood behind Cerise. His eyes lit on Valadon's. For a moment, it appeared he was going to massage his niece's shoulders to get her to relax. No one expected what he did next. In a move too quick to stop, he wrung her neck. The sound of bone crunching reverberated throughout the room. Cerise's dead body slumped down on the table, her head at an impossible angle. Renworth nodded to Valadon. "Justice is served."

"Christ!" Miranda's heart was thudding against her chest.

Tears started down Nick's cheek as he clung to her.

"Smart move." Katya sneered in Renworth's direction. "Kill the only one who could implement you further."

Miranda was horrified. "He gets away with that?"

"In our court system, yes. Blood pays for blood. Rather than have to make a monetary payment to Valadon for the insult of conspiring to murder Nick, he killed Cerise before any testimony could damage his position. If anyone accuses him, he can simply deny he had any knowledge about what his niece had planned." Katya sucked on her teeth. "Pretty crafty."

Miranda thought it was barbaric. She watched as Renworth and Cantrell packed up their papers and left, leaving Gren to retrieve Cerise's body.

Nick and she were not allowed to leave the room until Renworth and the others had taken the elevator down to the lobby. When Valadon tried to approach him, Nick turned away from his uncle. Miranda spoke mentally to Valadon, *"I'll stay with him for a while. He was devastated by the testimony and then watching Cerise die."*

"Please do. Miranda, however harsh, it was necessary for him to see."

Miranda wondered about the truth of his last statement but said nothing.

Chapter Sixteen

"Shhh, he's asleep." Miranda smiled as Remare entered Nick's living room. Her voice was barely a whisper. "He asked Dr. Amira for a sedative. She left a little while ago." Reclining on the couch, she brushed Nick's hair away from his face as he lay against her side. "He was emotionally drained after watching the inquest." She exhaled. "So was I."

Remare nodded in sympathy. "None of us expected Renworth to do what he did."

Miranda wondered if Valadon had known, or at least suspected, what the Were King would do. "He asked me to stay with him for a little while." She moved her feet from their tucked position on the couch to the floor and winced at the weight of Nick's head on her shoulder. She'd been happy to just hold him, give him the comfort he needed, but dead asleep, he weighed a ton.

"Let me put him to bed. He'll be more comfortable there." Remare's voice was soft as he lifted Nick as though he weighed nothing and carried him to his bedroom. Remare removed his shoes so that Nick could sleep peacefully. He stood over him as Nick curled in on himself.

"He looks almost angelic."

"He has suffered much for his young years." Remare tenderly pulled the duvet over him. She was impressed at how paternal Remare was toward Nick. But growing up an orphan, Miranda knew others often tried to compensate for the lack of parents.

Remare lowered the lights and led her from the room. "You look exhausted, Mir-randa. Have you had anything to eat?"

"I couldn't keep anything down." But she knew if she didn't eat something, she'd awake during the night starving. "Do you think Escher could send up some soup?"

"I'll see that he does." He took out his phone and started texting. "What kind would you like?"

"Anything." She shrugged. "Chicken soup sounds good about now. Make sure he sends some up for Nick, too. In case he gets hungry later on." Since the kitchenette had a mini-fridge and microwave, he could reheat it later.

Remare joined her on the couch. But she avoided his gaze, tucking one foot beneath her. "Do you find vampire justice so disagreeable, Mir-randa?"

"I know Were justice can be vicious. Lizandra's told me as much. I know there are a lot of things she doesn't discuss with me, but..." She rubbed her forehead. "I've killed before." She'd incinerated members of the HOL who took part in Remare's torture and were responsible for Dane's brutal death. "But they were grown men. Evil. I think it got to me because Cerise was so young."

"You think evil only exists in those who are older? I can tell you, from experience, evil knows no age limit. The very young are also capable of great acts of malevolence."

She always felt stronger when Remare was near. Grateful, she took his hand in hers.

"Will you come to my rooms later?"

"No." They'd been lucky no one had seen her leaving his rooms the last time she'd been there; she wasn't going to take the chance someone saw her tonight. She ran a finger down his thin line of beard. "Maybe you could come to my place later tonight?"

His eyes darkened seductively. "I'll try my best."

God, she liked the way he smiled at her. Being naked in his arms made her euphoric, but sometimes, just the simple act of holding hands, feeling his thumb sliding over her knuckles, was all she needed to feel complete. As if he was the missing piece to her puzzle. She was about to lean over and kiss him when the door opened.

"Valadon." She moved back to her side of the couch as Remare's back straightened.

"How is he doing?" His voice was deep, melodic, but mellower than she'd heard before.

"He asked me to stay with him. Said he didn't want to talk to anyone. But he didn't want to be alone either."

"I put him to bed a few minutes ago." Remare rose. "Dr. Amira gave him a sedative so he could sleep."

Valadon nodded. "Yes, I know. I spoke with her earlier." He studied Miranda's face. "You look tired. You should stay the night."

"I think that's what Nick wants, so if he wakes, he has someone here to talk to."

Valadon frowned. "You do realize I have several spare bedrooms. From what I hear, very comfortable and accommodating."

"I've slept on couches before." She patted the cushions. "Someone should be here when he wakes. I don't think it should be either of you."

"Yes. I tried contacting him before. He doesn't want to speak to me. I expect he'll feel that way for a few days." The High Lord sighed. "You don't have to sleep on a couch in my home, Miranda. I'd be a poor host if I didn't provide suitable sleeping quarters for you. I'll get Tristan to stay here. Of all the Torians, he's the one Nick is closest to."

There was a light knocking at the door. Escher strode in with a tray of soup and crackers. And a few snacks. "I brought Miranda and Nick some soup." He laid the platter down on the coffee table.

"Consider my offer, Miranda. Escher will show you the available rooms if you should choose to stay the night."

"It will be my pleasure," Escher said, winking as he bowed toward her.

She gazed down at the food. "Thank you." *Chocolate chip cookies. Good man!* She wondered if Valadon would ever lend her Escher for just one weekend. *Probably not.*

Valadon signaled for Remare to join him, and they left together.

Miranda contemplated Valadon's offer, but somehow, she didn't think she'd be able to sleep tonight. Not having seen Cerise's execution. After finishing her soup, she washed out the bowl. Tristan had come and told her he'd stay the night should Nick want someone to talk to. However, instead of taking Escher's offer of showing her the spare bedrooms, she decided to go to the one place that offered her some semblance of peace.

When she reached the lower level of the archives, Morel was thumbing through the stacks. Even though she'd seen him here once before reading, it still surprised her. "Fancy meeting you here."

"Miranda. I didn't know you were still here." He kissed her forehead. "I heard about the inquest. How's Nick doing?"

"He's resting. It took a lot out of him."

"I'm sure it did." He glanced downward for a moment. After a while, he asked, "So, what are you doing here in the archives? Are you working for Valadon, again?"

"No. He said I could use the archives as much as I wanted." She exhaled. "I like to tell myself I'm here to find some long-forgotten artist I can do a dissertation on, but I'm not quite there, yet." Miranda wondered if she'd ever be ready. "Instead, I'm interested in history."

"Human or vampire?"

"Both. But someone told me you have volumes on vampire history."

"Yes, down this way." He led her down the row of stacks. "Vampires have very long memories, so no one really reads these books much."

"What do you read?"

"I've been studying philosophy, spiritualism. It gives me comfort." At her disconcerted expression, Morel laughed. "What? You didn't think vampires had great thinkers? Philosophers, mathematicians, historians. We do." He spread his arms wide. "A whole world of it."

Miranda blushed. "That's not what I meant."

"I know. We do have a certain image." He laughed. "I guess we do at that." He took down a volume from the highest shelf. "Ah, here is Toussaint. He was one of our early philosophers. It's said Descartes was a follower and adapted some of his ideas"

Miranda took the book and leafed through it. "I wish we had learned more of this in school."

"Yeah, me, too. Maybe, then, the world wouldn't have been so frightened of us."

Miranda nodded. "Okay, I'll check out Toussaint."

"You know, if you're curious, you should meet our sage, Victor. I study with him sometimes. He's the most brilliant man I know. He could probably answer any questions you might have." Morel rubbed his jaw as he gazed around the library. "I think he's read just about every book here, probably wrote some, too."

She'd seen Victor when he'd acted as chief magistrate at the inquest and wondered what kind of man he was. "You don't think he'd mind?"

"Nah. You once saved Valadon's life and protected Nick when he needed it most. I should think he'd be happy to meet with you and discuss history or philosophy or whatever it is you're curious about."

"Well, okay, then. Maybe I will. But, for tonight, I think I have my reading material. Thanks."

"You're welcome."

Miranda was turning to leave when a thought occurred to her. "Would you like to have dinner with me sometime soon? I know I'm not the best cook around, nothing like Escher, but I haven't killed anyone...recently."

He smiled. "Sure. That sounds wonderful. If you want, I could bring Victor along to meet you."

"Sounds good. I'd like to meet him, as well."

***

When Nick woke, his mouth was dry and his head was hazy from the knock-out meds Dr. Amira had given him. You would think, between the sedatives and the pain pills he'd taken earlier, he would have been out for the night. But, then, his stomach started growling, and he remembered he hadn't eaten anything for most of the day. He made his way to his kitchen when he noticed someone sitting in his living room.

Tristan looked up as he was about to swallow a bite of his meal. "Hey, Nick, how you feeling?"

"What are you doing here," he sniffed the air, "and what are you eating?"

Tristan finished chewing. "Valadon said he wanted someone here when you woke up, and I got nominated."

Nick rubbed his head. "Where's Miranda?"

"Not sure. I think Escher cooked her something to eat." He handed Nick a piece of paper. "She told me to give you this when you woke."

Nick smiled at the note with her number, *"Whenever and wherever you might need me.—MC"*

"Escher left some soup and medallions of beef for you in the fridge. It's really good. He used those great spices we like so much. There's some potatoes and gravy, also."

"Thanks." Nick grabbed the food container and a bottle of cold water out of the fridge and guzzled it down. His throat was dry. Probably from the meds. He took the lid off the soup and sniffed, then placed it in the microwave. When the soup was finished heating, he joined Tristan on his couch.

"Listen, Nick, I'm sorry about Cerise."

"Yeah, me, too." He tasted the soup, grateful it soothed his throat. Nick wasn't sure he wanted to talk to him or anybody else, but Tristan had always been a good friend. "I just can't believe she set me up like that."

"Yeah, I know it must sting like hell. But the main thing is you survived."

"What?" He feigned surprise. "You're not going to lecture me on why I shouldn't have been dating a Were? Everyone else has."

"No. I figured Valadon already gave that speech. I'm just glad the creature didn't kill you." He shook his head. "I can't believe the rumors about those humans who were trapped underground for so long are true."

"It's true. Believe me." He swallowed more soup. He hesitated, his voice strained, then asked, "How did you deal with losing Zoe?"

"Yeah, that was tough. Remember, Valadon had abjured her years ago, so I had time to adjust. We'd been tight for a long time, I loved her, but she'd broken Valadon's prime directive." He stretched out his legs over the table. "I knew it was over, then."

No one had ever told Nick what Zoe had done to get thrown out of House Valadon, but he knew it had to have been something really bad. A betrayal of some sort. For Valadon to permanently ban one of his Elite soldiers, he had to have had a solid reason. A disgraced Torian, alone, without the protection of a House, was an easy prey for any of their enemies to kill. "Tristan, what did she do that got her shunned?"

"Shunned?" He sat up quickly. "Valadon wanted to kill her." He closed his eyes in bitter memory, his face twisted in agony. "Her brother had been badly beaten. He was dying and needed blood. Her own blood wasn't enough so she went in search of a source." Tristan peered up at him. "They fed on a child. By the time Kai was finished with her, the child was dead. He died sometime later."

Zoe had not only fed on a human child, she was responsible for its death. No wonder Valadon had renounced her. "Do you still think about her?"

"From time to time," he rubbed his hands together, "something happens, stirs up a memory. But I'm with Katya now. We're good together."

"Do you love her?"

"Not sure. I could. We've both been in long-term relationships that went south, so neither one of us is really ready for that deep a relationship." He shrugged. "Who knows? Maybe, someday, we'll have that connection, but for now, we're happy, and that's all that matters, right?"

"I was happy. I loved Cerise."

"I know you did." Tristan put a hand on his shoulder. "But you're a Blueblood, in case you've forgotten." He shook his head. "You are so friggen young, my friend. You'll find others."

"I don't think so. Not like her, anyway."

"No. Not like her. Someone better, who won't try to get you killed. Give yourself time, man. I know it hurts, now, but..."

"Time heals all wounds? Yeah, I never really believed that. Look at Gabriel."

"Let's not. Gabriel digs his own hell." Tristan stood and took their empty plates into the kitchen. Nick hadn't even been conscious he'd finished eating.

"What are the others saying?" He put the back of his hand over his eyes. "They must think I'm the biggest fool going."

"No one thinks that. Don't be so hard on yourself." Tristan stood with his hands on his hips. "You got played. I think everyone goes through that, or something like it, at one time or another. Learn from it! Look at it from every possible angle. Then, fucking let it go."

"How?"

"One day at a time, Nick. One day at a time. You *will* find another woman to love. I'm sure of it. Listen, after Zoe, I didn't think I'd ever find another I could connect with. Really feel that tightness that's so fucking rare in our world. But I'm pretty damned tight with Katya now."

Learn from it, huh? He was not going to fall in love with another person for a very long time to come. "Yeah, I'll give it some thought. But, right now, I just want to go back to sleep. Those meds Dr. Amira gave me are messing with my head."

"Get some sleep, Nick. You'll feel better tomorrow."

He gave him a sideways look. "Really?"

"Maybe." Tristan smiled sympathetically. "I do know this: Each day, it gets a little easier."

"Hope so." Nick turned and closed his bedroom door behind him. He laid his head against the door. "This fucking sucks."

He tried to process everything Tristan had said. Knew what he said made sense. But, right now, the pain was too real, too raw. He wondered if the pain would still feel as bad tomorrow. And how was he going to face the others when they knew he'd been played? He didn't even want to think about that. At this point, he wasn't even sure he wanted to return to NYU. He just wanted to be alone for a good long while.

Chapter Seventeen

Miranda wanted a bottle of cold water from the fridge, but she didn't think her legs would work. Her body felt like Jell-O, and she couldn't muster the strength to move. When she turned her head to look at Remare, he wasn't in much better condition. The last few hours of exertions had perspiration rolling off their bodies. She enjoyed watching him sleep; he so rarely did when he was with her, as if he were afraid he'd miss something. She rested her hand over his heart. No wonder vampires got to live so long. When they slept, it was as if their bodies shut down, their heart rates incredibly slow, almost as if they were dead.

She smiled. Vampires may be cold-blooded, but when they worked out, the blood pumping vigorously, oh yeah, they got as hot as any human.

She ran a finger down the center of his chest. "You know, for a vampire, you work up a hell of a sweat."

One corner of his mouth lifted. "Is that a complaint?"

"Hardly. I think you nearly gave me a heart attack the last time."

"Yes, you did scream particularly loud. I thought I might have hurt you, but you made that whimpering sound you make after you come."

"I do *not* whimper."

He turned to her. "Yes, you do, Mir-randa." His smile was wickedly sexy as he drew lazy circles on her stomach.

"Okay, okay, maybe I whimper a little, but you're the one who growls."

"I know." He nipped her lower lip. "And I plan to growl more often." Laying his head back on the pillow, he said, "I was a fool to have stayed away so long."

"You're here, now. That's all that matters."

Frowning, he gazed around her room. With his aristocratic background, she wondered if he looked down on her place. "What's wrong? Don't like my home much? Sorry, pal, I don't make the bucks you do, and for your information, this house has been in my family for generations. I'm lucky to have it."

"Your house is fine, Mir-randa. That's not it."

"What is it, then?"

He grimaced. "The windows."

Miranda turned to look at the moonlight shining outside. "What's wrong with them?" She couldn't remember when they'd been cleaned last, but they looked fine to her.

"Have you ever considered getting bars on them?"

"Hell, no. I'm not going to be a prisoner in my home. Why would I need bars?"

"It would be safer."

"And if there's a fire? I'm not going to be trapped inside."

He seemed to consider that. "How about screens?"

Miranda thought back to the place where they'd been attacked. It had been a vampire home so some of the windows had black screens on the inside. "Like the house we were in with the creature?"

"Yes."

"I'm not a vampire, Remare. I actually like the light coming in. Sheesh, next thing you'll be complaining about is me taking the subways." At his raised eyebrows, she knew she spoke too quickly. "Don't. Start."

As if in shock, he asked, "You take the subways?"

"How did you think I got up to Werehaven and other places?"

"I thought Orion drove you or you borrowed his car when he was on tour."

"Nope. Besides, I've been taking the subways since I was a teenager. There's nothing to worry about."

Remare's look of revulsion almost made her laugh. And she thought only Max made the Brussel sprouts face.

"I am only concerned for your safety. I can't be here every night, and I don't like you living by yourself."

"I'm not alone. There are two Weres sleeping upstairs." Max and Sasha were still waiting for the fumes from the extermination to lessen in their apartment. Miranda was saddened at the prospect of them leaving. Sasha was a fantastic cook, and Max really knew how to organize her stuff.

"Yes, I met them earlier tonight." His frown was back. "They're awfully short for Weres and not what I would call protectors."

"You've never seen Max fight. She might be pint-sized, but that girl packs a wallop. And, besides, Orion will be back soon, so you need not be concerned."

"I do worry. You didn't see the pictures of the victims after the HOL was through with them. I'm halfway tempted to assign bodyguards to you."

"Don't bother. I'm sure Valadon needs them more. How many guards does he have, anyway?"

"Besides the Elite Torians, he has an army of three hundred mid-level soldiers." Remare folded his hands behind his head. "One hundred for each eight-hour shift. They are always on call at ValCorp and have different jobs within the company." He seemed to be reflecting. "There's one young soldier. Handsome devil. ValCorp's leading model. He's a cut above the rest. Less than a hundred years old, but he moves incredibly fast for one so young, and he has very sharp instincts."

"Jeremy?" She'd met the stunning vampire briefly at her so-called engagement party at Nightshade.

"Yes. He told me he doesn't plan to model much longer. He just did it to pay for his college, and once he has his MBA in finance, he hopes to join Valadon's junior executives. I'm thinking of taking him on my next mission."

Concern made her stomach contract. "And that would be...?"

"I'm going to be busy the next few nights checking out warehouses and other locations Gregori and Irina have discovered as being registered to prominent members of the HOL."

"Tell me you take back-up and don't work solo." Now, she was the one to feel anxious. She didn't need photos to know the horrors the HOL inflicted on its victims. They'd delivered a gift box to her containing the head of her former lover.

"Only a fool would work alone. I'm not a fool, Mirranda."

"I know." He'd told her earlier of the ongoing investigations he'd been conducting on known members of the HOL. Now, she understood his concerns for her. "Hey." She turned his head to her and made her voice soothing. "I'm not defenseless." She spied Toussaint's book on her desk across the room and summoned it to her.

His brow rose in surprise. "Your abilities are improving. I thought you could only move small objects, like pens and keys, those sorts of things."

"I've been practicing. Paper, wood, anything that's made of natural elements, I can manipulate. Metal is a challenge, though; it's denser. Not so much with plastics. I can't move items made of synthetics."

"How long have your powers been growing?"

"For a while now." She didn't want to tell him she'd been concerned for Lizandra when there'd been skirmishes with the Red Claws or that she'd been training with Blu to hone her skills in case she ever had to deal with another vampire like Vivienna.

He thumbed through the book. "You're reading Toussaint? Why?"

"I was curious. I wanted to learn about your histories, philosophies." She took the book from him and laid it on her bedside table. "You know, I met Morel in the archives. He's studying philosophy, says it gives him comfort. He recommended Toussaint."

"I read him while at University. Brilliant vampire."

"That's what Morel said. I had dinner with him and Victor last night. It was good to see Morel out."

"You're one of the few that's been able to do so. Ever since Cyra died, he hasn't been the same."

"I know." Miranda glanced down. "That's why I made him my specialty, Veal Francaise with pasta. It came out pretty good."

He clasped her hand. "Thank you for getting him away from ValCorp. He needs to get out more."

"Yeah, he's pretty tight with Victor. The two of them seem to get along pretty well. I liked Victor; for a scholar, he has a pretty good sense of humor."

"Victor has been our sage for some time now. He's very well-respected." He kissed her hand. "I'm glad you decided to learn our histories."

"Yeah, me, too."

Caressing her biceps, his thumb brushed the underside of her arm. "What's this?"

"It's an implant. Birth Control."

He sighed. "Miranda, you need not worry. I am long past the age of fathering children, and vampires don't carry discascs."

"I wasn't sure. You told me your father was a Blueblood." She knew purebreds like Valadon and Nick could father children for a very long time. Just how long, no one knew for certain.

"But my mother was not."

At times, she could sense his emotions, and other times, he seemed to shut down. Now was one of those times. "Does it bother you not having kids?"

"You assume I never had any. I did."

Miranda's ears perked up; she leaned up on her elbow. "Where? Who?"

"A very long time ago." He closed his eyes in memory. "Nearly nine hundred years ago." His voice sounded husky. "I was barely a hundred years old, and I was enamored of a woman who lived near my father's winery in Tuscany. We courted, married. She became pregnant with our first child, a boy, and then, two years later, presented me with a girl."

Miranda sensed this had an unhappy ending. "What became of them?"

"When I was sent to Rome to learn military tactics, a rival family attacked and murdered them." Absently, he drew circles on her wrist. "Later, I hunted down the killers and had them slaughtered."

That was nearly a millennium ago. She knew vampires rarely married, but in a thousand years, she'd suspected he might have had a wife or two. Still, it stung. She wondered if he'd ever re-married. "Did you ever have any other children?"

"As you discovered in Paris, I nearly married Vivienna until I learned of her treachery. At the time, I remember thinking we would have had beautiful children together."

Miranda scoffed. "They would have been ruthless as she."

"True. I'm glad I spared the world that horror. Centuries later, I was stationed in India. I met a princess, Indira, who captivated me with her beauty and whimsical ways. We married and had two children—again, a boy and a girl. It had been agreed upon before the ceremony, when our High Court summoned me back to Paris, she would accompany me with the children. That did not happen.

"On the day of our scheduled departure, she decided not to board the ship. She became hysterical, refusing to leave her homeland. I petitioned her mother, the Madame Lord of Bombay, to intercede. But even she could not persuade Indira to join me. When I suggested taking the children with me, she threatened to cut my throat in my sleep.

"After much negotiating, we agreed I would visit often, when my duties permitted. But revolutions broke out in Europe, and I was away at war for long periods of time. When I returned, she had found a new husband and had two other children. Her mother had dissolved our marriage on the grounds of abandonment. However, I was welcomed into her new family. My children called me papa and asked me to tell them stories of the great courts of Europe. I enjoyed that very much." He linked their fingers as if seeking support. "Even Soorah, her husband, bore me no ill will, no jealousy. There was none to be had, by either of us.

"On my successive trips East, I was treated, at first, like a welcomed member of the family and then, over the years," his exhale was silent, but lengthy, "as a distant relative. When my children became teenagers, they no longer called me papa, but Remare instead." He closed his eyes in memory. "It was apparent Soorah had become their father, and they no longer asked me for stories about the European Courts."

Miranda's heart was breaking for her proud warrior who would not allow his agonizing disappointment to show. She fought the tears threatening to break loose. Her hand over his heart, she sensed the bitter, emotional turmoil he'd experienced, the scars he kept so carefully covered. He'd been rejected by his own children. Replaced by another. *How did he survive such a grievous loss?* She knew nothing on God's green earth could ever replace what once was. "I'm so sorry you went through that."

"It was my own fault. I knew Indira was headstrong." He exhaled. "Part of me knew she would never get on the boat when it was time to leave, but I wed her, regardless." He turned to her, his eyes dark and deep. "Do not feel sorrow. There is no ill regard, Miranda. They are a united family, quite content and live very well. Gradaya, the Madame Lord, was a shrewd businesswoman and made certain their fortunes were well preserved. I sent them money for many years to ensure they were well taken care of. They have been.

"Do you still see them?"

"Not anymore. We live separate lives." His voice was heavy with emotion. "The last time I visited, it was as if I was a stranger. Everyone was polite, considerate, but there was no familial closeness. I was as foreign to them as they were to me. Any bond we might have shared was long over." He sighed deeply. "It's better that way, I think."

Miranda hated seeing sadness in his eyes. No matter what he said, she knew there had to be pain. She'd lost her family at a young age, and that was not something you ever got over. Sure, you learned to deal with it, but the scars were always there.

"You're not alone, Remare. You belong to a wonderful House, and...you have me." She bent over and kissed him soundly, relishing the way his arms embraced her. Cocooned in his warmth, she wanted him to feel what she did when she was with him. Other men may send chills through her, but only Remare made the world drift away.

Sliding her leg over him, she took him deep inside her, loving the way her body welcomed him. No other man could ever fill her the way Remare did. She began to move, emulating the way he rocked inside her with that little rotation of the hips. When his eyes started glazing over, she whispered, "I'm your family, now, and I won't ever leave you."

He smiled up at her with male satisfaction. "I know." In one quick move, he reversed their positions. He penetrated her deeply, slowly and retreated, the ebb and flow of his rhythm seducing her into a world where only pleasure existed.

She slid her hands up his tight, firm abs enjoying the feel of his cool, smooth skin. When she reached his pecs, she caressed his muscles and stroked his nipples with her thumbs. That one simple gesture brought a smile of contentment. She knew his body well enough now to know what he simply enjoyed and what drove him insane with lust. When he bent to kiss her, her hands circled his neck and brought him closer, their bodies slick with perspiration.

There was nothing else that mattered, no monsters hiding in closets, no HOL to contend with. Through their lovemaking, they created a world of their own, a sacred place filled with only passionate sensations. The sensual awareness so intense, she'd never felt more alive.

Remare broke from the kiss, his hands braced on either side of her, and increased the speed of his thrusts. His control was admirable, driving her insane with his unrelenting desire to make their time together last as long as he could. When she'd risen so high, the potency of their lovemaking so strong she didn't think she could bear any more, he'd slow down enough to cradle her in wings of warmth that caressed her very soul.

In those dark orbs of his, she saw her life, her death and her world. But not as she saw it, but rather how he saw her. And, in his eyes, she was beautiful, magical and she owned the part of him he rarely showed to others, his heart.

Tears started rolling down her cheeks as her body trembled from the sheer force of the magic they were creating. His eyes glazed over, the red rims pulsing with desire. His breaths fierce as his body contracted. When she came, she screamed his name and heard the echoes of his growl roaring in her mind.

Her heart thundering, it took several moments for her breaths to even out. Safe in his embrace, exhausted from their intimacy, the darkness claimed them.

Chapter Eighteen

"You know, it wouldn't hurt if you smiled."

Leaning against the bar, Miranda grinned. "Jordan, you know how I feel about these galas." Though, as far as parties went, the showing of an Artemisia Gentileschi painting at the New York Art Institute was pretty good. And, as far as bosses went, Jordan Knox was fantastic, even though he did come off a bit too fatherly, at times.

"Yes." He sighed. "That's why I accommodate you when you ask for time off. With little notice, mind you."

She raised her drink to him. "And that is why I come when you beckon."

"I should be so lucky." He looked at her ponytail and frowned, but said nothing. "And couldn't you wear regular high heels like every other woman here?"

"What's wrong with my boots?" She looked down at them. "They're very fashionable." Maybe not the best choice, given her evening gown, but still very comfortable. The black suede clung to her calves, and the silver heels added a spark of sophistication.

Shaking his head, he just exhaled in frustration and sipped his champagne.

Amused, she asked, "Really, Jordan, when are you going to do the retrospective on female artists? Poor Artie looks miserable there all by herself. One of her *Judith and Holofernes* series is a treasure."

"Well, my dear, it's a little difficult selling the board on an artist who was known for her female decapitations of men, especially when the board is comprised mainly of males."

Miranda smirked. She knew it was a hard sell; though, eventually, the retrospective would happen.

"It's on the backburner for now, but before you protest, yes, I am in the planning stages. Look, there's Eliot Harper, a major contributor to the museum. I want to speak with him. Now, for God's sake, mingle and try to be pleasant."

"Yes, I'll be sociable and offer my expertise when requested."

"Good. And promise me no sarcasms."

Laughing, she feigned surprise. "Who, *moi*? Not tonight, Jordan."

He cleared his throat. "We'll see how long that lasts."

Miranda accepted a canape from a passing server and circulated through the room. Everyone seemed to be involved in conversation, so she admired the institute's classic paintings. Although Mannerist works weren't her specialty, she could appreciate the techniques and styles of the artists.

An attractive woman with long dark hair she hadn't seen in years approached. "Hello, Miranda."

Her breath almost caught. "Terese Laines. I haven't seen you since..."

"God, what is it, nearly ten years, now?" She hugged Miranda, doing the air-kiss thing. "NYU was a blast; I have great memories."

Yeah, Miranda had memories, too, not all good. Terese had been one of the best artists in NYU's fine arts department but had dropped out in her last year. She'd fallen prey to some of the seamier underground clubs of NYC and relished the lifestyle. An expert in shading, her monochromatic paintings of erotic figures were fascinating to behold. Miranda admired them for their composition but always wondered how much more talented Terese could have been if she'd chosen other subjects. "Did you ever go back to get your degree?"

"No. I made enough money and developed enough of a clientele I didn't have to. I do some secretarial work, now and again, just to get out of the studio." She shrugged. "And you? Do you still work for the museum? That was always your dream."

"Yup. Still do. I'll leave the creative stuff to you; I prefer doing the histories and authentications. Boring to some, I know, but I like it."

"You should come by my place sometime and see my newer work. My style's become more sophisticated." Terese took out a card from her purse and handed it to her. "I better find my date; he's around here somewhere."

Miranda tucked the card away, glad Terese seemed happy. For a long time, she hadn't been.

"Good to see you, Professor. I hoped you would be here."

"Gabriel." He kissed her cheek. "What are you doing here?" She hadn't seen him in a while. For some old lovers, meeting up at some social gathering might be awkward; that wasn't the case with them. She'd had dinner with him once or twice since she returned from her Paris trip and enjoyed his friendship, as he did hers.

"One of the contributors to the foundation sponsoring my grant invited my director, who insisted I get out of the lab and accompany him. He's here somewhere, hobnobbing with God knows who." He scrutinized the black diamond necklace Valadon had given her after she'd been nearly burned at the stake by an evil ancient. "Nice rocks."

"Thanks. You're looking pretty debonair, yourself." She stepped back to admire him in his elegant dark suit. With his light brown hair and golden eyes, he was a looker. "How've you been?"

"Pretty good. Research is going well. I have no complaints. But I did want to ask you something."

"Shoot."

"It has to do with your profession."

Miranda was intrigued. In the six months they'd been together, Gabriel had shown only mild interest in her work. She suspected that was only because he'd felt obligated to do so. "Ask away."

"Recently, I came across a painting that has raised my interest." His eyes seemed to narrow in reflection. "I would like you to take a look at it and give me your opinion."

"Sure. Where's the painting, now?"

"In the archives."

Her brow lifted. "Valadon's archives?"

"The one and only. *Dad* and I have been having some conversations, and he told me an intriguing story about the woman in the painting."

She was glad to hear father and son were talking, again. "So, are you on better terms, now that you've been on your own for most of a year?" She knew their relationship had been strained, and Valadon had *not* wanted his turned son to leave the safety of House Valadon. For the longest while, Gabriel had refused to refer to him as his father, and even now, sarcasm veiled his voice when he did.

"Let's just say we have an understanding. Oh, look, speak of the devil."

Miranda turned to see Valadon and his entourage arriving. He was flanked by Irina, on his right, and Gregori, on his left, and several other Torians she didn't recognize. Miranda was barely aware of heads turning in his direction as the High Lord walked toward them. Her body stiffened, and her breath caught. Valadon was still one of the handsomest men to walk the planet; with his dark hair and piercing emerald eyes, he was a sight to behold. His face had to have been carved by the angels. Every angle, even the cut of his lips, was male perfection.

And Valadon had the arrogance to know it.

She'd never seen him in a tux before, but the vampire filled it out stylishly with his wide shoulders and trim waist. Every muscle moved with liquid grace as he walked, but Miranda knew him for the predator he was. In public, he could equal the social poise of any human, but when he was enraged, the monster within surfaced. She'd seen firsthand when he'd had to battle an evil ancient—a fight she was glad he'd won.

With a little help from her, of course.

"Miranda, you look striking as always. The necklace complements your beauty," Valadon said in his deep, resonating voice, sending shivers up her spine. "Gabriel, good to see you, again."

Nodding to Gregori, Miranda tried to avoid Irina's icy gaze as she faced Valadon. "I didn't know you'd be coming here tonight. Somehow, I didn't think Artemisia was one of your favorites."

"She is. You haven't seen my entire collection as yet, Miranda. I have homes throughout the world with several of her paintings on display. Perhaps, one day, you'll see them."

"Perhaps, someday." But Miranda doubted it, especially if Valadon ever found out about her relationship with Remare.

"I checked out the painting you told me about." Gabriel smiled graciously at his father, but Miranda could detect the rising tension in his body. "I would like to talk to you about it when you have time."

"Of course, but not tonight. This evening is for socializing, and there are a few people I need to speak with." He tilted his head. "Miranda, I hope you save a dance for me later."

"Maybe." The problem with Valadon was that no one ever said no to the High Lord, either out of fear or respect. However, she'd once told him no, and what frightened her was not that he'd been angry or hurt, but under that calm, tranquil façade of his, she knew he was planning something. What that was exactly, she didn't know.

And that concerned her. Gravely.

"Miranda." Gregori bowed his head in her direction then followed his lord.

All she got from Irina was a frosty glare. Miranda had never warmed up to Remare's former lover, and the feeling was mutual. Somehow, she didn't think *The Ice Queen* would ever be fond of her either. And that was fine with her.

However, the one female Miranda was very fond of came bouncing up to her. "Miranda, how lovely to see you." Rosalyn, with her mane of beautifully styled red curls hugged her. "You must stop by Nightshade sometime soon. We have a new chef, and he makes the most amazing appetizers. He's from the Caribbean. Jamaica, I think."

Miranda's face lit up. *She couldn't mean, Lawe, could she?* Any ill feelings she'd sensed from Irina were now replaced with warmth and affection from Rosalyn. "I will. Now that the semester is over, and I have some time, we should do dinner."

"Love to."

Rosalyn's urbane boyfriend, Jason Morgan, joined them. With his light blond hair and attractive face, he was certainly handsome; together, they made a stunning couple, and their happiness shone brightly between them. Jason handed a flute of champagne to Rosalyn and shook Gabriel's hand. "With the New Year approaching, we should be celebrating. Gabriel, you should join us at Nighshade."

"It would be a pleasure."

After much small talk Miranda had never been comfortable making, Rosalyn and Jason left to socialize with friends and Gabriel went in search of his boss. Needing time away from people, Miranda started perusing the paintings and casually strolled down a quiet corridor. She admired the institute's collection and was glad she remembered her glasses.

As she turned a corner, she spotted a dark-haired man also studying the works of art. He was fashionably dressed in a designer tux and she guessed his age to be about early forties. He was of medium height and build and appeared in good shape.

When he turned in her direction, she was struck by the intensity of his gaze. Cold, penetrating eyes seemed to be studying her. When he smiled, his features softened. As harsh as his stare was, his voice was even-tempered with a hint of Europe. "Caravaggio was a master with his shading. You can really see his influence on Gentileschi's work."

Miranda was amazed at his understanding of technique. "Yes, Artemisia's father, Orazio, was a devout follower of Caravaggio, even though his earlier works were Mannerist."

When he pointed to another painting next to Orazio's, Miranda glimpsed his ring. It was similar to the caduceus Gabriel and other doctors wore. But, instead of the two snakes facing each other, they faced outward. *How odd!*

He was rapt in the painting. "I think the daughter surpassed the father."

Miranda felt comfortable discussing art with someone who was not only knowledgeable, but seemed to have a deep appreciation of the old masters. "*Susannah and the Elders* is considered her masterpiece, one that had her ranked as one of the world's premier female painters."

As they casually strolled down the corridor, he pointed out another painting, "What do you think of Antoine Caron's work?"

Miranda examined the painting. "He was certainly daring for a Mannerist; look at his exaggerated figures and overly bright colors."

"Daring, yes. Did you know, besides his depictions of battles and massacres, Caron had an affinity for magic and the occult?"

Miranda had a vague memory of her professors in college mentioning that.

"Darling, they're waiting for us." A woman with short blonde hair and a severe expression approached them.

He looked at his watch. "Quite. It was a pleasure discussing art with you. Perhaps we'll meet another time."

Before Miranda could ask him his name, he turned and left with the blonde. *What an intense couple for the crowd there!* She wondered if they were art thieves. She shook off the bizarre thought. After studying a few other paintings, she made her way to the stairs and spotted Gabriel in the main ballroom.

As she neared him, a malevolent voice entered her mind. *"Enjoying the party, Miranda?"*

Her breath caught, and she slammed her mental shields down hard, but not before she heard his mocking laughter. Her hand went to her stomach as bile began rising. Immediately, her skin turned cold, and sweat rolled down her back. She'd never heard that voice before. It was old, like something from the grave. As if a veil of darkness had lifted to reveal a sinister quality suggesting evil in its purest form.

She gazed around the room, anxiously trying to figure out whose voice it was. Then, she spotted a man halfway down the stairs, tilting his head in her direction. Tall, mid-fifties, she guessed, light brown thinning hair, neatly trimmed beard. With a cruel twist to his lips, he raised his flute of champagne in her direction as if saluting her.

She blinked, trying to clear her mind. In the next instant, the figure was gone.

"Earth to Professor Crescent, are you there?" Gabriel joked.

The voice echoed in her mind. *"Grab the redhead and let's leave."* Inadvertently, whoever it was hadn't completely closed the psychic portal he had opened.

Miranda's heart started beating out a staccato. There was only one redhead she knew of at the party. "Let's leave. Wait a minute. Is Valadon still here?"

"Yes." He pointed to the corner. "He's over there talking to Jason."

Miranda made her way to the High Lord, giving herself credit for walking slowly. "Hello, Valadon. I just wanted to say goodnight before you left with Jason and Rosalyn."

At their confused looks, she tried to maintain an air of graciousness, hoping Valadon saw through her façade. She wasn't taking any chances the stranger could get into her mind, again. "Rosalyn told me about the welcome home party you're planning for Orion at Nightshade." When Rosalyn joined them, Miranda grasped her hand. "I'm so glad you're hosting the party for Orion's return. We really enjoyed what you did the night of our engagement."

Miranda tried to will understanding in Valadon. When he tried to silently question her, she locked her mental shields down. His eyes darkened, but his voice was evenly modulated. "I'm sure whatever Rosalyn has planned will be astounding, as is her usual. There's room in my limo; would you like to join us for a nightcap at ValCorp?"

Miranda shook her head. *"I can't."* "Have a *safe* trip home."

"We will." He turned away with his people following close behind.

Miranda wanted to go with them but feared she'd be leading enemies into his territory. Even worse, she had a perverse feeling she'd been marked, somehow. Whoever had gotten through her natural shields was either a very strong telepath or...a vampire. But why would a vampire mark her?

Gabriel joined her. "Miranda, is everything all right?"

"Yes, I'd like to go home, now. Would you mind giving me a lift?"

"Not at all. Just let me say goodbye to someone, and we'll go."

She watched as Valadon departed with his entourage. "Miranda, have you seen Irina? Valadon wants to go, and I can't find her." She turned to see Gregori's concerned face.

Her breathing quickened. "Something's wrong."

"What?" He grabbed her arm.

"Something's wrong. I can't explain it." She made her way to the door and yanked it open. Flying down the outside stairs, she searched the block, Gregori on her heels. Nothing was happening to her right, but when they searched left, men had grabbed Irina and were trying to force her into a car. She was fighting like a banshee, as one man was trying to put a cloth over her mouth, and another was trying to inject her with a needle. She flung off one, and Miranda heard the sickening sound of bone cracking.

She heard Gregori's enraged roar and barely made out his shadow as he used his vampire speed to get to Irina. A dozen men joined in from two waiting cars, and a fight broke out. Sensing her eyes darkening, Miranda noticed one of the spikes from the wrought iron fence of the nearby building was loose. She summoned the metal spear to her hand and joined in the fracas. Although everything was moving at a rapid pace, Miranda saw the events unfolding as if in slow motion. How odd that, instead of hearing her heart racing, it seemed to quiet and became tranquil.

Remembering Remare's dancing technique, she extended the spike like a sword and used it to attack the assailants. Her steps were graceful and lightning quick. On instinct, as if some ancient voice was guiding her steps, she ducked, evading when necessary and attacking with a strength she didn't know she possessed. From the corner of her eye, she saw Gabriel had joined them and was fighting off one attacker after another. She'd seen him fight before and knew, as a Blueblood, he had more strength than most people realized.

What happened next, happened so fast, it was impossible to track. Gabriel must have summoned Valadon. The High Lord appeared like some avenging angel and dispatched one assailant after another in deadly fast movements that had bones crunching and blood flying in all directions. One of the attackers was thrown through the air and landed, impaled, on the fence. Sounds of utter agony rent the air, and the men, limping, fled back to their cars. The sound of tires screeching reverberated through the night.

Valadon pointed to the impaled man. "Grab that one! Make sure he's taken to the interrogation room." His men promptly obeyed his orders and ushered the injured man into a waiting car.

Tossing the spike away, Miranda went into the High Lord's open arms. Exhaustion and fear had her feeling emotionally bruised. She looked up at Gabriel and tried to smile in gratitude. When she turned, she saw Gregori leading Irina to Valadon's limo. Both were covered with cuts and bruises. His caring manner was evident as he kept his arm protectively around her shoulders. Her arm appeared broken.

"I want everyone back at ValCorp. Now! Gabriel, my limo. You, too, Miranda."

Jason burst forth. "How did you know, Miranda? Is this what you were warning us about? How did you know?" he demanded.

"I overheard them talking," Miranda whispered, not sure if she was still in shock.

"We'll discuss this once we're at ValCorp." His arm still shielding her, Valadon led her to the limo. "Let's go."

Miranda glanced down at her hand. The tips of her fingers were still glowing.

Chapter Nineteen

Miranda was glad someone had lit the massive gas fireplace in Valadon's living room and lowered the lights on the grand chandelier. Cold had seeped into her bones, and her eyes were tired. In the limo, Valadon had assured her he never traveled with less than a dozen guards and they were safe; she didn't relax until they were within the walls of ValCorp. Escher had been kind enough to make her a cup of hot, steaming green tea, which helped soothe her.

When Valadon joined Miranda and the rest of his Torians, he took the centermost position on the luxurious couch. "We interrogated one of the attackers. He was able to give us vivid descriptions of his employers, but at this point, he has not revealed any names." His voice was cold as steel and just as deadly. "I trust *The Scorpion* will elicit more information before dawn."

Miranda shivered at the techniques they would be using to retrieve those details.

When he saw her tremble, he asked, "Would you like another cup of tea?"

Foolishly, she had not taken a coat this evening, thinking the black and gold quilted jacket would keep her warm enough. "No. Thank you. I'm just stunned by what happened."

Gabriel, Gregori and Irina, whose arm was now in a sling, joined them.

"How is Irina's arm?" Valadon asked Gabriel.

"It's fine." Irina added, "Not broken, just sprained." She glared at Gabriel. "I'm not sure why you insisted on this sling. It will be completely healed by morning."

"It was a hairline fracture. And you're lucky I didn't put a cast on it. But I know, with rest, you will heal quickly."

A low growl emitted from Irina.

"Irina!" Valadon's voice did not invite discussion. "In all medical matters, Gabriel has the final word."

She nodded as Gregori tenderly stroked her back.

Once they were all seated, Valadon addressed Miranda "Now. I would like to know exactly what transpired tonight."

"It all happened so quickly." She rolled the warm cup in her hands. "One minute, I was walking toward Gabriel, and then, I heard a voice in my head."

"Whose?" Valadon demanded.

"I don't know. Vampire, I think. Or one hell of a telepath." She sipped what was left of her tea. "He broke through my natural walls. His voice was...cold, vicious almost." She met Valadon's eyes. "He knew my name and welcomed me to the party. But there was something calculating in his voice, as if he was mocking me. I searched the room to see if I could locate the voice. He was on the stairs. Tall, middle-aged, light brown hair, beard. He was there for a moment and then just," she waved her hand in the air, "gone."

"Did anyone else notice a man fitting Miranda's description?"

Miranda scoffed when everyone shook their heads. "Now, you think I'm imagining things."

Valadon continued with his questions. "How did you know they were after Rosalyn?"

"I didn't. I heard the voice commanding another to grab the redhead. I assumed it was Rosalyn."

"And, when they couldn't get Rosalyn, they went after Irina." Valadon leaned forward. "You're human, Miranda. You could have been injured tonight. You shouldn't have helped in the fighting."

"I saw the way you fought," Gregori interjected. "You were extraordinarily fast, lithe on your feet, and yet powerful. Your timing was incredible and almost reminded me of..."

"A Were." All heads turned as Remare walked toward them. "That would make sense since Miranda has spent much of her adult life among the wolves."

Valadon addressed his second. "Remare. How did your mission go tonight?"

"I checked out the warehouse on the West Side. Although it had once been used, it is now abandoned. As was the hanger near the airport. Our people are dusting for prints, but Archer believes both places have not been in use for some time."

"They seem to prefer out-of-the-way places where no witnesses are around."

"True." Remare said, "I understand you had some excitement tonight."

"Someone made a grab for Irina."

Remare gazed in her direction, as if noticing her for the first time. "Are you all right?"

"Yes, a few scratches. Nothing major."

Miranda admired the woman's pride. Her arm had been wrenched, and she'd been covered in bruises, but she refused any pity. Her determination and fortitude were strong, as was the longing in her eyes for Remare.

He noted the sling. "Your arm?"

"Barely a sprain."

Gabriel rolled his eyes.

Valadon continued, "Miranda made contact with what may be a Rogue vampire."

Remare's eyes met hers, his voice matter of fact. "Do tell."

"I'm fairly certain it was a vampire. An old one. He got inside my head."

Remare's brow knitted. "What did he say to you?"

"He welcomed me to the party, and then, I heard him say something about getting hold of a redhead, which I believed he meant Rosalyn."

"Rosalyn? Where is she, now?"

"She's home safely with Jason Morgan. I offered them the hospitality of my house, but they preferred their own. They wisely accepted some of my guards for their protection."

Remare poured himself a drink. "Jason and Rosalyn each have their own security personnel, as well."

"Yes. That is why I allowed them to leave. After the fight, we were able to get hold of one of the attackers. He's down in the interrogation room. No doubt he's one of the HOL's foot soldiers. We will have more information by dawn." Valadon exhaled. "Did any of you happen to notice the license plate number on any of their cars?"

Silence ensued. Miranda closed her eyes in memory. "SBE 45... The last letter was either a one or a seven, I couldn't tell which. Range Rover. Late model. Black." When she opened her eyes, everyone was staring at her. "Hey, I notice things." She smiled up at Remare. "The devil's in the details."

Valadon smirked. "Anything else, Miranda?"

She shook her head. "I'm exhausted." She rubbed her neck. "I can't think of anything else tonight."

"I know you've refused me in the past, but I think it would be a good idea if you stayed here tonight."

Miranda was afraid to meet Remare's eyes for what they would reveal. She nodded. "Okay."

"The same goes for you, Gabriel. Tomorrow, we can sort the rest out. In the meantime, I suggest we all get some sleep. Escher?"

"Yes, sir?"

"Please show Miranda the guest bedrooms. Let her pick which one she wants and see to it she has everything she needs."

"Of course."

Everyone rose and went in their separate directions.

"This way, Professor Crescent." Escher led her and Gabriel down the hall.

"Remare, stay for a minute." Valadon requested. "There's something else I want to discuss with you."

Remare watched as Escher led Miranda and Gabriel down the corridor. "What is it?"

"I got a call from *The Castilian* earlier tonight."

"Asanti?" The artist had been a friend of his for centuries. He'd been an incredible general in many of the wars they had fought together in until Asanti had grown tired of the carnage and retreated to a life of solitude and painting. He'd moved to New York not long after Valadon had established his base of operations here. Many of his paintings hung in Valadon's archives, as well as in several of Remare's homes.

"Yes, he's coming tomorrow to meet with me. He requested you be present."

"Did he say why?"

"Only that it was a personal matter, and he wanted us together when he told us so he wouldn't have to repeat himself."

Remare sipped his wine. "He's lived a reclusive life for decades now."

"Yes, though, we have been in touch over the years. His son, Jacob, should be about Nick's age by now."

"And he didn't say anything further?"

"No. But I guess we'll find out tomorrow what he wants." Valadon rose and put his hand on his shoulder. "Go. Get some sleep. We've all had a long night."

***

"Any room is fine." Miranda was too exhausted to visit the others. If they were anything like Nick's or Remare's, she knew they would all be stylishly elegant. When Escher opened the door, Miranda saw a room swathed in green. It was soothing. Rich verdant drapes hung over mood screens emulating windows. The Aubusson carpets looked plush, and the king-sized bed was an ocean of tropical colors beckoning her. But it was the chaise lounge that caught her attention. "Beautiful."

"Everything you may need is already in the closets, and there's fresh linen in the bath."

When Gabriel made a motion to join Escher by the door, she stopped him. "Gabriel, please stay." At his inquisitive look, she added. "I'm not offering sex; I just don't want to be alone tonight." She flopped down on the chaise and pulled the throw over her. "That vampire who got inside my head scared the hell out of me."

He grinned. "Thank you, Escher. I'm sure we'll be fine here."

"Very good, sir."

After Escher left, Gabriel sat beside her. "I'm sorry about the Rogue." He patted her leg. "Valadon will take care of this; he always does." He raised a brow. "You know you could sleep in the bed. I do know how to behave myself."

Miranda laughed. "I know. But I don't think wild horses could pull me out of this lounge. Besides, I like sleeping with my back up."

"Liar. You're a stomach sleeper." He examined the contents of the dresser drawers and retrieved a set of dark pajamas. "Let me know if you want anything. I'm sure Escher can get you anything you might need. Right now, I'm going to take a shower." He closed the bathroom door after him.

Exhaustion tugging at her, Miranda pulled the blanket up to her neck. There was a soft knocking, and then, Remare entered the room. He took one look at her and then the bed and didn't look happy.

"You think this wise?"

She gave him the look Lizandra often gave her, the one that said, *"As if."* "Nothing is going to happen tonight, Remare. I just didn't want to be alone." She lowered her voice. "And I couldn't go to you, so I asked Gabriel to stay with me. A vampire so easily slipping inside my head got to me."

He sat beside her and took her hand. "You could come to my room later."

"And get you in trouble. No. We were lucky, last time, no one saw me leaving your rooms. I won't risk it, again."

"Who was this vampire," he brushed a strand of hair from her face, "who got inside your head?"

"I wish I knew. I'm not entirely sure he was a vampire. He could be a powerful telepath." She held his hand between hers. "Whoever he is, he's evil. I felt it in his voice and, later, when I looked up at him."

"Describe him."

She did. "I've never seen him before. Do you know who it might be?"

"Your description is vague, Miranda. It could be anyone. Sleep. I will check on you later." He kissed her forehead then rose to leave.

When he reached the door, she said, "Thank you for understanding." She knew he didn't like the idea of her sleeping in the same room as Gabriel. "You're the only cave I go to when I need comforting. When it's cold outside and I'm exhausted from dealing with all the hells the fates have thrown my way." Smiling, she rose and met him by the door. "And you're the only bear who gives me warmth when I'm chilled to the bone." She hugged him tightly. "And strength when I need it the most."

"Bear, huh?"

"Oh, yeah, my savior, my heart."

He held her closely to his chest then let her go. "Just make sure he knows that." He kissed her once more then left.

***

Gregori lit a few candles in the bathroom then tested the water in the tub to make sure it wasn't too hot. The steam was already coating the walls and mirror. "All right, the bath's ready."

Inhaling her scent of lilacs, he helped Irina slip out of her robe and into the soothing water, careful to keep her injured arm on the tub's ledge. He inwardly growled at the scar on her lower back. For the abuse she'd suffered at Ivan's hands, he wanted to kill the son of a bitch.

"There's some Smirnoff in the fridge, why don't you get us some?"

Gregori returned with two shot glasses of the vodka and handed Irina her drink. "A short one for you. With the pain meds, it's better not to drink too much."

She laughed. "I've drunk far more than this when I was a child." She gulped down the drink. "Thank you."

"What a night, huh?" He sat on the toilet seat. "When I saw the men on you, there was no way I was going to let them take you."

"There was no way they were going to take me." She glanced up at him, her eyes held fatigue and something else—pain, he thought. "You fought bravely. I'm glad the cut over your eye has healed."

"A scratch, nothing more." Gregori sipped his vodka. "I tell you, I was surprised how Miranda fought. She was much faster than I thought possible for a human." His eyes narrowed. "There was a moment, when the light from the lamp post hit her eyes, and I thought they glared red." He shook his head. "A trick of the light, I suppose."

Irina closed her eyes. "She didn't flinch, not once. How many humans do we know would fight for vampires?"

"A few." Gregori had seen Irina's expression when Remare had joined them. Exhaling, he bowed his head. He knew Irina still had feelings for her former lover, and that just frustrated him. He also remembered Remare hadn't even looked at her until Valadon had mentioned her injury.

Irina used the sponge to wash her good arm. "She fought like Remare."

"I thought so, too." Miranda's twists, turns and lunges reminded Gregori of the sword master's techniques.

Irina's sorrowful words broke into his thoughts. "Why do you bother with me? I'm not whole. You would do better to be with a woman who is."

"You're my partner." His eyes met hers. "We take care of each other."

"You saw the scar on my back." She lifted the sponge to stroke her leg. "You know what Ivan did to me."

He nodded. "I know. It doesn't matter to me." Shaking his head, he leaned forward. "The only thing that matters is your safety." He took the sponge from her and washed her lower leg and foot. Then did the other one. Her skin was smooth as the finest silk.

"Remare once told me we all have our scars. In all the time we were together, it never mattered to him that I wasn't whole."

He held her eyes. "It matters to me." He wanted her whole, again, but that was something she would have to want first. He bent and kissed her soft lips. "We may have scars, but maybe we become whole when we open ourselves to another."

She raised her good arm to him as if she would say something then changed her mind. "Help me up. The water's getting cold."

He took a towel from the shelf and wrapped it around her. He used another towel to dry her hair. When she took a step and faltered, he lifted her up in his arms and brought her to her bed. "All tucked in. Get some sleep." He gazed over at her couch. "I'll sleep here tonight. Make sure you get the rest you need." He undressed until he was only wearing his black boxers. When he turned to her, he hoped she would invite him to join her but knew she would not.

"You'll get cold. There's extra blankets in the closet."

He retrieved one and then turned off the light, the bedroom's only illumination coming from the one remaining candle in the bathroom. As much as he wanted to join her on the bed, he knew, with her injury, she was better off sleeping alone. "Good night, Irina."

She was silent for a moment then spoke Russian. "*Debroy nochi,* Gregori."

She'd said his name, and that made him smile. She may not be ready for a lover to love her completely as he would, but he was going to make certain she would want to.

Someday.

***

Seething in rage, Blackmore marched toward Peralt's lab. They'd been so close to getting a female of high status, one of Valadon's Elite Torians, when his men were attacked by the other Torians. He'd had his eye on the red-headed Blueblood, but when that was no longer an option, the blonde would have made an excellent specimen. He'd hoped to mate her with his other vampire. Without knocking, he entered his chief chemist's lab. "Increase your experiments. I want the timetable moved up."

Peralt gazed up at him. "That is not possible. The tests take time. We can't rush the results."

"Do whatever is necessary. Have Anya assist you." Blackmore turned and left. Soon, he would have the toxin necessary to destroy the vampires. As for the man they had left behind, either he was already dead or would be soon. He didn't fear his soldier giving up any information. He smirked. He'd already taken measures to make sure that would not be a possibility.

Chapter Twenty

"Are you asleep?"

"No. I keep closing my eyes, hoping the dream fairies will visit, but so far, they haven't shown. Damned bitches must all have hot dates." Miranda thought, having taken a hot shower and switching into pajamas, she'd fall asleep easier. She hadn't.

Gabriel lifted up on his elbow. "You were always a terrible insomniac."

"Still am." Miranda turned toward him, his face illuminated by the dim light coming from the bathroom. "How come you're still up?"

"I have a lot on my mind. It's that damned painting I can't stop thinking about it."

"What painting?"

"In the archives. God, it looks so much like her."

"Who?"

Gabriel got up and retrieved the antique gold watch in his pants pocket. Opening it, he brought it to her. "This was my father's. He left it to me when he died."

Miranda examined the miniature picture. "Turn the lights on brighter."

After he did, he sat beside her on the lounge.

"She's a looker, all right. Who is she?"

"My mother." He exhaled. "Valadon told me he'd once fallen in love with a woman near Marseille centuries ago. I swear, Miranda, she looks just like her."

"All right. Let's go see." She grabbed a robe from the closet and tied it around her. Preferring to wear the thick socks that kept her toes all toasty, she left the slippers by the lounge.

"I didn't mean for you to get up, now." Guilt marred his face. "This could wait until tomorrow."

"Neither one of us is getting much sleep, so let's go check it out."

Gabriel led her down the stairs to the Biographies section of the archives. Even though the massive chandelier illuminated the libraries, he turned on the little light over the painting.

Miranda put on her glasses she used for validations. "You're right. She does resemble your mother." She looked at the nameplate on the frame: *Marlena de Avignon*. There was no date on the painting, but there was the artist's signature—Asanti.

"That's odd. From what you told me, I would have thought this painting was much older."

"How old is it?"

"There's no craquelure, no scent of mold." Miranda lifted the painting and examined the stretchers. "The wood hasn't faded, and there's no rust from the staples. My best guess: This was painted in the last fifty years. No earlier." She replaced the painting on the wall and studied it.

Gabriel checked the stacks until he found the book he wanted. *Journal de Marlena de Avignon*. "I read some of this the first time I came down here. She was in love with Valadon, but her father had promised her to a wealthy merchant."

Miranda took the leather-bound tome. "It's dated sixteen-forties." Sitting on the carpet, she carefully thumbed through the old yellowed pages. "There's a drawing of her in here. I think it's the same one as the painting." She studied the painting and then asked to see the portrait in the watch, again.

"Hell, they could be twins. Gabriel, they are nearly exactly alike."

"I know." He slumped down beside her. "I was kind of hoping you would tell me I was wrong. That I was imagining things."

"But why?"

Closing his eyes, he exhaled in frustration and laid his head back against the bookshelf. "Don't you see, Miranda? Valadon was always going to turn me. It wasn't that I'd been attacked and lost too much blood. I'm Marlena's last living relative." Bitter sarcasm laced his words. "Bastard planned it all along."

Miranda grasped his hand. "I don't think so, Gabriel. You told me, on the way down, he always kept track of her descendants. Watched over them, made sure they never wanted for anything."

"Yes. So?"

"You had children. You weren't the last of your line. He didn't plan anything." She looked back at the painting. "He must have really loved her. Deeply."

"My children died." His voice was pained. "I was the last one."

"No. Not necessarily. You're a young vampire. What? Maybe a hundred years old? You can still have children. I don't think he planned anything, Gabriel. Imagine what he must have been going through when he saw your bloodied body dying on the street. He had a decision to make and not much time to make it."

"He didn't give me a choice."

"I know," she said softly. "You were unconscious at the time. I think you wanted to hate him. Wanted a reason to resent him because...you hated yourself. It doesn't take a brainiac to figure out you had survivors' guilt. I know. I had to deal with mine for a long time." Lizandra had pointed out Miranda's more daring episodes in college were due to her own guilt of surviving when her family had died in a car crash. Sometimes, people were just too close to their own problems to see the truth.

"You're wrong."

"Am I? You made it. They didn't. Have you ever forgiven yourself, yet? Isn't it time to just let go?" She took his hands in hers. "I care about you, Gabriel. I always have. But I think you've been letting your resentment kill you a little bit each day. You hide yourself away in your lab; you socialize very little. It's as if you've been punishing yourself by refusing to enjoy the life you've been given. Valadon didn't wish you any harm. He wanted you to have a second chance at living."

Gabriel hung his head in despair. "I've hated him ever since he turned me. I refused to call him father because I knew it would irritate him. I wanted him to feel the pain as deeply as I did."

"It's been over a hundred years, now. Isn't it time to let it go? Talk to him, Gabriel. It's the only way you're ever going to find peace." She took him in her arms and tried to give him the warmth he had shut out.

"I will." He wiped away the tears that streaked his face. He looked one last time at the painting as he stood. "I'll talk to him tomorrow."

"Good." As Miranda turned, she knocked a book off the shelf. Something caught her eye. "What's this symbol? I saw one earlier tonight. It looks like the caduceus you docs wear, but the snakes are facing outward instead of inward."

Gabriel took the book from her. "It's a history on the early stages of medicine. In the seventeenth century, there was an ancient cult that broke away from traditional medicine. They thought they could find cures through alchemy and mysticism. The Brotherhood of Hermes, they called themselves."

"I thought Apollo was the god of healing."

"He was. But Hermes was the messenger of the gods, and they thought they had some divine message. They adopted the symbol but changed the snakes. They're defunct, now."

"I don't think so." She took the book from him. "I met a man earlier tonight who was wearing this symbol on his ring. What happened to the cult?"

"I can't imagine why anyone would wear that. In the beginning, they were heralded for their revolutionary ideas, but as time passed and their beliefs became too radical and too outlandish for conventional medicine, they were expelled from the universities and branded charlatans."

When Miranda turned a page to a picture of one of the leaders of the Brotherhood, her breath hitched. "Oh, my God! This is the man! Gabriel, this is the man I met tonight."

Gabriel took the book from her. "It can't be. This is Francis Peralt. He's been dead for four hundred years."

"No, he's not." She put her hand over her heart. "I know because I saw him. I talked to him tonight."

"You said the guy had light brown hair and a beard. This man has dark hair and eyes."

"Nuh-uh." She shook her head. "No. Not that guy. I met another man earlier in the night. We discussed art history. Oh. My. God. This is him. We were talking about Artemisia and her father. Gabriel, do you know who Peralt was?"

"Yes. He was a brilliant doctor but, later on, became a deranged alchemist. Instead of searching for ways to change metals into gold, he searched for a way to prolong life. He never found it. It drove him mad."

"Last year, I found a book about the experiments he performed on vampires and humans. It was barbaric. Horrible, gruesome operations he did on what he called 'demon children'."

A voice sounded from above them. "Isn't it a little late to be conducting research, Professor?"

"Remare." Miranda sprung up and threw her arms around him. "I'm so glad it's you. Gabriel and I were discussing a madman who lived centuries ago." Recovering herself quickly, as if she just remembered Gabriel was there, she caught her breath. "It spooked me. I almost thought you were him."

Remare held Miranda to his side. Graciously, he addressed Gabriel. "What did you find?"

"A history on the Brotherhood of Hermes. Miranda met a man tonight who resembles Peralt. I tried to tell her it's impossible because he's been dead for centuries."

"Not impossible. Remare, remember the book we fought over last year? It was a compendium of poisons used in the seventeenth century by Peralt. He's alive." She showed him the portrait in the book. "This is the man I talked to tonight."

"I don't think so, Miranda. Peralt was caught by the Vampire Nation's army. Execution orders were dispatched by our king at the time. I'm sure no mercy was shown the infamous '*Angel from Hell*' as he was called for his many crimes against vampires and humans alike."

Miranda breathed deeply. "I hope you're right. Maybe the guy is just a descendant or something."

"I think you two need to get some sleep." Remare gestured to the stairs. "We'll talk more about this in the morning after you've had some rest."

"You two go ahead. I want to stay here and read some more. I'll be up later."

Miranda grimaced. "Gabriel. That stuff will give you nightmares."

"I'm a doctor. I've seen pictures of autopsies and other atrocities. I'll be fine."

Remare nodded to him and led Miranda away.

Chapter Twenty-One

"Those drawings were horrible. I can't believe what some people could do to others in the name of science."

"You haven't lived long enough, Mir-randa. I've seen what trained assassins can do to enemies. Put it out of your mind for tonight."

"Okay. Let's stop off at the kitchen. I know where Escher keeps the cookies." When there, she opened the cupboard and frowned. "Oh, no!" Her shoulders sagged. "Someone must have beat me to it. There aren't any left."

Smirking, he stood, leaning against the fridge. "Don't look so glum, Mir-randa. I, too, know where Escher hides the treasure of treats. He opened the freezer and, reaching in the back, retrieved a box of Girl Scouts Thin Mints.

Miranda nearly drooled. *Vampires like Girl Scout cookies?!* She didn't wait for him to open the box, grabbed it and tore open the sleeve. "Mmm! The best!"

He must have read her mind because he said. "We have several employees whose children are scouts. Escher buys several cartons he keeps tucked away in the pantry." He rubbed his jaw. "We also have several tins of popcorn we open when we watch movies." Remare took one of the mint cookies and munched. Somehow, Mr. Badass vampire didn't seem so badassy with a few crumbs on his lower lip. Smiling, Miranda wanted to lick them off. Realizing she could, she reached up and ran her tongue along his lower lip.

A warning growl, throaty and seductive, rose up. His eyes heavy-lidded, he quickly kissed her. "Not here."

After he put the remaining cookies back, they continued down the corridor. When she turned to go down the hall leading to her room, Remare grabbed her arm and pulled her to his side.

"Where are we going?" She spoke mentally so that her voice wouldn't wake any sleeping vampires in House Valadon.

"My apartment."

"Is that wise? We'll be caught!"

"No, we won't. Everyone is asleep, except for one inquisitive researcher."

When they reached his door, he glanced back down the corridor before entering. Once inside, he shoved her against the door and, securing the lock, kissed her passionately. The familiar tickle of his mustache and beard rubbing against her face had her moaning. Inhaling his intoxicating scent of the forest, Miranda ardently returned his fervor.

"I've missed you." His voice was husky. "You tortured me with images of what you and Gabriel might have been doing tonight." The red rims of his irises were glowing.

"Nothing. We did nothing. Will never do anything. He's a friend, Remare. That's all." Grabbing his face in her hands, she kissed him soundly, their tongues tangoing as his hands ripped open her robe and undid the buttons of her pajama top.

His hand was cool to her too heated flesh. He trailed kisses down her neck to her breast then sucked her nipple into his mouth. Miranda's nails dug into his back as pleasure soared through her. When he bit down, she saw stars. Somehow, he managed to remove her top and robe and toss them aside.

Miranda's hands shook as she undid his buttons. Impatiently he pulled his shirt over his head and discarded it behind him. Flesh to flesh, she kissed him soundly, loving the way the smattering of his chest hairs caressed her breasts. The scent of their combined arousals permeated the air as they fumbled to get quickly undressed.

Once naked, Remare carried her to the edge of his bed and set her down. Laying her back, he brought her ankles up, spreading her legs wide. He stood, watching her, his dark eyes glowing with intensity as his red rims pulsed with desire. Miranda groaned when he thrust inside her. Their passion spiraling higher and higher. Remare was a talented lover who knew the best way to quench a hunger was to increase the need. As he stared into her eyes, his fangs lengthened, and that dangerous aura of his drew her ever higher, teasing her with the promise of an earth-shattering orgasm.

Miranda's heart hammered in her chest, her voice a throaty whisper. "You're going to kill me if you don't let me come soon."

"We come together or not at all." His voice held the fiery eroticism of a man possessed. Unexpectedly, he pulled out and turned her over. Her feet sank to the floor as he bent her over and entered her from behind. Leaning over her, he stretched out her arms and whispered in her ear, "Take all of me, Mir-randa."

Miranda couldn't think, wasn't sure she was even breathing. Her nails dug into the sheets as he pounded into her. His hand traveled down her spine, pinning her to the mattress. Then, his fingers dug into her hips as he held her in place as he continued thrusting. Lights started swimming at the edge of her eyes. The force of her climax was so strong, when it hit, she turned her face into the sheets and cried out his name. Her arms shook from the force of their lovemaking.

Remare's growl of release reverberated through the room.

When his panting subsided, he pulled out and went to the bathroom. Remembering to breathe again, she could hear the water running. When he returned, his face and goatee were still wet. He used a washcloth to clean her then tossed it aside. He lifted her up then pulled the sheet back. After tucking her in, he joined her and covered their bodies with the blankets.

She snuggled into his embrace. "We're going to kill each other someday."

He snickered. "Hardly."

"You're a passionate man." Smiling, she traced the line of his beard. "I like that about you."

He returned her smile. "You like a great many things about me."

She laughed at his vanity. "Yes, I do."

"I'm going to tell Valadon. I don't know when. But soon. I don't like all this hiding. It feels too much like betrayal."

"It's not." She placed her hand over his heart. "We didn't betray him. We simply fell for each other. I don't know how he's going to take it."

He caressed her hand. "I think it wise to wait until this business with the HOL is over. We're getting close to finding their installation. The investigation is progressing. It shouldn't be much longer, now."

"Good."

"Tomorrow, I want you to join Valadon and me for breakfast. An old friend is coming to visit. He's an artist. Someone I think you will like meeting very much."

"Who?"

"His name is Asanti. He painted several of the paintings in the archives."

"Yes, I saw some of them." She balanced on an elbow. "Did you know there's a painting down there of a woman who looks just like Gabriel's mother?"

He slid his fingers through her hair. "Really?"

"Her name is Marlena de Avignon. She lived in the seventeenth century. Ever hear of her?"

"Yes. She was a woman who Valadon loved very much."

"What happened to her?"

"That is a very long and sad story. One, I think, Valadon should tell you. All I really know is that she married someone else and had three sons. She later died. It devastated Valadon," he exhaled, "for a very long time."

"Gabriel knows about her. He told me Valadon told him the story of her." Miranda massaged his chest. "He thought Valadon turned him because he's the last of her line."

"That is simply not true. I was there when we found the bodies. Tristan was first on the scene. He called us to the site. Gabriel's wife and children were already dead. And Gabriel was barely breathing. Valadon was emotionally torn on whether or not to turn him. He knew Gabriel would hate him for it. But they had been close friends. He'd helped us whenever one of our people became injured and needed medical assistance. He never once betrayed our secrets. Valadon did what he thought was right. Bestowing vampirism on a human is a gift. A very rare fete." He rubbed his brow. "I believe Rosalyn will soon give the gift to Jason."

"Seriously?" Roz hadn't mentioned anything to her.

"Yes, she's petitioned Valadon for permission. But Valadon wants Jason to meet with our sage, Victor, so he has a clear understanding of what will happen."

"Does Jason want to become vampire?"

"Yes. He is desperately in love with Rosalyn and wants to spend his life with her. I believe it is only a matter of time, now."

"How long have they been dating?"

"For years, now. Three, I think. Maybe four."

"Wow. Big step."

"Yes, one you are not ready for." He smiled seductively. "But, maybe, someday, you will be."

"Maybe." She ran her fingers through his smattering of chest hairs. "You said you wouldn't pressure me."

"I won't. I'm not." His eyes gleamed. "But I'd be lying if I didn't tell you the thought of having you for decades appeals to me."

"Just decades, huh?"

"Well, one decade at a time." He lifted a leg and covered her body with his. His erection, already hard and throbbing, pressed into her stomach. "Or should I say...one night at a time." He smiled and whimsically kissed her nose then her lips and chin. When he got to her neck, he gave her a naughty grin and licked the piece of amber then sucked it completely into his mouth. Her jaw lowered. Blu had once told her just touching it affected him. She could just imagine his reaction, now, and tried not to burst out laughing as Remare moved farther down her body.

***

It was just before dawn when Miranda slowly opened the door to her room. Making sure Gabriel was still asleep, she grabbed the jeans and sweater she'd picked out earlier and made her way to the bathroom. The steaming hot water of the shower was heaven on her skin, and she laid her head back to let the soothing water cleanse her sore body. She smiled. Yes, she ached, but not in a bad way; she was just tender. Remare could be a vigorous lover, but he could also be slow and romantic.

Rinsing off, she shut the faucets off and stepped out.

Her breath caught. Gabriel was already dressed, and when his eyes met hers, she knew in the pit of her stomach, he knew. Unable to read him, he handed her a towel and closed the door behind him.

Miranda quickly dried off and dressed. When she opened the door to the bedroom, he was sitting on the bed, hunched over, putting his watch on. He didn't bother looking up at her. "Does Valadon know?"

Any attempts at subterfuge would be useless. "No one knows, and we're keeping it that way." Even though Orion and Rosalyn were aware of her relationship, they would never betray her confidence. That went double for Lizandra.

Concern marred his voice. She'd expected censure, but there was none in his voice. "Do you have any idea what you're doing?"

Besides having the most passionate affair she'd ever had? One that made her feel more alive than anything that had come before? "It wasn't something we planned." She bit her lip. "It just happened."

He stood and grasped her arms. "Do you think Valadon is going to be pleased when he finds out? And make no mistake, Miranda, he *will* find out."

"You're not going to..."

He rubbed her shoulders then released her and turned away. "I won't say a word."

"How did you know?"

He faced her. "Miranda, his scent was all over you when you when you walked in. So was the aroma of sex." He ran a hand through his hair. "Jesus, of all the vampires in House Valadon, he's the last one I would ever imagine you to be with."

"Yeah, me, too," she mumbled. "I can't explain it." She threw her hands in the air. "We were attracted to each other. Tried to deny it. Avoided each other, but..."

He shoved his hands in his pockets. "Do you love him?"

That was a question Miranda had asked herself many times. But how did she tell a former lover, one she had great affection for and knew he still cared for her, that she'd found love with another? She bent her head and nodded.

He snorted. "I think I would have preferred it if you told me it was just some lusty affair you were having. Then, I wouldn't be so scared for you."

"Don't be." She paced a few steps. "We know to be careful."

"Do you? You know you called out his name in your sleep." He resumed sitting on the bed and, avoiding her gaze, rubbed his hands. "It wasn't the first time. Even when we were together, there was one night you breathed out his name."

Miranda didn't know if his look of hurt was more of dejection or genuine concern. "You never told me. I'm sorry."

"Yeah, me, too. Forget it. That's not what I wanted to talk to you about. While you were otherwise...engaged, I found out some interesting things. Want to come to the archives with me? There's something I want you to see."

Chapter Twenty-Two

Remare quickly took his place at Valadon's side at the morning table. All the members of the Elite Torians were already settled and enjoying their breakfast. The aroma of freshly cooked spinach and mushroom omelets was only surpassed by their delectable taste. Opposite him, Morel nodded, as did Victor. Escher served Remare his morning cup of Moroccan mint tea.

"Thank you." After sipping the soothing tea, he asked, "Have there been any new developments?"

"You're usually here before me." Valadon joked as he passed the basket of croissants to him. "Rough night?"

"Not particularly." He knew Valadon was referring to the warehouses he'd checked out last night but smiled inwardly. Last night he'd had an unusually high level of activity with Miranda. After changing the sheets, he'd thoroughly showered to make sure her flowery scent was clear of his skin.

"Asanti will be here momentarily. He rarely travels this far down in the city, and traffic was heavy. Now that we're all here, I think it's time for some updates." Valadon gestured for Aiden to go first.

"We traced the license plate from last night to a holding company. There are several subsidiaries, and we are narrowing the field as we speak. We should have more information soon."

Remare nodded as Valadon continued, "Let me know ASAP. Gregori."

"The interrogation last night of one of the assailants went about as well as could be expected. The addresses he gave us coincided with the ones Remare already checked out. When pressured for more information, he either didn't know or refused to share." He smirked. "Scorpio assures me every tool of persuasion was used. Exceedingly. He thinks the guy gave us everything he knew."

"Keep on him." Remare sneered. "If anyone can elicit information, it's Scorpio."

Leaning toward Irina, Valadon asked, "How is your arm, Irina?"

"Healed." She rotated her shoulder. "It was a minor injury."

Remare grinned as Gregori cleared his throat but said nothing. *He's learning!*

Escher returned with more coffee and filled Valadon's cup. "Your guest has arrived."

"Good. Show him in."

A tall vampire whose broad shoulders were almost as wide as Valadon's entered. Older than most of the vampires present, Asanti had fought with Remare centuries ago, and there were few he respected as much as *The Castilian.* Since moving to New York nearly two centuries ago, Asanti had stayed in his Upper West Side home, creating some of the world's most beautiful paintings.

His long, straight black hair fell down his shoulders from a widow's peak. His complexion was dark, as was most vampires who came from his area of Spain. His face was stern but handsome. Remare wondered what had disturbed the vampire so much he'd traveled this far downtown.

"Asanti." Valadon rose and shook his hand. "Please, join us."

Remare embraced him. "Old friend, it is good to see you, again."

"Thank you." After sitting, he accepted coffee from Escher.

"We've all been eager for your presence." Valadon sipped his coffee. "You rarely visit ValCorp, even though I have extended several invitations."

"Forgive my reticence. I know I've developed a reputation as a recluse. After all the wars I've fought in," he nodded in Remare's direction, "I now prefer the peace of the West Side."

"How is your son, Jacob?" Remare inquired. He knew Asanti had a close relationship with his only son. "He must be close to finishing his university studies by now."

"Jacob is the reason I'm here." Asanti closed his eyes and hung his head in despair. Remare sensed his anguish. "Two nights ago, he went out with friends of his from Columbia and hasn't returned since." He shook his head, as if confused. "This is not like him. When I tried to contact him, I've gotten no responses at all, either through his phone or our blood connection. I'm worried about him. Severely. And came here today to seek your assistance."

Remare stifled the low growl deep in his throat. "Have you contacted any of his friends?"

"Yes, of course. There's two who I know of, Skylar and Jenson. Neither one of them has seen him since that night. And before you ask," he turned to Valadon, "I've had my personal guards out searching for him. As yet, they have not been able to ascertain his whereabouts."

Valadon made eye-contact with Remare and spoke mentally. *"Asanti needs to know what's been going on in the vampire community."*

"I agree, but the news will devastate him. Ever since his wife died years ago, his son has become his world."

"That is why we must do everything to help him."

"Of course, we'll assist in any way we can." Valadon exhaled. "Asanti, there are certain things you should be aware of."

As Valadon relayed the reports of the missing vampires, Remare could feel *The Castilian's* growing agitation. He gave the vampire credit for maintaining his composure.

"I'd heard the reports before." Asanti's fist tightened. "I just thought they were rumors. But, if what you say is true, my son is in grave danger. What can you do to help me?"

"As much as we can. Remare."

"We'll start by having our people canvass your area. I know your guards are good, but they're not Torians. Tristan, I want you and Katya to do a search of the area in and around Columbia. Someone there might have seen something." He met Asanti's eyes and smiled. "Tristan has a way of having people open up to him."

"We're on it." The youngest Torian rose, wiping his mouth on his napkin.

"Katya, assign some of our mid-level Torians to check out the local bars, taverns where the students hang out. Report in as soon as you find anything."

"Consider it done." Bowing to Valadon, she left with her lover.

"Is there anything left over for breakfast?" Nick sauntered in. "I'm starved."

"My nephew, Nickolas." Valadon informed Asanti. "Good of you to join us. A week ago, he went missing, as well. Remare was able to track him down with the assistance of one of his professors. This is Asanti, an old friend of ours. Two nights ago, his son disappeared."

Nick swallowed his juice as Escher served him a steaming plate of mushroom omelets. "I'm sorry to hear that. Is there anything I can do?"

"Your uncle tells me you're a student at NYU; do you have any friends at Columbia University?"

"I'm sorry. Most of the students I know at NYU hang out with their own friends." Nick shook his head. "Columbia is so far Uptown, I don't know any students who go there."

Deflated, Asanti leaned back in his chair. "Thank you."

"We'll find your son, Asanti." Valadon's voice was stern. "My people have been relentless working to track down our enemies. We'll continue to do so."

Gabriel entered and looked like he'd gotten little, if any, rest. "I've just come from the archives. There are some things you should be aware of." His eyes lit on Asanti.

"Gabriel, join us." Valadon gestured to the seats Katya and Tristan vacated. "This is Asanti, a very old friend. His son has gone missing."

"I see." Gabriel rubbed his jaw, which he'd yet to shave. "Maybe this should wait, then."

"I've already informed Asa of the vampires who've been recovered."

"All right, then." When Gabriel was seated, Escher served him his tea. "I've been doing research on an old alchemist who lived in the sixteen hundreds. Francis Peralt." He rubbed his neck and sipped his tea. "I've read through his biographies and the experiments he performed. I looked over the photographs taken from the sites where the bodies were recovered, and there's a striking resemblance to what was in Peralt's journal."

"If you're implying there's a connection, that's highly unlikely." Valadon exhaled. "Peralt was killed over four centuries ago for the crimes he committed against vampires and humans both. After King Robert became aware of his atrocities, he ordered his execution."

Victor, silent for most of the meeting, coughed. "That may not be *exactly* true."

All heads turned in his direction.

"What do you mean?" Remare asked.

"Before I entered the Order and became a sage, I was a soldier in King Robert's army. I was part of the group who apprehended Peralt. I wanted a quick death for the monster. But I was overruled by an aristocrat who felt death was too good for someone who'd been known for his tortures."

"What happened to him?" Valadon's tone turned deadly.

"The noble wanted to see him suffer for his crimes. Slowly. What could be more fitting than to make the monster who hated vampires one himself?" Victor sighed. "The lord transformed him, relishing the man's screams and pleas for death. Peralt was many things, but he still believed in his religion; the thought of becoming vampire terrified him. He'd once named us 'demon children' and feared becoming one. When the transformation was complete, the aristocrat had him sealed in a cave with a huge boulder blocking the entrance. There was no way one person could move the stone."

Remare demanded. "Did he survive?"

"For several nights, we heard his blood-curdling screams and howls of pain. I wanted to end his misery, but the lord would not allow it."

Remare remembered how Gabriel had no warning of his transformation and handled it with terrific fright. "How did Peralt feed?"

"He didn't. Our commander wanted him to suffer, excruciatingly. He had him starved."

Remare knew the pain must have been unbearable, but he had no sympathy for the monster who had conducted such horrific experiments. "What happened afterward?"

"It was days later when our leader was called away. When we heard only silence from the cave, we went to retrieve the body. But someone had gotten there before us, because the boulder was pushed aside. When we explored the cave, there was no sign of him anywhere. We thoroughly searched the grounds. He had escaped."

Valadon's eyes turned a turbulent green. "Who was the commander?"

Remare had his own suspicions, confirmed when Victor's gaze shifted downward. "I'm sorry to inform you, but the aristocrat was your brother, Brandon."

All heads turned in Valadon's direction as the temperature in the room dropped substantially. Remare felt Valadon's fury vibrate against his skin. "And you're *absolutely* certain it was Brandon?"

"Yes. Unequivocally. No one would defy him. They were too afraid Brandon would have them tortured or, worse, they'd be sealed up in the cave with Peralt."

Morel posited, "It's possible his body was carried out and buried by one of his disciples."

"I don't think that happened." Miranda stood by the dining room's entrance with a book tucked under her arm.

"Miranda."

"Hello, Valadon. I've been studying alongside Gabriel in the archives. You forgot to tell him about the ring."

Gabriel addressed the group. "Peralt was disillusioned by the physicians of his time. Considered them inferior. He even publicly burned the writings of Galen and Agrippa. He broke away from the traditionalists and started his own group of acolytes. To show his disapproval of their beliefs, he wore a ring with a caduceus opposite of the customary one. As did his followers."

Miranda walked toward Valadon and showed him the book she was carrying. "The traditional design is having the two snakes face each other; Peralt's faced outward."

Remare was confused. "What does this have to do with anything?"

She took a deep breath. "I saw that ring at the party last night. A man was wearing it."

A collective sigh sounded in the room.

"Wait, it gets worse." Gabriel rubbed his brow. "Anyone want to venture a guess what the name of Peralt's group was?"

Remare was seething in rage. "Tell us."

"*Ordo Lucis*. In Latin, it means..."

"I know what it means." Remare sneered. "The Order of Light. Or more correctly, The Human Order of Light. The HOL."

"Son of a bitch! He should have been executed!" Valadon slammed his fist on the table. "Well, if Peralt is alive, it shouldn't be too hard to find him." The High Lord stood. "Aiden, search the databases for him. Then, tap into the NYPD's files. He may have Americanized his name if he's here. Do cross checks."

"I'm on it." Aiden threw his napkin on the table and quickly left the room.

"Gregori, Irina. Go through your computer files, see if you can find any mention of Peralt's name or any references to physicians, historians, philosophers."

"At once." They nodded and left, as well.

Valadon faced Gabriel. "Thank you for your hard work. You look exhausted and should get a few hours' sleep."

He nodded. "There's still some books we didn't get to. But I'll work better after a nap."

"Morel, Victor. I need you in the archives, dig up whatever information you can on Peralt and his brotherhood. Gabriel, can you tell him which books you've already read? Let them know where they should start."

Gabriel nodded.

"Miranda, I want you to work with Asanti. His son has gone missing, and I want us to find him before anything happens to him. Describe the man you saw wearing the ring. Be very specific and let him construct a drawing. We'll then circulate it to our people."

"All right."

"Remare, join me in the interrogation room. We have some new questions to ask of our guest." Nodding to Asanti, he left.

Remare smirked. "It will be my pleasure." He nodded to Miranda and then to Gabriel. "Thank you for your combined efforts. You may have helped us more than you know." His hand barely brushed her shoulder as he addressed Asanti. "Rest assured, we will do everything possible to locate Jacob."

Chapter Twenty-Three

"These are the drawing pencils and pad left over from my fine arts course. I really enjoyed those classes." Nick handed the art supplies to Asanti. When *The Castilian* had asked Escher for drawing materials, Nick had volunteered to retrieve some of his own. "I'm sorry about Jacob. But Remare is relentless in tracking down people, and so are the other Torians. They'll find him. I'm going to go to my room and use my laptop to check NYU's databases to see if they have any information on Peralt." Bowing to Asanti and Miranda, Nick turned and left.

After finishing breakfast, Gabriel returned to his room for a few hours' sleep. Asanti suggested they go to the main living room and sit near the fireplace. "This is the portrait of Peralt back in the sixteen-hundreds." Miranda handed Asanti the old book. "He looks a little different, now, though."

"Vampirism can slightly alter the way a person looks."

"How so?"

"Bones elongate; muscles lengthen. Essentially, the person is the same but more enhanced. Nature's way of ensuring the survival of our race by making us more attractive."

Sure. Vampires are predators. It makes sense. They need to be more beautiful to be able to seduce their prey in order to survive.

Asanti only needed to glance at the portrait once and listened to Miranda's descriptions. He drew the lines of Peralt's face quickly with skill and accuracy.

"His face was narrower, and his nose more aristocratic."

After Asanti made the altercations with a few shadowing techniques, Miranda gasped at the man staring back at her on the paper. "That's him. That's the man I spoke to at the party. Look at the intensity in his eyes. He's either brilliant or mad."

"Perhaps a little of both. And that is what frightens me." Asanti took out his phone and snapped a picture of the drawing and sent it to Aiden, who would distribute it to the Torians.

Escher served them tea with biscotti. "Can I get you anything else?"

"No, thank you." She sipped her tea, grateful for the soothing aroma.

Asanti shook his head.

"May I offer you my sympathies of the disappearance of your son." Escher's voice held genuine concern and compassion. "Valadon and Remare are working assiduously on the investigation. They will not stop until Jacob is found."

Asanti smiled up at him. "Thank you." After Escher turned and left, Asanti seemed to be studying her. "Valadon told me you assisted in finding Nick."

"Yes. Nick's been a student of mine for the last few years at NYU and was my assistant when I worked in the archives. I was able to help Remare track him down, but Remare's the true detective, not me."

"But he would not have been able to locate Nick without your help."

"Debatable." She shrugged. "I think Remare would have found him eventually."

"Without being too forward, I would like you to come to my home for dinner tonight. I have a fantastic cook, and she prepares wonderful dishes."

Miranda leaned back in her chair.

"You need not be frightened. I simply want you to inspect Jacob's room." His look of despair was heartbreaking. "There is a long age gap between Jacob and me. I don't always understand everything about his generation. You work with college students; your understanding of them is far better than mine. You know their habits; maybe you can pick up on something the others have not."

"I'm not sure what good that would do. I was only able to help in finding Nick because I know the students at NYU. I don't know anyone at Columbia. From what I hear, most students stay within their cliques. Valadon has good people working for him." She put her hand on Asanti's wrist for comfort. "I'm sure they'll be able to do a thorough search."

"Yes, but they are considerably older and may not have the insights you do. What are you, a few years older than the students?"

"Almost a dozen, if you count the freshman."

"Still, much younger than any of our people. If it comforts you, I will also invite Remare or Valadon to join us."

Sensing his anguish, she didn't want to disappoint him. And the thought of having dinner with Remare in the home of his old friend appealed to her. "All right, then. But I think Remare is the one you should call. His instincts are sharp, and he usually coordinates the workings of the Torians."

"I will. Thank you."

***

Miranda flopped face down on the bed in her guest room. The adrenaline rush of researching Peralt was wearing off, and fatigue was setting in.

"I thought I might find you here."

"Gabriel."

"Don't get up. He joined her on the bed. "I found a translation of a book Peralt wrote. I think you may want to read it."

"I don't think I could read another thing." Her voice was groggy.

"This will interest you. He has a whole chapter devoted to *Elementals*."

That perked her up. "What does it say?"

Gabriel leaned against the pillows for support. "Look here." He pointed to a page in the book. "He separates the four elements and their abilities. Among his many interests, Peralt had a fondness for things considered magical or the occult back then. He traveled all over Europe, collecting stories from the ancient world. He stayed in Constantinople for a while, studying under mystics; after that, he disappeared. No one knows what became of him."

"What did he say about *Elementals*?"

"At first, he thought they were spirits. Heavenly creatures who inhabited the earth. In each of the groups, he mentions there were good, as well as evil. The first group, he called Undines—they had power over the oceans, rivers, any water source. Secondly, he names Sylvestris as having control over the air. Third, he mentions the Gnomes, who could manipulate the earth. And last, he discusses the Vulcanus, who could invoke fire and use it at will."

Miranda was shaken by the last category. "What else?"

"He mentions a fifth group, the most powerful of them all, the Chameleons. They were supposedly the rarest of the rare and had incredible power over *all* four elements." Gabriel lifted her hands in his. "This might explain why you have the powers you do." He kissed her knuckles.

Chameleons? Blu? Miranda's heart was racing. She wasn't sure she wanted to hear more, but her curiosity was too strong. "Can I borrow this book?"

"Sure." He scratched his brow. "Peralt wasn't always evil, Miranda. In his early work, he created medicines from various combinations of minerals. He tried to prolong life, not end it. From what we could tell, he attended several universities and accumulated a wealth of knowledge. Some of it was really out there. His radical thinking got him in trouble with the medical society and the church. I think he was searching for a way to cure his vampirism."

Miranda met his eyes. "By carving up people? You saw those pictures of what he did."

He shook his head. "I don't condone his methods. It's true he was a monster. Anyone who could perform the heinous experiments he did is a psychopath. All I'm saying is that his madness had to come from somewhere, and...I have some insight why he did what he did."

"You almost sound like you admire him."

"No." He shook his head. "Not at all. I could never excuse what he did."

"There's a lesson in there for you, doctor. Look where his obsession got him."

"I'm not evil, Miranda." His voice softened. "I just want answers."

So did she. "Okay, I'm going to go home, get some rest, then do a little studying of my own." She rubbed his arm. "It was nice seeing you. I think Valadon liked having you back."

"I know. I won't tell him this," he chuckled, "but it felt kind of good."

"Will you two ever reconcile?"

"If, eh—*when* I get my answers."

Miranda exhaled. Both vampires were two of the most stubborn men she'd ever met.

"Be well, Gabriel."

"You, too. And be careful."

Chapter Twenty-Four

Alone, Miranda walked along the terrace to Bethesda Fountain. This place always gave her a sense of peace—something she needed now more than ever. She took the steps down to the fountain and sat on the stone rim. This late on a Sunday afternoon, the park was nearly deserted. The sky was overcast and dismal, like her mood. The two eagles Felicity was so fond of flew in circles overhead, creating a shadowy image on the ground before Miranda. Soon, it would be dusk, and any humans left in the park would soon vacate. *Humans. Was she even one of them?* She wasn't sure anymore.

She slid her hand over her messenger bag containing the book Gabriel had given her. What she had read frightened her. She checked her phone to see if there'd been any more messages. Remare had texted her he'd meet her at Werehaven that evening; from there, they'd go to Asanti's West Side home. Missing him, she wished he was with her, now, but he was busy trying to track down the HOL's main facility and hopefully discover the whereabouts of Asanti's son.

As she looked over the lake, good memories of her family having lunch at the Boathouse came to mind. God, how she missed them. And the stupid model boat races she and her sister used to have fun watching. *Cassie, I wish you were here, now. I have so many questions.*

Miranda shuddered when a cold breeze blew across the lake, causing it to ripple. A thought came to her she'd been too scared to contemplate. *Blu, aka The Chameleon.* She wondered how much he knew and hadn't told her.

Taking a deep breath, her resolve returned, she took out her phone and called him.

"Hello, Miranda." His voice sounded his usual casualness and incredibly clear for someone sailing in the Mediterranean. "I trust all is well."

"Not exactly. Valadon's been having trouble with some missing vampires. He thinks the HOL is involved, as well as Peralt. Remember the book of poisons I once showed you?"

"Are you wearing the necklace I gave you?"

She pulled the blood amber out from under her sweater. "Yes."

"Switch, now." Abruptly, he ended the call.

Miranda closed her eyes and pictured Blu in her thoughts. She hadn't thought, at this distance, mental speak was possible.

"What is this about Peralt?"

"He's alive. I've met him. Last night at a party." When there was only silence on the line, she asked, *"You're not surprised."*

"There were rumors he'd escaped the king's justice. Over the centuries, I've heard stories he'd been traveling through Bucharest, Varna and, eventually, what is now Istanbul. After that, the reports were sketchy. Are you certain it was him?"

"It's in his eyes. It's the same man whose portrait was in your book."

"What did he want with you?"

"Nothing. As far as I could tell. We just discussed paintings at an art gala. I only talked to him for a few minutes."

"I see. Miranda, listen to me. Peralt conducted atrocious experiments on vampires and humans alike. He's very dangerous. Do not allow yourself to be alone with him."

"*I won't.*" She trembled at the thought. "*I read a few other books in Valadon's archives. Peralt had a lot to say about Elementals: the Undina, Sylevestris, Gnomes, and Vulcanus.*" Lifting a hand, she flexed her fingers. "*And those who can command all four—the Chameleons.*" Waiting for his reply, she could almost sense the smile in his response.

"*Ask your question.*"

She hesitated only briefly. "*Are we related?*"

Silence. And then, "*Would it be so bad if we were?*"

Something inside her shattered. "*Why didn't you tell me?*"

"*You weren't ready to hear it. Many generations separate us. But I knew, when I met you, you were of my blood.*"

"*How?*"

"*Blood recognizes blood.*"

"*Then, how come none of the other vampires at Valadon House can?*"

"*You're not of their blood. Only mine. My line is a very old one, and I've been 'under' for some time. I'm sure they've forgotten my scent by now. And your blood is much more human than vampire; I wouldn't expect any other vampire to scent you.*"

Miranda exhaled as a wave of relief rushed over her.

"*This is a conversation I thought to have in person with you. Is there any chance you can come to Sardinia? I can arrange a flight for you, if you wish.*"

"*No. I'm helping Remare track down the son of a friend of his who's gone missing. Asanti. Have you heard of him?*"

"*The Castilian? Yes, I know him. I'm sorry his son is unaccounted for. Miranda, please be careful. The last time you tried to help Lord Valadon, you were severely injured. I don't want to see a repeat of that.*"

"Yeah, I don't either. Remare is meeting me soon, and we're going to have dinner with Asanti."

"It is best to keep your lineage a secret for now. I know you and Remare are lovers," he coughed loudly, *"but this is not something I would share...with anyone."*

"He's tasted my blood."

"Yes, I thought he might have. He won't be able to sense your heritage. I have much to tell you, Miranda, but it will keep until I return to New York. However, if circumstances are such that you need to reach me, contact me at will. Now, is there anything else I can do for you?"

"Yes. Peralt mentioned two other authors, Draxton and Courant, as his source of knowledge on Elementals. I can't find mention of them anywhere. Do you know where these books are?"

"No one does. Peralt had many enemies and had to flee cities under cover of darkness. It was believed they were left behind but never located. I, as well as several others, have searched for the tomes, but no one has ever found them."

Miranda's shoulders sagged. *"Okay. Just one more question. Does Felicity know? About me?"*

"Of course. There are no secrets between us."

Miranda closed her eyes. Felicity had known and hadn't told her. Somehow, it felt like a betrayal. *"I'll be in touch."*

"I am so sorry you found out this way." His voice was strangely soothing. *"I had intended to tell you myself. Do you believe me?"*

Did she? She wasn't sure. *"We'll talk when you get back."* Her head began to hurt, and she rubbed it. She snorted. *"So, do I call you Granddad, now?"*

Something like a mental shudder appeared in her mind. *"I would prefer you didn't, but if you must."*

"All right, GD, later."

"Be well, Miranda."

She let her head drop in her hands. Vampire blood. She had vampire blood in her veins. How was she supposed to deal with this? It certainly answered a lot of questions she'd had about herself.

"Well, aren't you a sight for sad eyes?" The Were Queen stood with one hand on her hip. "Wanna tell me what's got you so down? You wouldn't say on the phone."

Miranda wasn't ready to confess her bloodline to her best friend. Not yet. It was too soon, but eventually, she would. "Liz, if I give you something, will you hide it at Werehaven so no one can find it?"

She sat next to her. "Sure. What is it?"

"It's a book by a seventeenth-century alchemist. He describes the origins of *Elementals* in brutal details. It's not something I want anyone to find." She'd thought about hiding it in her wall safe but nixed the idea. As far as the Draxton and Courant books were concerned, she wondered if Blu had been telling her the truth. Maybe he didn't know, but with almost everything on databases, maybe she could locate the lost volumes. Smirking, Miranda imagined breaking into museums to retrieve those books, as well. Hell, she'd even considered hiring a professional thief.

"What's it say?" Liz thumbed through the pages.

"Apparently, my kind goes all the way back to the ancient Greeks and Romans. He discusses my abilities." Raising her hand, Miranda shook it for emphasis. "Goes on to say how they thought us spirits of some kind, descendants of angels, and later, *'humans with gifts'*."

Miranda gazed up at the statue of the angel. *Descendants, huh?* There were good angels and then The Fallen; which one did she derive from? Their powers were supposed to be for good, for healing, but what if one of them chose to use their gifts for evil? She shook her head free of the thought. "It seems women long ago had talents like mine."

"Yeah, they burned them at the stake." Liz raised one brow. "Ancient Greeks, my ass! They used to believe we were cursed by Zeus himself." She huffed. "Shows how much they knew."

"I know. I just didn't comprehend how many or why." Her voice sounded pained. "Liz, thousands—maybe hundreds of thousands—innocent women and men were killed because some fanatical religious sect thought us evil."

"Or they were terrified of our powers enough to wipe us out." Liz's eyes narrowed. "There's always been men who were fearful of powerful women. They hunted down Weres and vampires, as well. Spread terrible and frightening rumors to scare people, enough so they had reason to exterminate us."

Miranda remembered some of those horrific rumors about Weres. Ignorance bred fear, and there were those who wanted the Weres quarantined so that they could study them, conduct experiments. *Like Liz or the Council of Others would ever allow that to happen.* "Yeah. I think so. Peralt hinted that *Elementals* were more complex. Part of some sort of cosmic energy field we draw our power from." Her head swam with all the new information. "Liz, my power's been growing."

"I know." Liz rubbed her arm for comfort. "I've often sensed strength in you that you kept hidden."

"What scares me most is that, if some government types ever found out about me, they would try to use me as some sort of weapon. I have enough nightmares. I don't want anyone to ever find out. Okay?"

"They've used werewolves and vampires in wars since the beginning. But don't worry; I've kept your secret for years. I'll never tell anyone." She hugged her. "Now, why don't you come to Summit Rock? Since the weather's been warm, we thought we'd have a barbeque." She playfully tugged a strand of Miranda's hair. "You look like you could use some food."

"I'm not hungry, but I'll join you."

Liz put her arm around her waist as they walked the trail to Summit Rock. "Wait 'til you smell what's cooking, then you'll get hungry."

Miranda sighed. "I know."

***

"Pity he couldn't tell us more, but I suspect he revealed as much as he knew." Remare accompanied Valadon down the hall to his room.

"Scorpio did his usual best of persuasion with him." Valadon agreed. "Before I shattered his mind, I saw blank holes, where someone had erased his memories. Not just veiled them but obliterated them. Someone didn't want us poking around in there. It would take a vampire of considerable strength to do that."

"Peralt."

"Yes. Irina and Gregori are meeting with her informant, William Tolliver, tonight. We'll see what they discover." The High Lord's eyes lit. "As for now...I have a surprise for you."

"Really?" Intrigued, Remare asked, "What is it?"

They stopped outside his room. "Far be it from me to overwork my people to the point of exhaustion. You've been working twice as many hours as the rest of the Torians. You need a break." Valadon opened the door to Remare's room. Before he even stepped inside, a feeling of dread gathered in his stomach.

"Ladies, I'm sure you've met Remare at one of our cocktail parties. This is Gloria, from accounting, and Chloe, from my advertising department."

Remare gracefully bowed his head in their direction. Gloria was a seductive redhead who had tried to hit on him at their parties. Beneath her charming smile was an ambitious bitch who would use anyone if she thought it would further her career. Chloe was a fun-loving blonde who excelled at public relations. Neither woman interested him. He suppressed his disgust at their invasion into his private quarters. Only Valadon had the master key to his apartment; he'd obviously arranged this little soiree beforehand. Distancing himself, Remare went to his bar. "Would anyone care for a drink?"

"Ladies?" Valadon never took his eyes off him. Sipping his wine, Remare realized Valadon had set him up. *He knows!* Remare knew, beyond any doubt, Valadon had found out about him and Miranda. Valadon's penetrating, green eyes bore into him.

"I'll have what you're having." Gloria sidled up to Remare and started stroking his shoulder.

He poured her a drink and remained calm. Rationally, he conversed silently with Valadon. *"As beautiful as these women are, I must decline your generous invitation. Irina could be sending us valuable information at any time. I would rather not be distracted."*

"Nonsense. You deserve some time off...for good behavior. The men tell me you haven't gotten laid in quite some time. How unfortunate for you. I think now is the perfect time."

Remare's stomach clenched; he gritted his teeth and smiled graciously. *"But you, my friend, have had to shoulder so much. I think it is you who needs the relaxation."*

"You first." Valadon's mental voice didn't brook any discussion. He wasn't making a request. The High Lord was giving Remare a choice, offering a penance for his crimes. He'd betrayed Valadon with Miranda, and if he wanted to

stay in House Valadon, he would have to comply with Valadon's wishes.

Or else, he could leave. Remare considered just that. But how long would he or Miranda survive in the world without the protection of a House? He'd have to make her a prisoner in his home. And that was something he would never do. In time, they would learn to hate one another.

They could become fugitives, traveling from one continent to another. Hiding, hoping his enemies didn't find them, but eventually they would and he couldn't bear the thought of what his adversaries would do to Miranda.

From the corner of his eye, Remare saw the two women disrobing and fondling each other. If he complied and performed his act of contrition the High Lord demanded, he could still protect Miranda, even though she would want to kill him if she ever found out. And she would find out. Valadon would see to it.

Unlike other vampire lords who peddled their people for political gain, Valadon never expected his people to prostitute themselves for gain. In the past, the thought had never bothered Remare. He'd been trained to seduce and be seduced. Sex had been a tool, a weapon to wield in the name of survival. Until he met Miranda, sex was an enjoyment, a pleasurable activity, but nothing else. With Miranda, it had been so much more. He'd finally found the peace he hadn't realized he'd spent centuries searching for. And, now, Valadon was destroying it.

Raising his glass, he saluted his lord, his oldest friend, his liege. *"Touché, Valadon. Touché!"*

***

Sardinia

Guy de Montglat gazed out over the Mediterranean Sea and inhaled the crisp, clean scent. From the top of Robert's tiered mountain home, the fig trees provided generous amounts of shade, as well as a delightful aroma. Guy could see below his beloved reading to the servants' children who lived on the lower levels. Felicity was one of the world's leading experts on art history, brilliant, yet she was enjoying herself reading a Harry Potter book to them. His heart melted as she glanced up and smiled at him. They'd been together for centuries, and she could still make him feel the way he did the first time he'd met her.

"There you are." Robert approached, dressed in his formal robes. He joined him at the lookout area. "A beautiful sunset, don't you think?"

"It is." Guy admired the colors of the sky. "Do you ever think about moving back to your home in Naples?"

"My home doesn't exist anymore. The last world war saw to that. Many of the European vampires fled their homelands for the safety of the islands here in the Mediterranean. I know few who went back and stayed. Besides, even it were possible, none of us are who we once were."

"You were a king."

"I was. But no longer. You're the only one who ever uses that term. You're in a sentimental mood this evening." Robert gestured in the direction of Montglat's ancestral country. "Are you reminiscing about your home?"

"Sometimes, I do. Rarely. As you say, none of us are who we once were." Guy reflected. "I went back several years ago for a visit. It was not the same."

"It never is." He nodded to Felicity. "She takes pleasure in reading to the children."

"She does. She's always had a fondness for children."

"You were lucky to meet her when you did."

"Yes, I was." A memory surfaced of how she had worked with him for Robert's court. She'd been deciphering the secret letters of a rival court and was nearly caught by Lord Acton, a vampire lord known especially for his cruelty. Montglat had had to rush to England and smuggle her and the documents out of the country to safety. It was the only time he'd nearly exposed his identity.

"How is your progeny doing?"

Guy closed his eyes in contemplation. Miranda had sounded so sad, his heart ached for her. "She's not ready, yet. She's only now begun to understand her origins."

"She'll need to become ready. Savinien will be waking soon."

"We still have time." He waved to Felicity. "When I return, I was thinking of leaving Felicity here with you. For her own protection. Things may become…complicated."

"Felicity has never struck me as one to back down from a fight. She is always welcome in my home as you are, but I doubt she'll stay here without you."

Guy sighed. He would have to do something about that.

Robert exhaled. "Have you heard from your son lately?"

"Not for some time. I've offered him several lucrative positions in Glatt Industries. But he continually turns me down, says he prefers his independence, wants to make his own fortune."

"And has he?"

"Not exactly. But he will." Guy smiled knowingly. "Someday, he will."

Chapter Twenty-Five

"Jesus! Who's the hunk? He looks like a Viking!" Miranda admired the physique of the new Were playing volleyball. He was the most enormous male she'd ever seen. Even though it was nearly winter, his muscle shirt revealed a body carved from granite. Exceedingly tall, with shoulders wider than Liz's personal guard, Lawe, who'd been the most muscular of the tribe, this new man was a force to be reckoned with.

Tongue between her teeth, Liz sniggered. "His name's Cyrus Lasker. They call him the white wolf. He's transferred in from Chicago. Got some kind of promotion to the New York offices and needed a clan to belong to." Lust nearly dripped from her mouth. "I made him an irresistible offer."

"I bet. He's huge!"

Cyrus' long white hair flowed down his back as he fiercely spiked the ball and then whooped it up with his new clan.

"I'll say," she moaned seductively, raising her eyebrows up and down. "What do you think of the twins?"

Miranda eyed the other two new members of Black Star. As Lasker was tall and brawny, the two young men were of average height and bulk. With their stunning looks and blond locks, they appeared to be a couple of surfer dudes. "What are their names?"

"Drew and Daniel Cott; they're from California. Got work on the same soap opera with Max. They're actors. Sasha does all their make-up."

"Sheesh, they're handsome."

"Don't you know it." Liz gestured to Miranda's new roommate. "Look how Max is salivating. I bet she can't wait to taste one of them. Or both."

Max was rooting on the sidelines for them, and each time one of the twins returned a volley, she applauded loudly, her smiling face flushed with excitement. Or lust.

Lasker spiked a ball so hard it nearly took Gavin's head off as he dove for it. The look Liz's former lover gave Lasker as he snarled spelled trouble. But Miranda knew this was the way of the Weres. The strongest led. Gavin, the red wolf, was a great leader, well-liked and respected, but he wasn't built as massively as Lasker. It must have stuck in his craw something fierce when Liz brought the Viking into the clan.

"Are you expecting more trouble from Red Claw?" Miranda suspected Liz was beefing up her army.

"It's possible." She shrugged. "You never know. Let's just say I like to be prepared. For anything."

Rotating his shoulder he must have jammed diving for the ball, Gavin let a replacement take his spot and walked toward Werehaven. Miranda decided to follow. "Gonna use the ladies room."

Liz nodded.

Once inside, Miranda spotted Gavin by the bar having a beer. He looked so alone. Liz had told her his only crime was in wanting to marry her. Liz had been married twice before. Once, when she'd been very young, to a soldier who later died in Afghanistan, and then, later, to an army captain who mistakenly thought, when he married Lizandra, he'd become king. That marriage hadn't lasted very long. After that, Liz had sworn she'd never marry, again. But, with Gavin, Miranda had hoped she'd change her mind. She hadn't.

"So that's the new guy, huh?" She sat beside him and gestured to the bartender to bring her what Gavin was drinking.

He didn't look up. "Yeah, that's the new guy."

"I'm so sorry, Gavin." She rubbed his arm then shrugged. "I don't always know why Lizandra does the things she does."

"No one does. That's why she's the queen." He faced her. "How've you been, Miranda?" He smiled and his bourbon-colored eyes seemed to light. "You haven't been around much."

"Busy. End of semester stuff. And other things." She wanted to offer Gavin comfort. Knew he was hurting, even though his pride forbade him to show it. Miranda knew he still loved Lizandra, probably always would. She had thought they were one couple to last the century. Her heart ached for him. It was one thing to get dumped. It was another to be demoted to beta after being Lizandra's alpha for so long. And having everyone know it in the clan had to bite.

"You did a great job on the gazebo out there. One of my new favorite places to visit in the park." She knew Gavin was a great chiropractor, but he was also one helluva carpenter. He'd helped re-build her pantry when a pipe had busted.

"Yeah, I like the way it came out. Lawe and the others helped. This way, when it gets too hot and sunny out, there's a place to get some shade." He downed his beer. "So, what do you think of the white wolf?"

"He's huge!" Miranda wanted to smack herself in the head. Size was important to the Weres. So was strength. And she'd just insulted him. "I think Liz is just trying to project a certain image. Maybe she's expecting more trouble from the Red Claws."

His eyes lit up. "Has she said anything to you?"

"No. Other than always wanting to be prepared."

"As do I." Remare joined them. "Gavin, a pleasure to see you, again." He shook the Were's hand. "Lizandra said I would find you down here."

Miranda's face flushed, her body in hyperawareness. She gave him the evil eye. "You're late."

"My apologies. Obligations arose that couldn't be averted. I hope you'll forgive me."

Miranda tried to be angry, but Remare's handsome face was too charming to deny. "Well, you did text me, so I think I can forgive you this time."

"I called Asanti to let him know we'd be arriving a little late. He's expecting us."

Miranda rose. "We'd better get going, then. Gavin, I'll be in touch." She bent and kissed his cheek as he returned her hug. She whispered in his ear, "I'm still on your side. Always."

He winked at her and watched as she left with the vampire.

Saddened for her friend, she didn't know if Gavin and Lizandra would ever get back together, again, but she hoped one day they would.

Remare opened her car door. "Was that a new Were I saw on the volleyball court?"

"Yeah, some new guy from Chicago. There are two other younger Weres who joined them, too." She adjusted her seat belt. "So, why were you late?"

He hesitated then said, "Unexpected surprises."

"All dealt with?"

His face betrayed nothing. "Completely. Let's not discuss business tonight." He turned north on Riverside Drive. "I want you to enjoy Asanti's hospitality. Besides being an artist, he has quite a collection of art, as well. One I think you'll enjoy."

"He's hoping I'll spot something to help with the investigation. I didn't want to tell him how unlikely that was. He looked so despondent."

"Yes. Asanti's son is his world. They have a strong bond." After reaching their destination, Remare parked the car. "His town house is up two blocks. We have a little time. Would you like to walk near Riverside Park? We have a few minutes, and I need to tell you something."

"Sure." Taking his hand, she crossed the street with him to the park with the fantastic vistas of the Hudson River. They casually strolled along, arm in arm, admiring the rolling hills. Their sex life had gone into overdrive, but Miranda also enjoyed their quiet moments, like when he cooked for her or they just sat together discussing art on his boat. She smiled at the romantic moment she was sharing with Remare. It was such a peaceful night, but when the silence seemed to lengthen, she said, "The sky's dark. New moon. There won't be any Weres doing the lunar run tonight."

"I know." Stopping, he turned toward her. His smile didn't reach his eyes as he moved a strand of hair from her face, his thumb trailing over her cheek. "I wish that I had granted your request of visiting The Cloisters."

"Hey, it's okay. You promised to take me in the spring, and that's good enough." She didn't need to be an empath to sense his morose mood. His face was drawn, but she had thought it was because of the stresses of work. She stroked his jaw. "What's wrong?"

"You were always so intuitive, *mia sorceratrice*. There's no hiding anything from you."

Miranda's stomach clenched. Whatever news he had to tell her was bad. Real bad. She felt it to the depths of her being. "What is it?"

"Valadon knows."

Her hand flew to her chest. "No!" The blood drained out of her face. "How?" She gasped. "How did he find out? We were so careful."

"It matters not. What's important...is the choice he gave me." He massaged the side of her neck. His eyes darkened. "Either give you up or leave House Valadon."

"No! He couldn't have!" She shook her head in denial. "You're his oldest friend. He wouldn't do that." But she knew in the pit of her stomach, Valadon was more than capable of being vindictive. He was a vampire lord, a high lord, who was used to his commands being obeyed. "What did you tell him?"

His hands slid down to her shoulders. "It wasn't so much what I said, Mir-randa. He wanted a display of my loyalty. Proof of my fealty." His fingers dug in to her arms. "An act of sacrifice on my part."

Tears began forming in the back of her eyes as she fought the quivering in her voice. "What did he want from you?"

"After our meeting broke up, we walked back to my apartment. I had no idea what he'd planned." He shook his head. "If I had, I might have had time to plan some counter-move." He seemed to be searching the trees. "But there was no time." Exhaling, he met her eyes. "He had women waiting for us."

"Oh, God, no." Feeling like she'd been sucker-punched, she stepped out of his reach, her hand clutching her stomach. "Do *not* tell me this! Do *not* tell me he had you fuck one of the women!"

His eyes were flat and as cold as the night. "Both."

Her world, the world that always slipped away whenever he was with her, came crashing down around her. Time stopped. Breaths ceased. Their dreams, their hopes, everything that was sacred to her was shattered, replaced by an inexplicable void without any light. Standing erect like a statue, part of her died in that moment.

She'd had other men in her life. Dane had been important, so was Orion. In the mansion of her mind, where she housed her inner most thoughts, desires and secrets, each had opened several doors, exploring her psyche. But they never got any further than the first floor. Even Gabriel had unlocked doors others had never even tried. He would have opened more if she had let him, but she had never given him the key.

Remare didn't need a key. Laughing with her, he simply took her hand and flew through each of her floors, discovering doors no one else ever did or ever would. Some of those rooms she hadn't even known about, herself. Tears burned behind her eyes.

Her entire body trembling with rage, Miranda swung out before she even knew what she was doing and slapped him hard across the face. The sound echoing in the night was not only that of hand meeting face, but the slamming of a thousand open doors, now forever sealed.

He took out his handkerchief and wiped the blood from his mouth. "Hit me, again. I deserve it."

"*Why?!*" she screamed. "Why didn't you refuse?"

"I tried, Miranda; I came up with every possible reason not to." His words thundered in the night air. "He wouldn't hear it! He insisted on it. My penance, you see." Sarcasm and bitter self-loathing laced his voice. "He knew how you would react, and that was the exact reason he did it. He wanted us to end. Will you give him that?" His eyes closed in silent pleading. "Can you not forgive me?"

Miranda saw nothing but red. It felt as if her eyes were on fire. She wondered if they were bleeding. She already knew her heart was.

"I would have gladly accepted a public whipping with barbed wires than go through that. I loathed every minute of it. I couldn't stand their hands on me. With every passing second, I hid my revulsion, and all I could think about was how much you would hate me for it."

Miranda remembered how he'd been whipped with chains dipped in liquid silver and how his back smoldered with pain and blood. "I hate you! Right now, I hate you for what you did. And I hate Valadon! The sick games you play disgust me."

"It is no game, Mir-randa." His voice quivered. "What did you want me to do? Leave Valadon House forever? How would I protect you? Keep you caged in my home? Forbid you to work, to be around your friends? You would hate me more than you do, now. I will not abandon Valadon so that you and I live a life of fugitives. We would not last long, I can tell you that much. Lone wolves do not last long in the wild. They perish. We will not."

Miranda turned from him and held her head in her hands as she leaned against the cement wall of the park. This couldn't be real. This couldn't be happening, she kept telling herself. Remare didn't sleep with those women. He couldn't have. She whimpered. The pain eviscerated her. What they had, what they shared was so sacred, so fine, they were magic together. Nothing could touch it.

Until now.

"Miranda. I am so sorry." He took her in his arms. "Hear me. I will cut off my own arm before I ever reach for another woman. I swear to you."

Miranda stared at him through tear-stained eyes. Her voice was bitterly harsh. "We were great together, Remare.

You polluted something that meant the world to me. Don't expect me to forgive you or Valadon. I'll talk with Asanti tonight. I'll hide the loathing I feel, right now, but don't ask me for forgiveness. My heart is shredded. You did that."

She shook off his hands and marched back across the street. She turned halfway to him. "Which one of these homes is his?"

He hesitated then sighed regretfully. "It's up ahead on the right. The corner house."

Chapter Twenty-Six

The fireplace burning, Valadon sat alone, brooding in his living room while most of his trusted Torians were out on assignments. Drinking his blood wine, he winced at what he had put Remare through. Why had he done that? He rubbed his forehead. Was his ego so huge he'd needed to punish the one Torian who had been with him the longest? His friend, his confidant, a man who he respected more than any other. One who had saved his life, time after time. Did Valadon need to torture a vampire like that?

His head thrown back, he ground his molars and closed his eyes. Even with his shields locked firmly in place, he'd sensed Remare's torment as the women shared him. Felt his self-loathing as he completed his act of contrition. Was it true misery loved company? Valadon pondered the thought and didn't like what was becoming apparent.

The bastard loved her. After all these long years, Remare had finally found a woman he could cherish. The one woman Valadon had grown fond of and intended to make his own, Miranda. And she'd chosen to be with Remare. *Beautiful! Just beautiful!* Oh, how the fates must have enjoyed laughing at him. How many times in the past had Miranda backed away from him, distancing herself? Had she been trying to tell him all along she didn't want him?

Of course, she had. He'd just been too proud to see it. He snorted in painful awareness. And, now, he'd destroyed their relationship and any chance either of them had for happiness. Sickened by what he'd done, he threw his wine glass into the fire, watching as it shattered into a thousand pieces. Disgusted with himself, he started pacing. It was over. He shook his head in aggravation. There was no way to fix this; the damage had been done.

Exhaling, he ran a hand through his hair. He'd been melancholy ever since memories of Lena started surfacing. Informing Gabriel of his ancestry had affected him more than he thought it would. At least Gabriel seemed to be taking his heritage in stride. After they had discussed it at length. He smirked. His prodigy was as stubborn as he was.

Deciding he needed some distance and refusing to wallow in his self-pity, he took the elevator up to visit his army of mid-level Torians. Those individuals who worked for ValCorp and would lay down their lives for him. He'd had a training area, similar to the one the Elite Torians used, built on their floor. As he neared the racquetball courts, he stopped by the glass to watch as Tristan played with Jeremy. He was pretty sure his top model wasn't supposed to engage in any sport that could potentially harm his striking features.

Valadon stood with his arms crossed. Jeremy was beyond handsome; he could give Adonis a run for the money in the looks department with his golden hair and sculpted face. No wonder sales in mens' products had grown substantially since they signed the vampire. Surveys indicated that his beauty appealed to females, as well as males. Valadon watched the action on the court grow vigorous. Both men were incredibly fast as they returned each other's volleys.

Remare had informed him of Jeremy's desire to become an Elite Torian. Besides modeling for Cesare, Valadon's top designer, Jeremy had started training alongside his soldiers. As a model, he needed to keep his body in shape, and Valadon thought he did a good job of it.

Tristan hit an impossible shot for Jeremy to return. He lunged but was a half-breath too short to reach it. When they noticed Valadon was watching them, they decided to take a water break.

He entered the court. "You play very well."

"Of course, we do." Tristan grinned at him. "We've been at it for some time."

"I understand you wish to become a Torian after you've completed your training."

Jeremy wiped the sweat from his face. "Yes. I'll be getting my MBA soon and hope to join your executive branch."

"I take it modeling's not exciting enough for you?"

"It's fine. I enjoy it. But it's not something I want to do the rest of my life." Jeremy tried to put his water bottle on the shelf near his watch and ring but accidentally knocked the ring to the floor.

Something about the gold band caught Valadon's attention, and he retrieved the ring. "Columbia. A friend's son goes there."

"I didn't know you went to Columbia." Tristan studied the ring. "I thought you went to Pace."

"Jenson goes to Pace. I go to Columbia. What? Didn't think a model could get into Ivy League?" he joked when he saw their surprised reactions. "I work hard for my grades."

"I'm sure you do." Valadon's eyes narrowed. "By any chance do you know a student by the name of Jacob?"

Jeremy's eyes squinted. "Jacob, Jacob. No, I don't think so."

"He's enrolled in the same MBA program you are. Jacob Asanti."

"You don't mean Asa? Dark-haired guy we sometimes hang with. His father's an artist, I think?"

"You know him?"

"Sure, we sometimes hit the clubs in the area after school. Last week, Asa wanted to go to a Were club. I wasn't thrilled with the idea, but I figured why not. Try something new."

Valadon's voice was cold as steel. "What club?"

"It's in Mid-town. Oasis, Club Oasis."

Valadon turned to Tristan. "Did your people check out this place?"

"It wasn't on the original list, but I'll check it out, now." Tristan swiftly left the court.

"Did I do something wrong? Is it taboo to go to a Were club?"

"Not at all." Valadon turned to leave. "You may have done something very right."

***

After a superb dinner that had been wasted on Miranda, her stomach too knotted to eat much, Asanti gave her a tour of his stunning Upper West Side town house. An old-world vampire, he had a thing for parquet floors and lots of wood paneling with wainscoting. Not only was he a fantastic artist, his collection was outstanding. Needing distance, she was grateful for the chance to be away from Remare. Even though the wine had settled her nerves, she wanted some alone time with Asanti to calm down.

"And here is an artist you might find interesting." Asanti gestured to his Mary Cassatt painting of a woman at an opera.

"Reminds me of *In the Loge.* I told my professor I thought it was Degas in the background, spying on the woman, and he laughed and said it might very well be."

"I don't believe anyone definitively figured out the identity of the man in the painting. But Cassatt was a great observer of people. And very talented. She had an eye for detail."

"One of my favorite artists."

They strolled down the hall until Asanti opened the door to his son's room.

"I'm still not sure what you expect me to find." She didn't want to disappoint him, but she didn't see any way she could help. "I never met Jacob; I don't know what his routine was."

"I know." He sighed. "Remare told me you were invaluable in finding Nickolas. I was just hoping." He waved his hand around the room. "A father's last request. My men, as well as Valadon's, have already gone through it. I thought you might find some little detail the others did not. As someone who works with young people, you might have a clearer insight. Excuse me, I did not mean to pressure you."

She saw the pain in his eyes he'd been bravely concealing during dinner. "You didn't." She wanted to offer him some measure of comfort, but she honestly didn't see what good she'd be. She'd never met his son, but what harm was there in looking? "Let me look through his room. I can't promise anything. Most likely, I won't see anything the others missed."

"Thank you. That is all I ask. I'll join Remare in the library." He turned and left.

Now that she was alone, she texted Max, who was close by at Werehaven to come pick her up soon. She did not want to be stuck in a car with Remare for the drive downtown. As far as she was concerned, after tonight, they were through.

Miranda studied the walls of what appeared to be an average room of a typical college student. Man, did the kid love economics. So many textbooks and magazines. Even though much of her own material was online, she still recommended certain art texts to her students. Apparently, the professors at Columbia agreed with her. She knew Aiden had Jacob's computer and was going through it for anything that could help in the search.

Jacob's wall showcased different awards he'd won for business competitions. "You're one talented guy. Incredibly bright. Driven. You'd love working for Valadon," she whispered to his picture. Everything she'd heard about ValCorp and Valadon's business acumen pointed to a tremendous business empire. She hoped they found Jacob in time so that he could realize his dreams of the corporate world.

She felt uncomfortable going through his personal items. Like a transgressor. What could she possibly see that the others didn't? She took a step back and, closing her eyes, breathed in the scent in the room. She looked at the room from every angle. She sensed nothing. There were no clues to his whereabouts. She searched his room, again, afraid to go downstairs and meet the sorrowful eyes of his father. After searching his dresser drawers and closet, she turned in frustration for one last look at the room then closed the door silently behind her.

Downstairs, in the library, Remare eyed her as she entered. She shook her head. She couldn't find anything that even suggested where Jacob might have vanished to. She moved toward Asanti. "I'm sorry to disappoint you, but I didn't see anything that could help."

"That's all right. I knew it was a long shot, but I didn't want to leave any avenue of hope unexplored. Thank you for coming tonight."

Remare put his hand on Asanti's shoulder. "Please be certain that Valadon and I are doing everything in our power to locate your son. We have close to a hundred men scouring the clubs, bars and any other place your son might have gone to."

As both men hugged, Miranda felt a pang deep in her stomach that they might already be too late. She accepted Asanti's embrace. "It was a pleasure meeting you."

"As it was for me. I hope we meet, again, someday, under better circumstances."

When they were outside, Miranda briskly walked to the corner.

"Why are you walking there? The car's over here."

"I called Max to come pick me up." She didn't want to meet his penetrating gaze but did. "Look, Remare, I just need some time alone."

"Don't be ridiculous. Your place is on my way. Of course, I'll drive you home."

Miranda shook her head. When he started arguing with her, Max drove up with Sasha in tow and double parked on the street.

Getting out of the car, Max hugged her. "We found the place. Your directions were spot on."

"Hi, Miranda." Sasha started moving foot to foot the way kids do when they are either chilled or have to use the bathroom. "God, it's cold out. Do you think your friend will let me use the facilities? I gotta go badly."

"I told you to go before we left." Max chimed in.

"I did. I gotta go, again."

Miranda glanced at Remare, who said, "I'm sure Asanti will accommodate you."

The group of them marched back to Asanti's house. He was surprised when two Weres looked up at him in hope. Remare made the introductions, and when he explained Sasha and Max were Miranda's friends, their host was more than gracious. He pointed down the hall to the bathroom. Sasha went quickly in that direction.

Max spotted Jacob's picture on the tabletop. "Hey, there's Asa!"

Asanti looked confused. "You must be mistaken; this is my son, Jacob."

"I know Jacob; all the guys at Oasis call him Asa."

"What is Oasis?"

Remare appeared intrigued but explained, "It's a Were club in Mid-town."

"My son does not frequent Were establishments."

Unladylike, Max snorted. "Yeah, right, he doesn't. You should have seen him last week."

All heads turned in her direction.

"What? What'd I say?"

Sasha returned from the bathroom. "Thank you. I'm sorry we disturbed you." She ran a finger lovingly over Jacob's picture. "Oh, it's Asa."

From the look on her face, Miranda knew there was more than casual friendship involved. "Sasha, were you at Nightshade about a week ago with Jac—ah, Asa?"

The look of guilt on Sasha's face was telling. "Yeah. Is that okay?"

Remare took out his phone and started texting. Miranda marveled at how fast his hand moved, but then, she had firsthand knowledge about how quick his fingers could be. She hoped her face didn't betray her thoughts. It usually did.

"Were clubs were not on the original list for us to investigate. I'm having our people search them, now."

"Is something wrong?" Max asked shyly.

"Jacob went missing a few days ago," Miranda explained. "No one has seen him since. Have you guys been in touch?"

Sasha spoke softly "He was supposed to call me to get together for dinner. He never did."

"This opens new possibilities. Let's go." Remare gestured to all of them. "I need to get back to ValCorp ASAP."

After Asanti invited the girls to stay with him and tell him more about his son, Miranda reluctantly joined Remare.

The ride South on Riverside Highway was a quiet one. She opened the window a little to let some of the breezes off the river in. She hoped the air would cool down her heated face.

Remare's jaw seemed hard as granite. "I understand you're hurt, Mir-randa." His voice was laced with pain. "But do you really want to destroy what we've been building for so long?"

Miranda wanted to say *she* wasn't the one who destroyed it. "I need time, Remare." Avoiding his gaze, she slowly exhaled. "Just give me time." She had a lot on her mind, not the least of which was her newly discovered ancestry. "Will it help? What Max and Sasha said—will it help with the investigation?"

"It very well might." He came to a stop in front of her house. "I don't have time to come in, right now, and discuss our situation. I wounded you. I know that. I've also sworn to never repeat my actions." The intensity in his eyes was almost frightening. "There is no one else, Mir-randa." He grasped her hand. "And there never will be. I want you to think about that."

Part of her wanted to touch him, to kiss him. But her pride wouldn't allow it. "I will think about it. I'm tired so I'm going to go inside and try to get some sleep. I hope you find Jacob. His father is quite a man. I liked having dinner with him."

"I'm glad for that." When he leaned in to kiss her, she turned her head slightly so that he kissed her temple. "I'll contact you as soon as I can."

Miranda nodded. "Okay." She strode up the steps to her door, unlocked it. When she turned around, Remare was already gone.

Chapter Twenty-Seven

"There's *girly* things in my bathroom!"

Recognizing his mildly annoyed voice, Miranda barely had time to lock the door behind her. As she turned, her face brightened, and her sullen mood dissipated. "You're home! We weren't expecting you until next week. I missed you! Always."

Rising from the stairs he'd been sitting on, Orion welcomed her embrace and hugged her tightly. "Thanks, Miranda." He kissed the top of her head. "It's good to see you, too!" Keeping one arm around her, he rubbed his head. "So, why is there girl stuff mixed in with mine?"

She needed a moment to take in his handsome face, inhale his clean, masculine scent. Orion's hair had grown longer since the last time she'd seen him. "Well, while you were away, Max and Sasha had their apartment exterminated. The odor was too much for them, so they crashed here for a couple of days." She had to admit she liked having the two Weres around for company. *Maybe it's time I rent out Aunt Meg's downstairs apartment.* "They're staying at a friend's tonight. I *promise* they'll be out soon!" She shuffled out of her jacket and hung it on the newel post.

He shrugged. "Okay." They walked into their living room.

Tucking a foot under her, she sat next to him on the couch. "Why didn't you call me? I would have picked you up at the airport."

"No big deal. I caught a cab." He stretched out his long legs. "Hey, is that your new Jeep parked outside? It's pretty snazzy. It looks a lot like mine, but the license plate is different. At first, I thought it was but then remembered I left it in ValCorp's garage."

Miranda shook her head. "I loved the postcards you sent me. Especially the ones from Amsterdam. Are you still thinking of buying a home there?"

"Not really. It was just a thought." His voice sounded tired, but after his flight, he would be. "But, out of all the countries we visited, I liked the Netherlands the best. Those villages were so goddamned beautiful. Made you fall in love with the place."

"Did anyone else fall in love?"

He smirked. "There are many different kinds of love, Miranda." He tilted his head. "Family, friends, lovers, and other things; some you can touch, and others you can't."

She wondered where Bastien fit. "So, how's Bas?" She knew they'd grown close, and Orion couldn't stop talking about how great the guy was as his manager and new best friend.

"He's fine."

When the silence dragged on, Miranda suspected something went sour. "Did Bas come back with you?"

"No. He's still in Paris, visiting his parents for the holidays. I'd had just about enough of family, so I came home early."

"They didn't invite you to stay?"

"Bas did. But not his family. Hey, it's okay. We kinda sprung it on them. Last-minute stuff. No big. Look, I'm a little tired, can I use your bathroom? I need a shower. Crash in your room tonight?"

"Sure, we're engaged, after all? Aren't we?" Her attempt at a joke at their *"arranged engagement"* didn't seem to register on him.

He leaned against the wall and folded his arms over his chest. "Do you still want us to be?"

Orion was one of those guys who was sexy even when he wasn't trying to be. With his tight black jeans and V-neck sweater, he was a looker, but right now, he seemed vulnerable. "Okay, what happened?

"Nothing. Nothing happened." He turned and walked toward her room.

Nothing, my ass! Something had happened. She followed him then leaned against the doorway to the bathroom as he ran the water in the shower. Pulling off his sweater, he toed off his boots and socks then pushed them into the corner. "It's not going to work between him and me. Man, I could just..." He hit his fist against the wall. Frustration and anger were evident in the way he clenched his teeth. "I feel like I just want to kill something."

"Yeah, I know how you feel."

"You couldn't *possibly* know how I feel." His breaths came hard and fast. "People say that all the time, but really, they have no clue how it feels; they just try to..."

"Remare slept with two other women." She hadn't meant to say it that way, but the words rushed out faster than she'd intended.

He looked stunned, confused for a moment, then at a loss for words. "Why?"

"That's the question, isn't it? Take your shower. We'll talk when you get out."

He unzipped his jeans and tossed them over the sink. Steam escaped as he stepped inside the shower, the warm water rolling off him. The muscles in his back were defined as were his biceps and triceps. As a Were, he was more muscular than any human, and because he was in the entertainment business, he kept his physique in outstanding shape. She left clean towels for him near the sink and closed the door so he could have his privacy.

After running upstairs and fetching him a pair of clean boxers, which she laid on the towels in the bathroom, Miranda shut the lights in the living room. Leaving only the night light on over the stove in the kitchen, she made her way back to the bedroom. Their deal had always been no nudity in the house, and if and when he slept in her bed, he wore boxers or he didn't sleep there at all. She heard him using the blow dryer and then shutting it off.

Wearing only a towel, he opened the door to her bedroom. He held the boxers with two fingers. "Do I have to?"

"Yes." She'd already changed into a T-shirt and pair of shorts and was slipping under the covers.

He complied then slid in beside her. "So, what happened?"

She lay on her side. "You go first."

"There's not much to tell. We were doing great. Dublin was fun, so was Glasgow and Copenhagen. All the northern European countries were fantastic. Bas has great organizational skills, and you should have seen the way he handled security at the different concert halls. It's a blast having someone backstage waiting for you, cheering you on. And I helped him on all the missions he went on."

"Valadon was smart using your cover as a musician to get you and Bas into all those cities. Meet with his confidants." After the events in Paris, the High Lord wanted to be kept aware of what was going on in the royal courts of Europe.

"It was exciting. Bas always kept me out of harm's way." Orion ran a hand down her arm. "But I liked being with him on assignments. It was a challenge and a rush. He's really good at what he does. The guy knows his shit inside out. What a turn-on to watch him in action."

"What went wrong?"

"Paris. Fucking Paris. Before we even got to France, he started acting, I don't know, more remote. Like he was distancing himself."

"Did you ask him about it?"

"Yeah, he said some of the people he had to meet with were dangerous, and he didn't want me with him."

"Sounds like he was looking out for you."

"Yeah, I suppose so. We stayed at his parents' place. They treated us pretty good. At least for a while."

"Giselle and Auguste de Rosemont. I remember them from the last time we were in Paris. They seemed like nice people."

"I liked Auguste. We hit it off okay."

"And Lady Rosemont?"

"Yeah. I don't think I'm what she would choose for her son."

"Did she say something?"

"She said a few things. I guess any mom wants grandchildren, someday." He shrugged. "They had a party for us, the holidays, whatever. Some of his friends may have had too much to drink. Said some things I could have done without."

Miranda rubbed his hand. "What did they say?"

"I had just returned from the bathroom, and they didn't realize I was close by. I think a lot of people forget Weres have acute hearing." His voice was tight and held hurt. "They called me *'Bastien's newest bitch'* and wondered if we took turns being on top. If I howled when I came."

Damn! "Did you talk to Bas about it?"

"He knew. He heard them and said...nothing. They ridiculed me, and he didn't say a damned word."

Miranda was surprised. She would have thought Bas would have set those guys right. "I'm sorry. I don't know why he didn't confront them."

"Fuck it! It was his house, and I guess he didn't want to start a fight. Lady Rosemont would not approve."

Miranda held his hand tighter.

"So, I hopped a plane the next day and came home." He kissed her hand. "To you."

"You do realize, sooner or later, you're going to have to talk to him."

"I know. I prefer later." Orion rose up on one arm. "Now, what the hell happened with you and Remare?"

Miranda lay on her back and closed her eyes. "I don't want to talk about it."

"Oh, no, you don't. I just spilled my guts. You don't get to shut down. Friends share."

She wondered if she just said it quickly, it wouldn't hurt so badly. "We had dinner with an old friend of his tonight. Before we got there, he told me he had sex with two other women."

"But why? I don't get it. Did you two have a fight?"

"No. No fight." Miranda's throat tightened. "He told me Valadon somehow found out about us and ordered him to fuck the women. His show of fealty." A sarcastic laugh escaped her throat. "He said he couldn't protect me if Valadon kicked him out of his House, so he did as commanded. Said we would never survive as lone wolves."

Orion looked out the window at the light of the streetlamp. "Is that why we have bars on our windows, now?"

"What bars?" Miranda rose from the bed and studied the new security. The black metal rods were bent in a graceful curly-cue design seen in some of the old homes built in the last century. She whispered, "When the hell did he get these installed?"

"They're on all the windows on the first floor. I think he takes your safety very seriously."

"Yeah, I guess so." She thought they had agreed on the possibility of screens, not bars. Exhaling, she returned to bed. "So, what do you think?"

Orion blew out a breath. "Don't get mad at me if I try to see things from his perspective. Okay? I am a guy."

Her eyes narrowed. "I'm listening."

"You say Valadon ordered him to?"

"Yeah, that's what he told me."

"Miranda. The vampires take their monarchs very seriously. I know; I've been in the courts in Europe. No one, and I mean no one, contradicts their kings and queens. Their law is final. I get it. Lizandra is a bit more democratic, but even her decisions are final, and no one challenges her."

"Lizandra would never ask her people to fuck someone they didn't want to."

"Debatable." He shrugged. "Maybe yes, maybe no."

Jaw open, she just stared at him.

"Anyway, I think you might want to cut him some slack. Obviously, the guy cares for you. I understand how he wouldn't be able to protect you if Valadon abjured him."

"He could have..."

"No. Hear me out. I was a lone wolf. Remember? Think back to how you found me after I'd been mauled by those pricks. I barely survived. If it hadn't been for you and Lizandra, I could have died. Vampires aren't much different. I saw unattached vampires in Europe. They didn't look good. Nothing like the court vampires."

"I still think..."

Orion sat up. "Did Remare lie about it? Try to cover it up? Or did he tell you as soon as he could?"

Miranda eyed him. "You are *such* a guy."

"Guilty as charged."

"He fucked two other women."

"Did he enjoy it? Did he get any pleasure from it? I doubt it."

"I don't like you, anymore."

"Why, am I beginning to make sense?"

Miranda turned away from him. She'd been nursing her ego for most of the night. Her inner voices started speaking. Her Dark Angel was seething as she stood with her arms crossed. *"He had choices."* Her Light Angel held her arms out with her palms open. *"Did he really? Have a choice?"* Miranda wasn't sure, anymore. "I need sleep."

"Come here." Orion pulled her to him and held her in his arms. "We both do."

His warmth seeped into her skin, soothing her. "You're getting breakfast in the morning."

He yawned. "Don't I always."

***

"I will tear his fucking head off," Gregori mumbled as he waited in the room next door to their key informant. The Upper East Side was swanky, but he'd seen more luxurious apartments. Irina's mark obviously had inferior taste. And when the fuck had he ever cared about furnishings? He ran a hand through his hair as he paced. She was driving him crazy.

William Tolliver, a known member of the Human Order of Light, had grown weary of their politics and tendencies toward violence. And, given the fact his finances had faltered in the last few years, he'd needed the support Irina had offered him.

So, he owed her or, more correctly, Valadon for the bailout.

Gregori ground his fist into the wall. But did she have to fuck the guy for information? Sure, they had seduced others in the past, but that was long ago, before he'd taken her to bed. Did what they shared mean so little to her?

"Dahling, it's what we do." Her words burned like acid in his stomach. Couldn't she show any hesitancy, any remorse? Or was she really *The Ice Queen* everyone called her? Could he have been so wrong about her?

That's it. His patience gone, he was going to march in there and garrote the guy. Watch as his eyes bulged out. Maybe then Gregori would feel one iota of satisfaction.

The door opened, and Irina stepped in with a smile on her face, a flash drive in her hand.

"Quickly, I was able to download everything he had about the HOL's facilities."

Gregori took the component and plugged it into his laptop. The layouts displayed an underground facility. Some sort of testing area. "Son of a bitch! That's on Governors Island, right here in the East River. The government used to own it." He tapped the screen. "Coast Guard occupied it for several decades." Irina leaned an arm over his shoulder, and he stroked her hand. "When they moved out, no one wanted it. Too expensive to construct a bridge there." His fingers flew over the keyboard. "I'm sending the data to Aiden in communications, as well as Valadon."

"Good! I penetrated his mind as far as I could go. He's only been there once when updated equipment was being brought in. Tolliver knows they do research and simulations there. He knew testing was going on but wasn't sure if it was done on people or just animals."

"He knew. On some level, he knew." Gregori turned his head toward her and inhaled. He couldn't tell if she'd had sex with Tolliver or not. Her arousal was evident, but he couldn't detect any male scent on her. "Was he rough with you?"

Irina snorted. "I didn't sleep with him. I merely replayed a memory with him so that he thought we were fucking." Her eyebrow arched. "I let him believe my hands were roaming his body, my breath tickling his skin. He gives better information when aroused."

The way she said aroused, with her thick Russian accent, did things to Gregori's libido. His burgeoning erection strained against his pants. He wanted to take her in the bedroom and make sure only his scent coated her body. But the residents of the apartment might soon come back, and they needed to be gone. He shut his laptop and packed up their equipment. "Let's ghost!"

***

"Chocolate croissants are the best."

"I know." In the kitchen, Orion took a bite of his own pastry. "That's why I get them for you." Sitting back in his chair, he seemed to be studying her. "You ever think of getting married? For real, I mean. Having kids, the whole package?"

"Not really." Miranda shrugged. "My life is complicated enough. Besides, Remare can't have children; he's too old."

"I'm not." He smiled. "We have a pretty good thing here going. I'd be a good husband and father."

Miranda sensed his need to belong. "You're on the road six months out of the year."

"I'd take some time off, spend time with the little ones. You could go back for your PhD. We could be a family."

Miranda empathized with him. Closing her eyes, she exhaled. "It's a dream, a pipedream."

"We could make it real."

She studied his face. He was serious. But she knew where he was coming from. He was hurting. Sure, they could go through the motions, play house, take the kids to the park, but how long before they realized they'd made a mistake and learned to resent the other? "It wouldn't work."

"Why not?"

"Because we both love other people."

"Think so?"

"Yeah. Know so. Unfortunately." She reached across the table and grasped his hand. "You'll work it out with him. Have faith." Miranda pointed to the small package as she finished her hazelnut hot chocolate. Usually, she preferred green tea, but on cold, overcast days, hot chocolate was necessary. "What's in the other box?"

"Not sure. It has your name on it. It was on the foyer table." He handed her the package.

She opened it. "It's a remote and a set of keys." Miranda held them up for him to see. "Whatever for?"

"Miranda, those are car keys."

"I know. But I don't have a car."

"Apparently, you do, now."

A buzzing sound started ringing. "Is that my phone or yours?"

"Mine." Orion read the text. "It's from Valadon. He wants me at ValCorp ASAP." He put their cups and plates in the sink and rinsed them out.

"I'll go with you. Valadon gave me free reign of his archives, and there's some research I want to do."

Sunglasses on, Orion wrapped a scarf around his throat as Miranda tossed on her jacket. When they were outside, he pointed to the shiny new black Jeep Wrangler. She'd rented a similar one when she'd been in New Mexico.

"There must be some mistake." She bent to check out the license plate: *SOR CRS.* Her jaw dropped. "You've got to be kidding." Closing her mouth, she smiled.

"Use the remote."

When she pressed the tab, the car started immediately, and then, the doors unlocked.

"Cool! I'm driving." Grinning, Orion got behind the wheel before she could protest, but since she hadn't driven in months, she let him. "There's an envelope for you."

Miranda read the note aloud. "I hope you don't mind the bars. They are to keep transgressors out, not to cage you in. They can be removed if you don't approve. But I hope you will keep them. I sleep better knowing you are protected. Also, a woman like you shouldn't be riding the subways. Enjoy, my sorceress—*R*."

A grin blossomed across her face.

"Sorceress, huh?!" Orion started laughing. "Oh, man, he is so fried."

"Shut up!" She chuckled. "Just drive."

Chapter Twenty-Eight

Valadon stood as Orion entered his office. "Good to see you. Thank you for coming so soon."

Shaking Valadon's hand, Orion spotted the vampire sitting in front of the High Lord. "I came as soon as I could."

"This is Asanti, an old friend." Orion shook his hand, as well, and sensed the vampire's despair. Sadness and concern marred his eyes. "His son has gone missing, and I wanted you to help us locate him."

"This is my son's shirt." Asanti passed him the material.

Orion inhaled the scent deep into his lungs. "I've got it." He returned the shirt to Asanti. "I'll help any way I can."

"Will you be able to track him?"

"Yes. As long as he's on the ground." Orion didn't want to alarm the vampire. If they airlifted or traveled by boat, chances were pretty slim to none of finding him.

"Good. We'll be having a meeting shortly, concerning our mission tonight. Make sure you're there." Valadon relaxed back in his chair. "Bastien arrived early this morning. He told me your concert tour was a great success, as was your assistance on his missions. He's eager to talk with you."

"I'll stop in to see him."

Valadon nodded once. "See that you do."

Orion strode down the corridor to Bastien's room. He hesitated before knocking, but before his knuckles touched the door, it swung open. An arm reached out and pulled him inside.

"What the hell were you thinking?" Bastien stood with his hands on his hips, his eyes on fire. "Taking off like that?"

"I just thought you may have wanted more alone time with your family." Orion removed his jacket and tossed it over a chair.

The veins in Bastien's neck stood out. "And what the hell gave you that idea?"

"Oh, I don't know. The fact that you seemed to enjoy the company of your friends more than mine at the party."

"Those were my father's friends. Long-time acquaintances necessary for his business."

Orion blew out a breath. The last thing he wanted was a fight with his best friend. "They didn't seem to like the idea of a Were in their midst. I got tired of their little innuendos."

"What insinuations?" Indignation marred his face.

Orion sat on the couch. Sullenly, he looked up at Bas. "Where would you like me to start? I didn't appreciate being called your pet. I thought our friendship meant more to you." He tried to hide his hurt feelings, but even he could hear it in his voice. "The best was when one of them called me a 'mongrel'. And you did nothing"

Surprise flickered in Bastien's face. "Why didn't you come tell me; why did you have to take off that way?"

"Tell you? You were standing right there. I'm sure you heard every word."

"I *didn't* hear them. If I had, I would have said something."

Orion's temper spiked. "How could you *not* hear them?"

"Because I've had to socialize with my father's associates since I was a child. I learned early to shut them out." He gestured to the air around him. "It's all white noise to me." He sat beside Orion on the couch. "I was worried about you."

He could scent no duplicity on Bastien. Remorse for leaving him started to gather in Orion's stomach. "What would you have said, if you had heard?"

"I would have asked him to leave." Bastien laughed. "Then, once outside, I would have decked him."

"And risk your father's business associates?"

"In my father's home, we don't tolerate insults like that. He doesn't appreciate violence either. That's why I would have waited until we were outside to introduce him to my fist."

Orion snorted. "Now, you tell me."

"So, are we good?"

"Yeah, we're good." He tapped Bastien's knee with his fist.

When Bastien moved closer to him, his nostrils flared. "How come you smell like Miranda?"

"I grabbed her scarf by mistake." He pulled out the black material from his jacket pocket. "What's this about a mission tonight? Valadon wanted me to confer with you."

"Let me get the folder. There's a lot to update you with."

***

"Did you finish reading the book I gave you?"

"Almost." Miranda had hidden the book beneath a plank in her closet at Werehaven. This way, whenever she stayed over, she could reread the sections most important to her. Lizandra assured her no one else had access to her room and it would be safe there.

She leaned against the bookcase as Gabriel sat near the desk at the far end of the aisle of books in Valadon's archives. "What are you reading?"

"Just perusing some old medical books by Galen and Agrippa. Peralt, who spelled his name *Perrault*, back in the day, got himself in trouble by dismissing the teachings of the older physicians."

"Find anything of interest?"

"Yeah. Peralt was quite an anatomist. Before he did experiments on live beings, he worked on cadavers. His work was rudimentary, but he was one of the first to realize the potential medicinal worth of minerals such as mercury, arsenic and antimony, instead of all the plant-derived medicines most of the doctors used."

Miranda joined him at the small table.

"The thing about all his experiments, before he went mad...I think he was trying to find an antidote for vampirism."

"Before he tried poisoning them?"

"That's just it. The degree of poison was in the dosage. I don't think he was necessarily trying to maim or kill vampires, just desperately trying to find a cure...for himself, for others."

Miranda sympathized with Gabriel's plight. He, too, never wanted to become a vampire. "You do realize it's been almost four hundred years, and he never found one."

His face was downcast. "I know. I'm just saying he wasn't completely bad or evil. He did do some good with his research. He made strides where no one else did."

"Feeling sympathy for him?" Miranda worried Gabriel's goal of one day becoming human again was clouding his judgment.

"Maybe a little. I know he's a monster. I know he must be stopped." He shook his head, as if clearing his thoughts. "What about you? Did you find anything worthwhile in your reading?"

"Yeah, Peralt mentioned two others, Courant and Draxton, who also wrote about *Elementals*. I'm going to try to find their books, see if I can learn more."

Gabriel moved toward the stacks and retrieved a book on the shelf. "Check this one out. It's mostly history and politics of the time, but it makes mention of Peralt's patrons and others who shared some of his beliefs. And you might find *The Mystical Beliefs of the Rosicrucians* interesting. They say Peralt was a follower."

"I'm also looking for more books, personal accounts of the Inquisition." She grimaced. "So many innocents died."

"Peralt classified *Elementals* according to their abilities. He thought they had great healing abilities."

"Yeah, he also said we might have been derived from angels. Good and bad. And that the *Dark Elementals* used their abilities to harm and torment humans." What had really gotten to her was Peralt believed *Elementals* were natural alchemists capable of various transmutations. She gazed down at her hands and remembered when they looked like an eagle's talons.

Gabriel put the books on the table and took her hands. "You're not evil, Miranda. Evil is a choice." He kissed her knuckles. "Maybe Peralt was right; maybe there were *Dark Elementals* who used their gifts for evil. You're not one of them."

"Thanks. It just scares me when Peralt goes on about power. Can you imagine what kind of weapon people would turn us into if they knew?" Valadon came to mind, among others. "Listen, I'm going to take these and read in the sitting area by the fireplace. Let you continue your research in peace."

"Okay. But you would never be a weapon. You'd be a healer."

She smiled quietly and turned away.

"I'll be here if you need me for anything."

Nodding, Miranda moved from the biographies section to the histories. She passed on the books written in Latin, but the ones in French—thank God Valadon was originally from France—she could read. She considered asking Nick to join her. He understood a dozen languages, but she nixed the idea. What she was reading was still too personal to share. When she had the books she wanted, she made herself comfortable on the couch and started sorting through them.

Hours must have slipped by, and Miranda started to doze off. Her head spun with so much information, and she still didn't have all the answers she wanted. She'd contact Felicity about libraries in Europe housing rare books. See if she could help locate Draxton and Courant. Closing her eyes, Miranda leaned back against the pillows.

She knew she was dreaming as if she were suddenly thrust back in time. Darkness surrounded her as her spirit floated, unrestrained, through a narrow passageway. Touching the cold, damp wall of the cave, she sensed the natural vibrations were much stronger at this depth, unpolluted with the technological world. Even the magnetism in her hand was more intense, more wondrous. She could smell the old earth, smoke wafting through the air from the torches lighting her way. Power, strong and glorious, emanated from here.

Following the path before her, she heard music. The tones and pitch unfamiliar to human ears. When she turned a corner, she discovered a girl singing as she played a dulcimer. Others, similarly dressed in robes, joined in her chorus creating a song so beautiful in its purity, so striking in its clarity, it sent shivers up Miranda's arms and caused tears to form in her eyes.

In the grotto, a coven of *Elementals* were chanting. Incense was burning, scenting the air with lavender. Crystals were glowing, pulsing with life at their feet as they sang songs of the woods and nature.

The women were centered around a fire of red flames. *How odd!* Fire burned yellow and blue, but these flames were crimson, blood red. A woman with long dark hair chanted in a language foreign to Miranda—possibly Celtic. She kept repeating the words over and over as she raised her hands, invoking powers Miranda had no knowledge of. And then, with startling confidence, the dark-haired woman walked into the fire—unharmed, as if she bathed in the flames.

Miranda's heart beat out a staccato. A veil of darkness appeared and covered the coven, blanketing them in cold. Her breaths came hard and fast, fear turning her stomach as the power, unlike anything she'd ever felt before, pulsed along her skin, penetrating her to the bone. The signature alarming in its vibrancy.

Without warning, the dark-haired woman, wondrous and beautiful, terrifying and ethereal, turned and faced her. Her eyes glowed red as she stared straight at Miranda...and smiled. The woman's spirit reached out to her, and with her icy fingers, touched her arm. The infusion of energy shocking in its potency. But it was her voice, hauntingly familiar, as if emitted from an undiscovered world that truly jolted her as she whispered, "Welcome, sister."

Her heart thundering, Miranda screamed and woke in fright. Her mind trapped momentarily in that halfway state between the dream world and reality. As she gasped for breath, her teeth started chattering.

Strong arms surrounded her and held her close. She burrowed into his chest. The ocean, fierce and stalwart, cleansing with the scent of brine enveloped her, chasing away the awful smell of sulfur.

"It's all right. It was a dream, just a dream." Valadon's deep, melodic voice penetrated the thick haze. "You're ice cold." He wrapped an afghan around her and rubbed her arms. "Drink this. It will help warm you." He handed her a cup of steaming tea.

The warmth of the gas fireplace heated her face. The flames, yellow and blue, offered comfort and relief. She inhaled the soothing aroma of the tea and tried to take a sip, but she was shaking too much. Valadon's hands covered hers, and his strength seemed to imbue her with a sense of calm she so desperately needed.

"Thank you." Her voice sounded gravelly.

Valadon picked up her books. "*History of the Inquistion in France* and *The Malleus Maleficarum.*" He tossed the books on the coffee table. One brow lifted. "No wonder you had a nightmare."

"It felt real." She blew on her tea and sipped. "Too real."

"I'm sure it did. Want to tell me about it?"

Miranda didn't want to discuss it with anyone, not until she had time to process it. "Not really." She sat up and distanced herself from him. "It's kind of fragmented." When her breathing returned to normal and she could think clearly again, her anger surfaced.

She put down the tea on the coffee table. "What you did to Remare was unconscionable."

He breathed deeply. "Perhaps. But I'm not used to having my orders disobeyed." His voice authoritative. "He's a member of my House and, like everyone else, subject to my rules."

"No matter who gets hurt in the process?" Her spine straightened. "He didn't betray you."

"He knew how I felt about you." His beautiful emerald eyes turned turbulent. "He never should have touched you."

"For your information, he didn't even *like* me when we first met. He thought I worked for the HOL. Tried to kill me." She pointed to the center floor of the archives. "Remember?"

"Yes, I remember. When did hate turn to lust?"

"It's more than that." She pushed the afghan away. "We never intended to hurt you. We tried to stay away from each other." She raised her hand dismissively. "That didn't work out."

"Why?" Visibly straining to control his anger, he asked, "Of all the men in the world, why my second? Why Remare?"

She huffed. "I wish I knew." But she did. If it had only been lust, she could have walked away a long time ago. But it was so much more, and something she'd given a great deal of thought to. "His courage, his unrelenting need to protect those he cares for most." She stared at Valadon. "His humor, however twisted it is at times. His resolute loyalty...to you. And to me."

"Remare's not known for his fidelity. At least not with the fairer sex. He's never stayed with a woman for long." Valadon shook his head. "This won't last."

Miranda thought differently. "That's my choice, isn't it?"

Hands tightening, he stood and moved to the fireplace, staring into the flames.

Miranda sensed Valadon's inner turmoil. There were so many conflicting emotions emanating from the High Lord. His anger was barely restrained, but underneath, he warred against himself. He loved Remare like a brother, more than he ever felt for Brandon; a bond he believed unbreakable. They'd laughed, lamented and celebrated their victories and defeats throughout the long centuries together. And each had worked side by side building ValCorp into the empire it was.

He peered over his shoulder at her. She was humbled by what she saw in his eyes. He loved her, too, was enchanted by her in ways she couldn't comprehend. Desire, strong and unyielding, beat heavily in his chest. His longing to hold, cherish and protect made Valadon who he was. He ruled over his vast empire the best he could, often making sacrifices that cost him dearly to ensure the safety of his people. Such sorrow and loss were ingrained in the very fiber of his being. Deep down, beneath the façade of the High Lord, beat a heart yearning to love and be loved.

Miranda had to breathe deeply to suppress her own need to give comfort to a being of such unfathomable power. She'd rarely experienced such profound sympathy for someone, and her own heart wept for the pain she'd caused. She looked away, taking solace in her own inner solitude.

"This is a conversation that will have to wait until another time. There's something you should know."

"What?"

"We're going to war with the HOL."

Chapter Twenty-Nine

Miranda had heard about Valadon's communications room from Cyra and Morel. Knew it existed but never imagined it would resemble something like NASA's operations room. Toward the rear of the room, Valadon and she stood behind the glass partition separating them from the Torians. All equipment was state of the art, high tech. A slew of computer monitors lined the rows of desks on either side of a huge screen dominating the far wall. In tiered rows, sat at least a hundred Torians. She smiled when she spotted Orion with Bastien. Apparently, they had resolved their differences.

Her breath caught when Remare made eye contact with her. He then continued discussing mission tactics. The Torians were rapt in his explanations. A pang of pride stirred in her belly for Valadon's chief strategist. Using a laser pen, he directed their attention to specific access points on the enlarged diagram of an island on the screen. "Our people will position themselves here, here and here."

"That looks like Governors Island." Miranda remembered the island from when she and Lizandra took a boat ride on the city's Circle Line cruise ship. "I thought it was abandoned."

"Very good, Miranda. It was at one point." Valadon crossed his arms over his chest. "Not anymore."

The schematic changed, and Remare gestured to a large room and two long rows of compartments. "We believe the main research area is on Level Two. If any of our people are still alive, they are being held in these containment cells."

Admiration bloomed in her heart as Remare continued with their plans. He was methodical, focused and precise in his approach. Whenever any of the Torians asked a question, he explained in as much detail as he could, showing respect and commendation. What a great professor he would have made! NYU would have been thrilled to have him teach classes on strategies and tactics.

She whispered to Valadon, "How were you able to access all this information?"

"We've had ongoing investigations and surveillance of known HOL members and their affiliates for some time now. Irina was most persuasive in convincing one of the Order's leaders to turn over certain documents. She and Remare once made an awesome team." He stroked his chin as he watched Remare. "But not all relationships are meant to last."

Miranda sullenly considered his words. Images of Gavin and Lizandra came to mind.

"Unfortunately, due to the injury she sustained in the attack the other night, Irina will be sitting out our endeavor. She's quite angry with me."

It dawned on Miranda their plans were far more imminent than she had thought. "When is your operation scheduled for?"

He turned and his turbulent eyes met hers. "Tonight, after nightfall."

Her heart lurched. *Tonight!* Fear made her skin prickle.

One of the Torians caught her eye. She gestured to a man in the back row. "Isn't that..."

"Jeremy. Yes, our spokesperson for many of our products. He said he was tired of being known for just his handsome face. He's been training alongside some of the Torians. Tristan says he's become an ace shot with phenomenal accuracy. He volunteered for this operation. Wants to prove himself worthy of becoming a Torian."

"Do you think he's ready? He looks so young."

"All reports suggest he is. Even Remare is impressed with his skills and intelligence."

At that moment, Irina looked over her shoulder at them. Ice formed in her eyes.

"She's livid."

"She'll have to deal with it. Tristan said she was off on some of her shots in the range. I won't send anyone out who isn't one hundred percent."

Miranda noted the look Irina gave Tristan. "I wouldn't put those two together any time soon."

Valadon nodded.

Remare ended his session. "If there are no further questions, everyone suit up. Meet in the armory. Make sure you have all the equipment I've outlined. Let's go." In farewell, he tilted his head in her direction.

Aching for him, she flattened her hand against the glass.

Valadon's next words surprised her. "I'll be going with them on this mission."

"You can't. You're their ruler." What little Miranda knew of battle strategies was that the king on the chessboard rarely moved. He sent out his pawns, his knights and bishops in the vanguard to fight for him while he stayed safely behind.

"Worried, Miranda?" He smirked. "I assure you I'm more than prepared." He bent to whisper in her ear. "I've been in continual practice. And I never stay in the shadows, for very long."

Miranda's breath froze as his power seared against hers.

When all the men and women had departed and Valadon met with Remare to go over a few last-minute details, Miranda waited by the elevator. She wasn't sure this was a good idea and considered leaving. But, as Remare approached, her heart sped up, and her stomach flipped the way it usually did when he was nearby. Part of her was still angry, hurt. But a larger part was worried for him. He was going into battle. What if he got harmed? She'd seen what the HOL was capable of. Witnessed how bloodied his back had been when they had captured and tortured him.

"I didn't realize you were moving against the HOL so soon."

His desire for her was palpable. "It was inevitable. The time for negotiations is long over. They've attacked us too many times. Killed too many innocents." One corner of his mouth lifted. "Concerned?"

Was she ever. There was so much she wanted to tell him, the words lost in her throat. She almost reached to palm his cheek but restrained her hand. Three simple words came to mind she'd longed to say to him. "Don't get killed." *I love you!*

He smirked, with a wicked glint in his eyes, as if reading her mind. "I wasn't planning to." *I love you, too!*

When the elevator dinged, he stepped inside, and before the doors closed, he blew her a kiss. "My sorceress." He nodded farewell. "I'll see you when I get back."

Miranda wanted to thank him for the Jeep, but the doors closed too soon. Biting her lip, she exhaled and leaned against the wall as Valadon and Irina walked toward her.

"I am in *excellent* condition." Irina's voice dripped outrage, her accent more pronounced. "It's because of me we have the information necessary to proceed."

"I'm not arguing with you. Sit this one out, Irina. I promise you, there will be other battles." Valadon bent to kiss her forehead.

"But—"

"My word is final." Valadon's resonating tone brokered no argument. "Help man the communications room with

Morel and Bree. This is our home, Irina. I'm trusting you to make certain of its security."

The threatening look Irina gave her made Miranda shudder. No wonder they called her *The Ice Queen*. She felt as if a thin coat of frost covered her skin.

As she stormed off, Gabriel joined Valadon. "Ready?"

Surprised, Miranda never imagined Gabriel went on missions, but she supposed a good medic was essential to their operation. "You're going with them?"

"Yes. You've seen me fight, Miranda. You know I can hold my own. Besides, if anyone gets injured, I can treat them." He hoisted his backpack containing his medical supplies.

When the two of them stepped inside the elevator, Valadon held the door. "I want you to stay here tonight. You can join Morel in the communications room or resume your studies in the archives, if you wish. But you might want to take a night off from your research."

Miranda nodded. "Be careful. Both of you."

Valadon bowed his head in her direction. "We'll see you in a few hours."

The doors closed, and a dread of ice formed in the pit of her stomach. *I hope so!* There was so much more she had wanted to say to them. But she'd been too frozen to even formulate her thoughts. She considered going back to the archives, but nixed the idea. She was probably going to have enough nightmares.

She sighed then smiled. Right now, there was only one place she wanted to be.

***

Miranda strode along the training area, admiring the swords mounted on the wall. She remembered how she and Remare had once danced with steel in this room. She could almost feel his touch upon her arm, his breath along her neck, hear his words of encouragement. Those moments were precious to her. She opened the door to Remare's museum-worthy sword room. She flicked the light on and was in awe of his collection of weapons. He'd fought in so many wars, survived so many battles. Strolling down the aisle, she perused his assortment of jeweled daggers when a sound had her turning.

Irina stood by the door. She took one of the long knives from the wall and started playing with it. "He's been acquiring these for centuries."

The hairs rose on her arm, but Miranda refused to give in to her fears. She knew she was in the presence of a predator, one who disliked her. Immensely. Cautiously, she said, "It's quite an assortment. Some of these should be in a museum."

Irina's eyes tracked her as she glided farther into the room. There was only one entrance, and Irina was blocking it. If she locked Miranda in, there was no way to get out. Her pulse sped up.

"Did he sword dance with you? He's quite remarkable with a blade in his hands."

Miranda wasn't about to be baited. "How's your shoulder?"

A growl emerged from Irina's throat. Her anger still tangible at not being allowed to see her mission through. "What do you care?" *The Ice Queen* moved steadily toward her with the knife in her hand.

"I can fix it."

That stopped her dead in her tracks. "How? The muscles were torn. The bone fractured. It takes time to heal, even for a vampire."

According to Gabriel, *Elementals* had great healing abilities. "Want to let me try?" She smirked with a hint of bravado. "Or are you too afraid?" She moved slowly toward her as Irina narrowed her eyes then lay down the knife. "I have certain...abilities." She raised her palm to hover above Irina's biceps to her shoulder. Her hand was glowing, and from the look on Irina's face, the heat was helping to mend the injury.

"How were Valadon and the others getting to Governors Island?"

Irina rotated her shoulder. "We have several Zodiacs—motorized rubber rafts."

Confident Irina wasn't going to kill her, she asked, "Want to join them?"

The curve of Irina's lips suggested they leave now. They made their way down to the parking garage, but the steel gates had sealed them in. Miranda shook the metal, but it remained firmly in place. She searched for the control mechanism as Irina cursed in Russian. Just as she was about to zap it, they heard footsteps approaching.

"Halt!" Morel advanced to them. "You know, I kind of expected this from Irina, but I did not think you would pull something so stupid, Miranda."

She offered the blond vampire a wry smile. "We thought Valadon and Remare might need some help."

"They've got it under control. If you were listening to the voice transmissions in the communications room, like you were supposed to be, you would know exactly what was going on. Now, if you'll accompany me." He didn't wait for a reply but took them both by the arm and escorted them back to the war room. "I suppose Valadon didn't tell you he put the place on lock down after they left?"

No, he hadn't mentioned that little detail.

***

"They've made it to the second level." Bree greeted them as they entered. "Encountered some resistance, but situation is dealt with."

"Have they located Jacob?" Morel resumed his seat at one of the monitors.

"Not yet. They're checking cells, now. Fuck! Gunfire! They're under attack!"

Miranda's heart was in her throat. She tried to read the blips on the computer but didn't understand the thermal images in different colors.

"We'll put it up on the main viewing screen." Morel gestured to the front of the room.

Erratic images of smoke and shadows appeared, obscuring the progress of the vampires as they infiltrated the facility. Lights flashed as more shots rang out. Bodies hit the ground. There was no sign of either Remare or Valadon. But Miranda heard one voice, Aiden, Bree's husband, giving orders for them to move out. The camera attached to his shoulder was recording the events as they unfolded. Sirens screamed in warning. Where the hell was Remare?

Her pulse pounded. She knew it was crazy, she wasn't a warrior, but she wanted to be there. With her power, she could have helped clear away the smoke so they could see.

Aiden used his equipment to electronically open a cell door. Through the static, she heard his voice. "Bring the body bags; these two are already dead."

Miranda's eyes were glued to the screen, searching for any sign of Remare.

Gregori came rushing up, and the view split into two images. "Get them out of there, now. This place is rigged to blow. Look at the cables." His camera pointed at the ceiling to something resembling C-4 explosives.

Morel shouted for them to retreat. "All units report in, now. Fall back. I repeat, fall back."

She could hear Aiden repeating the message to the rest of the Torians.

Bas' voice sounded in the distance. "We got him." Gregori turned and captured an image of a black wolf running alongside Bas. "We found Jacob; he's alive. Gabriel's treating him, but he's in bad shape. He's been shot with some sort of dart, but he's breathing."

Miranda watched as the screen split, again, and two Torians she didn't know half-dragged, half-carried a prisoner out.

Remare's voice rang out. "We've located Peralt. In pursuit. No shots fired. Any shots you hear will be coming from us."

Aiden shouted into his mic. "The place is wired with explosives! You have no time, no time at all. Get the hell out of there!"

Bastien must have decided to assist Remare, because more images from his camera appeared on screen. He was running toward the end of a long corridor then turned down another. When an enemy soldier attacked him, Orion jumped up and tore the man's arm with his fangs and then went for his throat. Blood filled the camera as the dead man fell to the ground.

Miranda watched in terror as Remare faced off against Peralt, who was trying to flee with a briefcase full of files. Images of Bas fighting an enemy soldier lit up the screen. Suddenly, a guard came out of nowhere and attacked Remare. She recognized him from the night of the gala. He was the human who had broken Irina's arm. A fight broke out with each throwing punches. Remare flung him against the wall, his attacker's body slumping to the floor. They were moving toward the back wall. Someone hit a switch, and a portion of the back wall moved to reveal a hidden passage.

Peralt quickly fled through the portal, Remare on his heels. He must not have been wearing a camera because things went dark. Where was Bastien?

More gun shots rang out. Glass started flying all over the place as explosions rang out.

Miranda was frantic. "Get them out of there! They don't know the place is exploding."

"They know." Morel's fingers flew over the keyboard. "Alpha team. Report."

Static sounded, then, "We got Asanti's son. He's safe with us. We're bringing him back to ValCorp. Prep the infirmary. We have casualties."

Bastien's camera showed Remare in pursuit of Peralt. Each was firing off rounds. Apparently, the HOL had motorized rafts waiting for them, as well. One was farther down in the distance. A man with a light beard and mustache came into focus. Miranda gasped. The same man at the gala who had raised his glass to her. She heard one of the men in the boat say, "We need to leave, now. We can't wait for the others."

He gave the signal, their boat disappearing into the night.

Peralt was running for his boat when, suddenly, Valadon appeared out of nowhere and stepped in front of him. "Peralt. You escaped the king's justice once. You won't again. For your crimes against the living, I sentence you to death."

Peralt sneered at him. "Kill me and you'll never get the answers you seek." His eyes drifted to where the boats had been. "He knows the formula. He'll use it against you. Only I know the antidote."

"Don't be so sure of that."

Miranda watched as blood began to seep from Peralt's mouth and knew Valadon was using his mental abilities to shatter Peralt's bones. Peralt raised his hand, in a desperate attempt to combat the High Lord's power, but to no avail. Valadon had him.

Peralt crumbled to his knees, blood spewing forth from his lips. Remare handed Valadon his sword. Miranda saw the steel glint as it rose in the air.

Gabriel came running up to them. "*No!* Don't!"

But it was too late. Valadon moved so fast his movements a blur on screen.

However, the image of Peralt's decapitated head rolling away had been clear enough.

Miranda slumped down in her chair. There were so many questions she needed answers to. About *Elementals*, about his research. In one fell swoop of the sword, those hopes had died.

Gabriel groaned. "You should have let him live. We could have questioned him." His look of despondency was clear to her. "We may have learned much from him."

"He escaped justice once before, and many suffered because of it." Valadon faced him. "I would not permit that to happen a second time."

Remare wiped the blood off his sword with a handkerchief and sheathed it.

Gregori came up to the riverbank and yelled, "We need to leave, now!"

Valadon, Remare and a few of their men entered the raft. Gregori reported in, "We killed most of their men. One of the prisoners died en route to ValCorp. Bastien and Orion were in pursuit of one of their boats, but they had a chopper waiting and got away."

"All right." Valadon gestured to the boats. "Let's get back to ValCorp."

Miranda heard, more than saw, the explosions going off in the facility as their rafts came back to Manhattan.

Chapter Thirty

In the infirmary, Gabriel finished applying a dressing to a Torian Miranda didn't know. She made her way to the far end of the room where a crowd of onlookers were watching as Dr. Amira desperately tried to halt the spread of the poison in Jacob's leg. "I can't get the toxin to relent. It's mutating too fast. We may need to amputate."

A tic started in Remare's jaw as Valadon's head lowered in sympathy.

Gabriel moved in to inspect the leg. "Aspirator."

Miranda moved closer for a clearer view.

"Done twice. We tried to suction the poison out, but we can't get it all. It's moving at an accelerated rate. I don't see any other recourse but removal of the leg."

"*No!*" Jacob screamed in agony. "I don't want to lose my leg! Father, don't let them." His plaintive cries were soul-searing and had Miranda's skin breaking out in gooseflesh. "Promise me, they won't cut my leg off!"

Asanti tried to sound reassuring, but tears formed in his eyes. "The doctors know best."

Amira looked to Gabriel. "Tourniquet."

He shook his head. "Temporary."

Empathy had Miranda gazing at her hand. The tips of her fingers were glowing. She remembered how she'd healed Irina. "Let me try something." She moved closer to Jacob's bed. She met Gabriel's eyes. "I might know a way to save the leg."

He nodded his encouragement.

"How?" Dr. Amira demanded.

"We need to clear the room." Miranda faced the High Lord. "Please, Valadon."

Nodding, he gave the command, and his soldiers left the area. The only ones remaining were Amira, Gabriel, Remare, Valadon and Asanti. She addressed Remare, "Remember how I helped heal your leg when you were injured?"

A small smile. "Let her work. I've seen what Miranda can do. If she can help, she will."

"Everyone get rid of all metal objects: keys, pens, coins, anything like that. Get it out of here." Miranda could feel the vibrations in her arm as everyone scurried, removing equipment, monitoring devices, and other objects.

"Remare, hold down Jacob's shoulders. Valadon, hold down his other leg. Asanti, stay behind me." She motioned for Gabriel and Amira to flank Asanti.

"I'm sorry." She stroked Jacob's good leg. "This is probably going to hurt. You may have to lose your toenails."

Sweat ran down his face. "Please don't take my leg." Pain lanced his voice. "Don't do it."

"I won't. I'm going to extract the poison."

"How?" Amira inquired.

"I've read Peralt's books. His toxins contained three base metals: mercury, antimony and arsenic. The sulfates he used act as a catalyst. Where other doctors of the time used plant extracts, Peralt experimented with minerals."

"How do you know this?" Dr. Amira questioned.

"It's what I do. I read, and I know things. Some useful, some not."

Miranda moved closer to Jacob's leg and ran her hand over his skin. Closing her eyes, she breathed deeply and focused on identifying the deadly elements until they were clear in her mind. When she opened her eyes, she signaled for Remare and Valadon to press down on Jacob's body, effectively pinning him to the mattress.

"Can we kill the lights a little, please?"

Someone had them lowered. "I'm sorry for the pain I cause you." She used the bio-magnetic energy in her hand, and his toenails were pulled out.

The scent of his blood rent the room. She inhaled. "I can smell the sulfur. It's pungent, so is the antimony. Pass me the plastic salver," she said to Gabriel, who handed her the small tray.

"The trick," she whispered, "is to separate the toxins from the natural elements in his blood."

Tiny globules of black emerged from the wounds in his toes.

Someone asked, "How is she doing this?"

"By scent. I had to take a class in paint artists used. I know chemical compounds and what they smell like." She didn't want to tell them she could identify the various metals by the pitch they emitted. Metal was part of the earth, and the earth's natural elements vibrated at different levels. *Try explaining that to someone!*

More black dripped down Jacob's foot. She used her power to transfer the toxins to the tray. "You may want to analyze that. If there's synthetics included, I don't know what they are." As long as the poison's base was metallic, she could work it. Anything not natural, she had no control over.

"Look." Dr. Amira pointed. "The poison is moving down his leg." His veins, which had appeared black, were returning to their normal color.

Asanti gently put his hand on her shoulder. Immediately, her power diminished. She shook, nearly screaming, "Don't touch me!" Her voice was harsh as she shrugged him off. "It throws off my ability to focus."

"I'm sorry." Asanti quickly apologized. "I just wanted to see my son's leg."

"Don't touch her, Asanti." Valadon's voice was soothing. "She needs to concentrate."

Miranda nodded her thanks to Valadon then continued drawing out the poison. Several minutes passed as she used her magnetism to draw the poison from Jacob's leg. Someone took the tray and replaced it with another. When that one was filled, another appeared. Miranda's arm began to tingle. She knew the backlash from using her gift was going to hurt, but she didn't care. She didn't want to see this innocent, handsome kid lose his leg.

When she was done, she turned to Gabriel. "Someone's going to have to bandage his toes. He might need stitches."

"I'll do it.' He exchanged places with her.

Miranda faced Valadon. "How'd I do?"

She never heard his response as gray covered her vision, passing out in his arms. The last thing she heard was Gabriel yelling, "She's having another brain bleed!"

***

Hours later, Miranda woke to the heavenly scent of country woods and the spicy aroma of cooked meat. "Something smells good." When she cracked an eye, Remare was hovering over her with a bowl in his hands. The Oriental décor of his bedroom was a welcome change from the infirmary.

"Most people ask where are they when they first wake from passing out."

"I'm not most people." She smiled. "And I know where I am."

He sat beside her on the bed. "How do you feel?"

"Groggy." Sitting up, she put a hand to her stomach. "And strangely hungry." Noticing her lack of clothes, she asked, "Why am I naked?"

"I do believe you are the first person in my bed to ever ask that." At her frown, he amended, "And the last." He handed her a glass of water, which she greedily drank. Then, Remare took a forkful of meat and brought it to her lips. "Here, taste this. Escher prepared you beef stroganoff. The protein will do you good."

"Mmmm, yummy. Is there wine in this?"

"Possibly. Escher put vitamin supplements in the food. Gabriel insisted you have them. He wouldn't leave until your vitals were normal."

"He worries." After another bite, she asked, "What happened to my clothes?"

"When your nose began to bleed, drops stained your shirt, and a few got on your pants. Escher is having them laundered as we speak."

Deciding she could feed herself, she took the fork and bowl from him. "How's Jacob?"

"Well. Gabriel said there's been no recurrence of the toxins in his blood. You were right about the metallic substances. While you were sleeping, Jacob and his father stopped by to offer their sincerest thanks for your efforts. I told them you were resting. When you are fully recovered, Asanti requests you come to his house, so he can thank you in person."

Placing the empty bowl on the bedside table, she had the strangest yearning for something sweet. "I think I could kill for a KitKat bar right about now."

"No need for bloodshed." He reached up on his dresser. "I think I have some chocolates here with your name on them."

She quickly undid the wrapper. "Thanks." When the last remnants of the fog in her brain cleared, she reached for his hand. "I was worried about you, earlier tonight. Morel let us watch the videos of your attack on the HOL facility. It was scary."

"Morel told me he found you and Irina trying to bust out of the garage after Valadon put the compound on lockdown. Exactly what was it you were planning to do?"

Miranda tried not to look guilty. "We were going to rent jet skis and see if there was any way...we could help you." She cringed when she saw his disparaging look.

He exhaled. "When ValCorp is on lockdown, there is no way in or out. You would not have been able to leave."

"Yeah, we kind of figured that out."

He massaged her hand. "Miranda, you are not a soldier." At her intended interruption, he added, "I know you can handle yourself in a tough situation, but tonight, we went up against trained mercenaries. I would not have wanted you there. It would have been impossible to concentrate on what I needed to do." He stroked her cheek. "It was difficult enough thinking about you."

"Likewise, watching you fighting with Peralt. When you ran into the dark passageway, and we couldn't see what was happening, it scared the hell out of me."

"There was no need to be frightened. All of the Torians were in constant communication with one another. However," he sighed, "there was one moment when I hesitated. I've never done that before in battle."

"Why did you?"

"Because, before I met you, I relished the chase and the ensuing fight. I never gave much thought to the idea of injury." He held her eyes. "Now, I have something to live for. A woman I very much wanted to get back to. And I knew you would be very much upset with me if I was harmed in any way."

"That's why I wanted to join you."

One corner of his mouth lifted. "Does that mean I am forgiven?" He reached for a book on his table. "I came across a poem I thought you might like. Have you ever heard of

Yevgeny Yeytushenko? He's a Russian poet. The title of his poem is 'Colors'. He read it to her, his voice soothing music to her ears.

"Lovely poem." The words echoing in her mind, she knew what he was saying. Without her in his life, he was a hollow man, who only saw the world in shades of darkness, a cold, desolate place. Alone. But, with her, the world was beautiful, alive in shimmering, vibrant colors. A world he wanted to belong to. His way of telling her that he loved her.

"Yes, you're forgiven." Of course he was; who wouldn't be after such a heartfelt poem? Her heart aching for him, she took his hand in hers. "As angry as I was, you're a part of me now. I don't think I'll ever be able to get you out of my system."

"As I, you." His hand caressing her cheek and neck, he brushed his lips over hers.

Miranda was lost in his embrace and returned his kiss, ever so grateful he survived the battle, knowing there was every possibility he might not have.

Breaking from him, she said, "I missed you. Part of me is still stung, but I want you, anyway." She smirked. "Even the bad parts. I talked to Valadon about you. I told him we didn't betray him; we both love him in our own way. He wanted to know why I chose you."

"What did you tell him?"

"The truth. I didn't like you much when we first met. You tried to kill me. Remember, on the archives' floor?"

"I remember." A sexy growl broke from his mouth. "Even then, I wanted you."

"Hmm. Strange way of showing it. I think it was then that I started caring. You were so fiercely determined to protect Valadon. Admirable trait. Later on, you sat with me. Explained your history. At my house. About the HOL. I liked the way you spoke. And then, when we were in the archives searching for the missing painting, the way you simply held my hand. It sent thrills throughout my body."

He kissed her knuckles.

"Pretty hard not to fall for you."

"For the record," his eyes glinted, "I would not have killed you."

"Your fangs were inches from my throat."

"I know. I desired to taste you. Badly. But, even then, I hesitated. A few moments before that, I watched how you stood rapt on the top floor of the archives in awe of the paintings. I thought you were an angel from heaven sent to torment me." His lids grew heavy. "I wanted you."

"You fought with me. Over Peralt's book."

"Yes. Foreplay. Frustrated that I couldn't have you. Angry at myself for coveting you so very much."

She stroked his jaw. "Why didn't you tell me?"

"Because you belonged to another."

"I don't anymore. Now, I'm yours. Completely." She kissed him, again, savoring his taste and the way he held her in his arms. "I think it's going to be okay with Valadon. He's hurting. He still has feelings for me. I told him what he did to you was reprehensible. He agreed. I think he's sorry for what he did. He acted out of anger, hurt. But I think he loves us too much to cause either one of us any more harm."

"That remains to be seen. But I will talk with him, soon." He smiled wickedly at her. "If I am very gentle and move very slowly, will you want me?"

Miranda's heart was racing. Did she want him? When *didn't* she want him? "I always want you, Remare. But let me take the top position. I want to make love to you."

He stood and slowly undressed. Standing naked, Remare was a work of art. Miranda breathed deeply. How the master artists would have loved capturing his likeness.

Every inch of him was male perfection. He lay down beside her.

Reaching over him, she lowered the lights. Her eyes were still sensitive from using her powers.

"Do not exert yourself, Mir-randa. You've had an ordeal tonight."

"You fought like a tiger tonight. You sure you're up for this?" she teased.

"Lay down, and I'll show you."

"Nuh-uh. I want to ride you." She slid on top of him.

"Okay, cowgirl." He stroked his cock for emphasis. "Your steed is waiting for you."

Smiling, she leaned over and kissed him. "I don't know what I would do without you."

"An unpleasant thought." Grinding his teeth, he growled. "Ride me or I will take you."

Miranda positioned his cock at her core. Keeping her eyes on his handsome face, she gently sank down on him, enjoying the way his eyelids slowly closed in silent joy. Her body, already damp with arousal, smoothly welcomed him. Every inch of his cock stroking against nerve endings ready and waiting to explode, crying out for the touch only he could provide.

Whenever they'd been in bed together, Remare's body temperature increased as if he were absorbing her warmth and reflecting it back to her. She lightly ran her fingers along the fine line of hair ending at his navel. She loved the way his abs tightened under her touch until her hands caressed his pecs. She bent and kissed his nipple. When he moaned in pleasure, she gently bit down then did the same to his other pec.

"Stop tormenting me, you sorceress, and ride me."

She laughed. "That reminds me. I like my new car. Thanks. I knew it was mine when I saw the license plate, SOR C RS."

His fingers bit into her waist in his attempt to make her move faster. "It was either that or WI C WO. Witchy-woman. I prefer my sorceress."

Miranda laughed then bent down close to him, her finger stroking his lips. "You are one sexy devil. I don't think I've ever met anyone who does to me what you do." Hands on his pecs, she emulated the way he moved when he was on top. He could reach inner nerves no one else ever had. He made her feel hotter and more alive than she'd ever felt before. Oh, God, she needed this. Needed him.

He used his hands to position her hips and helped her with her circular motion. When she was able to maintain a rhythm pleasurable to them both, he stroked her nipples, teasing and tugging, until she threw her head back and moaned.

Sitting up, Remare increased their pace. He always knew when she was on the verge of coming and would slow things down to make it last, but not tonight. When she almost screamed out his name, he covered her mouth and kissed her senseless. Three strokes later, he shuddered inside her, his release coating her inner muscles.

Miranda inhaled his masculine, woodsy scent. He tilted her head to face him as he made a small cut over his left pec. "Drink, Miranda."

She hesitated for just a second, the longing in his voice encouraging her to do what he desired. She latched onto him and sucked down his life's essence. Her old aversion to blood no longer viable. He needed to have her feed from him. His instinct to provide for his mate was incredibly strong. So, she gave him what he wanted then closed the tiny wound with her saliva.

"Thank you, Mir-randa."

She laid her head on his shoulder, holding him close to her. "You're my heaven."

"Mine, too." He kissed the top of her head. "You're the only who makes me forget the rest of the world when we make love." Slowly, he disengaged from her and went to the bathroom. He used a warm washcloth to clean her then covered her with the blankets.

"Could you get me some more water or juice? I'm thirsty."

He returned with a small bottle of cranberry juice. "I remembered you liked to drink vodka and cranberry juice." He opened it and handed it to her.

She drank nearly half the liquid. "Thanks."

He joined her under the covers. Miranda stroked his chest, enjoying the beat of his heart under her hand. With Remare beside her, she really did feel like she was in heaven. Even the air around them smelled pure and good, as if their lovemaking created a perfume like no other. It was peaceful, serene, and lulled her into a deep sleep.

Chapter Thirty-One

Lord Valadon sat back in his chair and reviewed the tapes of the raid on Governors Island. From the report on his desk, Remare had done his usual exemplary job evaluating the performance of his Torians. Each had done his or her job splendidly, according to their procedures. Even the younger soldiers had done remarkably well, special mention given to Jeremy, who had turned out to be quite a marksman. However, Valadon's attention was focused on another. Smaller than most of his soldiers, the young female was almost as adept with weapons as Jeremy, but she moved stealthier, lighter on her feet, more cautious. The others barely saw her.

He pulled up her file. She had been working for him for nearly five years in his fashion department under Cesare. Her work was unique and a hit with the younger clientele. He was curious why someone with such creative tendencies would want to become a Torian. Apparently, her brother was one of the missing, and she wanted to do what she could to find him. He almost granted her request to continue training with the mid-level soldiers when another idea surfaced. *She would make an excellent agent!*

After information circulated about the missing vampires and the carnage the HOL was capable of, several of his employees had requested to join the Torians. He was proud of them and their desire to protect all that was precious to him. Presently, he had enough soldiers. But, as for Carla, he would see to her training, make sure she could handle the demands his operatives had to deal with. He gazed over her report: Highly intelligent, resourceful, analytical. Her scores were off the chart. He nodded. Yes, he would assign her to a very special unit.

A knock at his door. "Gabriel."

"I have the preliminary reports you wanted on the toxins." He shook his head. "Miranda was spot on in her assessment of the base metals found in Jacob's blood." He sat and handed Valadon a file. "But there were also some synthetic chemicals. I've isolated some of them as compounds used in common household cleaners."

"I see."

"I still think it unfortunate you couldn't keep Peralt alive long enough for questioning. Coming up with an antidote to such a fast-moving catalyst will take some time, if one is possible at all. I've never seen anything mutate quite so rapidly."

Hope arose in his heart for his son. "So, will you be staying on with us, then?"

"No. My work at the foundation is very important to me."

"You could work on this at your leisure. No pressure will be put upon you."

Gabriel sighed. "Has it escaped your notice we get along better without me living here?"

"You wouldn't have to live here. But you could continue with your research in the labs. All resources would be made available to you."

Leaning back, Gabriel seemed to consider his offer.

"We have several apartments throughout Manhattan if you so choose to move closer."

"Let me get back to you on that one. I must admit, it was great seeing the guys, again. And Miranda."

"She is healthy, yes?"

"Yes. Unusual heartrate, though. Her biorhythms slowed down a great deal when she was sleeping; I almost thought she was one of us."

"The body does what it needs to repair itself. No more bleeding?"

"No, it's as if she was in some sort of stasis. I monitored her vitals. They're all within normal tendencies, now." He snorted. "Remare watched over her until I said she was doing well, then he moved her to his room."

"He did what?"

"Said she could relax better in his room than in the infirmary." Gabriel sat back in his chair. "You knew about them, didn't you?"

"I had my suspicions. He's quite fond of her."

"It's more than that, and she feels the same about him. Even when we were together, she called out his name in her sleep."

"Even then?" *How long had they been lovers?* Valadon's eyes narrowed. "Did she ever talk to you about him?"

"No. And I never asked." Gabriel scoffed. "Probably should have, though."

"You've done good work; you should get some sleep."

"I will. I'm going to go back to apartment now. My East Side apartment."

"As you wish. Thank you." When his son turned to leave, he stopped him. "Gabriel. My offer still stands if you should ever reconsider."

He nodded. "I know."

"Did you ever forgive me?" Valadon lightly brushed his fingers over his neck. He knew Gabriel understood what he was referring to.

"I don't dwell on it as much as I used to." He shrugged. "I guess letting go is part of the forgiving process, huh?"

"It is." Valadon kept his emotions in check. "I wish you good fortune in all your endeavors...son."

"I wish you the same, *Dad.*" He winked and then was gone.

For the first time in a long time, Valadon felt hopeful, one day, Gabriel would, indeed, return to him. Reaching inside his desk, he retrieved the leather-bound book Tristan had found buried under some debris during the raid. The fringes had been burned a little, but the title was clear enough: *Journal de Francis Peralt.* His lips curved. Perhaps, when he was finished reading, he would make it a gift for Gabriel.

Not wanting to be alone anymore, Valadon decided to visit his Torians. It was nearly daybreak, and most would be asleep, but some would still be awake.

When he got to Remare's door, he hesitated and thought about knocking but decided to pull the shadows around him and enter furtively. The aroma of sex greeted him. Gliding up the stairs, he stared down at Miranda. Remare spooned her from behind, the sheets covering them from the waist down. They were naked.

Valadon closed his eyes as his heart thundered, his emotions threatening to strangle him. Anguish, frustration, jealousy assaulted him from different angles. But the one emotion surprising him more than all the others combined was...love. He had deep affection for Miranda, wanted her, prayed she would come to him. She hadn't. Instead, she had chosen another.

Remare was his closest friend, his brother in all things, save blood. He'd never meant to betray Valadon's trust, but he too had fallen for the beautiful *Elemental.* Something died inside Valadon at the sight of his two beloveds together; he wondered if it was hope.

He left before his warring emotions got the best of him. Once outside the room, he breathed deeply. The way Remare held Miranda lovingly in his arms stung him. Lust, he could understand. Over the long centuries, Remare had desired many women and they, him. It was an expected emotion. But Valadon hadn't truly accepted that they had fallen in love. The way Miranda clasped Remare's hand in hers to her heart wounded him; even in sleep, she wanted Remare.

Valadon's hand covered his heart as a solitary tear threatened to break free. That would not do. He was a king.

And kings didn't cry. He strode down the corridor to the safety of his own rooms.

***

"Ouch, that hurts!"

"Big baby." Bastien continued removing the glass from Orion's back. "It wouldn't hurt so much if you hadn't jumped through the window."

"How else was I supposed to get into the office? Open the knob with my teeth?! I was still in wolf form."

"You were *supposed* to wait for me." Bas drolly glared at him. "That's what partners do."

"You were lagging behind. Besides the smell of gunfire was burning my eyes. Oww, Jesus, Bastien, can't you pull them out without grinding them into my flesh?"

"The pieces are jagged. I'm doing my best. Some are barely slivers. It's a good thing Katya loaned me her tweezers. I'm almost done. Just a few more."

When the last shards were removed, Bas used a damp cloth to wash away the streaks of blood. "Your skin is all smooth." He ran his hand slowly down Orion's back. "You heal up almost as fast as vampires do."

"I know. I've always been a quick healer. I'm going to take a shower, now. I can't stand the smell of smoke." Orion ran the water until it was hot enough then stepped under the spray.

Bas sat on the commode. "The operation went pretty smooth tonight. I wish we had known sooner where the installation was. We could have saved more people."

"Yeah," Orion reveled in the heat of the water penetrating his skin then, bending his head back, rinsed the shampoo from his hair. He repeated the action to make sure he got the stench out. "I couldn't believe the shape of those bodies we found." He knew Bas was watching him. Knew his body was in great shape as he used the cloth to stroke down his skin. Bas had seen him naked many times before on their tour of Europe. As a Were, nudity was no big deal to him. If Miranda had allowed it, he would have walked around their home naked plenty of times. He smiled. He still did when he knew she wouldn't be home.

"Hey, you going to use up all the hot water or you want me to come in and help search for any more glass shards?"

Did he want him to come in? Hell yeah! But they'd agreed on the trip to keep their relationship platonic. Even though they had shared a few women during their tour. Those moments were precious to him. He enjoyed the way Bas looked as he thrusted. He'd never known such pleasure until he watched as Bas came. Those guttural moans of his were sweet music to Orion's ears. His hunger had been steadily increasing for him. Did he dare tell Bas how much he wanted him? Would it destroy what they already had? Orion didn't know. And he wasn't sure he wanted to take the chance.

He'd known enough rejection in his life. Sure, his female fans craved him, screamed out his name. But all they really wanted was to fuck Orion, the rock star, not Orion, the man.

And the man only yearned for one person—Bas.

Chapter Thirty-Two

"Gregori's in the training room." Bastien closed his phone. "He texted me Valadon and Remare are going to sword play. We should go watch. It's rare when they spar, and it's really something special to see."

His hair still damp from the shower, Orion shrugged. "Okay." Relaxed from the soothing heat of the water, he rolled his shoulders. His frustrations and feelings of longing abated when he considered how lucky he was to have Bastien as a friend. Sure, he had urges, probably always would, but at least he got to spend time with the guy. And that he valued. Dearly. "Hey, how come you never taught me how to handle a sword?"

"Because, *'Swordsman of the Sky'*, you never asked. You wanted to learn how to fire a pistol, so I taught you that, instead."

"Hey, you researched the constellation I'm named after." Orion mockingly put his hand over his heart. "I'm impressed. And I got to teach you how to sing. Though, in your case, I'd stick to running missions." Chuckling, he ducked, just in time, when one of the sofa pillows Bas threw at him went soaring past his head.

"Not everyone is blessed like you." Bas sighed. "But I can still skate circles around you on the ice in the hockey arena."

"Oh, get real. I outscored you."

"Only because I let you."

"In your dreams." Orion closed the door behind him as they left. "We should get some shots in at the rink in Central Park. I always liked the outdoor ones better."

"Sounds good."

When they reached the training room, Bas nodded to Gregori and Irina, who were on the other side of the room. Orion watched as Valadon stretched out. The vampire king's physique was fascinating to behold. A work of art, as Miranda would say, but nowhere near as enticing as the vampire next to him.

"How about a match?" Valadon asked Remare.

"I thought you might have decided to sleep today. You gave much of your time to ensure the success of our mission last night." Remare leaned against the wall of the training room as Valadon worked out with a foil.

"Your reports were very thorough." Valadon saluted him with his sword. "As always, such a brilliant strategist."

"I do my best in service to ValCorp."

"Grab a sword. Let's see how well you perform, now."

Orion thought he detected something odd in the way Valadon had phrased his words, but shrugged it off.

Remare took down a sword mounted on the wall. "All right, then." He positioned himself on the mat. Legs spread, he bent his knees and flexed his shoulders in preparation for the match. With a few quick flicks of his wrist, he seemed ready.

"Ready, *mon ami*?" Remare asked.

"Always." The vampire lord's voice was melodic, yet cold.

Tristan, Katya and other Torians entered the room, wanting to watch the fearsome vampires spar.

Bas leaned closer to whisper, "The only one who can truly challenge Remare is Valadon. Wait until you see their speed."

Their game of thrusts and feints began. Valadon started with a series of feints and parries, but his eyes stayed focused on Remare. Orion admired their fierce level of concentration.

Gradually, their speed of attacks and ripostes increased. All was silent except for the sounds of steel clashing against steel. Orion could barely detect their breathing as they stood rapt watching the two vampires on the mats.

Orion had read up on the sport after watching Bastien spar with his father in Paris; Lord Rosemont had explained the particulars to him afterward, so he knew some of the moves.

He watched as, first, Valadon would take the offensive, effectively maneuvering them down the length of the mats, then Remare would be the aggressor and reverse their momentum. Fencing truly was an engaging game, a carefully choreographed dance whose opponents exhibited precise skill with a blade. They'd have to be with the speed in which they moved.

Out of the corner of his eye, Orion noticed Morel entering with Victor. Each stayed on their respective sides, providing Valadon and Remare with plenty of room to spar.

When Aiden and Bree arrived, the match had significantly increased in intensity. Orion's body tensed with exhilaration. This was way faster than the match with Bas and his father.

Morel mistook his reaction and smiled. "Don't worry, Orion. They often spar like this. They like to challenge each other's skill and acumen."

"He's never seen them fence before." Bas added, "No one moves as fast as they do. Not even my father. And he was one of France's top fencing masters."

Orion let out a breath he hadn't realized he was holding. Valadon's speed was incredibly rapid with his series of thrusts. And Remare moved in concert with him, but no faster. Orion wondered if he was purposely holding back.

A solitary bead of sweat ran down Valadon's face.

"You're in a mood today." Remare's voice was barely a whisper, but as a Were, Orion's hearing was acute.

Valadon growled. "Yes. I am."

"Anything I should be aware of?"

"I would think you'd be cognizant of *exactly* what I'm feeling." Valadon went on the offensive, backing their contest farther into the room.

"Enlighten me."

Valadon smirked. "Did you sleep well last night or did your exertions wear you out? You're rather slow today."

"You're angry." Remare sighed. "Miranda told me she had spoken to you and that you had accepted our relationship."

Oh, crap! Valadon knew about Miranda's relationship with Remare? Since when? Orion's heart started beating out a staccato. No wonder the tension level seemed strained between them.

"Accepted? I wouldn't say that." Valadon's green eyes were turbulent. Orion thought them a fitting color. "Perhaps acknowledged is a better word." He thrust fiercely, barely avoiding cutting Remare's ear.

Remare's eyes were glued on Valadon as he began to move in a circle. "Would you prefer we have this conversation in your rooms?" His demeanor seemed subdued as was his voice.

"No. I like the thrill of the pursuit."

"If we move any quicker, one of us is going to get hurt."

Venom coated Valadon's voice. "Don't hold back."

Concerned, Orion whispered, "Are you hearing them?" If he could hear them, surely, the others did, as well.

Bastien stood silently, his stance rigidly alert. "Yes. I am."

Remare exhaled then resumed his ready position. "As you wish."

The crowd began whispering their confusion as the match proceeded at a brutal pace. Apparently, far more fiercely than anyone had seen before. The sounds of the clanging metal reverberated louder through the room.

Morel grimaced. "Something's not right. I've seen them spar many times, but not like this. Not with both of them fighting without holding back."

Orion's instincts had him questioning Morel's words. From what he could tell, Remare was pulling in his hits. Perhaps there was some code about not injuring their king he didn't know about.

After a series of twists and turns, in a move impossibly fast for most to follow, Remare drew first blood—the piercing scent of it invaded Orion's nose. It was a slight sting to Valadon's arm, causing his shirt to redden. Remare, breathing heavily, took a step back and waited. Defiance etched deep in his countenance. A collective gasp sounded from the onlookers.

Morel unfolded his arms and whispered, "This can't be. He never makes mistakes."

Orion heard Tristan mutter, "This is turning into a nightmare." Katya squeezed his hand, worry evident in her eyes.

Valadon eyed the wound, then his gaze lingered on Remare. Orion had the nauseating feeling that was exactly what Valadon had been waiting for. His breath caught at the look Valadon was giving Remare. Envy to the ninth degree mixed with controlled rage. Then, the vampire king smiled, his fangs emerging to their full length. Something in Orion's gut clawed at him. He wasn't sure he wanted to witness how powerful Valadon was when he unleashed the full extent of his fury.

Miranda rode the elevator down to the level where the Torians were working out. She was looking forward to having dinner with Remare. Her body still tingled from their previous night of passion. When the doors opened, immediately, she could hear shouting from the crowd. Something was wrong. She rushed from the elevator to the training room. Heart pounding, she saw the way Valadon and Remare were engaged with one another, their faces savage in determination, their fangs more prevalent than she'd seen before. This was no sparring match. Remare and Valadon were fighting without reserve, each covered in sweat and blood. Their shirts cut in various places. Then, in a blinding move, Valadon slashed Remare across his stomach, and blood seeped onto his shirt.

She quickly stepped between Bastien and Orion. "Stop this," she hissed at Bastien.

"I can't." He seemed as shocked as she was to see them in this manner. When she looked at the horrified faces of the Torians, she marched forward, fully intending to stop the match.

"Put her in the sword room!" Valadon instructed two Torians she didn't know. Miranda fought fiercely against them and tried to pull free, but they had been too strong and too quick.

When Orion tried to go to her, Bas held his arm, shaking his head. "No." He turned to watch the combatants.

Remare wiped the sweat from his brow. "She will not be happy with you."

"For her own protection. Shall we continue, or do you concede?"

"It's not in my nature to back down from a fight."

"Neither is it in *mine.*" Valadon's voice was heavy with authority.

The fight was on, again, as each of them swung out in rapidly blinding thrusts. The cut on Valadon's arm started bleeding, again, but he would not relent. Remare's stomach wound began oozing, but Orion knew, however painful, their wounds would eventually heal.

Relentlessly, Miranda banged against the door and screamed for someone to let her out. She looked at the mechanism on the wall. She could fry the circuitry, but then, she might be sealing herself in. She quickly looked around the room. *Where's an air vent when you need one? They always had them in the movies, why couldn't there be one here?* She looked around the room at all the swords and daggers. Could she use one of them to pry open the door?

Let's find out!

Breathing heavily and wanting to free Miranda, but unable to tear his eyes from the mesmerizing fight, Orion stood his ground. He knew the match had spun terribly out of control. Would Valadon truly run Remare through with the blade?

As if hearing Orion's thoughts, Remare bellowed, "Let go of this! Would you really kill me over Miranda?"

"Why not? You killed me with your betrayal." Valadon then addressed the crowd. "Remare has defied me by sleeping with a woman he knew I had claimed as my own." His eyes cut to Remare. "This is how I deal with infidelity." Valadon attacked Remare in a series of hits much faster than Orion had ever seen the High Lord instigate. It was only a matter of time, now, he thought. Valadon was a purebred vampire, a full Blueblood. Miranda had told him

Remare was only half-Blueblood. Eventually, he suspected Remare's strength would falter.

Miranda growled in frustration loud enough that the walls seemed to vibrate. She'd broken a third knife in her attempt to pry open the door. She banged against it with her fist. It was solid steel. Her breathing frantic, she searched the room, one more time, for something to break down the door. She was going to kill Valadon for locking her in this room. She wasn't claustrophobic by nature, but she was sure beginning to feel like it. She could feel her eyes turning red. Not good! Instead of exhausting herself trying to beat down the door, Miranda eyed its edges. She couldn't break the metal door itself, but maybe she could manipulate the hinges.

The fight continued raucously. When the Torians pleaded for Valadon to relent, he only increased his strokes until in a *botta secreta*—a secret move taught only by fencing masters, one Remare hadn't anticipated—Valadon was able to get the upper hand and tripped Remare so that he'd fallen prone on the mats.

Heart pounding, Miranda drew on the energy from the lights in the sword room. Lock her in a room! Did Valadon know who she was? Her hands glowing from her power, she released the hinges and blew the door out. The Torians quickly scattered. When she saw Remare, bloodied and breathing raggedly on the mats, she flew to him, shielding his body with hers. Gazing up at Valadon, her Dark Angel wanted to kill him for what he'd done to Remare.

"*Why?*" she screamed.

"Because he took what belonged to me!"

"I'm not a possession, Valadon. It was *my* choice!

"You're in *my* House, Miranda." He waved his arms around the room. "Everything here belongs to me."

"That's what you would like to think." Her voice was vitriolic. "How kingly of you!"

When he raised his sword over her, Orion broke away from Bas' hold and flew to protect her and Remare.

Valadon laughed. The bastard *laughed.* "How right you are. And as king..." He pointed his sword at Remare. His voice, full of venom, reverberated around the room, "I order you to leave my House."

Irina fell to her knees, tears streaming down her face as Gregori held her back. "Mercy, my lord. Do not banish him. We need him as much as you do."

"I will do as I wish." Valadon pointed his sword around the room. "Any other objections."

Miranda watched as the Torians bowed their heads. She could feel their frustration, anguish, but to defy their king would be a death-sentence.

He was about to speak when Morel confronted him. "You cannot do this. Think, Valadon, think! Don't let your anger cloud your judgment. Remare has been your friend for centuries. One indiscretion does not merit banishment. You need him! We all do!"

"How noble of you, Morel, but I decline your request." He turned to Remare. "You will leave my House before midnight. Pack your things. You are to report to Madame Lord Dione's court in Montreal. If, after six months of service, you prove your loyalty, I *may* reconsider rescinding your orders. That is all." In his fury, he threw the sword against the wall and stormed off with the two unknown Torians.

In shock, the rest of the Elite Torians watched as Morel and Orion helped Remare up. No one said anything as they aided him to his room. Once there, they made sure he was comfortably seated on the couch.

Visibly shaken, Morel palmed Miranda's cheek. "I am so sorry." He gazed at Remare. "For all of this. He'll calm down. He has to."

Remare nodded but didn't say anything. Leaning forward, he held his head as if in pain.

"Is there anything you need?" Orion asked, his voice full of emotion.

Miranda shook her head.

"I'll be close by if you need me." He pulled her into a tight hug and kissed her temple. "Just text me."

"Okay."

After they left, she went to Remare and heard him mutter, "I'm ruined."

Her heart ached for him, but the damage had been done. He had stopped bleeding, but his wounds were still raw. She peeled off his shredded shirt. "I'll get you a new one."

She went to his closet and chose one of his black silk shirts. After laying it on the side of the sofa, she went to the bathroom to retrieve a wet cloth. After wringing it out, she knelt by Remare. "He cut your stomach pretty good."

"It's almost healed." He took the cloth and washed his wound then tossed it on the coffee table. "Do not fret, Miranda." He managed a weak smile. "He didn't kill me."

"He exiled you."

"At least, he didn't abjure me."

"What's the difference?"

"A person who is in exile can be recalled. Someone who has been abjured is shunned, permanently. A few decades ago, one of our Torians, a female named Zoe, was abjured. She was never allowed back into House Valadon."

Her voice hoarse, she whispered, "What did she do?"

"She killed a child. A young girl. Took too much blood. The girl died."

"You need blood." Miranda offered her wrist to Remare, who shook his head.

"There is a bottle of blood wine beneath the bar. Please bring it to me.

She poured him a glass and watched as he drank. His color seemed to be returning. She sank to her knees beside him. "I am so sorry, Remare." Tears threatened to break free. "I caused this. It's my fault he exiled you."

"What's a little fight between friends?" he joked.

"Little? It looked like he wanted to kill you."

"But he did not. He could have if he had wanted to." He sipped his wine. "He was merciful."

"How?"

"Montreal is fairly close. He could have sent me to any of the courts in Europe or Asia, and for a much longer period of time." He used his thumb to wipe away her tears. "Do not cry, dear one. I knew the risk when I first kissed you. You are not to blame." He kissed her forehead. "I would gladly do it, again."

Miranda snorted. "I'm going to talk to Valadon. Maybe I can talk some sense into him."

Remare massaged her neck. "My brave sorceress. It is not wise to talk to him while his emotions are wound so tight."

"He nearly killed you." She shook her head. "He won't harm me. He *supposedly* loves me."

Remare pulled her down so that she was sitting in his lap. "I will talk to him, not you. I'm the one he believes wronged him."

"Oh, no, you, don't. He sees you, the fight might start up, again. I'll talk to him, try to reason with him."

"Stay with me for a little while. It will be difficult enough not seeing you for six months. We have a few hours before I must leave."

Miranda couldn't even comprehend what it would be like without Remare for so long. She wouldn't see his sexy smile, hear his seductive voice. Wouldn't be able to hold his hand like she was doing, now. Six months? She couldn't do it, and what was more, she shouldn't have to. "I don't want you to go."

"I don't want to leave either." He held her close to his chest. "I will miss you immeasurably."

She bit back the tears threatening to fall. "Isn't there some kind of appeal we can make? File a petition or something?"

"Hardly."

"There must be something!"

"He is our ruler; there is no other recourse." Silence ensued, and then, his eyes turned dark. His hand stroked her cheek. "The only thing that will placate him is...you."

Miranda's emotions seemed to whirl and expand. Thoughts and feelings foreign to her began to surface. She stared at Remare, her jaw dropping as understanding suddenly bloomed. Backing away, she felt as if an anvil just fell on her. "You want me to go to him." Her eyes narrowed in realization. "You want me to be...his lover."

He shook his head and reached for her.

"Yes, you do. That way you could keep your status here and have me, too." Her body was trembling. "You *want* to share me with Valadon."

His eyes betrayed nothing; only pain and fatigue marred his face. He sighed. "I would be lying if I said the thought never crossed my mind. But, no," he shook his head, "that is not what I want."

"God, Remare," she huffed as she moved away. "If that's what you were pinning your hopes on, you're going to be disappointed." She glanced back over her shoulder, her voice was searing. "I'm not wired that way."

"And I would be very disappointed if you were." He held her shoulders and met her eyes. "I could not do what you accuse me of. I could not bear to see you in another's arms. You're my heart...and I do not share."

"Good to know." She held him tightly to her as if she could absorb some of his strength.

"No, Miranda," he sighed. His voice was soothing, his words not so. "There is no other option. Valadon is our king. His word is final."

Miranda exhaled. *Final, huh?* Well, she'd see about that.

Already thoughts were forming in her head as to what she was going to say to High Lord Valadon, King of the Vampires.

Chapter Thirty-Three

Valadon sat in his darkened room and brooded. The only illumination was from the computer screen. He thought about going up to his penthouse office; at least there he could stare out at the moon over the river. His arm still hurt where Remare had slashed him. Son of a bitch was fierce with a sword. The wound stung, but not as much as his heart. He'd fought with the one vampire he'd trusted more than any other. Memories of the many battles they had fought on the field and in the courts surfaced in his mind. Centuries upon centuries of watching each other's backs. Remare had always fought bravely and fiercely against his enemies. And always with his sarcastic humor.

Valadon closed his eyes in pain. None of his Torians wanted to see Remare leave. He'd seen the looks on each of their horrified faces as their match had turned vicious. Only he had been brutal with his thrusts; Remare had just used defensive strokes. Not once had he tried to harm Valadon. Bastard was a demon with a sword. He wondered how much damage Remare could have inflicted if he hadn't held back. Valadon inspected his arm, the wound nearly completely healed. Memories of his Torians' expressions of grief and remorse when he'd sentenced Remare haunted him.

A knock on the door. He didn't want to see anyone but knew he couldn't stay hidden. "Enter."

Katya closed the door behind her. "You know I would never criticize you in front of the others, but do you think you made the right decision, regarding Remare?"

"You were his lover for a long time; you're thinking with your heart, not your head."

She moved closer to his desk. Valadon admired her courage. "You once told me a house divided could not stand. Remare is the strongest of us all. We need him. All of us do. Even you. Could you reconsider your decision?"

"He insulted me."

"Remare didn't disrespect you. He fell in love."

"And you're at peace with that?"

"Yes. We all are, except you."

Valadon swiveled in his chair. "Did they send you here to try to change my mind?"

"Tristan and I discussed it. I would imagine Irina and Gregori feel the same, maybe more."

Valadon sighed. He knew, one by one, the Torians would plead their case before him. It was not something he was looking forward to. "Tell the others I will consider your request." He knew he was only pacifying her; he would not change his mind, but he did not want to see anyone else. In time, they would understand why he did what he did and accept his ruling.

"Thank you." Katya turned and left.

He'd barely had time to close his eyes when another knock sounded at his door. "Yes?"

Miranda entered, her anger seething just beneath her skin. He gave her credit for controlling her passions. He wasn't sure he would have if he'd been in her position. He was impressed with the way she'd flown to Remare's aid—like some sort of avenging angel. She truly was magnificent.

"Miranda."

"Was that necessary? Did you have to *prove* to everyone you're the king?"

"Of course not. They know who I am and to respect my commands." He rose and moved to his bar. Turning his back on her, he poured himself a drink.

"Remare didn't betray you."

"He slept with you!" He faced her. "In my House, under my roof!"

She shook her head as if fighting to control her rage. "You need him. He's your second. Who else will you get that can do what he can?"

"That's not your concern." His voice sounded rougher, deeper, even to him. "You should leave, Miranda. There's nothing for you to do here, anymore."

"Someone needs to talk sense into you. You acted out of hostility. You need to think this through. I know your pride is injured, but why would you hurt one of your own people?"

"I said this is no concern of yours. I've been king for centuries; I think I know how to rule my own House."

"Apparently not. Not when you make decisions that cost you."

Something she said must have hit a nerve. Valadon pushed her shoulders against the wall. His body effectively trapping hers. There were times Miranda wished she wasn't an empath. Valadon was feeling so many emotions: anger, hurt, frustration, and sorrow. But the one emotion blanketing the others was his unrelenting lust. He still wanted her, and he hated himself for it.

Miranda knew their emotions were heated. Too heated, because, in that instant, in that one terrifying moment, she realized a part of her wanted him, too. He still loved her, and that melted something inside her.

The King of the Vampires was in love with her. His emotions brushed up against hers, and she could sense his feelings as much as her own. Panting, he bent his head, trying to steady his breathing. He knew his emotions made him volatile. He was fighting a war inside himself to control what he didn't want to feel. When he looked at her, his beautiful emerald eyes were filled with pain and longing.

He'd been alone for such a long time. He was afraid he would forget what it was to love and be loved, and that fear was riding him.

When he bent his head to kiss her, when his lips were close enough to hers that she could almost taste them, she turned her head. She was unsure of what to say to him, but words seemed to come to her she hadn't considered before. "I'm not her."

His eyes narrowed in confusion. "Who?"

She moved away from him, grateful for the distance. "Whoever it is you want me to be." Her hand waved nonchalantly in the air. "I'm not her."

His look of anguish was palpable. "I never wanted you to be anyone else."

"I almost wish that I could be." Sighing, she leaned against his desk. "Remare almost wished for it, as well." His look of confused despair gnawed at her. "Remare toyed with the idea of inviting you to our bed. He wants both, you see. Loves you as much as he loves me."

Valadon snorted. "He would never share you."

"I told him I wasn't wired that way. I think I disappointed him, on some level." Miranda didn't want to contemplate that idea any further. "But don't you see how much he cares for you? He never meant to hurt you. Neither did I."

Valadon let his head fall back and closed his eyes as if in pain.

Miranda wanted to go to him, offer him comfort, but she wasn't the one for him. She could not fill that awful, soul-stealing void threatening to swallow him whole. In some respects, he was so alone, even though he had legions of loyal Torians who would die for him. It wasn't enough. His unrelenting yearning for someone to hold, to love overwhelmed her. Her compassion mixed with other emotions. She almost reached for him but let her hand drop.

At the door, she turned and faced him. "Don't hurt us, anymore. If you must send him away, banish me, as well. Let me share in the punishment. Make it three months instead of six."

"You're a terrible negotiator. Most people would offer something in exchange."

"I'm not most people."

"No, you're not." He pointed to her hand. "Your powers have grown substantially."

"Yes. I've been practicing."

"I'm glad." He offered her a weak smile. "Leave; I will consider your suggestion."

"Thank you."

"Send Remare to me." At her concerned expression, he added, "I won't harm him; I give you my word."

Miranda nodded.

Outside his room, she'd barely taken a few steps when she held her stomach and leaned against the wall. He'd gotten to her. His emotions had bled into her own, causing a dizzying effect. That was the only possible reason for her reaction. She took a few calming breaths. When she got back to Remare's room, she hesitated before entering. Sensing Valadon's emotions had played havoc with her own, as if they'd become crisscrossed in some way, she needed a moment to gather her thoughts. Breathing deeply, she opened the door.

Remare was sitting where she left him. He looked up at her expectantly.

"Your friend is very stubborn."

His shoulders relaxed, and Miranda couldn't tell if he was relieved or disappointed she hadn't fallen into Valadon's arms.

He rose. "What did he say?"

"I think it was more what he didn't say. He's hurting. I wanted to hate him for what he did, but I couldn't. I just couldn't." She went to Remare and put her arms around him. He was the only cave she sought out when she wanted comfort. "He wants to see you. He's waiting for you." She smiled up at him. "He promised me he wouldn't hurt you."

His smile didn't reach his eyes. "All right, then."

"Do you want me to go with you?"

"No, it's better I speak with him alone. Man to man." He kissed her forehead then left.

Remare was glad no one was in the halls when he walked down to Valadon's rooms. While Miranda was gone, Katya had visited him to offer comfort and relayed the well wishes of the others. He didn't want to have to say goodbye to anyone else. It made it too real.

He knocked and then entered. Valadon was staring at the blank screen on his wall.

"She will hate you for this."

"She will have to learn to deal with it, now that you've mated with her. I played back part of the tape you wanted to see." He pointed to the screen and flicked the remote. The smoke from the gunfight cleared as a man positioned himself behind Valadon. His gun was aimed, point blank, at Valadon's neck. A kill shot. "You were right. He almost fired at me. Instead, he shot the HOL soldier when he saw you approaching."

"Why haven't you given the execution orders?"

"Not just yet." He swiveled in his chair. "We'll wait it out. Let our little spy report back to whoever it is pulling his leash. See who he reports to."

"You don't think he was one of Peralt's?"

"No. Look at the gun he's using. It's a European model. I think our would-be assassin has another superior."

"Then, why make him a Torian?"

Valadon smirked. "I like to keep my enemies close. Speaking of which..." He pressed the remote so that more images appeared on screen. "Notice how he keeps his back to the camera as if he knows someone's watching." He gestured to the screen. "Here, here, and here."

"Yes, we saw these earlier."

"Ah, but now, take a look at the sketch Asanti drew. Miranda gave him not only the descriptions of Peralt, but of the man who had saluted her at the art gala, the one who broke into her mind. Look how he holds his shoulders, very aristocratic. Now, look at the images taken during the raid."

"He keeps his body turned away from the cameras."

"Yes. But he made one mistake. Look carefully at the window in the office. His head is down when the assault began, but for one second, he glanced up."

Remare smiled. "His reflection is in the glass."

"Yes. I had Aiden run it through the facial recognition program." The face of a man, light brown hair, early fifties, appeared. "Now, look at Asanti's sketch." Valadon transposed the drawing over the man's face. It was identical.

Remare growled. "Who is he?"

"His name is Stuart Blackmore Ehrlich, president and CEO of Ehrlich Pharmaceuticals." He paused. "Also, known to us as...*The Regent.*"

Remare uncrossed his arms. The idea of hunting down and killing the bastard thrilled him. "Where is he, now?"

"He boarded a private plane to Austria hours after the raid."

"Have our people there been notified?"

"They have." Valadon used the remote to shut off the screen. "He will be under constant surveillance."

"You're not going to have him killed?"

"Not just yet. All in good time. We kill him, another will take his place. Let's see who slithers up to him. Learn who his strongest allies are, here and in Europe. Then, we'll take care of them, once and for all." He rubbed his bicep. "You nearly took my arm off with that blade of yours."

"You told me to make it look real. There was a moment when I thought you were going to run me through."

"I might have...if you hadn't come to me earlier. None of the others suspect?"

"No. I don't like deceiving them."

"Neither do I. But, for the time being, it is necessary."

Remare groaned. "Six months?"

Valadon smirked. Remare was convinced Valadon was enjoying his discomfort.

"Yes. Punishment enough. Do you think you can keep it in your pants for that long?"

Remare smiled sarcastically. "I've gone far longer without. But it is not fair to Miranda. She's human, and time moves much differently for them."

The High Lord's tone was melodic. "She almost succumbed to my charms tonight."

"She would not have. Don't confuse her compassion with affection. Miranda is mine."

"And you ask why I'm sending you away for six months?"

"Do you really think it will take that long for our enemies to surface?"

"It may. Now that word of our House division is spreading, the sharks will come feeding."

"And we'll be waiting for them."

"Yes. And you won't be alone in Montreal." He sighed. "Nick came to me and expressed his desire not to return to NYU. Too many memories of the girl who tried to have him killed. He will be finishing up his undergrad work at McGill University. I'm hoping he likes it there enough to finish his MBA, as well. You'll see to his safety."

"Of course."

"When the spring semester is over, you can come home and resume your duties here. In the meantime, you will have no contact with Miranda. That is your punishment."

"You could not have created a more gruesome hell for me."

Valadon's lips twisted. "Oh, I'm sure I could have, after the hell you put me through."

"And who will be my replacement when I'm gone?"

"I've asked Aiden to be my second in the interim. You should know he did not want it and argued against your leaving. Finally, he reluctantly agreed when I told him you would return."

"Why not Morel? He's your third."

"After the way he confronted me in front of the others? How would that look?"

"He is sentimental where Miranda and I are concerned. He will not want her to suffer."

"She won't. She's free to use the archives as she sees fit. Her protection will be well-provided for." Valadon sat back and swiveled in his chair. "Were you aware of how much her powers had increased?"

"No. I had no idea." Though Remare suspected Miranda drinking his blood had escalated her abilities.

"There's one other thing." Valadon started playing with his letter opener. "I heard from Magritte. She's displeased with my refusals to return to Europe. It appears, now, she wishes to torment me further."

"She's been the Queen of All Vampires for a long time now."

"Too long. And too used to having her will imposed on others."

"What's her latest threat?"

"It's not a threat; it's more a negotiation." He sighed. "Remember when I told you Lena bore me a son."

"Yes, you said he died days after he was born."

"It appears Lena was lied to. Magritte swears a noblewoman paid for the child. Raised him as her own. That he is very much alive."

"Do you believe her?"

"I do. She was too smug, too certain of herself."

"Where is the boy?"

"She refuses to reveal that piece of information unless I submit to her whims."

"What does she want?"

"Since I refused her offers of mergers with the European Union, she's come up with another idea."

"What?"

Valadon ran his finger along the edge of the blade. "A marriage between me and one of her choosing."

"Who?"

Valadon pushed a file toward him and opened the flap. Remare's skin crawled.

"What do you plan to do?"

"Track down my son, of course. I've instructed Victor to check all birth registers around Marseilles and the outlying areas. Marlena was Catholic. She may had him baptized in a small church outside the main city. I'm also having our historians check anyone who was associated with the courts who may have adopted a child at this time. I *will* find him."

"I have no doubt." *No doubt at all!* "Is there anything I can do to assist in your investigation?"

"Before she claimed Canada as her territory, Madame Lord Dione was familiar with many of the women in our High Court at the time. Find out if she knows anything or anyone who might. She's expecting you."

Valadon shoved the file inside his drawer and locked it. "All right, then. Arrangements have been made to transfer Nick's courses to McGill. Both of you will live at her court. When he graduates in the spring, he can choose which apartment he wants, if he so desires."

He rose. "I think this calls for a toast." He went to his closet and retrieved his golden chalice and an old bottle of wine. Cutting his wrist, he let his blood drop into the goblet.

Remare did the same with his wrist.

Contentment lining his face, Valadon mixed the blood together with the wine and saluted Remare. "Always and forever." He sipped the mixture then handed the cup to Remare.

Repeating the words, Remare lifted the chalice and drank. Their blood bond, always fierce, was cemented, again. He hugged his liege, his oldest friend, his lord. "I'll see you in a few months, then." He sighed. Without Miranda by his side, it was going to be a long six months.

Chapter Thirty-Four

"I'm not staying here a moment longer."

"You can't leave. You took a blood oath to Valadon."

"Yeah, well, that was before he raised a sword to Miranda." Orion stood with his hands on his hips.

"He didn't touch her. Valadon has never shown violence toward women." Bas ran a hand through his hair. "Look, I don't agree with all his decisions, but he always has reasons for what he does. He just doesn't share them with us." He sounded vexed. "Don't go. Please, I'm asking you to stay."

Seeing the anguish in Bas's eyes, part of Orion wanted to relent. He knew Bastien was upset; all the Torians were grieving in their rooms, trying to come up with some sort of plea for Remare to stay.

"I can't." He exhaled. "At least not for tonight. I stay here any longer, I'm going to have words with Valadon. It's better I go." He texted Miranda he'd wait until she was ready to leave. "I just want to make sure she's all right. She shouldn't be alone tonight."

"Will you come back tomorrow? With Remare gone, Valadon's going to need his Torians close to him."

His hand on the door knob, Orion glanced back and saw the pleading in Bas's face. It almost undid him. He nodded. "Yeah, I'll be back."

***

Miranda watched as Remare finished packing. "This is wrong. Wrong on so many levels." Her fury was boiling just beneath her skin.

"It won't be forever." He smiled reassuringly and rubbed her shoulders with his thumbs. "Before you know it, I'll be back." At the knock on his door, Remare turned and said, "Come in."

Morel entered. "The helicopter's fueled and ready for departure. Valadon ordered me to take you to the airstrip. When you are ready." He leaned against the wall. "I don't like this. No one does. I know he's upset, but he had no right to exile you. None of us want to see you go."

"Thank you." Remare nodded. "You and I both know his punishment could have been much worse. He showed mercy. I'll be back in six months. Count on it."

"Do you need help packing?"

"No, I've taken everything I need." He gestured to his two black suitcases. "If I've forgotten anything, I'm sure arrangements can be made to have it sent to me."

"You shouldn't have to be going at all." Miranda was still fuming. "You have the most obstinate vampire for a ruler."

Remare caressed her arm. "But he is our king, Miranda."

Morel grabbed his bags. "I'll be waiting for you on the roof. Take your time." He bowed to her and to Remare then closed the door behind him.

Miranda held Remare to her. "I don't want you to go." Breathing his scent deep into her lungs, she thought, if she held him tight enough, he would become immersed in her. She couldn't let go. Not yet. He'd become a part of her, and she felt as if someone was tearing her heart out.

"I don't want to go either, Mir-randa, but I must." He glanced over at the bed. "Stay here tonight. They say the weather will be turning brutal. You'll be safe here."

"I'll walk you up to the roof."

"No. If you do that, I won't get on the chopper. Let me say goodbye to you here." He leaned her against the wall and stole her breath away with a kiss so hot it made the butterflies in her stomach take flight.

A tear formed in her eye. She promised herself she'd be strong for him. Not break down and let him see her cry, again. Remare needed support, right now, not a scene. She wiped away the tear. "Do you think, if I slipped away for the weekend to visit you in Montreal, he'd find out about it?"

"I'm sure he would." He managed to grin. "I think I've had a positive influence on you. You're becoming devious."

She snorted.

"Six months, Miranda." He grabbed his laptop. He gave her one last smoldering look. She kissed him with all the passion she knew, pressing her body tightly against his. "Okay."

When he reached the door, he turned. His half smile was wickedly sexy. "I bought you a few gifts for the Winter Solstice. I'll make sure they are safely delivered to you." He blew her a kiss and was gone.

Miranda's heart sank, and she leaned against the wall for support. The tears she'd been holding back now fell. She wiped them away. *God, how did the wives and girlfriends of soldiers do this?* Her back straightened. If they could endure it, so could she. She sniffled and went to the bathroom to clean her face. The cool water was soothing against her heated skin.

In the bedroom, she looked lovingly at his bed and closed her eyes in regret. She could still taste him on her lips, smell his incredibly intoxicating scent of the woods. It gave her the strength to leave. If she slept in his bed, she'd be reaching for him all night long.

***

Gregori had said all he could to get Irina to calm down. He'd never seen her so upset before. Pacing back and forth, Irina was more than seething—she was out for blood. And

God help anyone who got in her way. She was lethal in devising ways to eliminate her enemies. He liked that about her, because so was he. He smirked. They were all distraught over Remare's departure, but he knew, in his gut, the leader of the Torians would be back.

At least her cursing in Russian had stopped. He'd known most of the words, but he had to admit there were a few creative choice terms he'd never imagined and knew were anatomically impossible. When she'd run out of Russian colloquialisms, she started using English, and those words he knew well.

"Irina, he'll be back."

The icy stare she gave him would have gravely wounded another. "I know he'll be back! He never should have gone to begin with! If he hadn't fucked that human cunt, he wouldn't have been exiled!"

Gregori winced. Her accent was far more pronounced than he'd heard in a long time. "It was his choice." He knew his words were painful for her to hear. "He chose to be with her." She'd been Remare's lover for decades, but it was time she acknowledged he'd moved on. "You need to let go."

She nearly hissed at him, and that only roused him more. He wanted to take her in the bedroom and make love to her. Fuck her until she couldn't remember Remare's name any longer, have her calling out his name instead of her former lover's. When he reached for her, she evaded his touch.

"I need to work this out. Alone." Angrily, she closed the door behind her.

***

On her way out, Miranda strolled through the training area illuminated only by the exit signs. She sneered when she saw someone had already repaired the door to the sword room. *How efficient!* Her night vision stronger than ever, she admired the swords mounted on the walls. Wishing to forget the ugliness of the earlier fight, she chose to remember Remare sword dancing with her. God, how she'd loved dancing with him. Remare was graceful and lithe on his feet, an excellent teacher. He'd taught her moves, helped her with her form and had become her partner in an erotic ballet that had her smiling and her body throbbing.

She had watched him before he'd even instructed her. Memorized his moves. Man, that vampire could move fast! She could match his movements, but his speed was incomparable.

An angry voice cut into her reveries. "What are you doing here? I would have thought you'd be gone by now."

Miranda turned to see the irate scowl on Irina's face as she leaned against the doorframe.

"Reminiscing."

"Didn't you do enough damage?" Her voice dripping venom, Irina came farther into the room. "Or are you here to gloat?"

Miranda knew all the Torians were hurting at their leader's departure, but Irina must have been wounded the most. She'd been his lover for years. "I'm not the one who sentenced him."

"No, you're just the one who caused it."

Her caustic remarks cut Miranda to the bone. She studied *The Ice Queen's* features, and something in her stomach froze. Irina was one of the most gorgeous women in the world. With her platinum-blonde hair, piercing blue eyes, cheekbones to die for and svelte figure, she was a stunning beauty. Miranda had once been jealous of the Russian goddess, but not because of her looks. Irina had known every inch of Remare's body. He'd made love to her countless times over the decades.

Insecurity singed Miranda. How many times had she overheard men talking in the museum about how vampire females were better lovers than human women? More beautiful, more talented, more captivating. How she hated hearing it.

Breathing deeply, she knew Remare had chosen her. He could have had anyone, but he'd chosen her. Still, there remained that one modicum of doubt. Was she good enough? Over time, would Remare lose interest in her? Would her features fade so much he would turn from her? Fear turned to anger. She watched as Irina circled her, eyeing the swords on the wall.

"What do you want, Irina?"

"Remare taught you how to handle a sword, didn't he?" Her eyes gleamed with anticipation.

"Yes, we danced with steel."

"How about a game? Let's see who he taught better."

Miranda wasn't sure she was just referring to fencing. She also knew Irina would cut her to ribbons. "Let's not." She tried to pass Irina, who bumped her shoulder.

"Coward. You stink of fear. You humans think you're good enough to dance in our world. You don't belong here. You're so much less than us." Irina's loathing was palpable. "I don't know what he saw in you."

A thin red haze covered Miranda's eyes. Not a good sign. Not good at all! She turned and, in a voice that wasn't hers, said, "I belong where I choose to be."

Irina took a sword down from the wall. "Really?" Her eyes sparkled. "Prove it."

Miranda sensed the animosity and jealousy vibrating in Irina. She would not be suckered into a fight. She was halfway to the door when Irina taunted her. "I heard Chloe and Gloria commenting on how well Remare fucked them last week. They said he was splendid, the best they'd ever had. I guess you didn't impress him, after all."

Closing her eyes, Miranda tried to blot out the images of Remare in bed with the two women Valadon had brought him. Laughter echoed in her ears. Pain lacerated her until she saw only red. Using her power, she summoned one of the swords to her.

Facing Irina, she smirked. "Let's dance."

Irina's lips twisted into an ugly parody of a smile as she took her position on the mats. She twirled her sword like a baton. Miranda knew this was foolish, but she'd been wanting blood ever since seeing Remare bloodied and bruised lying on the mat with Valadon standing over him. Something in her had finally snapped. Surprised she wasn't pulsating with rage, Miranda gazed down at her hand. She was perfectly calm, as were her breaths.

And that scared her even more.

The dance started off slowly. Irina wanted to see what she was made of. So, she would show her. Irina's thrusts were aimed at finding a weakness. Miranda parried each of her jabs skillfully as Remare had taught her. She measured each of Irina's steps, knew Remare had taught her, as well, and that he'd had decades with her.

Miranda didn't need decades. She'd memorized his moves and the moves of the Olympians so she could impress him. She had.

"Gee, Irina, is that the best you've got?" Was she insane? Had she lost all of her reason? Why was she taunting *The Ice Queen*?

"Why move too quickly at first? It rushes the pleasure."

Miranda wondered if that was something else Remare had taught her.

Irina started to quicken her strokes. The woman was impossibly fast; Miranda had to concentrate hard to follow her steps. The vampire liked trying to confuse her, but Miranda could sense more than see her opponent's moves.

Thrust, parry, evade. They danced like that for a while, swords clashing, each studying the other. Occasionally, one of them would offer a riposte, an attack immediately made after a parry. Miranda knew she was being fucked slowly. Irina was purposely wearing her down.

And, then, she would strike a killing blow.

The clash of swords must have woken the others; Miranda sensed shadows moving into the room. She decided not to wait for Irina's death strike. She added a few moves of her own. Irina had been right about many things, but she forgot one crucial aspect. "Having fun, Irina? Have you forgotten I'm the one who healed your shoulder?"

She lunged at her. "Your stupidity."

Possibly! Miranda skillfully deflected the blow. *More than likely. No good deed goes unpunished.*

Finally, in a move Miranda couldn't track, Irina spun around and cut Miranda across her jawline. Had she aimed a little lower, she would have slit her throat. Memories of another vampire slicing Orion's throat haunted. Miranda glanced at the blood on her hand and then at Irina. Without warning, her eyes turned black.

Even Irina took a step back when she saw Miranda's eyes.

Her Dark Angel, patiently waiting on the sidelines of her psyche, whispered, *"Set me free!"* She knew the Light Angel would not fight her on this one.

"First blood, Irina. I needed that scratch to wake me up." Holding her sword in front of her, eyes closed, Miranda summoned her *Elemental* abilities. Powers she'd been too frightened to invoke, had kept hidden for far too long. Unleashing her fury, she gave free reign to the darkness.

Miranda attacked with a confidence foreign to her and, yet, strangely familiar. She quickened her thrusts with a speed she didn't know she was capable of. They fought as savages fought, each screaming their hatred of the other as hits landed with resounding clashes. Back and forth, they challenged each other to the utmost.

Finally, Irina tripped on a fold in the mat and went down on one knee. Miranda loomed over her and held her sword pointed over her neck. "Had enough?"

With a shriek Miranda could only imagine a wraith making, Irina sprang forward and attacked her. The swords went flying away from them as they fought viciously. Miranda used her power of air-bending to deflect Irina's blows. Then, in a move too quick to follow, Irina grabbed her in a binding hold and licked the blood from Miranda's jaw. Fangs elongated, she tried to sink her fangs in Miranda's throat. Repulsed by her actions, she broke the hold. When Irina lunged for her, again, Miranda calmly raised her hand and blasted her with her power.

Irina went flying across the room into the wall. The sound of bones cracking reverberated in the room. From the corner of her eye, she saw Gregori rushing toward Irina.

Someone flicked the lights on, and Valadon bellowed. "What the *hell* is going on?"

All the Torians turned toward him.

Miranda slowly bent to retrieve her sword. She tried to make her eyes revert back to normal, but they refused to shift. She took several calming breaths, but to no avail. Evading Valadon's gaze, she placed the sword back on the wall.

Valadon marched to her and tipped her chin up. His voice held concern. "Your eyes are black."

Keeping her lids lowered, she whispered. "I know."

His voice was deep, authoritative. "What happened here?"

"Ask Irina; she started it."

"She attacked me first!" Gregori helped Irina stand. From the way she was clutching her side, Miranda guessed she'd broken a few of her ribs.

Miranda pointed to her jawline. "She drew first blood. I merely defended myself."

"By attacking my Torian?" Incensed, he shouted, "In my office. *Now!* Everyone go back to your rooms. Gregori, take Irina to the infirmary."

Irina protested, "I don't need to go."

"Do *not* challenge me! I've had enough defiance for one night. Gregori take her, now."

Miranda watched as Gregori helped Irina leave the training room. The others followed suit.

Orion came to her. "Are you all right?" He kissed the top of her head.

Only now did her eyes begin to turn their normal brown. "Yeah. Wait for me, okay?"

He nodded to her and then to Valadon.

In silence, Miranda walked with the High Lord down the hall to his office.

Chapter Thirty-Five

Once inside, instead of taking his seat behind his desk, Valadon crossed his arms over his chest and leaned against his desk. He was patiently waiting; it was as if he was willing her to speak.

Miranda wasn't sure what she should say, so she said nothing. Saying, "Oops!" probably wouldn't go over very well, right now.

The storm in his eyes seemed to abate. "As long as you're a guest in my House, you will not attack one of my Elite Torians. Is that clear?"

Miranda rubbed her hand. It was still tingling from the fight. "And if one of your Torians attacks me?"

"I don't think any of them will challenge you after that little demonstration you just gave them."

Miranda had known she acted foolishly. Now, all his Torians knew what she was. "Do they all know? What I am?"

"Yes, I'd think so. I would have thought you were intelligent enough to conceal your abilities. The last time you attacked a Torian, you threw a fireball at Remare."

Miranda smirked. She'd nearly forgotten. She shrugged. "He made me mad."

"Is this going to happen every time you get angry at someone?"

She sighed. "No. I lost control. I'm sorry. Irina hates me because I'm with Remare, now. I had to accept her challenge or I'd be constantly looking over my shoulder."

"I sincerely doubt you'll have to worry about Irina in the future." His voice softened. "I'll speak to her in private. Get her assurance she won't seek retribution on you."

Miranda lowered her eyes. "Thank you."

"You've left me in quite a conundrum. I should punish you for what you did."

Inwardly huffing, Miranda wondered if she'd done anything different from what Valadon had done earlier to Remare.

"But, instead, I want to offer you a proposition."

Miranda's eyebrow rose. "What?"

"The archives. You wished access to do your research, didn't you?"

She nodded, hoping he wouldn't bar her from her studies.

"I want you to do something for me. You found Peralt and the experiments he performed."

"Yes, I did." She wondered where he was going with this.

"I want you to search the archives. For anyone else Peralt may have worked with. Anyone who might have shared his beliefs, his philosophies, his practices."

Miranda was surprised. And intrigued. "Gabriel read more than me. He may have come across more than I did."

"I know. I've already had extensive conversations with him about it. He has his own research to focus on but said he would help me when he can."

Miranda considered his offer; she'd wanted to discover anything else Peralt may have written about *Elemental*s. "I have off a few weeks before the spring term starts."

"I think you should know Nick will not be returning to NYU. He's transferring up to McGill University."

She was outraged. "You can't! He only has one semester left. Let him graduate from the school he's attended for the last three and a half years!"

"It wasn't my idea, Miranda." He softened his tone. "Nick came to me and told me he didn't want to return. Too many memories of Cerise. Madame Lord Dione of Montreal is a good friend of mine and a strong ally. McGill has already accepted him."

Miranda was crestfallen. She'd wanted Nick one more time in her class. "I'll miss him."

"We all will. He'll be back late spring. Think of it this way, at least Remare will have someone to talk to up in Montreal, though, knowing Dione, neither will be at a loss for companionship."

Her molars grinding, she lifted one eyebrow. "You enjoyed that last barb."

"I did. Yes," he said unapologetically. "So, will you accept my offer? You will be compensated, generously, I might add."

Her thoughts started tumbling over one another. "Peralt mentioned two other authors who influenced him. I've checked all over your archives. I can't find any books by them, and when I searched the databases, I couldn't find them at any research library."

"Not all libraries put online every book they have in their possession."

Miranda wondered if libraries were like the museums. Only a fraction of their works of arts were displayed. Far more marvels were in their vaults awaiting restoration and reconsideration.

"Give the names to Aiden. He'll find them. Or at least someone who would know where they can be found." He moved closer to her. "Do we have an accord?"

"Yes. But understand my work at the museum comes first. I'll need an assistant."

He smirked. "I'll provide you with one, possibly two."

She wondered who he would pick, now that Nick was no longer available.

He surprised her with what he said next. "Morel and Victor share their love of philosophy. I'm sure Morel would love to work with you."

She sighed. Of all the vampires at House Valadon, she trusted and liked Morel the best.

"Shall we have a toast, then?" He went to his cabinet and retrieved a golden chalice encrusted with jewels and a carafe of wine. "This is a special blend I think you will enjoy."

Miranda looked at the goblet. "A little ornate, don't you think?" Meeting his eyes, she sipped. It was sweeter than she liked, more full-bodied and robust. She handed the wine back to him and saw his lips curl before he drank. A strange sensation of being caught in a web crept over her. "Orion's waiting for me. I'll start work on your project next week."

"I'll look forward to it."

Miranda turned when she reached the door. The High Lord's face betrayed nothing. Except a subtle smug smile of satisfaction. But, at what, she had no clue.

Other than she'd just been played.

Valadon sat back in his chair. Miranda was a powerful *Elemental*, more powerful than any of them had guessed. What a welcome addition to his arsenal. If the other Houses or courts in Europe learned of her abilities—and, in time, they would find out—they would try to seduce her to their covens. He would not allow that to happen; he would take steps to insure she remained loyal to him.

He contacted Aiden. Every member of his Torians would be informed Miranda's welfare was paramount to House Valadon.

And God help anyone who thought otherwise.

***

Aiden walked down the hall to Irina's room. Straightening his spine, he exhaled then knocked. When Gregori opened the door to reveal a prone Irina, Aiden stepped inside and asked her, "Do you require further medical attention?"

She sat up. "No, Gregori finished taping my ribs."

"Dr. Amira says she has three broken ribs and bruising around the rib cage." Gregori exhaled. "But she'll be fine with bedrest."

"That's good, because you're on seclusion for the next two weeks."

"What the fuck?" Irina roared, clutching her middle.

"Valadon's orders. He wanted me to remind you, and all his Torians, Miranda is 'Friend of the Court' and not to be touched by any member of his House. You violated that covenant."

"That bitch attacked me first!"

"Be that as it may, you're secluded." He turned to Gregori. "You may bring Irina her meals and visit occasionally, but no one else will be allowed contact."

Irina cursed in Russian.

Gregori's eyes narrowed as he crossed his arms over his massive chest. "He made you his second, didn't he, while Remare is in Montreal?"

Aiden sighed. "I did not want the position." He shook his head and grit his teeth. "I told him I would only accept the assignment on a temporary basis. Until Remare returns." He addressed Irina directly. "He told me to advise you Miranda is under his protection, and any attempts at retaliation toward her will result in your expulsion."

Irina gasped in trepidation.

"I'm to stress his word to all the Torians."

Gregori nodded. "Thank you for informing us."

Aiden returned his nod and closed the door behind him.

***

It was nearly dawn when Jeremy watched his spy move through the thinning crowd at Nightshade. House Valadon's chief interrogator and jailor, Scorpio, made an imposing figure with his dark hair and long black leather coat. He was one of the most solidly built vampires, probably due to his Were blood, but even with his muscles, he wasn't as strong as Jeremy.

He didn't need muscles to implement his will; his powers lay elsewhere.

"You think it smart to meet here?" Scorpio sat across from him in one of the VIP booths that circled the near-empty dance floor. "There could be other Torians still here. I'd have thought your father taught you better."

Jeremy kept his voice low and waited for a dark-haired girl to pass by. He recognized her as one of Cesare's assistants at Valadon Creations, Carla or Carol or something like that—he didn't give a fuck; she was of little consequence. Scorpio had been his father's mole at ValCorp and now reported to Jeremy. "My father taught me never to have his orders questioned by those who served him."

Scorpio leaned forward, his musky scent permeating the air. "You're not your father."

"No. Mulciber trusted the wrong people. I won't make the same mistakes."

"So, what went wrong last night? You had a perfect shot to take; why didn't you?"

"His second came upon me too quickly. I shot one of Peralt's soldiers, instead. Valadon was impressed with my ability to protect him. Complimented my skill. Little did he know."

"What are your plans, now?"

"Word throughout ValCorp is that he banished Remare because he was fucking his human. With his second gone, Valadon is vulnerable."

"He still has his Elite Torians protecting him."

"Not for long. After my heroics in the field, I've been accepted into the Torian program. I plan to become one of his personal guards. And, with my upcoming MBA, I will become one of his executives. I can get close to him. Learn everything I need to about him, and when the time comes, I'll execute him."

"What do you need me for, then?"

"Are you still in contact with Mulciber's allies in our High Court?"

"Yes, of course."

"Good. Let them know they have a powerful ally at House Valadon. I will need friends there when I ascend the throne."

"Caltrone will be glad to hear it. Magritte is eager to meet you. They plan on visiting next year."

"Good, it's time I met them both."

"I'll arrange it."

After Scorpio left, Jeremy watched as his sister, Kaylee, danced with the others. His heart still ached that Mulciber hadn't been able to fully turn her before he'd been murdered. Her mind was still fractured, but at least, now, he could take her out in public. She could tolerate being around others for short amounts of time. And, for that, he was grateful. Half-human, half-vampire, she would never be completely whole.

And he blamed Valadon for that, as well.

"Ready to come home, Kaylee?" He sidled up to her and danced a few steps with her.

"Oh, yes, brother." She rubbed her body suggestively against his. "I'm always ready for you."

He'd introduced her as his sister, even though they'd had different human parents. Mulciber had adopted them, made them his. So, even though he thought of her as his sister, she was also his lover, and tonight, he wanted her.

In time, he would release his other sister, who had been locked away in Valadon's dungeon. From their blood bond, he knew she slept. *Soon, Persephone, soon!*

Chapter Thirty-Six

Miranda tossed and turned in her sleep. After Orion and she had returned home, they discovered Max and Sasha still there, reluctant to leave. They'd asked if they could stay on. Moved by their hopeful faces, and knowing she'd be lonely with Remare gone, Miranda welcomed their companionship. In the morning, she'd offer them the basement apartment that once belonged to her Aunt Meg.

Orion said he was sleeping in his own bed tonight and they could either join him if they wanted or sleep on the couch. Neither one hesitated. Weres often slept in puppy piles when they were troubled and just needed the physical contact of pack members. Outraged Irina had attacked Miranda, he said he wanted to spend more time with her. She suspected Valadon put him on guard duty.

Her body craving Remare, she turned, again, unable to get comfortable. A specter of him appeared in her mind. She smiled as she imagined him being there with her. Even his woodsy scent permeated the air around her. She knew she was dreaming; she'd had other erotic dreams about him visiting her in the night. The one in Paris had felt so intense she'd thought it real.

She turned toward the apparition. "What are you doing here?"

"The flight's been delayed due to the bad weather." He smirked in his usual suggestive manner as she undulated against the mattress. "Miss me?"

Her voice was husky. "Always."

He joined her on the bed and kissed her passionately. Then, he stood, removing his cashmere sweater and the rest of his clothes. Miranda loved watching him undress. Remare was solid muscle, not an ounce of fat anywhere on his marvelous physique. Moving the blankets aside, he covered her body with his.

After another searing kiss, he peeled off her T-shirt and shorts and tossed them casually on the floor. Her breath caught. "I don't know how I'm going to get through the next six months without you."

"We have hours. The pilot says they won't take off until after sunrise." His hand slid down the center of her body until he reached her core. "You're warm and wet. Just the way I like you." Burying his head in her hair, he then laved the vein along her neck, his fang lightly grazing her.

Breathing heavily, her body on fire from his touch, she welcomed him deep inside her. Her fingers traced a trail down his back, loving the smooth, cool feel of his muscles rippling under her touch. She kissed him, again, wanting him to stay with her always, knowing it wasn't possible. If this was her dream, she was going to have as much of him as possible. She reversed their positions, pushing him down into the mattress.

He threw his head back in joy, his laugh was full-throated, not holding anything in reserve. She loved seeing him happy. She pressed her hands into his pecs and rotated her hips, watching as his eyes sparkled with mirth.

In a move too quick for her to follow, he reversed them, again, so that he was on top. "Not too fast, Mir-randa. I want this one to last."

She growled in frustration. Remare could take her to the peak and ride her like a surfer does a wave. She was the water; he was the glider and rode her for as long as he could, keeping her on that beautiful crest that stole her breath and nearly bordered on pain for its volume of intensity. Sensing she couldn't handle any more, he thrust hard inside her and covered her mouth with his so that her scream would not wake the others in the house.

They made love for hours, each fighting for the top position, each ebbing and flowing over the other in sacred communion as their bodies gleamed in the cool night air.

Miranda woke feeling thoroughly relaxed. Damn! She sighed. What a dream she'd had. She smiled. Her body was still tingling from the aftershocks of her imagined sexathon with Remare. If he knew the kind of erotic dreams she had of him caused her to come in the night, he would have laughed in smug male appreciation. A vision of his laughing face came to mind. Happiness engulfed her. Hungry, she made her way to the kitchen.

Halfway there she realized something was off. She was cold. Miranda rarely got cold. She looked down at her bare feet. No slippers. Not unusual, she usually didn't wear them. However, the rest of her was naked. Miranda shook her head. She never slept naked, especially with others in the house. Rubbing her neck, she realized it was tender to her touch. And so were a few other places. Her jaw dropped. That was no dream! She giggled at the realization. Grabbing a robe from her bedroom door, she moved into the kitchen.

There were three packages lined up on her kitchen table. The top one marked, *Miranda*.

She didn't have to open the bakery box to know its contents; she could smell chocolate a mile away. Sliding the strings off and opening the lid, she found a chocolate croissant. Biting into the fresh pastry, she moaned. *Heaven!*

When she moved the bakery items aside, she found a note.

"*Sorceress, I could not leave without giving you your presents for the Winter Solstice. Always remember all good things come in threes.*"

Miranda chuckled. She wondered if Remare was referring to the orgasms he'd given her the night before.

She opened the second parcel and removed the tissue paper. Another card, but this one wasn't from Remare. *"Thank you for helping to find my son and healing his leg. There are no words to express the depth of my gratitude. Please accept this gift as a token of my appreciation. If you should ever find yourself in need, I will assist you in any way possible. Please feel free to contact me whenever you wish."—Asanti*

She removed the covering to reveal Mary Cassatt's *In the Loge,* the beautiful painting of the woman at the opera Miranda had admired in his home. She gasped. Her heart beat furiously. *My God, where am I going to put it?* If anyone knew she had this painting, they would break in to steal it. Miranda exhaled. Good thing Remare had installed bars on her windows. After admiring her painting, she placed it aside. She reached for the last box and read the notecard.

"I noticed your purse was looking a little worn, so I bought you a new one." Sliding the red ribbon off, she removed the top of the box. It was a beautiful Bellini black leather messenger bag. Very expensive, very chic. It would have set her back a few paychecks. She loved it!

Glancing at her old one, she said, "Sorry pal, but you've been replaced."

She held the new one up and then looked inside at all the compartments. She found two smaller boxes. One contained a shiny new fountain pen, a Montegrappa, also very expensive. *Thank you, Remare!* After kissing it, she laid it aside and opened the third box.

It was a key with a note. *"Miranda, I want you to stay at my Sutton Place town house from time to time. I like the idea of you sleeping in my bed, even though I cannot be there to keep you warm. I know your house is reasonably safe with* the security system and bars, but my place is more secure. Paul will see to any requests you might have, and Emma is a fantastic chef; she will cook anything you wish. Try not to have any wild parties while I'm away. I know how your Were friends like to enjoy themselves."—R

Ecstatic, Miranda couldn't stop laughing. For a moment, she was despondent. She hadn't gotten him anything. *What did you get a vampire millionaire who had everything?* No matter, she would put her mind to it and get him something he'd love and have Morel send it to him. She held the key to her lips and grinned. *No wild parties, huh?! Well, he didn't say I couldn't invite a few friends over.*

She reached for her phone. "Lizandra, what are you doing for the holidays?"

Epilogue

A few months later—

Inside the communications room at ValCorp, Aiden stared at the computer screen and frowned. He moved in closer for a better look then enhanced a section of the picture. "Oh, fuck! This is not good. Not good at all."

After the last war, the NYPD had set up cameras at all the major tourist locations: the Statue of Liberty, the Empire State Building and the New York Public Library. As well as the major transportation areas. Aiden had tapped into some of those feeds, hoping to ascertain Brandon's whereabouts, but instead, he found something entirely different.

"What's wrong?" his wife, Bree, asked as she moved from her terminal to his.

"Look at the image on screen."

"I am. What's wrong? It's Miranda leaving the library. So, what?"

"Look closer at the guy she's with."

"He looks like a college grad student. Why are you so upset?"

"That's right." He leaned back as Bree sat in his lap. "You weren't in the courts at the time he was."

"Who is he?"

"I'll tell you when I get back." As she rose, he patted her butt. "Keep my seat warm. I've got to talk to Valadon."

As he approached Valadon's door, Aiden took a deep breath and then knocked.

"Enter."

"I found something you need to see. I sent it to you in an email."

Valadon adjusted his computer and opened the email.

"Look closely at the image. I enlarged it on the next slide."

Valadon moved in closer. His breath ceased. "It couldn't be!" He clicked on the next slide. "Son of a bitch! Where's Remare? Right now. Find him."

"I will. He's still in Dione's court."

Valadon's breaths intensified as if he were a locomotive. His voice was icy as he whispered, "I will kill her with my bare hands."

A picture of Guy de Montglat, *Le Cameleon*, the High Court's number one spy stared up at him.

And Miranda was arm in arm with him.

Available Soon

Veil of Secrets, Seven Deadly Veils, Book Four

Caught in Queen Magritte's snare and forced to wed someone he loathes, Lord Valadon, King of the vampires in New York, enlists the aid of two of his most powerful allies to thwart the plans of the Queen of All Vampires. Learning that his son survived, but unable to ascertain his whereabouts, he will call upon his trusted friends to locate the one person who can stop his upcoming marriage.

Meanwhile, Remare's return is hardly what Miranda has been dreaming about. With her association with Guy de Montglat revealed, her relationships with Remare and Valadon are strained. If she wants to keep her dreams alive, she will have to choose who to give her oath of loyalty—to her own bloodline or to the vampire who holds her heart.

Everyone has secrets, right? Remare knows this, but the secrets Miranda has been keeping from him threaten to tear them apart. Only through trust can their love survive. Now he must find a way to earn her trust or risk losing her forever. A situation that will not bode well for House Valadon.

Diana Marik is the author of the Seven Deadly Veils Vampire Series. She grew up in New York City and has her MA in English Literature from Hofstra University. Before becoming an author, Diana worked as an educator, mental health therapist, yoga instructor and camp counselor.

Among Diana's passions, traveling is her favorite. One of her favorite places to visit is the American Southwest and her home away from home, New Orleans. When not writing, Diana loves discovering museums. In her leisure time, she enjoys going to the movies and hanging out with her friends.

Diana is currently at work on her latest novel in the Veilverse and would love to hear from her fans. She can be contacted at www.dianamark.com

www.ingramcontent.com/pod-product-compliance
Lightning Source LLC
Chambersburg PA
CBHW021303250626
47155CB00002B/352